Revenge

A Travis Mays Novel

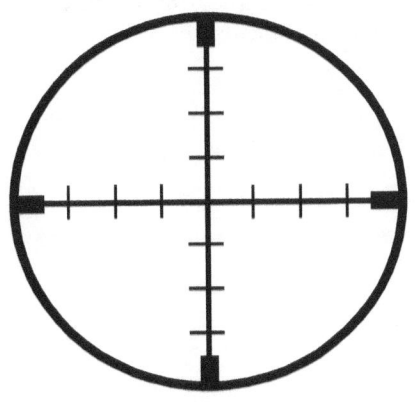

Upcoming Novel by Mark Young

Off The Grid, A Gerrit O'Rourke novel (Winter 2011)

Visit www.MarkYoungBooks.com for more information about Mark Young and his writing. Readers may also connect with him at http://hookembookem.blogspot.com/ where readers, writers and law enforcement connect.

Revenge
A Travis Mays Novel

Mark Young

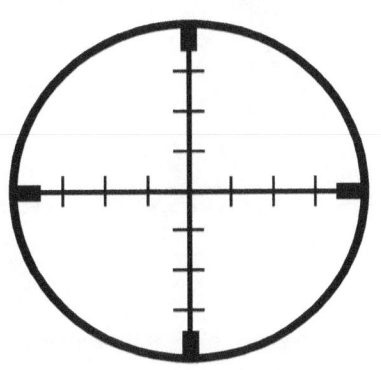

Mark Young Books
www.MarkYoungBooks.com
http://hookembookem.blogspot.com/

Mark Young
P.O. Box 504
Garfield, WA 99130
www.MarkYoungBooks.com

First edition: January 2011

Revenge is a work of fiction. The characters and events in this book are fictitious. Any similarity to real persons, living or dead, is coincidental and not intended by the author.

Mass market © 2011 ISBN: 978-0-9832663-1-0
EPub Edition © 2011 ISBN: 978-0-9832663-0-3

Library of Congress Cataloging-in-Publication Number: 2011900434

Katie,
The love of my life.

 **Prologue**

Santa Rosa, California, December 2004

Raindrops splattered the windshield as Travis Mays raised his binoculars. *Come on. Come on. Where are you?* He squinted, trying to catch a glimpse of any movement near the building through this infernal darkness.

Nothing.

Travis flicked the glove box open and snatched a bottle of antacids, tossing a handful into his mouth. Jaw muscles ached from gritting his teeth. These tablets did little to ease the burning inside. He raised the glasses once again.

Carlos shifted in the passenger's seat. "She's still inside, dude. Don't get your shorts in a twist."

Travis ignored his partner, straining to see through the windshield's fogged-up glass. A two-story building loomed in the darkness fifty yards away. A black-grated fence circled the office complex. A droopy-eyed security guard—sheltered from pelting rain inside a lighted shack—sat twenty yards away, scanning all vehicles coming and going. No way to sneak inside to check on her safety.

He glanced at his watch. Ten o'clock.

Travis gripped his binoculars, searching for any signs of life in the darkened building. "Something's wrong. I told Michelle to get out of there before everyone went home. Get in. Get the documents. Get out. This is taking way too long."

"Chill out. Maybe she's just waiting until everyone leaves. Then she can grab and run." Carlos chuckled. "Michelle, is it? Sounds like this is more than business. I saw you making eyes at her. She's just a snitch, man. Business is business. Don't let it get personal."

"That *snitch* is risking everything. She's putting it all on the line. We get paid to take these risks. Not her. She gets nothing out of this."

"Okay, Okay. She's a saint. What do you want from me?"

"I want you to give her some respect. Michelle willingly came forward to tell us what she found out. No one forced her. And now, we're about to nab one of the most ruthless traffickers we've ever hunted down—because of her bravery. Who knows how far this network reaches." Travis lowered his voice. "She went back in there—knowing the danger—because I asked."

Carlos raised his hands. "Whoa, man. Lighten up. To set the record straight, the suits higher up the totem pole sent her back in. Not you. They forced your hand."

"I had a choice. I could've told them to take a hike."

A car emerged from the parking garage beneath the office building. Two on board. He scanned the car as it slowed at the guard shack. Two burly men, no one else. "I'm telling you something's not kosher."

"Okay, maybe you're right," Carlos said. "What are we—"

Travis' cell phone emitted several sharp beeps. He glanced at the digital screen and grimaced. His sergeant, Timothy Heard, supervisor for Santa Rosa Police Department's criminal intelligence unit, was calling. "Yeah, sarge."

"Need you to break away right now. We just received a call from the county. Their VCI dicks are working a homicide near Goat Rock. I need you and Carlos to eighty-seven with them."

"We're still waiting for the CI to come out. Once we connect, we'll head out—"

"—I need you out there *now*. Your CI's a no-show, right?" Heard barged ahead, not waiting for an answer. "Their victim is a female. Description matches your gal."

"No way. She is still—"

"—I need you to get out there immediately, Travis. That's an order. The victim matches your snitch, that's all you need to know. We may have some damage control issues."

"It can't ... what do you mean 'damage control?'"

"I mean if your informant turns up dead, we've got to cover ourselves."

"You ordered me to send her back into that killer's den. Damage control? You mean protect your sad —" He felt a hand squeeze his arm.

Carlos leaned over, silently mouthing the words, "Be cool."

Travis snapped the cell phone shut, jamming it into his pocket. "The SO found a body out at the coast. They want us to check it out."

"The boss thinks the body might be our gal? And we're just supposed to drive away? What if she's still in there?"

Grimacing, Travis fired up the engine. "Orders are orders. But if this victim is Michelle ..." He let the words dangle, not wanting to give them life.

Only six hours ago he'd held her in his arms. They'd met in a motel room where he gave her final instructions. *Get in, get out.* Carlos stood guard outside. It had been eight exhilarating months since she breezed into his life, gave him a reason to get up in the morning. The way she teased and cajoled him into doing things he never tried before—ballroom dancing, or using a palate machine with her instead of going out for a beer with the guys. Michelle squeezed joy and excitement into every day they spent together. For once in his life, Travis began to think about the future, about spending his life with her. It had been a long time since he thought about anything other than police work. She changed all that. Before they parted ways today, she reached up and drew him close, almost like a premonition. Jasmine perfume still lingered on his clothing. A few moments later he followed Michelle to her car, watching her taillights disappear into the bowels of the garage across the street. The last time.

Travis gunned the engine, cutting through the darkness. Rain and wind rocked the car as he slowed at the next intersection. He pressed the accelerator to the floor, activating emergency lights embedded in the grill of his car. It would be a long drive to the coast.

Travis tautly gripped the steering wheel until his fingers became numb, careening down River Road from Santa Rosa until they reached the coast thirty-minutes later. Red, white and blue emergency lights stabbed the darkness like flashing fingers as he pulled off Highway 1. Patrol cars and unmarks huddled together in a parking lot a quarter-mile below, flashing lights from several emergency vehicles acting as beacons.

He guided the dark-blue Crown Vic—almost black from a moonless night—down a single-lane leading to the mouth of the Russian River. The road split at the bottom of a steep grade. One lane continuing to the left, leading motorists toward a rock-climbing attraction called Goat Rock, a hump of rock rising from the ocean floor. To the right, another sliver of asphalt snaked toward where the river met the Pacific Ocean. He followed this second roadway, parking near the closest police car.

Grabbing a flashlight, Travis swung the door open and heaved himself into the night with a grunt. Bitter winds pushed him across the asphalt parking lot as if he was a child's toy. The ocean pounded the shoreline. Crashing waves—churned by storms far out at sea like a witches' brew—stirring the water into a white froth. Rain lessened for a moment, sporadic drops adding to the gloom.

A voice cut through the windy darkness. "Travis, over here."

He flashed his light toward the familiar voice. A heavyset man—decked out in a dark rain jacket, denim trousers, and cowboy boots—plodded toward them. Jim Davis, a VCI investigator from Sonoma County Sheriff's Department.

Travis grasped the Jim's outstretched hand. "Hey, my man. My boss said you needed our help." The two men endured the police academy together some fifteen years ago. Jim later joined the Sonoma County Sheriff's Office, earning his way to the homicide unit.

"Need you to take a look at my victim. Dispatch advised you might know her?"

Travis felt his stomach tighten. He shot a quick glanced toward Carlos, standing a few feet away. "Can't tell until we take a look."

Jim nodded. He turned his back on the ocean, leading them across the parking lot until the pavement gave way to sand dunes. Here, they began trudging through the sand toward the river's edge.

For a moment, Travis tried to focus on other things. Like the mountain he knew stood guard around them in the blackness. Even in the blackest of nights, Travis could picture these coastal mountains embracing the powerful Russian River, standing watch over the centuries. The river's slow-moving water—clear and refreshing—normally continued its sluggish journey to the sea without interruption. At this time of year, however, the river's cadence began to heighten as recent rainstorms pushed water higher up the banks. He knew from experience that rain-swollen creeks began to empty loosened soil and debris into the swollen water, giving the river a menacing look. Sand dunes—draped with scraggly brush and green ice plant—separated the ocean from the rising river until the two bodies of water met further west. A man's cough brought Travis back to the crime scene. Back to the task at hand.

Jim cleared his throat. "A couple of lovebirds came out here to swap spit. They stumbled across this." He shot his flashlight across the wet sand. Yellow evidence tape fluttered in the wind. Ahead, Travis saw a body sprawled on the sand.

Jim handed him paper booties. "Here, put these on. Maybe your partner better stay back?"

Carlos nodded with a look of relief.

The homicide detective waited for Travis. "I'll lead you in once you're ready."

Travis finished and gave him a thumb up.

Jim held up the crime tape to allow Travis to slip underneath, and then dropped the fluttering yellow tape, grasping Travis by the shoulder. "This way, my friend." The burly cop ploughed through the sand leading them closer to the river.

Travis felt a fire raging inside. The blaze began when Michelle failed to come out of the building as planned. Now, he felt a forest fire raging inside that medicine could no longer curb. As he drew closer, Travis felt his legs begin to shake and his feet felt like to cinder blocks. He'd visited hundreds of scenes like this, always able to wall himself from these emotions, never letting his feelings get in the way of the job.

Tonight, everything changed. Those walls he carefully built inside seemed to crumble.

At first, Jim's bulk hid the victim from view. Silently, Jim stepped aside and signaled for Travis to continue alone.

A howling wind swept over the sand dunes as Travis edged closer to the woman's body. He raised the flashlight with icy fingers and pointed it toward her upturned face.

Michelle's lifeless eyes stared at the darkened sky.

Her body—like a crumpled doll discarded by a child—lay with arms outstretched as if beckoning to the night. Unlike a doll, a bullet hole marred her forehead, a single shot to the head. Travis froze as thought struck him. Michelle saw the killer moments before the gun fired.

His legs buckled, knees sinking into the sand. Darkness crashed into his soul—as hard and cold as those ocean waves pounding into the shore. Everything inside him seemed to die.

 **Chapter 1**

Lochsa River, Idaho, five years later

A dark image flickered over emerald waters. Travis Mays glanced skyward to see a vulture searching for carrion, its tip feathers spread like blackened fingers against a hazy-blue sky. He crouched by the river, listening to rushing water as he eyed the scavenger winging a path above the Lochsa River.

A flash from the mountains caught his eye across the water. Travis turned away from the river, scanning the forest behind him.

Zilch. Nothing.

He tried to turn his attention back toward the water, though his thoughts kept wanting to drag him to another place, another time. Travis closed his eyelids for a moment, forcing his mind to shed the past and return to the present. That flash a moment ago troubled him. A feeling that had been plaguing him for several weeks.

A woman's light footsteps forced him to smile. *Ah, yes. The river guide. Jessie White Eagle.* He twisted around as she approached. She drew close with almost effortless movement, although rocks, pebbles and boulders made for treacherous footing. Her long raven-black hair—normally reaching to her waist—had been tucked beneath a gray helmet.

Drawing closer, Jessie peered down at him for a moment before giving him a soft nudge with her hip. "Hey, professor, waiting for the Lochsa to run dry?" She tugged on straps of her safety helmet—headgear straight out of an old WWII movie. The ugly helmet somehow made her more attractive. "You hired me as a river guide, Willie boy. Can't teach you anything just sitting here!" Jessie flung him a get-down-to-business look before turning toward the river. Two orange kayaks, partially in water, rested on the shoreline. She leaped into one of them while simultaneously shoving the bow into deeper water in one graceful move. She made it look simple.

Travis cringed. Where'd she come up with his middle name?

Then he remembered. Three Rivers Company. The name printed on his driver's license when he signed up for this trip.

Travis Willie Mays.

He grimaced. "My name is Travis. Only my momma calls me Willie." He fought the urge to say his mother became a die-hard Giants fan, worshiping the ground Willie Mays played on. Thanks to her, Travis got tagged with the ball player's name. "Everyone else calls me Travis."

"Okay, Willie," she yelled back with a fleeting smile. "I've got a lot to teach you. Let's get cracking."

Travis grasped his paddle and stepped toward the remaining kayak.

Jessie's smile a moment ago reminded him of the first time they'd met. A woman burst into the front office at the raft company while he spoke to one of the co-owners about a week ago. Moments before, he'd confided to the owner that he'd never tried whitewater rafting before and needed a trustworthy guide. He failed to mention he'd never set foot in a kayak. The office door swung open before the owner responded. Jessie strolled in, giving him a smile that seemed to brighten the room. The owner pointed at Jessie. "That is the person you need to speak to." He chatted with Jessie— who described their whitewater trips with enthusiastic animation—for a few minutes. They agreed to meet in a week and he signed up with a little less hesitation.

Everything felt different today. Jessie's smile a moment ago was her first since they started up the river at dawn. Before dragging their kayaks to the river's edge, she'd pulled him aside and meticulously covered all the information to safely navigate down the river. Unlike last week, she spewed out regulations and procedures with less emotion than a pre-recorded voice on an automated phone directory. Her first attempt at a joke—calling him *Willie*—seemed contrived, almost listless.

Something seemed off.

Travis turned once more and glanced up the mountain slope. He felt that strange sensation returning, tugging at his insides, calling for his attention. He heaved his own craft partway onto the water, stern still resting on the rocky shoreline. He straightened for a moment, rubbing the back of his neck.

Surveillance? Was that what he was picking up?

An uneasy feeling continued to nag at him. It felt like when he was a kid on his own, walking home from a friend's house late at night, knowing someone or something lurked in the shadows. He couldn't define it or put a name to it. He just knew it was out there. As a kid, he knew his imagination kicked into overdrive.

His childhood melted away a long time ago, but over the years those childish instincts—alerting him to danger—became honed to a fine point as a man. Those years in foster homes and orphanages forced him to grow up fast, and his years in police work taught him do know the difference between imagination and real danger. His danger needle had been flickering in the red zone for several weeks even though he could not come up with one rational fact to justify these feelings. He just knew.

Recently, every stranger that crossed his path earned a second glance as he struggled to put a name to these feelings. But nameless they remained, like nightmares one barely recalls when morning finally comes.

Jessie's voice brought him back to the present. "Hey, professor, time to get wet. Move it along." Jessie feathered her paddle, watching from midstream.

He eased into the kayak, hands gripping both sides of the cockpit for balance. The boat wobbled as he shoved off and he struggled to stay upright. For a moment, he thought he might lose his balance. Catching himself, Travis shifted his weight to stabilize the craft. He felt like a drunken sailor trying to walk a gangplank after shore leave.

This was a long way from the university— his classroom, his comfort zone. But like everything else he tackled, he'd attack it until he felt at one with the river. Just like he finally mastered these mountains after five years of plugging away, building his own cabin. Creating a safe haven to start all over, finally burying the past.

Until these premonitions returned. He must not lose his grip. Not this time.

He paddled a few strokes in the water, getting a feel for how the craft handled. As Jessie drew near, he remembered something he meant to ask earlier before they'd left the Three Rivers lodge. "Jessie, I overheard two guys this morning talking about a search party. No details. You know anything about it?"

Her face hardened, eyes narrowed. "My brother's missing. Been gone for two days. Never showed up for work." She looked away, masking whatever was going on inside.

"Oh, wow! You should've said something. Need to go back?"

She shook her head. "We've searched everywhere. He's just vanished." Her eyes glistened. "His car turned up near here about a mile away. Keys missing. We don't know what happened."

"Maybe he just wanted to take a hike by himself. Get away from everything." He knew how that felt. "I'm sure he'll show up soon."

"Maybe. All we can do now is wait."

"You want us to break off and help them search? We can do this kayaking any time. A few more days won't matter one way or the other."

"I've already searched everywhere I can think of and came up empty. Now, I'm just waiting to see what Dad and the others find out." Jessie brushed a hand across her eyes, straightened her shoulders and turned toward him. "I just need to keep doing my normal stuff until he comes home."

"Whatever you want, Jessie. It's your call."

Her face softened as she offered him a smile, eyebrows raised. "Losing your nerve, cowboy?"

"Losing my nerve? Never happen, Pocahontas. Show me your stuff."

She rocked his kayak, dashing snow-chilled waves across his lap. "Watch yourself, *paleface*. This is Nez Perce country. You're in my house now."

In that brief moment, he felt they might be able to cast aside their problems and enjoy the river in all its beauty. Leave their troubles for another day. He began following Jessie downriver as she led them around the first bend. In the distance, he heard the roar of whitewater.

Chapter 2

Travis felt like his arms were going to fall off. He figured they'd only been on the river an hour and already he needed a break. Miles down the canyon, he spotted several vultures circling like aircraft stacked in a holding pattern. He yelled over at Jessie, trying to get her attention as he paddled toward shore.

Fingers of sunlight painted the river's canvas with shades of green and sandy yellow until overhanging trees cast a foreboding net of darkness across the water. Like a dividing line between the seen and unseen worlds, sun-flecked waves became pools of mystic gloom beneath these leafy behemoths.

Jessie glanced back and began paddling toward him. She pulled alongside as they neared the shore. Pearl-white sand cushioned their craft as they eased onto a clam-shaped beach nestled among granite boulders. Brightness of the sand contrasted with shadows of the forest shadows further inland. Ferns and huckleberry bushes created a gray-green hedge between the beach and the woods, where towering pines and firs stood defiantly.

They dragged their crafts onto the shore before stretching out on the sand.

Travis peered over at Jessie, who seemed to be studying the river's current. He leaned closer. "Do you mind me asking if your brother's ever—"

"—been in trouble before?" Jessie looked irritated.

"No. I was just going to ask whether something like this ever—"

"—No." Her eyes flashed. Then she looked away.

He drew back, leaned on one elbow and picked up a handful of warm sand, letting the granules slip through his fingers.

The forest seemed unusually quiet. No birds. No animals. Just silence. The river gave the only symphony of sound, always running, always moving, always giving and taking on its path to the Pacific Ocean.

Jessie's voice cut through the stillness. "I didn't mean to be rude, Travis. I'm just worried ..." She turned toward him as if unable to finish.

He raised himself up and dusted off his hands. "No problem. You've got a lot on your mind."

Jessie sat and crossed her legs. "Nothing like this ever happened before. He's always been so dependable, the one I lean on." She looked away before continuing. "He graduated from law school with high honors. Started his own practice. Our pride and joy. Local boy makes good."

Her face relaxed for a moment. "One of the first clients he picked up was the Whitewater Casino. He loves working in all that glitter and excitement."

"Must make your parents proud."

She glanced at him, a faraway look in her eyes. "Mom passed when I was little. And Dad ... he's not thrilled about Tommy working at the casino. One of many things they fight over. "

"Your father's against gambling?"

Jessie seemed to ponder the question. "Says gambling takes the heart and soul out of our people."

"You agree with him?"

"A few people get hooked, Indian and white. But our people need this economic boost. They've been struggling for generations trying to survive, trying to give our people a way to stand on their own in this changing world. People like my dad... well, they just look at it differently." She lowered her voice, mimicking a man's voice. "Says 'a man's work ought a have eternal perspectives.'"

"Part of your tribe's beliefs?"

Jessie's frown softened. "Not really. Dad took it from the Bible. Pounded that into us since childhood."

"Sounds like white man's religion." He grimaced, wondering if his words might offend.

Jessie smiled. "Yeah, well, Dad claims God is color blind."

A twig snapped.

Travis whirled just as a man emerged from the forest, a shotgun cradled in his arms.

He sprang to his feet.

The man jerked the gun up and pointed the barrel at Travis' chest. "Whoa there partner. Don't be so jumpy."

"I get nervous when someone points a gun at me." Travis estimated the man stood about ten yards away. Too far for him to get the jump.

The man seemed to read his mind. "Hey, stud, I don't know who you are. You and your girlfriend here might be Bonnie and Clyde for all I know." He glanced at Jessie as she slowly rose to her feet. "Hey beautiful, just stay next to your boyfriend and don't get all hysterical on me."

A car passed on the Highway 12 across the river. No one in the car could see them from the roadway. Overhanging trees on both sides of the river obscured any view.

The gunman appeared to be in his late thirties, heavyset, wearing a green-plaid woolen shirt, denim trousers, and a matching denim vest. His scalp—as much as Travis could see—carefully shaven to the skin. A baseball cap advertising 'Hank's Towing Service' shielded the man's eyes from the sun. Those eyes shifted toward Jessie.

Travis tried to ease himself between her and the gunman.

The man swung his attention back. "Hey, Daniel Boone, I told you to stand still."

Slowly, Travis raised his hands. "Look, Hank. We've got no weapons and we're not looking for trouble. What say you lower that thing before someone gets hurt?"

"So you can jump me? No thanks. And my name's not Hank." The man seemed confused. He kept looking over at Jessie. Travis did not like the way the man stared at her. He edged closer, putting himself directly in front of Jessie.

"Name's Travis," he said, trying to draw the gunman's attention. Start with the ABCs of hostage negotiations. Build a rapport with the suspect. Make him think of you as a person. "Mind giving me your name?"

The stranger hesitated. "Harold. Name's Harold. Where'd you come up with Hank. They're not even spelled the same way."

Travis relaxed, starting to understand Harold. Not exactly an Einstein. "Okay ... Harold. Tell me what's going on here?"

"Whadda you mean?"

"I mean ... why you holding a gun on us? We're no threat to you."

Harold lowered the weapon a few inches. "I came out here to shoot me a few rabbits. You guys surprised me."

Travis chuckled.

Jessie glared at him a look like he'd lost his mind.

Travis turned toward the rabbit hunter. "Surprised *you*? Harold, you walked up on us. Remember?"

Harold's eyes suddenly widened. "You guys think I'm trying to rob you or something? Man, you're crazy." He lowered the weapon, cradling it in his arms like a baby. "A man's got to be careful out here. I heard all kinds of nuts might be running around."

Travis looked at Jessie, trying not to laugh. "Harold, we're perfectly sane. Or at least I am." He winked at Jessie.

She threw him a look colder than the river.

He turned toward Harold. "Just taking a trip down the river. Stopped for a breather. No crazy stuff."

Harold scratched his ear, still clutching the shotgun. "I can see that now, Travis. But you jumped up like a red ant might be taking chunks out of your behind. I wanna make sure you guys weren't turning weird on me."

"I understand, Harold. We're not turning weird. And we'd like to shove off now, okay? Hope you find Peter Rabbit."

"Thanks, Travis. You and the missus have a good day." Harold gave him a brisk salute and stumbled back into the woods, shotgun resting on his shoulder. Travis heard the man trip stumble, cutting loose with a string of profanities. "I think all the rabbits are safe today."

"Hey, he got a drop on you, Daniel Boone." Jessie laughed and let out a long sigh. "I almost feel sorry for the guy. I hope his family isn't counting on him bringing home dinner. They might starve."

"The gut on Harold tells me he doesn't lose out on too many meals." Travis gestured toward the river. "Shall we take off?"

They shoved their kayaks off the beach, allowing them to float free in shallow water. Jessie faced him. "You trying to be my knight in shining armor?"

"Huh?"

"Before you knew Harold was only interested in rabbits."

He eyed her for a moment. "I don't know what you're talking about."

"The hero thing," she said, touching his shoulder. "Thanks."

"Old habits die hard." He reached down and drew his kayak closer. *Hero*. He fell off that pedestal a long time ago.

Jessie easily swung into the cockpit, moving out to mid-stream in a few strokes. Travis tried to the same move, almost falling in again before he balanced himself. He paddled out to join her.

"I think I got this down, Jessie."

She shook her head, laughing. "Watching you trying to squeeze into that kayak reminds me of that movie with Mel Gibson. That one where he knows what women are thinking. He gets drunk and tries to cram himself into women's nylons to better understand what they put up with. He winds up falling all over the place."

"Well, I'm not drunk and I got in without falling into the water."

Jessie smirked. "The day isn't over yet, Willie. It is a good thing you're wearing a wetsuit. You're going to need it."

Chapter 3

Two hours later—and still dry—Travis jubilantly felt he'd mastered the river until rounding the next bend. A cluster of boulders straight ahead lay in his path, each granite outcropping rose like teeth above white churning froth, waiting to grind his small craft to splinters. Doubt began to return.

Jessie tried to yell above the river's thunder. "They call this the Grim Reaper. A class three plus rapid."

"A class what?" he yelled back. "And why do they call it that?"

She grinned, ignoring his question. "Start to the right, then move to the middle to avoid that large boulder." She pointed with her chin. "Once you've cleared that rock, scramble to your right unless you want to get slapped silly by that monster on the left," pointing to a mass of sheer granite rising from the river like a giant carved in stone.

"And give me plenty of space," she said, turning away. "You're going to get wet."

Travis saw Jessie position herself for a moment, watching as she dug deeply into the water, squaring up, paddling faster and faster to gain speed. He backstroked to give distance between them, listening to the roar. It reminded him of watery thunder he once heard at the base of Niagara Falls. It was all he could do to keep from being swept downstream, the current gradually sucking him toward the rapids.

Jessie dipped and slid into white turbulence without any hesitation. Graceful. Effortless. A bird soaring over dangerous waters.

It was now his turn to face the Grim Reaper.

He took a deep breath and lunged forward, already feeling his kayak shudder from powerful disturbances beneath the hull. Water flowed downward like smooth glass and then rose in a white, churning mass. A savage wave struck the side of his craft, thrusting him violently toward the boulder Jessie warned about. He clawed at the water with his paddle trying to avoid a collision.

Smack.

His stern struck a submerged rock, jamming the bow forward, burying him in a shallow grave of water. He fought to right himself, but the current corkscrewed him into its depths and he lost his balance. Roaring sheets of water buried him, pounding his head with icy fists. For what seemed like an eternity he remained trapped beneath the surface as near-freezing currents burned his skin.

Bubbles of white madness hurled around him as if he'd wandered into a major snow flurry, the storm's white fury blinding him. A maddening roar of angry water hurled past. Deafening. A crescendo finally offering muffled quietness amidst a horrendous storm. He felt locked inside the eye of a hurricane and everything became a quiet roar. He locked his mouth closed, trapping the air inside until he reached the surface.

Bam.

His helmet smacked a submerged boulder hard enough to send shock waves through his ice-numbed brain. Dizziness crept in like a thief as he momentarily seemed to glide into a surreal world where gravity no longer mattered. Darkness in one direction. Sunlight in the other. Light became the only clue where he might reach the surface, where life itself held its breath waiting to see whether he might rise once again from this cold tomb.

He began to panic, thrusting and turning to free himself.

Frigid water became his savior, bringing clarity back to his jarred mind with a jolt.

He wrenched his body to the left, trying to use the thrust of this rushing torrent to heave himself upright. He struggled against the force as tons of pressurized water swept body and soul downstream. He fought against the river's powerful violence, against its wrath, as he sought to claw himself toward the light.

Slowly, reluctantly, the river relented, releasing its hold on him.

Travis burst to the surface, gasping for air, his kayak breaching like a nuclear sub after a long dive. Disoriented, he weaved between several boulders, surfing on the remaining whitewater until he reached calmer waters. He looked with surprise at his hands, still clutching the paddle like some extension of his arms.

His heart seemed to be pounding harder than the force of the rapids he just survived. Slowly he gained control of his breathing, and his pulse slowed. He looked around with awe. Here, the river became as meek and gentle as a lamb, no longer a raging torrent trying to drag him under. He gratefully eased into a calm eddy where the river widened, its current slowing to a crawl.

Jessie waited twenty yards away. She smiled as he drew near. "You're all wet, Willie. Grim Reaper got you?"

For a moment, he felt like lashing out until he spotted concern in her eyes. "Yeah, me and Mel Gibson have something in common. We both made fools of ourselves."

"You want to call it quits? Can't blame you. I should have prepared you better for that run."

"Forget it. I survived," he said, glancing downstream." Beside, the worst is over. All downhill from here, right?"

She tilted her head to one side, pursing her lips before speaking. "You've got guts, professor. I've seen others throw in their paddles and walk away after less than what you just went through. Let me know when you're ready to move on."

Water seeped under his wetsuit and oozed into his rubber booties. His face still stung from his frigid baptism. He turned toward Jessie. "Ready when you are."

They drifted for a few minutes, enjoying the quiet calm before continuing. Jessie straightened, lowered her paddle into the river. "Okay. Let's move on."

They angled downstream and began the journey once more. Travis spotted more vultures circling down the canyon, black dots circling on a blue-canvassed sky. He estimated they'd reach the birds in a half hour. More flesh eaters seemed to be circling.

Chapter 4

Roaring water alerted Travis of trouble, no longer tame like a lamb. For the last several minutes he observed the river became narrower and the water rushing faster. As he cleared the next bend, he saw where the river began to cascade down a steep decline.

Jessie glanced back. "Relax, cowboy. This part is much tamer. Just watch yourself, okay? Follow my lead."

He trailed behind, keeping a few yards behind her until whitewater started frothing ahead. He dragged his paddle in the water to slow his speed, allowing her to pull ahead.

A few minutes later, Jessie's craft became an orange blur as she worked her way between jutting rocks and pounding waves. He watched her fighting the waves until he realized he needed to pay attention to his own craft.

Travis reached the rapids quicker than he expected. He clenched his teeth and braced himself for another pounding. Residual panic from the Grim Reaper began to return. His training kicked in as he fought against this fear and he began to feel growing excitement. He was starting to enjoy this.

Maybe he was becoming Daniel Boone.

Scanning the rapids ahead, he chose a path which seemed to offer safe passage. He dug deep into the green water with each stroke, fighting to gain speed to match the river's power. He battled to put his bow between two jutting rocks. As he shot between them, his kayak seemed to collapse like aircraft in heavy turbulence.

Whoomp.

He felt the hull slam a wave as hard as concrete. He stayed afloat.

The craft regained buoyancy before slamming downward again. Time seemed to stop as the craft bounced from one drop off to the next until the river's fury finally relented just as quickly as it struck.

He survived.

Travis realized he was yelling. This challenge was not like the Grim Reaper, but it still got his blood running hot. He felt the tingle of excitement as he cleared the last hurdle.

Jessie floated a few yards away, motionless, staring downstream.

Puzzled, he guided his kayak toward her. "Hey, I made it, Jessie. I actually enjoyed it."

She remained motionless as if she never heard him.

Travis followed her gaze and saw a cluster of turkey vultures gathered on the far bank, their red heads bobbing as they picked and clawed at something in the brush. Other vultures perched in lower tree branches, waiting their turn to feast.

"No! No!" Jessie's cries echoed over the water as she began to furiously paddle toward them. "Get out of here!" Her screams filled the air above the sounds of the river.

Travis thrust forward, trying to catch up. As they neared the bank, he saw something lying in the brush. Waving Timothy grass obscured whatever drew the birds. He slid his bow onto the rocky shoreline just as Jessie rushed forward. Vultures clumsily scurried away, taking flight before the two kayakers reached the shore.

Jessie froze. "I can't ..."

He gently grasped her arm. "Stay here. Let me check it out."

Flies swarmed and buzzed as he forced a path through the brush. He heard Jessie following. He thrust aside stalks of grass to see large chunks of flesh—torn by feasting animals—lying at his feet.

Jessie gasped. "Oh, thank God." She grasped his arm, sobbing.

A large elk's carcass lay stripped almost to the bone.

He felt Jessie shaking as he put his arms around her. Muffled sobs filled the air as she clung to him. He watched as vultures still circling above.

Centuries of patience bred into them, they would keep a lofty eye until the humans vanished.

"Come on, Jessie. Let's get out of here." He guided her to the river's edge. As they started downriver once more, he glanced back and saw several birds already settling down to continue their feast, following nature's dictates. Life begins. Life ends. And the cycle continues.

Travis threw his gear into the truck bed and started the engine. As he stomped on the accelerator, he glanced in the rear view mirror to see Jessie following his departure. Any enjoyment they might have gained on the river ended after they found the dead elk. Spotting the carcass forced them to realize Jessie's brother was still missing, a fact that the river and Harold's blunder rabbit hunting briefly allowed them to forget. The dead elk brought reality back in full force. Jessie slipped back into a sullen quietness on the trip home. They parted ways at the Three Rivers office as he started for home.

A gravel driveway—more dirt than gravel—cut through the rafting company's property. He followed the driveway past a campground and RV center, and onto a blacktopped road. He jerked the wheel to the right as his tires struck pavement and drove over a narrow bridge spanning the Lochsa River. Off to his left, the Lochsa merged with the Selway, two rivers becoming one single tributary—the middle fork of the Clearwater River.

Travis turned west on Highway 12 and drove a dozen miles along the Clearwater before realizing he was almost home. His mind kept wandering back to Jessie's face as she approached the dead elk. He pulled onto an oil-stained turnout that served as a parking lot. After killing the ignition he listened to the truck sputter and cough, glancing down at the Clearwater and his cabin beyond.

Home at last.

A welcoming growl rose above the sound of the river as he crossed the roadway. A dog joyously bounded into the air on the other side of the river. Sam—part wolf, part mutt, part crazy—bounced along the bank in frenzied anticipation.

At least Sam seemed excited to see Travis.

He unlocked a switch box, pressed a button, and watched as the lift came to life. Two concrete poles, supporting a heavy cable spanning the river, provided a link between his home and the highway. A metal platform, suspended by thick steel coils, gently rocked in the afternoon breeze as it slowly inched toward him.

This was the easy way to his cabin.

The other route led through the forest behind the cabin to his back door. A roller-coaster fire-break—some call a road—snaked through the mountains for fourteen dusty miles. Rain or snow made the road impassable. Once the firebreak ended, he still needed to hike a mile to reach home. Too much effort.

Cradled across the river seemed the easiest way to travel.

As he waited for the lift to draw near, his mind returned to Jessie. The look he saw in her eyes—as they approached the elk—mingled fear and helpless rage. Fury. She was not a weak person. The way she tackled the Grim Reaper without any hesitation, fighting the river's fury with confidence and agility. But then—when faced with feasting vultures—she became paralyzed with fear.

Everyone becomes vulnerable when loved ones are in danger. He knew that feeling. After all these years, nightmares still haunted him. Dark memories of someone snatching Michelle away forever. The woman he loved. The woman he swore to protect. That night her death tore into his soul. He swore never to allow anyone to get close again. Guilt dragged him into this darkness where he chose to hide from the world.

So why was he still thinking about Jessie?

A car approached at a high rate of speed just as the lift creaked to a stop. The driver ground through the gears and hit the brakes. A yellow VW bug drew close and the driver leaned out the window to wave.

Jessie White Eagle.

Travis grabbed onto the lift and waited as she crossed the highway. "I was just on my way to Kamiah and saw your truck." She glanced across the river. "That your place?"

He sensed she knew the answer. Sam's renewed barks carried across the river as if the dog was trying to remind Travis to come on home. Travis watched the dog running back and forth, bounding with energetic strides.

"This is a long way from college, professor."

"I've got a place in Palouse, a short drive from the campus. I stay here weekends and summers."

"Must be tough getting over there in the dead of winter."

"I manage."

She looked away, gazing across the Clearwater. "Can I see your place?"

Reluctantly, he opened the gate and helped her into the single-person cage. Jessie cleared the river a few minutes later. Travis used the controls to reverse directions, sending the lift back to him. As Travis traveled over the river, he saw Sam gave Jessie a wide berth. Once Travis joined them, Sam slowly approached her, tail barely wagging, ears raised with curiosity. She slowly stretched out her hand palm down and let the dog sniff. She reached over and stroked the animal's head. Sam's tail beat the air vigorously.

Travis strolled toward the cabin. "Looks like you've made a friend. His name's Sam," he said, leading her up a path liberally sprinkled with crushed rock. "Sam Spade."

"Cute. You a mystery buff?"

"I teach criminology at WSU. Crime sleuthing comes with the territory."

Thick red fir planks, planed smooth and stained, creaked under their weight as they climbed rustic stairs leading to the porch. Soaring pines and firs cast lush shadows across the dark-stained deck, providing cool relief from the afternoon's heat.

"How'd all this building material get over here?" she asked, looking back toward the water.

"Most of the lumber came from around here. I brought what I needed across the river."

"You built this?"

"With my own hands. Enter at your own risk." Propping a screen door open with his foot, he unlocked the front door and listened to the hinges squeak as he thrust it open. Jessie and Sam paraded past as he held the screen open. Travis walked inside, letting the screen door slam shut. He glanced around the cabin. It had been a while since he'd cleaned up the place; bed unmade, dishes stacked in the sink, laundry piled in the corner. He tried to remember the last visitor. Grimacing, he realized the cabin looked like a frat house after an all-night bash.

A stone fireplace stood as the center attraction to his one-room abode, smooth river rock mortared along an entire wall of the cabin. Near the fireplace, a well-worn sofa and two easy chairs clustered around a low wooden coffee table. The weathered-gray table bore an array of magazines and books.

He glanced at the sofa, cringing. Clumps of white dog hair peppered the brown-suede leather where Sam spent most of his time while inside. Crammed against the far wall, a king-sized bed stood, its frame carved from downed trees he'd found in the woods.

Jessie wandered toward the kitchen, glancing at a used sink he'd salvaged from another house. Above the sink hung yellow-pine cupboards he'd built from scratch. A counter beneath the cupboards angled out like a crooked finger next to a wood-burning kitchen stove he'd dragged through the woods with a great deal of sweat. A large rough-hewed table with a couple of homemade chairs completed the décor.

This was his place to escape. Never meant for entertainment.

A pair of windows graced every wall but the fireplace. All were shuttered except for the two on either side of the front door. These windows offered a glimpse of the river below and the highway beyond, clouded only by smudged panes of glass.

Jessie scanned the kitchen. "This could use a woman's touch," she said, drawing a line across the dusty counter top and grimacing as she held up a grimy finger.

"You volunteering?"

Laughing, she shook her head. "I'm not the domestic type. Sorry."

"Can't blame a guy for trying."

"Trying to do *what*?" She said, smiling.

Travis motioned toward the sofa, taking one of the chairs. "Make yourself comfortable. Sorry for the mess."

REVENGE   25

She seemed to relax, sinking into the cushion. Sam jumped up beside her, nuzzling his head onto her lap. She looked down at Sam, gently stroking the dog's head.

Travis saw a car flash past on the highway, followed by a motorcycle. The bike rider revved the motor, the four-stroke engine howling as it overtook the car. Silence crept back into the cabin after they passed. He turned his attention back to Jessie.

Still petting Sam, she said, "When do you head back to the university?"

"Tomorrow. First thing in the morning."

She looked up, hand still resting on Sam's head. "Did you enjoy the river today?"

"You mean getting dunked and almost drowning, Harold pointing a shotgun at me, and finding—"

"Okay, except for all those things."

He saw she was trying to smile. Jessie appeared to give up, glancing down at Sam resting his head in her lap. He stretched out his legs."Actually, I did enjoy it. After the Grim Reaper, I thought I could survive anything."

Jessie's smile returned, her eyes sparked. "I love it on the river. Just me and the water. At times, very peaceful. At other times ... well, you found out, Willy-boy. Not so peaceful. I never take the river for granted. Ever."

Her soft brown eyes drew his attention. Something he'd failed to see before, a gentleness in the way she looked. She gazed at him—head to one side, eyes searching—waiting for a response. Travis looked away, not sure how to respond.

"Thanks for ... being there today, Travis. Seeing those vultures, I just sort of lost it. And Harold ... well, thanks."

Something across the river caught his attention. Travis glanced toward the highway. "We've got company, Jessie."

A marked police car slowed down and pulled off the highway. The patrol car bore Nez Perce Tribe Police in dark letters beneath a painted arrow with feathers attached. Travis knew the car was off the reservation by a few miles.

Jessie eyed the man climbing out of the car. Her face tightened. "That's one of the guys who works for my dad. Joseph Baptiste." She looked worried.

"Your dad's a cop?"

"Didn't I tell you," she said, still staring at the officer across the high-way. "My father is the Chief of Police."

Travis glanced back at the patrol car as the officer got out, first looking Jessie's car over and then staring toward the cabin. The officer shielded his eyes from the sun as he scanned the far side of the river.

Jessie rose from the sofa, her face tense. "I wonder if it's about Tommy?"

Travis followed her to the door. "I'll go with you if you'd like."

She glanced back. "Thanks. I'd like that very much."

Travis closed and locked the door behind him as they headed toward the river.

Chapter 5

Clearwater River, Idaho

One rifle shot—not more than a hundred yards—could take out the target right now.

Creasy knelt in the shelter of a giant fir, grasping binoculars in one hand and a parabolic dish in the other. He aimed the bionic ear toward two people further down the mountainside, straining to capture snatches of conversation. A man and a woman stood alongside the river bank. He saw the patrol vehicle pull up, but the officer did not seem suspicious. He turned his attention back to the couple on the far side of the river.

He bit his lip. *Patience, my man.*

Sweet revenge demanded his target must suffer. To writhe in pain—physical and emotional—before death came and claimed its prize. To feel every exquisite jolt of pain before darkness finally fell like an axe. That man must learn why Creasy wanted him dead.

A late-morning breeze rustled branches just enough to allow rays of sunshine to spear the gloom. Creasy shifted his position while peering through field glasses.

Flash.

He grimaced as the man below reacted. A gleam of sunlight must have caught the lens of Creasy's glasses, alerting those below. The target below whirled, eyes searching the mountainside for the source of the flash.

Instinctively, Creasy drew back into a cocoon of darkness beneath the tree, clamping down on his breathing to control any further movement. He prayed these shadows and his camouflaged clothing would be enough to conceal him from prying eyes.

Seconds clicked off like minutes before the male target turned toward the woman.

Creasy wiped his brow with a sleeve and slowly released air trapped in his lungs. One more stupid move like that and all his plans might vaporize. This was the second flash today. First, above the Lochsa as he watched Travis and Jessie starting their kayaking trip this morning. And now, a second mistake. Must tread carefully. No more mistakes.

Squatting, Creasy rotated his shoulders to work out stiffness. A blue Steller's jay scolded him from above as if trying to draw attention to his position. Pinholes of sunlight shot through heavy foliage, offering a variance of muted color. Below him the Clearwater River slashed a path through Idaho's Bitterroot Mountains. Rising from the river's edge, steep mountainous slopes stood clothed by forests of trees—firs, pines, cedars, and occasional hemlock—standing like an army dressed in varying shades of green, ascending to greet an early-June sky.

Slowly, he raised the glasses to resume surveillance.

He adjusted the lens until the face of the male loomed clearly—late thirties, a Tom Cruise build with smoke-blue eyes and coffee-brown hair cut neat and trim.

Travis Mays.

Fingers tightened around binoculars as Creasy focused on this loathsome face.

He swept the glasses over to focus on the woman.

Jessie White Eagle. A beautiful face. Striking, with almost Asiatic features.

Creasy's mind sifted through detailed reports he'd pored over before locking them away in a file hundreds of miles away. He compared what he remembered to the woman he saw below. Field glasses confirmed his intelligence reports. American Indian. Nez Perce tribe. Tommy's sister. Long silk-black hair caught by a breeze. Almond-shaped eyes, golden-brown skin that reminded him of South Pacific sunsets. She seemed to walk with a hint of attitude.

Jessie White Eagle—unwitting bait he planned to dangle before Travis.

Creasy lowered the glasses and reached into a trouser pocket, withdrawing an Idaho driver's license. The DL belonged to Tommy White Eagle, Jessie's brother. He glanced at the photo and saw their resemblance.

Raising the glasses once more, he saw lines of worry wrinkled on Jessie's brow as she clambered down the rocky slope toward the river. Travis trailed behind.

Jessie had every right to be worried. Tommy turned up missing. Everyone frantically searching, but no one knew where he might be found.

Well, almost no one.

Creasy knew. In fact, he was the only person who knew where Tommy might be. All that would change. He chuckled to himself. The trap's baited, ready to slam shut.

Travis would soon be within his grasp.

Briefly, Creasy closed his eyes and savored that moment soon to come. His fingers—like eagle's talons—closing around Travis' neck, slowly squeezing life from the man he so despised.

A man who stole the only thing Creasy treasured.

 **Chapter 6**

Sam started barking before they reached the river.

"Shut up, Sam," Travis said, turning to Jessie. "I'll go first, okay?"

She nodded as he reached up and opened the cage. Once across, he sent it back and waited until she reached his side. As they struggled up the bank toward the highway, Travis saw the cop glaring back. Something about the officer put Travis on edge. The uniformed officer leaned against his car, muscular arms crossed and flexing. His nose—broken at least once—and coal-black eyes gave Travis the impression this guy possessed zero patience.

Baptiste squinted at Travis as if eyeing a suspect, before turning toward Jessie. "Your dad's been looking for you, Jess. Called Three Rivers. They said you left for the day."

"Have they found ..."

Baptiste hunched his shoulders. "Your father wants you back at his office. Something came up."

"About Tommy?"

"He'll tell you himself."

"Joseph, if it's about Tommy, I want to know right now."

Baptiste thrust a finger at her. "Don't start telling me what—"

Travis stepped forward. "Officer, don't—"

Jessie placed a hand on his arm and turned toward the cop. "Please. I don't want to wait until we get back to Lapwai. Did they find Tommy?"

Baptiste seemed to relish her agony. "Orders are orders. Mine is to find you and hook you up with the chief." His eyes glinted.

Jessie turned toward Travis. "Would you come with me? I ..." She let the sentence trail off, her eyes filling in the blanks.

Travis glanced at Baptiste. The man's broad face loomed impassive, unyielding. "Okay. I'll follow in my truck."

She softly touched his arm. "May I ride with you, Travis? I'll leave my car here. I'm coming back to Three Rivers."

Baptiste scowled.

Travis nodded, smiling grimly at the officer as he opened his truck. Jessie climbed inside and slid to the passenger's side. She leaned forward, hands clenched on her lap. He grabbed the steering wheel and pulled himself inside, closing the door.

"You okay?" he said, starting up the truck. Travis saw her eying Baptiste as the cop strode toward the patrol car. "I'm fine. Just get me there quick. Please."

He heard the other vehicle start up, tires churning up rocks as the patrol car fishtailed onto the highway. Travis slipped off the brake and followed. Ahead, he saw a rust-crusted van parked off the road about a quarter mile away. Travis glanced into the van as they passed. No one in the driver's seat. He'd seen this vehicle earlier further upstream after leaving Three Rivers. He assumed it belonged to a fisherman working the river.

Late afternoon brilliance pained his eyes. He jerked down the visor to shield his eyes, and saw Jessie scrutinizing the patrol car ahead. Her expression seemed fixated on the car ahead as if she saw something that frightened her.

Looking at the silhouetted driver through the rear window, Travis wondered if Jessie feared what her father might have to say or the man driving the car ahead. Baptiste's anger and Jessie's anxiousness told Travis those two shared history. But she appeared unwilling to divulge anything, keeping it inside, her fists still clenched.

He understood fear, a beast everyone struggled with at some point in their lives. For him, fear died inside a long time ago. Instead, he struggled with another beast, another monster, whose powers haunted his nights and dreams, never letting go.

Guilt was this monster's name.

"**Boss. Mobile One, here.** They're headed your way."

Creasy's voice crackled over the radio. "You still in the van?"

"Yeah. But I think the guy spotted me twice now. I may have burned this ride."

"Then pull out and switch with Mobile Two."

"Okay. Anyway, nothing came up on the wire when they were in the cabin. Just chit chat. They will clear your location in about twenty. My guess, they're headed toward her old man's place."

"The cop shop?"

"Yeah. And they're following one of the local guys, a tribal flatfoot. Like some kind of escort."

"Gotcha. Clear out and let Two take over."

"Okay, boss. The wires still hot in the other places?"

"Yup. And the cop shop's equipped with rabbit ears. We're catching everything."

"Over and out." The van driver crawled from the back and wedged himself into the driver's seat. Another day, another dollar. But this sure beat a nine-to-fiver and Creasy paid a lot more dinero. He watched the cop car and truck disappear in his rearview.

"Did you get all that?"

Another man climbed to the passenger seat from the back of the van. "Yeah, I heard. Creasy's on a roll."

As the driver made a u-turn, he thought of his boss. The guy wanted the team to call him by that handle, *Creasy*, even though everyone knew his real name.

Strange hombre.

The passenger hunched forward. "I just wish I knew what this job is really about. It makes me a little hinky."

As the driver slowed down—letting the vehicles ahead pull further away—he glanced at his partner. "That makes two of us. Remember that job in Frisco? The hacker that tried to get money from Creasy's client?" The driver glanced over and thought he saw the passenger shiver.

"One sick puppy. You see what he did to that hacker? Nothing left when he got through."

"Yeah, and he torched the guy's apartment and the whole building went up in smoke. Innocent people could have got wasted."

"Exactly. If the money wasn't so good, I'd have jumped ship a long time ago."

"Yeah. This kind of job keeps me in the game. After all, none of us are saints. And women …" He rolled his eyes. "They like guys like us who dare to walk on the wild side. They get tired of those boring 8-to-5ers. Know what I mean?

The driver nodded. "We like to walk on the dark side sometimes. But this guy …"

The passenger thrust a pudgy finger at him. "That's my point. This guy—Creasy—lives and breathes the dark side. He takes everything to the extreme."

As a reflex, the driver checked the radio to make sure he'd turned it off. The last thing he wanted was to have an open mike and have Creasy listening to this conversation. The money was good and he'd let Creasy do whatever the creep wanted as long as no one got hurt on the team. But his partner was right. Creasy did like to take things to the extreme.

And death was always one of Creasy's favorite options.

The driver looked down the road and saw the truck and cop car disappear. Mobile Two would be tailing them soon. And Creasy would not be far behind.

 **Chapter 7**

Lapwai, Idaho

Travis heard Baptiste's goose-stepping boots behind them as Jessie led them through the police station. Footsteps slowed. Turning, he saw the cop veer off across the room and squeeze behind a desk.

"There's my dad," Jessie said, pointing to the man in a private office at the far end of the building. "He's expecting us."

As they approached, he studied the man behind the desk. The police chief's salt and pepper hair hinted at age, but his face seemed weathered by life without too much erosion. He glanced up as they entered. Travis saw a few wrinkles spreading across the man's features like small cracks in concrete after a hard winter.

"Travis, I'd like you to meet my dad, Frank White Eagle."

Frank's eyes, tired and drawn, sparked with interest. "So you're the professor." He rose and extended a hand, his grasp firm, his eyes missing nothing. "Thanks for bringing my daughter here. Now if you'll excuse us for a minute, I need to speak to Jessie alone." He gestured toward the door.

Jessie cut in. "Wait a minute, Dad. I want him to stay and ... how did you know he was a professor?"

An amused look crossed Frank's face. "You forget I'm a cop."

"You spying on me?" Jessie looked upset.

Frank glanced at her, eyes narrowing. "I'm jumpy since Tommy turned up missing, Jessie. I wanna be sure my daughter's protected. You can't fault me for that, can you?"

"I can take care of myself, Dad. I've been doing that for a long time." She shot him a look that matched his glare.

The police chief shrugged. "Okay, Travis stays. Shut the door and grab a chair." They sat down after she slammed the door closed.

Travis winced.

Frank sank into a wooden swivel chair and leaned forward, resting both elbows on a gray Formica-topped desk. Travis saw a Bible sitting on the shelf behind Frank. He watched the man steeple his hands as if praying. "No word on Tommy yet, Jess. Everybody's out looking. I've called in all the favors I've earned over the years and then some. We're looking everywhere."

Jessie nodded, staring at her father.

Frank unclasped his hands, gesturing. "Honey, we're doing everything we can. I've been up for two days straight. We're running out of places to look." He shot a look at Travis, then returned his attention to Jessie. "But that's not why I asked you here."

Jessie straightened as if preparing for a blow. "Yeah, Baptiste wouldn't tell me anything."

"In all fairness, I didn't tell anyone why I wanted to see you."

"You're scaring me, dad. What is it?"

"Remember Tommy's friend, Pete?"

"Pete Axtell?"

"Yeah. He's turned up missing." Frank studied her face before continuing. "Failed to show up for work yesterday. No one's heard from him since."

Jessie gripped the desk. "You think this has something to do with Tommy?"

Frank lowered his head before answering. "I don't believe in coincidences. There might be a connection." He shifted his attention toward Travis. "You were a cop once, right?"

Jessie glanced quickly at Travis and then back to her father. "No, Dad. He teaches at WSU—criminology, right?" She looked back at Travis.

He waited a moment before answering. "You're both right. I teach criminology at WSU and—yes, Frank—I once was a cop."

Jessie looked puzzled. "You never told me—"

"—we never got around to sharing our past, Jessie." He turned to Frank. "How'd you find out?"

Frank shrugged. "I told you. Ran a check and found you were in law enforcement in California for a number of years. Five years ago, you came up here and started teaching."

Jessie looked from one to the other.

Travis fidgeted in his chair.

Frank hunched his shoulders. "Got me curious why you'd drop out of law enforcement and come all the way up here to teach. So I made a few calls."

"Okay, I used to be a cop. No big deal."

"Actually, my contacts said it was a big deal. Worked on several joint task forces targeting organized crime. Worked undercover for seven years. Cited for bravery several times, including saving a child's—"

"Okay. Okay. So I have history. Let's leave it at that."

"So, professor, I'm interested in what you might bring to the table. My son is missing and I'm running out of options. What would you do if you were in my shoes?"

Travis stiffened. He glanced at Jessie, a puzzled look still on her face. He felt the walls of this office were closing in. He wanted to get up and walk away. Instead, he gazed at Jessie for a moment as he leaned back and tried to relax. "I don't know what good it will do, Chief, but tell me what you have so far."

A sigh escaped Frank as he placed both palms flat down on the desk. "Two days ago, Tommy left his office in Orofino about 4 p.m., according to a witness who saw him getting into his car. Another witness, a woman working in the same complex, saw him drive off. Those are the last two people who saw Tommy."

Frank shifted in his chair before continuing. "Yesterday, we located his vehicle abandoned along the Clearwater River. Twenty-four hours later. A deputy from Idaho County found the car in a grove of trees and called it in. They found it parked off the highway, in a pullout that dipped down near the river. The vehicle was locked up tight and the keys missing. No sign of a struggle."

Frank paused as if to invite questions. Met by silence, he continued. "Sent a BOLO statewide for my son, as well as Washington, Oregon and Montana. So far, we've got no responses."

Travis shifted in the chair. "What about credit card activity, acquaintances, neighbors? Anything?"

"Nope. Credit reports show no activity, and we can't find anyone—other than two witnesses near his office—who saw or talked to him since that afternoon. He just vanished."

"Who you working with?"

"Right now, no one except a cop from Orofino PD and the Idaho County Sheriff's Office. Talked to a friend with the FBI, but they won't really get involved unless we get something specific—crossing state lines, abductions, whatever might trigger federal involvement."

"And locals, state?"

"Again, we need to substantiate something beyond a missing adult report. Anything that might suggest foul play. As a courtesy, Orofino PD took the missing person report."

Travis shrugged his shoulders. "Sounds like you got it covered. Unless something else surfaces, I'm not sure what else to suggest."

"Come on. Give me something to work with." Frank's eyes hardened.

Travis tensed. "Look, Frank. I'll be honest with you. If I were working this case, I'd need to put my personal feelings aside and look at this objectively. Can you do that?"

Frank met his gaze. "You're asking the impossible, but pretend I could be as cold as ice. What would you do?"

Travis took a deep breath. "I'd start by thinking the worst. I take it this disappearance is out of the ordinary for your son. Right?"

Frank nodded.

"I'd approach it as if something *did* happen. The very worst you could imagine—that's where I'd start."

"You mean ..." Frank faltered.

"I'm sorry, but you asked what I'd do. Start looking at his life for any evidence of anyone who might want to harm him. Someone who might benefit if he disappeared. Start looking at all his friends and acquaintances as suspects, not just possible leads to his whereabouts. Continue trying to track his movements, his credit card use, his leisure hours, his business appointments. Look at everything. Believe no one."

Frank looked back impassively.

Travis continued. "The fact Tommy's friend is now missing should raise all kinds of flags, chief. I'd start turning over every leaf, every rock, till something pops up. Time is critical. Look for ties between these two men—beyond friendship."

Frank's face seemed to age in minutes, pain evident in his gaze. "I want you to help us, Travis. Help me find my son," he said, his voice raspy and hoarse.

Travis straightened his back. This was not going to happen. He could not risk it. He gave them his two-cents worth. That's all he could give. "I can't, Frank. Look, you got access to a number of law enforcement agencies, all of whom I know want to help. They're better equipped. Better trained. I've been out of this game for years."

"How can you walk away like this?" Frank said, forcing the words out between rigid lips, the man's pain turning into anger. "I'm asking for your help. Cop to cop."

Travis could not meet Frank's glare. "I just ... can't, Frank. I'm not a cop."

"What are you afraid of?" The chief pressed on, scowling. "Is that why you're no longer a cop? Lost your nerve?"

Jessie edged forward. "Dad, please. Travis did me a favor coming here." She turned to Travis. He saw she was trying to balance everything. Her dad. Travis' past. Tommy's disappearance. She seemed adrift, floating in uncertainty.

Frank shoved himself back from the desk. "My son's missing and another boy has disappeared." He stood, jabbing a finger toward Travis. "Like you said, time is running out. I need help right now!"

Travis tried again. "I know you're tired and worried about your son, but—"

"Don't tell me how I feel." Frank leaned on his desk with balled fists, his voice thundering through the office.

Travis tried again. "I wouldn't presume to know how you feel, sir. The truth is ... I'm not a cop anymore. I've got nothing to offer."

Frank's face hardened, his squinting eyes filled with rage and hopelessness. It was the same look Travis saw in Jessie's eyes by the river.

Travis rose and pushed back his chair. "I hope you find your son." Not knowing what else to say, Travis turned toward Jessie. "I'll be waiting outside when you're ready."

He left the door ajar. Someone slammed it shut. He glanced back to see father and daughter gesturing at each other. Even with the door closed, their raised voices rang through the building. Everyone in earshot hushed as they listened to the family squabble.

Baptiste sat smiling to himself.

Travis finally reached the lobby still hearing Jessie and Frank arguing. Once outside, a soothing breeze washed over him as he walked toward the truck. He could not calm down. Shadows danced across the valley floor as mountainous skylines stood colored in deep purples against a darkening sky. He climbed inside and found himself clutching the steering wheel, knuckles turning white. He loosened his grip and tried to relax. Frank struck a nerve, a cord that Travis thought died years ago. It surprised him that he still cared, that he was still tied to what he'd left behind.

Life as a cop.

He saw the station's main door fling open. Jessie came flying into the parking lot, heading for the truck almost at a run. Frank emerged in the doorway, watching her leave. Jessie yanked the passenger door open, hurled herself onto the seat, and slammed the door shut. The sound reverberated off glass.

"Hey, take it easy on this old clunker. This has to last me a few years."

Jessie peered at her father, the police chief still standing on the other side of the parking lot. "He makes me so mad I could scream. I see why Tommy fought with him so much. I can't believe he was spying on me. I'm almost thirty years old." She crossed her arms.

"Does your dad always have this effect on people?"

"To be honest, he and I always got along pretty good. Today is just not one of those days."

They traveled in silence until they were several miles north of town. He expected to see tears by now. He glanced over, surprised to see Jessie smiling.

"What?"

She shook her head. "I was about to say I'm almost as old as you, but that would be a lie. You're not as old as my dad, are you?"

Travis flicked a turn signal and maneuvered around a family van piled high with camping gear. "Getting people riled up, is that a gift that runs in your family?"

Her smile broadened. "Yeah, it's a gift I've inherited."

"Well, I'd better step on the gas and get you back before I get another dose." He glanced in the rear view and saw he'd cleared the van. As he pulled back into the right lane, he looked over at her.

Jessie's smile was gone.

He turned onto the highway paralleling the Clearwater River and headed due east. He saw her looking at the river, apparently lost in thought.

He thought about what Frank revealed and looked over the river, watching the water glistening from the last rays of sunlight. He knew what Jessie thought. Tommy White Eagle disappeared somewhere along this tributary. He just vanished without a trace, except for his empty car.

Travis turned back to study the road ahead. Frank's glare after Travis turned him down cut to his core. A hurting father asking for help. Travis bit his lip, disgusted with himself. What happened to him over the years? How did he turn out like this? Afraid to a take a chance. Afraid to step out and live life on the edge once more.

Quietly, he slumped down in his seat and peered into the rear view. Daylight slipped over the mountain range behind him. Darkness began reclaiming it right to reign once again.

 **Chapter 8**

WSU, Pullman, Washington

"You okay, professor?"

Travis cracked open tired eyes to see one of his students looking back at him with concern. "Yeah, I'm fine. Thanks, Brenda." He dismissed the classes minutes ago, but some students still lingered. Travis reached down and picked up a large paper cup of Starbucks' finest. He sipped and grimaced, lukewarm coffee leaving a bitter taste.

Brenda seemed to accept his answer, joining other students leaving the room.

He forced down another swallow, hoping caffeine might chase away his lingering weariness. All he wanted right now was to put his head down somewhere, anywhere, and sleep.

Two weeks ago, he'd dropped Jessie off at his cabin and left the solitude of his mountain retreat to return to the university. Once back at WSU, his paperwork kept piling up. He struggled to complete a research paper due in a couple months, spending every waking hour on the project between teaching, eating and sleeping. He thought working a summer teaching gig here would be lightweight and allow him to get caught up on his research project. Time seemed elusive.

Even Sam seemed to be getting irritated.

Like his dog, Travis wanted to flee back to the mountains, to his cabin in the woods. Quiet and peaceful. No people. No pressure.

The idea of pressure brought Jessie to mind as he thought of Clearwater River. Tommy must still be missing. He had seen very little about the search, as if everyone finally gave up.

Traversing Terrell Mall, he trudged into the main hallway of Wilson Hall, choosing the stairs rather than the elevator. A little exercise might just wake him up. Reaching the third floor, he entered the Department of Social Sciences by a rear entrance and sauntered toward his office.

He heard a cough just as he sat down at his desk.

Kent McPeters, department chairman, stood in the doorway scanning the tiny office before turning his scowl toward Travis. Bifocals gave the man's eyes a split-level look. "Professor Mays, thought you'd be up at your cabin."

"I've been back two weeks. My presence on campus obviously leaves a big impression on you, professor."

McPeters uttered a chuckle that sounded more like choking, his expression somewhere between a grimace and a belch. "I thought you slid up there every weekend." He seemed to be fishing.

"Whenever I can, McPeters. Why the interest?" Travis eyed his boss suspiciously.

McPeters cut loose with more choking sounds. "Oh, just trying to stay in touch. Wanted to see how everything's going," The chairman slapped his forehead. "Oh, I forgot. You have a visitor. Want me to send her back?"

"Her? Who is it?" He glanced at the papers on his desk, waiting for a reply. Silence made him look up again. He stared at an empty doorway.

Everything about McPeters made Travis edgy. The man seemed to spend all his time lurking in the hallways. Travis knew little about him, but what he did know made him want to spray the room with disinfectant.

He pulled a file from the in-basket filled with research on theories of criminal deviance. As he thumbed through the findings, his mind kept returning to his conversation with McPeters. He set the file aside as he heard footsteps approach and turned toward the doorway, expecting McPeters.

Jessie White Eagle emerged. "May I come in?" She looked ashen.

He started to rise. "Please. Have a—"

"—they found him, Travis." She crumpled into the chair as if those very words sapped her strength. "They found Tommy's body this morning."

Travis sank back down. "Oh, Jessie. I'm so sorry."

Jessie hardened her face, fighting back tears. "Hikers found him above

Lochsa, near Split Creek Ridge." She clutched her hands. Sorrow seemed to shove her deeper into the chair. "They shot him and then dumped his body in the mountains on federal lands like a piece of garbage."

"I don't know what to say."

Her eyes glistened. She rocked back and forth, as if the motion might ease the pain she held inside.

He clasped his hands. "Can I—?"

"We need your help, Travis." Her eyes searched his.

"I'm sorry."

"Help us find who did this."

"Even if I could—"

She leaned forward. "Please. I'm begging you. Dad tells me you were one of the best. Help me find the animals that killed my brother."

Travis gestured with his hands. "I can't walk into the middle of an active homicide investigation, Jessie. That's not how it's done."

She reached over the desk and grasped his hands. "Please, just shut up for a second and hear me out. Dad talked to the tribe's executive committee. They're making a formal request to the university, asking the school to let you work with him on this case ... if you're willing."

"Jessie, this is murder. The FBI and local cops will be all over this since the body turned up on federal lands. The tribal police won't even be involved."

She shook her head. "You don't know my dad very well. He's going to investigate what happened to his son—no matter who has jurisdiction."

Travis hunched forward. "Even so, your father won't work with me. You saw the fireworks between us."

Jessie gripped his hands harder, tightly, as if the intensity of her grip might make him cave in. "Travis, he made some calls himself. Found out what you did as a cop. You must have impressed him. He's asking for your help." She gripped so hard her nails almost cut into his skin. "He swallowed a lot of pride to make this happen. Please—I'm begging you—work with him."

As he looked into her eyes, the walls of protection he'd built over the last five years began to weaken. The urgency of her words and the vulnerable look in her eyes made him clench his jaw. His mind screamed *No*. His heart wasn't as sure.

Travis saw a shadow in the doorway. McPeters appeared. "Can I see you for a moment, professor?"

"Not know, McPeters. I'm right in the middle of something here."

"I need to see you in my office right now. It's urgent." McPeters wheeled around and stalked down the hallway. Travis found the chairman in his own office, staring out the window.

"What is so important that it couldn't wait a few minutes?"

McPeters turned and leaned on his desk. "Administration just shipped me a request about you. They say the Nez Perce tribe wants your help to investigate a murder."

"The woman in my office is the victim's sister. I really need to go back and—"

"You really need to tell me what's going on, Travis. What do you expect to accomplish? I mean, you're a ... teacher. The arrogance to think you can provide more help than all the other law enforcement agencies involved—"

"—Look, I didn't know anything about this until a few minutes ago. Jessie just told me about the murder."

"Jessie? On a first names basis, are we? I trust this is a *professional* relationship." His eyes narrowed, his lips curled back a grimace as if he'd just stepped in something disgusting. "And do they know about your past?"

"My past?" Travis glared at his boss, jaw clenched tightly.

McPeters sneered. "You know what I'm talking about. I heard you washed out of police work. Couldn't handle the stress."

Travis rocked back on his heels, struggling for control. "I didn't wash out. I chose to leave. I got tired of people like you who've never put a case together trying to tell others how to do their job."

"Sounds like you couldn't handle it."

Travis exhaled, looking out the window and focusing on the clock tower in the distance. Once he felt under control, he glanced back at McPeters."It sounds like this came from the top, well beyond your pay grade, Kent." Using the man's first name caused Travis to smile.

"It doesn't really matter what you think. The decision's been made, so live with it."

Travis realized this conversation with his boss helped settle his own mind. Jessie would get her wish.

McPeters look at him for a moment, his shoulders sagging in defeat. "I'll make sure your classes are covered Travis," he said. "Just don't embarrass the university out there. There will be a lot of eyes watching you."

"A lot of eyes? What are you talking about?"

McPeters was no longer aggressive or angry. It was as if a switch inside had clicked and McPeters became almost human. "You carry the name of this university with you. Everything you do will reflect back on us. Just watch yourself."

Travis nodded, taking one more look at McPeters before leaving. The man's expression made Travis pause. The man's eyes look as vacant as the dead. The change was startling.

As Travis walked back to his office, he thought of what had just happened. There was only one word that fit.

Weird.

 **Chapter 9**

Split Creek Ridge above Lochsa River, Idaho

Travis saw three police vehicles, bumper to bumper, along Highway 12. The lead vehicle was an all-terrain four-wheel-drive with sheriff's markings. The other two were unmarked.

He pulled off the road and braked.

Jessie leaned forward on the passenger's side. "Dad's car is the third one in. The others must be FBI and Idaho County sheriffs."

They got out of his truck and stood along the highway. He saw Frank and two other men standing down by the Lochsa River. The men below began walking in Travis' direction, the trio shoulder to shoulder with Frank in the middle. All three wore plain clothes.

Travis zeroed in on the man to Frank's right. Must be FBI, but the way he dressed J. Edgar Hoover would have rolled over in his grave. The agent looked like he lived in the woods—close-cropped hair, logger's shoulders, stocky build—and dressed in clothing straight out of a Sears catalogue; heavy red-plaid shirt, denim jeans, and a pair of tan ankle-high boots caked with mud. He looked familiar to Travis.

The man on Frank's left walked like a deputy who'd spent more than a few years in patrol. Slimmer than the other two men, much younger, with closely-shorn blonde hair. Compared to the FBI agent, the other man looked like he just graduated from college.

Travis took a deep breath. After his last face-off with Frank, he wondered how the tribal police chief might greet him. Jessie said her father pulled strings to get Travis here, so maybe the guy had a change of heart.

Jessie leaned closer, whispering. "I never met the guy in the red shirt. My dad's worked with him before. Name's Clay something. Italian. The other guy is John Steele from the sheriff's office. Nice guy."

So he was right on the money.

The three men crested the slope, stopping for a moment. They appeared to be caught up in a heated conversation, each taking a turn glancing his way. Travis felt like a person who walked into a party and realized he wasn't invited. Maybe Frank was having second thoughts about working with him.

Travis turned his attention to the river, watching the water cascading over granite boulders as it flowed down the canyon. He recognized this part of the river. He and Jessie shot past this point a few weeks ago on their rafting trip after their encounter with Harold the bunny killer.

As the men closed in, Travis braced himself. The FBI agent's expression seemed to tighten as he drew closer: skin—darker Mediterranean, olive—pulled taut by rigid facial muscles. The sheriff's detective, on the other hand, seemed relaxed, his boyish looks a striking contract to the tired-looking federal agent. A crooked nose—apparently broken and healed in his earlier years—was the only blemish on Steele's young face. Travis turned his attention to the police chief. There were dark circles under Frank's eyes, shoulders slumped like a man carrying more than his share of burdens. Tired and wasted.

Frank nodded a greeting, gesturing to his right. "This is Special Agent Clay Lafata from the FBI." Turning to his left, he said, "And this guy here is John Steele from the Idaho County Sheriff's Office. John's department handled the crime scene. I've asked him to show us where they found Tommy." Almost as an afterthought, Frank added, "These guys know I've called you in as a ... consultant."

So Frank was acknowledging his part in getting Travis here.

Lafata stepped closer. "Just to make it clear, Frank. This guy's not part of the investigation," thrusting a finger at Travis. The agent spoke in a terse, New York accent. Travis flashed on Robert De Niro in *Taxi Driver*. Lafata thrusting a finger in Travis' face, still looking at the police chief. "This guy can take a look and then we're out of there. Agreed?"

Ignoring the agent, Travis looked at Steele. "Your forensic team finished?"

"Yeah, they're done," said the younger man. "But I do want to minimize contamination in case they need to return. In and out. Okay with you?" The deputy sounded nicer than the agent.

Travis shrugged. "Your call, detective. I don't want to get in anyone's way." He sensed both men might be humoring Frank by allowing a *consultant* on the case. He saw only conflict ahead.

The federal agent glowered at Travis. "Listen up, profess-ahh." Again, heavy East Coast, drawing out 'professor' as if he was hanging a question mark on the end. "Just because you once were some kind of local hotshot in California doesn't mean squat with me. Our case, our rules. Got it?" His eyes flashed with hostility.

"Got'cha. Your rules, your case," Travis said, realizing he'd just mimicked Lafata. Another thought came to him. The agent's remark about Travis and California—now he knew where Frank got information on Travis' past.

As if to break the tension, Steele stepped forward, gesturing toward the river. "The killer dumped Tommy's body up there," he said, pointing across the river toward the nearest mountain peak. "There's a faster way to the scene that gets us around the river. Let's jump into my four-by since I know the way. We'll need to head downstream, cross over the bridge at Three Rivers, and then work our way back on a fire trail. Take us about a half hour."

As promised, a half hour later they stood above the crime scene. Travis saw a well-traveled trail, marred with heavy boot prints, leading down the hill and across a gulley before rising to a bare ridge. Patches of late-winter snow still clung to the ground. Steele led them across the gully and along a path to the ridge.

"The body was found there," Steele said, pointing down a slope littered with boulders. The body lay sprawled face up further down the slope.

Travis tried to imagine how the killer got the body to this spot. The terrain was treacherously rugged. He saw two parallel grooves leading toward the victim. He looked up to see Lafata eyeing him.

"Yeah, we already figured they used some kind of stretcher, probably made out of branches, to cart him up here. They didn't care about leaving any marks—just the boot prints. Brushed 'em out clean."

"They?" Travis asked.

"Whoever. Can't tell how many. One person might have pulled it off with some kind of stretcher. The problem is, whoever did this took his time sweeping up the scene and erasing any footprints. All the prints you see on the path were left by deputies and rangers hoofing it up here."

Travis continued to search the ground. "Cause of death?" He looked at the agent, hearing a pause.

Lafata glanced at Frank and Jessie, looking uncomfortable. "Still waiting for the coroner's report but it's pretty obvious. Death by gunshot, chest and head."

"How many shots?"

"Three. One to the head." Lafata looked at Frank and Jessie as he spoke.

Travis waited until Lafata looked his way. "Anything else?"

"Yeah, the ... Tommy's hands were tied behind him. Duct tape. At least until he was dumped here. Found bits of tape still clinging to his wrists. And we found what looked like gunpowder stippling on the skin. We assume it was up close and personal."

"What else did the body tell you?"

Irritation flashed across Lafata's face. "You mean postmortem lividity and all that mumbo jumbo?" He glanced at Frank. "You two wanna hear all this. I can ..."

Frank waved a hand. "Jessie and I will be going. Catch up to us when you're through." Father and daughter began to retracing their steps to the deputy's vehicle.

Lafata turned on Travis. "Look, pal. I'm doing this as a favor to Frank. Anything to help him get through the night. But, personally, I think it's a bad idea sharing information with someone like you."

"Like me?"

"Yeah, like you. I hear you refuse to follow orders. I also heard that when you didn't get your way, you packed up your marbles and skipped town to become a professor. Well, this ain't a classroom, school boy. This is the real world where real people get hurt."

Travis warily eyed Lafata. "You know nothing about me, Lafata. I'm doing this as a favor to Jessie. If I had my way, I'd be back at the university. Since we're stuck with each other—tell me about the body."

Steele chuckled, eying the two men. "This might be fun to watch. I feel like you guys are dying to jump into the ring and have at it. This could get real interesting."

Lafata relaxed as if he just declared a temporary truce. "Here's what we've surmised from the evidence. The victim was shot somewhere else and brought here. Time of death is going to be hard to determine. At least three days, maybe more based upon the condition of the body. Coroner and lab will tell us more later. No clue where the murder happened. We're still trying to track the victim's movements before he disappeared."

"There's a gap in time between when he disappeared and when he was killed, right?"

The agent nodded. "A huge gap. He was killed just before the body dump, maybe a couple hours or less. The onset of rigor became evident after they tossed the body. They must have held him captive for nearly two weeks before offing him. We found some markings on his chest. Looked like he was tased, but I'm waiting until Steele's people have a chance to study the body more closely."

"What about his car?"

Lafata shook his head. "Nothing that helps us right now."

Steele turned to leave. "I'll let you guys know when those reports are ready." The deputy began following the path taken by Frank and Jessie.

Lafata turned to leave, but Travis grabbed his arm. "I don't know where you got your information, but I never skipped out on a case in my life."

Lafata scowled at him, jerking his arm back. "Tell it to someone who gives a rip, Columbo. And don't ever lay a hand on me again."

Travis held the man's gaze.

The agent rubbed his arm before continuing. "I don't give a flying leap why you quit, professor. Just stay out of my way." He edged closer to Travis. "And if you withhold information from me, I'll hit you with obstruction. I'll come down on you like a ton of bricks. I don't care if you are Frank's friend."

"I wouldn't call us friends."

"Or whatever you're doing with Frank's daughter on the sly. Get my drift?" The agent started down the trail. He looked back with a sneer. "Just don't get in my way again."

"Again? What're you talking about?" Travis struggled to remember where he and Lafata crossed paths. He came up empty.

Lafata stalked away, following the others back down the hill.

Chapter 10

Orofino, Idaho

Creasy adjusted the police scanner, listening to conversations between tribal police officers and dispatch. One officer squawked to another about the FBI, a sheriff's deputy and a body found above the Lochsa River.

A source already whispered into Creasy's ear that police found a body. He wanted more information, but there were no further details broadcast over the air.

Frustrated, he flicked off the radio and crawled out of his car. Striding toward an earthen berm ahead, he heard the soothing white noise of the Clearwater River as it rushed past. A mound of soil held back the river's floodwaters from swamping a nearby parking lot where he now walked. Only one other car was in the lot, a vehicle he recognized. As he reached the grassy lip of the earthen barrier, he saw a man standing on a bicycle path alongside the river a few yards away.

Shane Foster. Client.

Foster glanced his way and turn back toward the river. As Creasy walked up, he saw his client slip a hand into a pocket of his denim jacket. He knew a gun must be hidden inside. Smiling, he eyed the bulge in Foster's coat pocket. "This is not a good idea. Meeting here in public."

The other man shrugged. "Just two men watching the river. Old friends passing time."

"We're hardly *old friends,* Foster. You hired my company to take care of your business problem. I told you I'd let you know when the job is finished. Until then, leave me alone. No contact. Those are my rules."

"Maybe I just want assurance you're working on *my* problem—not someone else's."

"What're you driving at?"

Foster stared back with cold green eyes. "I heard about that body they found upriver last night. Along the Lochsa. Your handiwork?"

"Why'd you think that?"

"Oh, I dunno. People just seem to die when you're around."

"You paid me to do a job. I'll get it done. That's all you need to know."

"I don't hire killers. Just ... reason with him."

"The body they found last night has nothing to do with you. Now, don't contact me again. Are we clear?"

Foster swung around, eyes narrowing. "Don't talk to me like that. You know the connections I have? The trouble I can cause?"

Creasy smiled without warmth. "And yet—you hired me. That says something about your so-called connections. So don't lecture me, Foster. That would be a mistake. A deadly mistake."

The man seemed undeterred. "You came to me and said you'd take care of this problem. People say you take care of business. Well? I wanna see some action."

Creasy faced the river, watching the white-capped water tumbling beneath the bridge. "Your situation is profitable to me because of other plans. You heard what I can accomplish and you jumped at the chance. Now, shut up and let me do my job."

"I'll have you taken—"

Creasy wheeled around and grabbed Foster by the throat, crushing the man's windpipe just enough to make him gasp for air. At the same time, he trapped the hand still resting inside the pocket. He felt the metal of a gun and turned the weapon inward towards Foster's gut.

"I'll kill you and everyone you love before anyone can lift a finger," Creasy hissed into the man's ear. "Are you really prepared for that kind of trouble?"

He shoved Foster away with contempt. The man staggered, still choking, glaring at him with fear and loathing.

Creasy turned away. "Don't call me again. I'll let you know when the job's done." He strode away, knowing Foster's hand rested on a gun. He also knew the man was too frightened to pull the trigger. Another gutless wonder.

Creasy walked as if he feared nothing. *A man on fire.*

Chapter 11

After leaving the crime scene, Travis followed the police chief back here to Orofino to begin their investigation. He followed Frank up a flight of stairs to the law offices they planned on searching. The police chief fumbled with his dead son's keys, struggling to unlock a glass-paned door. As Travis waited, he read *Thomas White Eagle, Attorney at Law* stenciled in black letters across the smoky glass.

This must be tough on him, Travis thought, watching the older man opening up his dead son's office. Going through these personal items must be like throwing alcohol on a fresh wound, he thought, stinging re-membrances of Frank's loss.

He heard the lock click open, and saw Frank swing open the door. A wave of musty old books and stale fried food lingered in the air, evidence the office must have been sealed up for awhile. As he entered, Travis caught a glimpse of the Clearwater River a few blocks away through a window. He glanced around the office; two rooms on the top floor of this second-story office building. Not a bad set-up.

He watched Frank hesitate before entering, as if the man was gearing up his resolve. A large oak desk, battered from years of abuse, dominated the room. File cabinets stood to one side, opposite the window overlooking the river. "What kind of law did he practice?"

"Criminal, civil, anything that came along. Whatever legal protection his people needed, Tommy jumped into it with both feet."

"His people?"

"We call ourselves Nimiipuu, the name my people used before Lewis and Clark and the others showed up calling us 'pierced noses, Nez Perce."

Travis grinned. "I can't picture you with a ring through your nose, Chief."

Frank rolled his eyes, sitting down behind the desk, staring outside for a moment. He uttered something under his breath that Travis could tell was not a compliment. "You know," Frank said, pointing toward the mountains with a look of sadness, "All this land once belonged to my people. Beyond where the eye could see—into Washington and Oregon. And now, people like my son struggle to hold on to what remains—the land, the water. All that my people swore to protect." Frank's voice sounded hoarse, words from a man whose world seemed to be collapsing.

Standing across the room, Travis stood in silence. Frank seemed to be reaching into the past, into a world of his father and his father's father. Or maybe it was a father struggling to come to terms with what happened to his son, a grieving parent trying to survive. Wrinkles in the man's face seemed deeper, more pronounced, as if thinking of the past aged him during this brief conversation. There was a framed photo resting on the desk, a black and white snapshot of a younger Frank and a small boy fishing along a river.

Travis felt like an intruder as he watched Frank work his way around Tommy's desk. Through an interior doorway, he saw another room. He walked in and glanced around: a small kitchen crowded into one corner of the room; a couch in the middle; and a queen-sized bed shoved into the opposite corner. To his right, a small television and bookcase loaded down with books. He ran a hand over some of the books. Tommy's reading interests seemed diverse—history and literary fiction, crime novels mingled with books on hunting, fishing, gambling and religion.

Travis glanced back at Frank still lingering near his son's desk. "Tommy lived here, too?" he asked, walking back into the office.

Frank picked up the photo, caressing its edge like a carpenter inspecting the smoothness of planed wood. "He lived to work. Always something in the oven. Kept all his own files, ran his own office to save money. And, yeah, he lived here. Tommy never needed much."

Travis glanced toward several file cabinets against the far wall. "When are they starting the search?"

"Steele said the prosecutor wanted to get a special master to help them search since Tommy was an attorney. You know, so they don't have to worry about attorney-client problems later if one of his clients turns up as a suspect."

"What about the search warrant?"

"They've got it signed, but they're waiting until the master's appointed."

"I thought they'd have this place sealed."

Frank grimaced. "Fortunately for us, they're anxious to get started on the case. Once a special master comes on board, it'll take days for them to get their hands on these files. I think they're hoping we'll give them something to roll on right now before the master takes over."

"Defeats the purpose, doesn't it?"

"Lafata's not one to let the rules get in the way of his investigation. I don't know how Steele feels about it. I guess the way they see it, there's plausible deniability if anything backfires and the defense finds out we got here first. They'll just say they never knew about it."

"Right. Well, let's get started. I'll start looking through the hard files. You take the desk?"

Frank just nodded and reached for a drawer. They began work in silence, each lost in their own worlds.

Nine hours later, darkness hid any view of the river. Travis needed a break. He glanced over and watched Frank using the computer, clicking through various programs. Earlier, Frank rifled through all the desk drawers, pulling out a number of files, thumbing through some and reading others more carefully. About an hour ago, Frank found a password to the computer in the bottom drawer, giving access to all programs. "Tommy seemed to have no appointments on the day he turned up missing," Frank said.

Travis shut a file drawer and sauntered over to the desk. He leaned over the older man's shoulder. Frank clicked on each day prior to the disappearance. "Look here," he said, pointed a particular day on the calendar. "Two days before he disappeared, Tommy typed in the words *'Jessie re: problem'* See that?"

Travis nodded.

Frank peered up at him. "She never mentioned it to me." Turning back toward the screen, he drummed his finger on the keyboard, apparently lost in thought.

Travis straightened and felt tightness grip his lower back. "Maybe I should be the one to talk to her, Frank." He knew what those words inferred.

Frank seemed to bristle. "We've got no secrets. She tells me everything."

"Trust me, Frank. Everyone has secrets."

The older man scowled. "Maybe in *your* family." Frank closed his eyes for a moment, slowly opening them. "Sorry about that. I don't know anything about you."

Travis walked over to the file cabinet. "Actually, you're right. I'm not the best person to give advice about families. I never really knew my parents."

"I thought you knew your mother? Jessie told me about that middle name your mother gave you. The one you try to hide." Frank tried to smile.

"She did, huh?" Travis returned the smile with a grimace. "I barely knew mom. She died when I was five. My father never entered the picture."

"Sorry about that." Frank looked up again. "If you don't mind me asking, who raised you?"

Opening another file drawer, Travis peered inside, not really focusing on anything as his mind strayed to his youth. "No other relatives that anyone could find. They just shipped me from one foster home to another until I was old enough to escape."

"Must have been tough on a little tyke."

Travis shrugged. "I survived." He peered at the darkened windows, catching his reflection in the glass. Frank kept pecking away at the keyboard, apparently searching for more information. The man seemed to know Travis did not want to take this journey down memory lane.

Frank's voice brought him back to the present. "I'll go back a few weeks. See if we can get a clue as to what Tommy was working on."

The clock on the wall showed midnight when Travis finished with the files. Frank still pecked away at the keyboard, hitting the down arrow as he scrolled through another program.

Travis blinked several times. His eyes burned from squinting over reams of legal documents without adequate lighting. The files revealed nothing of importance. It seemed Tommy's work load consisted of a smattering of criminal cases, water rights issues for the tribe, and representation of the Whitewater Casino.

He glanced at Frank, still bent over the computer. "Tommy's hard files show a lot of work regarding water rights and treaties research for the Nez Perce executive council. Could any of this make someone angry enough to harm him?"

Frank rubbed his eyes. "Sure. Just the Snake River Basin alone had about 150,000 water rights claims, each one significantly impacting people's lives."

"What was his involvement?"

The man looked haggard. "Tommy did a lot of work on that settlement along with other attorneys representing the tribe. In 2004, they reached an agreement that recognized the Nez Perce water rights claims all along the Snake, the Clearwater and other tributaries. A huge step forward."

"Enough motive to make someone want to murder him?"

Pain filled the older man's eyes. "Yeah. It might fire up someone enough to kill. Tommy rode point on some of these claims. But so did other attorneys and they're still breathing. And if it were one of these claimants, where do we start? There are hundreds of potential suspects here."

"Whatever happened to that other guy, Axtell. He ever show up?"

"Pete Axtell?" Frank sat up, resting on his elbows. "Still missing. Nobody's heard hide nor hair."

A thought crossed Travis' mind, something he spotted in one of the files. He picked up a file labeled *Whitewater Casino* he'd set aside earlier. Grasping it, he opened it and found what he was searching for—a handwritten note lying loose inside. "Frank, I saw this earlier. Someone wrote here 'Pete called. Problems at casino. Meet at his trailer. 8 p.m.' You think this refers to Pete Axtell?" He laid the note on the desk in front of Frank.

A frown creased Frank's face. "Could be. Maybe someone got to Pete too?"

Travis slipped the note back in the folder and jammed the file into the cabinet drawer. "Who knows? No date. Could have been written anytime. You know where we can find Pete's trailer?"

"Yeah, upriver near Kamiah. We've already searched his place when he turned up missing. Found nothing."

"Let's take another look in the morning. Your guys might have missed something." Travis closed the cabinet drawer slowly until he heard it click before turning toward Frank.

The older man's eyes missed nothing. "What's troubling you, professor?"

Travis leaned his back on the cabinet, staring at the floor for a moment. "As you know, in a homicide investigation we're suppose to look at everyone. Anyone who might have problems with the victim."

Frank nodded, still watching.

"I've got to ask you, Frank. I heard you and Tommy argued a lot. Did things ever get physical between you and him?" He saw Frank's hands clench, forearm muscles bulging.

"You think I could have hurt my own son?" His voice, low and terse, sounded menacing.

"I've got to ask, Frank. I know there was some conflict."

"Jessie tell you that? That I might've killed my son?" He sounded angry, hurt.

"No. She didn't say anything like that. Just mentioned you and Tommy argued a lot. About the casino, religion, stuff like that. Maybe there was something you two argued about that might shed light on what happened." Travis knew he sounded lame. He dreaded raising this issue, but it needed to be dealt with now. Before Steele and the other others started poking around.

Frank clenched his teeth, jaw muscles rippling. "You ever have kids, Travis?"

"No."

"Since you are such an expert, let me tell you about parents. No matter how proud you are of your kids—someday, someway, somehow—they will do something that will disappoint you. Might even hurt you. Something that you know deep down will do them harm."

"Like working in a casino?"

"That's not what I'm talking about. That's just a symptom. I'm talking about what really makes someone tick. What does a person hold on to when everything is on a downward spiral?"

"You mean religion? God?"

Frank nodded, grasping the photo on the desk as if somehow this might connect him to the past. "Tommy was very strong willed. That's what made him a good attorney. That's also what made him a real pain. Like his old man."

"That sounds like a good thing. People might call it determination."

"Yeah," Frank said, "Unless your direction has no purpose, no substance. Then, you can have all the determination in the world and still be headed nowhere."

"I take it you and Tommy traveled in different directions?"

Frank tried to smile but the effort seemed to hurt. "Like two boxers at a prize fight. And we'd go at it over those differences. I said things I wish I could take back now. It only made him more bullheaded. Drew us further apart."

Travis shifted against the cabinet.

"Now my boy is gone." Anguish on the man's face made Travis cringe. This father's torment seemed to fill the room "To answer your question ... No, I could never harm my son."

Travis focused on the darkness outside. The night seemed lighter. Moonlight sparkled on the river like flecks of diamonds cast upon black velvet.

"I know you didn't harm your son. We'll find out who did." He pushed off the cabinet. "Maybe we should get going."

Frank rose to his feet, still staring at the photo. He reverently picked it up, taking it with him as they walked toward the door.

Outside, a chilly night made him draw his coat tighter. He heard an owl shrieking in the distance, lonely and haunting, a sound meant to startle prey down below.

Frank trudged slowly toward his car, moving at a tired gait, shoulders hunched forward. "See you in the morning," he said, without looking back after giving Travis directions to Pete Axtell's trailer. "Get some shut-eye."

Travis waited until Frank drove off, listening to the night sounds around him. Again, he heard the owl's call. It was as if the bird raised the very question troubling both men.

Who? Who killed Tommy?

Maybe tomorrow they'd find a clue.

Chapter 12

Selway River, Idaho

The rider savagely kicked the Appaloosa on both flanks, whipping the horse's blanketed white rump with the reins. Startled, the animal high-stepped into the swollen creek and clambered up the far bank. Once across, horse and rider followed a narrow game trail paralleling the rushing stream.

Brian Wyatt swatted at a fly on his neck and leaned back in the saddle. Heat from the mid-afternoon sun seemed to fuel all his anger pent up inside.

He glanced at the forest around him. For almost a century his family vigorously protected this land, an inheritance handed down through generations from father to son. Surrounded by the Bitterroot National Forest, his family faithfully sheltered these lands from civilization's encroachment. All these years, they ruled and protected their ranch. Never giving an inch. Even when government agents came poking their noses into family business.

Never giving into pressure. Almost a family motto. He must not break tradition.

Water—and in particular, this creek—became the Achilles heel threatening everything his family worked toward. Today, everything depended upon who controlled this water. The government and other interests fought to pry control from Wyatt's hands. In the distance, he saw where the Selway River joined the Lochsa further to the north. He felt like a king looking over his forested kingdom, a fiefdom threatened by invaders seeking to tear it from his grasp.

Thieves armed with an agreement—a piece of paper government

forced down his throat—between governmental entities, businesses and ranchers.

And the Nez Perce tribe.

Trouble arose over this very creek, whose water his family dammed years ago higher up in the mountains. And now, a project he'd slaved over for ten years was about to collapse because the government wanted him to release all that water.

He kicked the horse in anger.

Shifting in the saddle, he felt a crumbled brochure for the Three Rivers Development in his back pocket. Thousands had been printed and distributed to anyone interested in the development. Potential buyers were beginning to phone in, despite the plunging real estate market, to put their name on the list. And now, he and other investors anxiously waited for the county to give final approval. Unsettled water rights issues might kill the deal.

A long ride should settle the fury that whirled around in his chest.

Four hours later, Wyatt still seethed inside. He wheeled the horse around and rode toward the ranch house along the river. The sun set just as he reached the barn. He turned the horse loose in the corral, after pulling off the blanket and saddle, storing them in the tack room, and giving the animal a quick rub down.

A red message light blinked on his phone as he entered the office. Pressing the play button, he listened to a gravelly voice giving him a call back number. He dialed, staring out the window.

The same voice answered.

Wyatt cleared his throat. "Got your message. What's up?"

"A slight complication. The cops are asking around about the ... problem I took care of."

"Yeah. So? You were supposed to *talk* to the problem, not make him disappear."

The other man continued. "One guy's father, Frank White Eagle, won't let go. He'll keep pushing until he gets some answers."

"Don't give me any details. Not over the phone." Wyatt's voice rose. "You took this further than I wanted. Now fix it. Permanently."

"It won't be traced back. You've got my word."

"Your word?" Wyatt struggled to control himself. "You already gave me your word this matter would be taken care of ... quietly. Now the cops will be breathing down my neck because of your stupidity."

The voice coughed. "So what'd you want? An apology?"

"What I want is for you to make this go away. And then for you to disappear." Wyatt gripped the phone. He detested men like this one. An amoeba had more brain power than this moron. "And don't call here again."

Wyatt slammed the receiver down. He hated incompetent people, especially when their failings came back to haunt him. Because of this man's blunder, Wyatt's neck might be stretched out by hangman's noose. Here in Idaho, hanging was still an option in the courts for murder. He'd looked it up when the news came about Tommy White Eagle's death. Just wanted to know how bad things might get if they caught him. Well, hanging was one of those options.

Wyatt sat down heavily in a chair. It was too late to roll back the clock. To undo what he had put in motion. He only meant to protect his family and the land. But now—he might lose everything. Even his life.

Bitterly, he thought how this came to be. Uncle Sam gouging the family's pocketbook year after year, demanding higher and higher taxes, while ranch income steadily declined.

Their financial salvation depended upon this development.

Now, a few protected fish jeopardized the entire project. The dammed up water—around which the entire development depended—allegedly obstructed natural migratory patterns of salmon and steelhead. They used terms like 'destruction of natural habitat.' Hah. His family toiled on this land and protected these *natural habitats* for decades. And now—when they really needed just a fraction of the land to keep things afloat—an agreement loomed in Wyatt's face, hammered out by politically-influenced outsiders. An agreement that directly affected his family's financial survival.

He would make sure the family survived no matter the cost.

Creasy replayed his conversation with Wyatt—made an hour ago—in his mind.

So that arrogant rancher thinks I'm stupid.

He'd learned long ago never to underestimate his enemy. Bitter experience taught him everyone became his enemy sooner or later. Only one person had been his friend, and that person lay six feet underground.

Now he was all alone. He must kill those responsible. It was time for judgment. Time for them to pay for their sins. And he would become their executioner.

Everyone has dirty little secrets. Those things they thought no one would ever find out about. They trusted him to help hide those secrets, always thinking they were smarter. That he would never find out the full extent of their secrets—but they were always wrong. He knew where everything lay buried. He made it his job to uncover these secrets. He chuckled to himself, thinking about all that money they paid to make them feel safe from exposure. Sooner or later, however, one of these mental midgets started thinking about what a threat he might become. Their little minds started clicking about ways to kill him. And when they got up enough nerve to whack him, they'd wound up in the grave alongside their own victims.

One nasty circle of clients.

Everyone underestimated his power. They never suspected he'd use all those secrets to gain his own objectives. To triumph in his own private war.

Ignorantly, they'd paid him a lot of money to seek his own revenge. When all the dust settled, his masterpiece would become apparent to all. His life's work. Like Creasy in the *Man on Fire* movie, he would ignite another man's world with destruction. He'd become like that man in the movie—a lily-white Denzel Washington. Unlike the movie, though, he had no one else to save.

This was all about vengeance and justice.

Creasy slipped his cell phone into a pocket, watching two men leaving Tommy's office. He already knew their identity. Travis Mayes. Frank White Eagle.

He followed Travis home.

Chapter 13

Clearwater River west of Kooskia, Idaho

"Travis." **Jessie's voice carried** across the rumbling of the river.

He stepped out onto the porch and saw Jessie's yellow bug parked behind his truck. She was standing on the far bank, hands cupped, shielding her eyes from the morning's brilliance. Sam was at the river's edge giving her a welcoming bark.

"Hey, lazy bones. Breakfast on me. At Lowell's?"

He waved back. "Be there in a few."

Jessie scrambled up the bank and into her car. He watched until she drove out of sight. Reaching inside the doorway, he grabbed a coat and strode toward the cabled lift.

Sam shot him an expectant look. "Not this time, boy. Stay here and guard the place." The dog lowered his head, his wagging tail slowing to a twitch.

Travis hoisted himself onto the platform. As the cable worked its way across the river, he watched the dog disappear among the trees. Glancing at his watch, he realized he must meet Frank at Axtell's trailer in a couple hours. Thoughts of the case kept him tossing and turning most of the night. He was working on two hours sleep.

Ten minutes later, he pulled into the parking lot of the only restaurant in Lowell, a mountain hamlet kept alive by passing motorists. Population, thirteen people at last count. He saw Jessie standing, arms crossed, under a sign that read 'Ryan's Wilderness Inn.'

Jessie smirked. "You city folk sure like to waste the day."

"Your dad kept me out late." He locked the truck and strolled toward the entrance.

Jessie pushed off the wall. "Well, you managed to miss the rush hour. I think we can find a vacant seat or two."

He followed her inside. A waist-high glass counter, just inside the entryway, supported a cash register and a rack of knickknacks, greeting cards, fishing gear, and maps. The dining room spread out to his right, and beyond that, another room—equipped with a pool table and bar stool—stood empty.

A woman yelled from the kitchen, "Sit yourself down anywhere, Jess. Be with you in two shakes."

A couple of customers sat around a table in the middle of the room. A man in a black cowboy hat sat at the counter, his back to them. The man turned and glared at Jessie, eying her from head to foot with a scowl. He turned back to face the counter.

Travis tapped her on the shoulder. "There's only a dozen people in town. How can you have a rush hour?"

"It's all those out-of-towners like yourself coming in here. You never know whether you can find a table."

He glanced at all the empty tables. "Out of towners? I live ten minutes away."

"Like I said. Out-of-towners."

Jessie picked a window seat overlooking the highway. The one-story restaurant offered a view of Highway 12. Beyond the road, he saw the Three Rivers Rafting company on the far side of the Lochsa River, its campground filled with patrons. He slid into a seat across from her. "Any recommendations?"

"Yeah, anything that's available." She glanced toward the river. "How'd it go last night?"

He lowered the menu. "We didn't fight. That's a good thing, right?"

"Anything interesting? Any leads?"

He laid down the menu and carefully smoothed the paper mat out with his hand. "Your father found an entry on Tommy's computer. Thought I'd ask you about it."

"Fire away."

He wrote *Jessie re: Problem* on a paper napkin and pushed it toward her. "Two days before he disappeared he typed this on his computer calendar. Do you know what this was about it?"

Her jaw tightened as her hand clenched the napkin. A waitress leaned over them, placing two glasses of water on the table and pouring coffee without asking before pulling out an order form from her apron. "What'll it be sweetie?" She glanced at Travis. "And who's this? Prince Charming?"

Jessie seemed flustered. "Huh, oh, ... Becky. This is Travis, he's a friend."

A crestfallen look leaped across Becky's face as she quickly grasped Jessie's arm. "Oh, hon', I just realized. Heard about Tommy. I'm sooo sorry." She lodged a pencil behind her ear. "What's the matter with me. I must have walked off and left my brains at home." She leaned over and gave Jessie a hug.

Jessie seemed to be fighting back tears. "Thanks."

Travis gave the waitress a smile. "Good to meet you." He looked toward Jessie. "Maybe we ought to wait to order?"

Jessie took a deep breath. "No, go ahead. I'll take the usual."

He watched Becky return to the kitchen with their orders.

Jessie took a drink of water, slowly lowering the glass. "This has nothing to do with Tommy getting killed." She shoved the napkin in his direction. "I'd rather not go into it."

Travis sipped his coffee before responding. "This is a homicide investigation, Jessie. Everything's going to be gone over with a fine-tooth comb. Everything." He paused, giving his words emphasis. "The FBI will be searching Tommy's office today or tomorrow. They'll see that entry and come knocking on your door. Count on it."

She rolled the edge of the paper placemat in her fingers. "I don't want Dad to know." Her eyes searched his, pleading.

"I'll try. But at some point he's going to find out."

Becky bustled toward the cash register where a man stood waiting. She and the customer started chatting.

The man in the cowboy hat rose, tossed money on the counter, slowly turning to face them again. His gaze seemed fixated on Jessie, a look of hate. He spit on the floor as if ridding himself of something foul-tasting and stalked toward the door, still staring at Jessie. "They let anyone in here," he said loud enough for everyone to hear.

Travis clenched his fist and started to rise.

Jessie reached over, gently grasping his arm. "Let it go, Travis. He's not worth it."

He sat down, fuming. "I hate racists."

She gave him a faint smile. "I've learned to ignore them Travis. My dad calls it 'turning the other cheek.' They have to live with themselves. I choose to rise above it."

"You're stronger than I am," he said, watching the man stroll across the parking lot. He turned and pointed to the note he wrote on the napkin. "Let's get back to this."

Jessie pulled back her hand. Eyeing it, she said, "Tommy helped me with a ... situation." She glanced toward the cash register.

Travis heard Becky flirting with the customer behind his back. He remained focused on Jessie.

Downcast, she continued. "Joseph Baptiste—the officer you met a couple weeks ago—and I used to see each other."

"You mean ..."

She nodded, eying him. "Dad never knew. I tried to keep it a secret. The relationship is not something I'm proud of. It just happened."

"Why was Tommy involved?"

Her eyes lowered once more. She poured more cream into her coffee, picked up a spoon and slowly stirred. "Joseph is a macho kind of guy. Tried to carry it over into our relationship but I wouldn't put up with it."

"Did he abuse you?"

She met his gaze. "Yeah. Once. He got angry at something I said and hit me. I kicked him where it hurt and walked away."

"And that was it? He let you go?"

"I wish it was that simple. He knew I didn't want Dad finding out about us."

"Why not?"

"It's hard to explain." She glanced up for a second, then looked away. "I was afraid our relationship would turn into an office joke."

"A joke?"

She glanced at him with irritation. "After I told him we were through, Joseph tried to force me back by threatening to flaunt our relationship at work. Make us an office joke if I didn't change my mind. I was afraid dad might be embarrassed." Again, she looked down, gripping her hands. "I thought he might be ashamed of me."

"Why would Frank—"

"—Like I said, Travis. It is complicated and I don't want to get into it right now."

"Tommy knew how you felt?"

"Oh, yeah. But that was over a year ago."

"A year ago? So why did Tommy have it on his calendar just a few days before disappearing?"

She shrugged. "I don't know. Once Tommy talked to him, Joseph just seemed to disappear from my life. He never bothered me again. I don't know what Tommy told him, but whatever they talked about it seemed to shake Joseph up. I've had no problems with him since."

Becky finished flirting with the customer and came over to refill their cups. "Can I get you guys anything else?" she said, slipping the bill onto the table.

He shook his head, waiting until Becky ambled away. "Maybe Tommy learned something about Baptiste he used as leverage."

"Like what?"

"I don't know." He thought for a moment. "Your brother represented criminal defendants, right?"

She nodded.

He leaned on the table, resting on both elbows and steepling his hands. "Maybe someone slipped Tommy some dirt on Baptiste, some information he could hold over the cop's head to keep that creep in line."

"I don't know. Tommy never discussed it with me. Just told me the matter had been handled. I never heard a thing after that."

After taking a sip of coffee, Travis picked up the bill. "Could it be possible Tommy found out something about Baptiste that got him killed?"

"I know he can be mean, but I don't see him killing Tommy. Too much to lose. Besides, I think he's afraid of my brother."

"Afraid?"

"When Tommy and I visited Dad at the station, Joseph would take one look at Tommy and hightail it out of there. Like he had some urgent business elsewhere."

Travis reached for his wallet. "I've got to meet your dad in Kamiah this morning. We're going to take another look at Pete Axtell's trailer."

"He and Tommy were good friends. I hope Pete is okay."

"Did Tommy ever mention any problems Axtell might be having at the casino?"

"At Whitewater? Never." She stood as Travis pushed back his chair. "Tommy always kept things to himself."

Travis walked toward the cash register after catching Becky's attention. Jessie tugged on his arm. "Hey, I promised you breakfast."

"I'll take a rain check. That way, I know we'll have another date."

"Is this a date?"

"What would you call it?"

"I'd call it breakfast ... for now." She glanced at him with tired eyes. "You know, the way you live—across the river in the cabin—it's hard to get in touch with you."

"Is that right?"

"Like you've planned it that way."

He grinned. "It doesn't seem to have slowed you down." He paid the bill, holding the door open for her as they left. Outside, a gentle breeze swept their way, morning sunlight warming a turquoise sky.

They stood near his truck for a moment. Jessie leaned back on the front quarter panel, closing her eyes as if listening to the sounds of the river. Her long dark hair hung loose around her shoulders, the beauty of her features highlighted by the morning's yellow brilliance.

Looking at her, Travis thought Baptiste had been a very stupid man.

Slowly, she opened her eyes. "When I make up my mind about something, I don't let anything get in the way. I just thought you needed to know that about me." Pushing her hair away from her face, she smiled at him before turning and slowly walking toward her car.

Travis waited until Jessie drove from the parking lot. A moment later, he saw the yellow flash of her car as she crossed the bridge over the Lochsa and drove into Three Rivers campground. He went back inside the restaurant.

"Becky, you got a pay phone here?"

"You bet, sugar. If it was a snake, it would have bit you." She pointed toward the wall nearest the counter. A pay phone hung on the wall between racks of postcards and gift items, the phone booth camouflaged with posters and handbills.

He pulled out a business card, dropped coins in the slot and dialed. A woman answered. "FBI, may I help you?"

"Could I speak to Special Agent Lafata. Tell him it's Travis Mays."

"Wait one moment while I see if he's in."

Travis waited, knowing he'd just been handed a line. Every FBI field office he ever visited seemed to have a mandatory grease board with every agent's name listed, the board hanging where everyone in the office could see it. Agents scrawled on the board the times they planned to leave and return, and sometimes even where they might be headed. The woman probably wanted to give Lafata a chance to decide whether to take the call. He imagined the agent sat a few feet away from the woman.

"Transferring your call, sir." Lafata must have accepted.

He heard clicking on the line. "Professor Mays, solved the case yet?" Lafata's voice boomed in his ear.

"Not yet. Even us local hotshots generally take a day or two to wrap up a homicide."

"Well, you got something for me?"

"Yeah ... but it's sensitive." He waited a moment, trying to decide how best to convey this message. "I want Frank White Eagle kept out of the loop. At least for now."

"Hey, keeping your partner in the dark isn't a good way to do business, Travis." He noticed the agent used his first name, dropping all pretense of formality.

"Well, Clay ... you want this information or not?"

"Don't screw with me, hotshot. You got something on the case, I want it right now. Don't play games with me."

Travis smiled to himself. "Do we have a deal?"

He could bluster as well as Lafata. For the moment, the agent lacked leverage. Travis enjoyed his advantage. The agent allowed Frank and Travis to traipse through Tommy's office, a possible crime scene. The court might call it an 'unsupervised fishing expedition.' Defense attorneys might yell and scream about cops planting evidence. This spelled leverage.

"We've got a deal." The agent did not sound pleased.

"Fair enough." Travis just bought Jessie some time to figure out what she'd tell her father. "On Tommy's computer, you're going to find an entry on the calendar a couple days before he disappeared. The entry reads 'Jessie re: problem.'"

"Frank's daughter? Big deal." The agent paused, then came back on the line. "You ask her about it?"

"Uh huh. This morning over breakfast."

Lafata laughed. "Frank know about you two?"

"Just breakfast, Clay. She showed up at my cabin and threw me an invitation."

"Okay, lover boy. What'd you learn?"

The agent's remark irked Travis. "She had a bad relationship with Officer Joseph Baptiste."

"The cop working in Frank's office?"

"Yeah." Travis relayed Jessie's information.

"That puts a spin on things. Keeping Frank in the dark might be tough. He has a way of finding things out."

"Jessie wants it that way. I promised."

"There you go again. Making promises you might not be able to keep. You ought to be more careful."

Travis bristled. "What are you getting at, Lafata?"

"Forget it. You better hope Frank doesn't find out. If he does ... I'd hate to be in your shoes."

"Just let me know what Baptiste says."

"That's not how it works, professor. Anything else?"

Travis remembered the note he found about Pete Axtell in the White-water Casino file. He started to tell Lafata and then stopped. The agent made it clear this was going to be a one-way exchange. Two could play that game. If anything turned up at the trailer today, he'd reconsider passing it on to the agent. "Nothing that seems important right now. We'll be in touch."

"Give me your cell number in case I need to reach you."

"Don't have one. You can reach me through Frank."

"What if I don't want Frank to know I'm talking to you?"

"Write a letter or come hunt me down. I don't use a phone, a computer, a pager—any technology created after Elvis Presley hit the big time. I distrust technology."

"Elvis Presley. Isn't that a little before your time?"

"The King is ageless."

"What about your teaching job? Don't you use technology there?"

"There are exceptions. But I won't be at the university in the foreseeable future. Find some other way to reach me."

"Paranoid, are we? Think big brother's watching?" Lafata laughed.

He hung up the phone. As Travis walked back to his truck, something the agent said bothered him. Keeping this information from Frank did not feel right. A partner did not keep his fellow cop in the dark about an ongoing investigation like this.

The promise he gave to Jessie made everything very difficult. For now, he must honor his word. He just hoped Frank never found out. If he did, everything might get even more complicated.

He opened the truck door and climbed inside.

Chapter 14

Kamiah, Idaho

The Clearwater River wrapped its boulder-strewn arms around Kamiah—an historic settlement nestled in a valley, carved by the river over centuries —and seemed to hug the life out of the tiny hamlet in some seasons, while giving it life in others. Today, this little village seemed alive. Travis drove to the north edge of town and followed a gravel road that snaked its way from the highway almost to the river's edge. He saw Frank's car parked in front of a single-wide trailer that nestled in a grove of yellowing pines.

Frank emerged as Travis climbed from his truck "Place is open. Thought I'd wait until you got here. Supposed to be here earlier, weren't you?" Irritation polished each word like sandpaper.

"Couple of errands to run," Travis said, glancing at the other man. "Sorry. Should we get started?"

"Why not," Frank said, turning toward the trailer. "Our officers went through this place when Pete turned up missing, looking for any evidence of foul play or anything that might suggest he left voluntarily. Came up with squat and started looking elsewhere."

Travis nodded, opening the trailer door. The place was surprisingly neat; sink empty of dishes, bed made tight enough to pass military inspection. Nothing seemed out of the ordinary. Even the trash can stood empty.

"You know this guy?" Travis watched Frank pulling drawers out near the sink.

"Nah. He came by with Tommy a few times. I knew they hung out together, but I really didn't know much about him. He worked in accounting at the casino. You know, a numbers cruncher."

"Was he a neat freak?"

"Couldn't tell ya. Like I said, didn't know the guy very well."

"Look around, Frank. This place look like a guy's been living here? I'll bet his laundry basket's empty. No guy is this neat. Not even Monk."

Frank cast a look around the trailer. "You may be right. I like things neat, and I don't live like this."

"It's almost as if someone put everything back in place. After they tossed it."

"So what are you saying?"

"We ought to go through this like Axtell stashed something. Whoever was here before us was looking for something. And it wasn't our missing guy."

"What're we looking for?"

"Who knows?"

Two hours later, the trailer had been neatly trashed. Every drawer pulled out and dumped. Every cabinet emptied. The bed stripped and turned over. Clothes strewn on the floor, the bathroom torn apart. They even crawled under the trailer.

Frustrated, Travis leaned on a fold-down table near the kitchen and eased himself into the chair. "Came up empty. Any luck?"

Frank plopped down across from Travis, squinting. "I don't know where else to look unless we start using a crowbar."

"If there's anything, it's got to be in a place where he could have got to fast—without tearing this place apart. Maybe there's nothing here. Or maybe whoever searched before us already found it."

Frank leaned back and studied the ceiling. A round opaque light fixture hung above the table. Travis watched Frank lean over and flick on the light switch next to the door. Nothing happened. He flicked it a few more times.

Nothing.

He glanced at Travis before standing. "I know this place has electricity."

"Maybe the light burned out."

Frank carefully loosened the screws holding the glass in place. Once loosened, he removed the glass bowl. There were no bulbs in the light sockets. As he moved the bowl, a solid object inside scraped across the glass. Frank peered inside and smiled. He reached in and withdrew a USB flash drive.

"Bingo."

"Strange place to hide your thumb drive."

Frank slipped it in his pocket. "Not if you're trying to hide it in plain sight."

"Now, we just have to find a computer."

"Got one in my office. Let's go."

Several hours later, they walked into Frank's office. Travis saw Joseph Baptiste working at his desk. No FBI agents around. The officer glanced up from his desk, giving Travis a slight nod.

Frank waved Travis into his office and closed the door. "Take a load off. I'll fire up the computer and see what's on this puppy," he said, withdrawing the drive from his pocket.

Frank waited for the computer to power up as Travis drew up a chair. The chief glanced at him for a moment. "By the way, Baptiste tells me he saw you and Jessie having breakfast together in Lowell this morning. One of the *errands* you had to run?"

Travis shifted in his seat. "She came by my place this morning and wanted to have breakfast." He never saw Baptiste this morning. Not even another police unit. Another red flag waved in his mind about this officer. "I think she wanted to find out how the two of us are getting along."

"And?"

"And what?

"How're we doing?"

"Just swell, Frank."

Something must have popped up on the monitor. He saw Frank shift his attention back to the screen. He breathed easier.

"Jessie tell you anything about the problem Tommy helped her with? The thing I found on the computer?" Frank looked over at him.

"We never got around to talking about it. I'll ask her later." He met Frank's glare, knowing if he looked away right now Frank would know he was lying. The room suddenly felt warm.

Frank looked back at the monitor, clicking the mouse as he appeared to scroll through the files listed on the drive. "He's got one file here, named 'Customer Information.' I'll just open ... whoa!"

Travis came around the desk carrying a folding chair he'd found leaning in the corner. He set it in place, sat down and peered over Frank's shoulder.

"Look at this." Frank pointed at the screen. "He's got hundreds of casino customers, listed by name and credit card number. Each name has a sub file, listing the customer's date of birth, social security number, mailing address, home address and buying habits. Why is he walking around with this kind of information?"

"Go back to the files menu and let's see what else he's got listed."

Frank clicked the back arrow until he came to the file directory. He scrolled down through the list.

Travis leaned forward, pointing. "Slow down, Frank. Go back up to the middle section there. See Tommy's name? Open that file."

Once Tommy White Eagle's file popped opened, they saw a video file listed in a sub-directory. Once opened the file activated a video recording of two men sitting at a table. Although a little grainy, Travis recognized the two men were sitting in Axtell's trailer where he and Frank found the thumb drive.

"That's Pete on the right," Frank said. He tried to zoom in on the man on the left. "I don't recognize this other guy."

Travis saw one of the men gesturing and realized one of the two men was speaking. "Do you have the sound muted?"

Frank leaned over and turned up the volume. "I always have that stuff turned off. Noise irritates me, all those bells and things they've built in."

Travis wanted to tell Frank to shut up as he tried to listen to the two men's conversation on the video. Once Frank stopped talking, conversation between the two men on the tape became audible.

"—I can't do this anymore, sir. They'll find out—"

"—You'll do what you're told until I say otherwise ... if you value your pathetic life."

Peter hung his head. "I can't. They're gonna find out any day."

The other man leered. "At least you'll still be breathing."

"They'll send me to prison. I can't do time."

"You don't have a choice. Get me the rest of that information by next Tuesday or my people will send you to the big burial ground in the sky." The speaker stood up and walked out of view, leaving Peter hunched over the table. They heard a door slam a moment later. Pete glanced toward where the hidden camera rested. He stood, walked toward the lens until he enveloped the picture. The recording went black.

Frank clicked the file closed, glancing up at Travis. "Interesting. We've got to get an ID on that other guy. This might be why Pete disappeared."

"Or he's dead." Travis rose and walked around the desk. "Two big questions. Did Pete disappear voluntarily? And, is this connected to your son's death?"

Frank yanked the flash drive from the USB port and slipped it back into his pocket.

"You going to call Lafata about this, Frank?"

The police chief smiled. "Speak of the devil," he said, gesturing toward the outer office.

A window gave them a glimpse into the next room. Travis turned and saw Lafata and another man walking up to Baptiste, sitting at his desk. They spoke to the officer for a moment. Baptiste turned toward Travis, tight-lipped.

Lafata turned and saw them standing in Frank's office. The agent grinned back at Travis and with two fingers gave him a salute.

So much for keeping secrets.

Frank turned toward him. "Anything you want to tell me, Travis? The FBI just gave you a look that tells me you might know something?"

Tension squeezed Travis' chest tight as he picked up his coat. "First, let's go find Jessie. Then we'll talk."

 **Chapter 15**

Santa Rosa, California

Creasy knelt at the gravesite and placed flowers next to the marble marker. *I have not forgotten you, Michelle. Revenge is all I can promise.* He heard footsteps on the path, but he did not bother turning around. "Did you get it?"

"Yeah, but it creeps me out meeting here."

Creasy rose and faced the visitor. The man stood a few feet away clutching an envelope. "Here. Everything from his personnel file. Complaints. Personnel investigations. Everything." He handed the package to Creasy.

"Does it mention anything about Michelle Scarsbourgh?"

The man looked at the tombstone at Creasy's feet, glancing at the name etched in marble. "You mean that lady?" pointing with his chin. "Yeah, she's mentioned in there. He got in a lot of hot water because of her."

"She's got a name. Use it."

"Why? She's dead and gone."

In a flash, Creasy kicked the man's feet from under him, kneeling on the fallen man's chest. "Would you like to join her?" Creasy said, shoving the man's face into the grass.

"Please, man. Lighten up. I didn't mean no disrespect." The man's voice quavered.

Creasy gritted his teeth and squeezed the man's neck. He smiled as the man thrashed and squirmed, unable to break free. Leaning closer, Creasy hissed, "One more word of disrespect and I'll end your life right here, right now." He slowly released pressure and watched the man stagger to his feet, gasping for air. "Now, get out of my sight."

Creasy rose and smiled as the guy scurried away like some frightened mouse. Death will soon knock on that man's door. He knelt once more by the grave. *Sleep well, my love. Soon, those who betrayed you will pay the price for their sins.*

Steve Kirkpatrick felt like he'd been sitting for days. This two-hour commute north from San Francisco's federal building to Sonoma County became a killer every day, a drive that should have taken half the time except for bumper-to-bumper madness. He pulled off the freeway in Santa Rosa and took the exit to Fountain Grove Parkway. As he climbed the hill, he saw the lights of the city spreading out below in his rear view mirror.

He and his wife, Linda, settled in this posh area of town knowing that he'd be shuffling off to the city every day. Linda wanted to enjoy suburban life, not the hustle-bustle of big city strife. And Steve wanted relief from her pestering, even if it meant fighting traffic every day.

Forty-five minutes ago Linda reached his cell phone to invite him out. She and a girlfriend wanted to dine at John Ash and Company and wanted to know whether he'd like to tag along. He declined. Exhausted, Steve knew he'd be dead to the world before she returned home. His bones ached at the thought of getting up early tomorrow morning and starting this all over again. He'd be back in the city before Linda ever woke up.

Such was their life together.

And now, after all this driving, he faced an empty house. Actually, a promise of a little peace and quiet felt good. Stress from his job took a lot out of him. Political fights and legal battles took its toll on him as chief of the U.S. attorney's organized crime strike force. Trial prep on a major human trafficking case needed to be finished next week. He'd head out early in the morning to get in the city before sun-up.

What a life.

One case seemed to flow into the next. Year after year, bad guy after bad guy, they all seemed to be jammed together as he flushed them down the sewer they called justice. Each case running into the next until he could no longer distinguish one from the other. Defendants and victims seemed to converge into one ongoing cycle of memories, each blending into the next.

One case still stood out vividly in his mind.

For a moment, his mind settled on that case. A case that almost came crashing down around his head.

Travis Mays.

Michelle Scarsbourgh.

Those names burned into his memory, never to be forgotten. One of the biggest cases he'd ever handled with everything on the line, everything to lose. Staggering collateral damage. He lost both Travis and Michelle in just a few days. Travis—one of the best investigators he'd ever known. Michelle—tragically slaughtered before she could testify. Travis turned in his badge the moment they found her body. Steve barely escaped with his job. Head hunters in Justice wanted to yank his job away, maybe even bring sanctions before the Bar.

Headlights illuminated scrub oaks and tall, dry grass as he pulled off Fountain Grove, and turned onto a smaller street leading to his house. He reached the crest of the highest hill and followed the street below, finally pulling into his circular driveway. He flicked the garage-door opener and drove inside as the door yawned open. Almost without thinking, he flicked the control and waited until the garage door closed before peeling himself out of the driver's seat. An interior door stood between the garage and the kitchen. Once inside, he deactivated the exterior alarm. Linda would know to reset it when she got home.

He grabbed a cold beer from the refrigerator and strode toward the back deck, his favorite part of the house. His elevated sanctuary—a Trex deck he'd built last summer—offered a sweeping view of Santa Rosa's skyline glittering below. To the west, lights began to disappear as the valley rose toward coastal mountains. In the other direction he saw more twinkling lights on Montecito Heights—more homes sprouting up on hilltops— and darkened mountains near Annadel State Park silhouetted by a rising moon. He collapsed on a lounge chair stretching out his legs. A tall pine tree at the

edge of his property rose up from his sloping backyard, partially blocking
his view of the downtown area. He meant to have an arborist trim it.

He took his last sip of the beer. A moment later—blackness.

Creasy slung the M40A3 sniper rifle over his shoulder and clambered down
the pine tree. Pop. One shot to the head. Neighbors might not even call it
in. People seemed reluctant to involve themselves. One single bang. They'd
justify it in their minds as just another vehicle backfiring. No reason to call.

No matter. Let the cops come.

He'd be history before the first patrol car swung through the neighborhood. Mrs. Kirkpatrick might have a heck of surprise when she got home.
Parts of hubby all over the new deck.

Let the cops try to figure this one out.

Creasy slipped to the ground, crouching for a moment as he scanned
the nearest homes. No one emerged. He quietly pulled the bolt back and
caught the spent cartridge as it ejected. He slipped the brass into a pocket.
One less piece of evidence for investigators. He slid the rifle into a camouflaged drag bag, took one last look around, then zigzagged his way to a car
parked a mile below in a shopping center.

He glanced around the parking lot and saw his car still parked where
he'd left it. A uniformed security guard eyed him from the door of the
market across the lot as Creasy reached the vehicle. He quickly opened
the trunk and threw his camouflaged bag inside. Slamming it closed, he
pressed the button to unlock the car. A patrol car entered the parking lot
just as he heard the locks click open. He glanced toward the security guard
and saw the guy still watching.

Only a couple minutes before the black and white reached the security
officer. All he needed was for some nosey rent-a-cop pointing him out to
the police as they drove by. Better to take the offensive.

He pulled a fire-engine-red sweater from inside the car and slipped
it on. The bright color would draw away any suspicion from his all-black
clothing underneath. He swiftly dusted off his pants around the knees
where he'd knelt on the ground moments after shooting Kirkpatrick. He
marched toward the market like a man on a mission.

The security guard warily eyed him.

Creasy grinned as he drew near. "Chilly tonight. Got to buy something to warm me up." He rubbed his hands together as if to make his point.

The guard seemed to relax. "Yeah, that's why I'm staying near the front doors. They got heaters blowing out warm air."

"Stay warm." He pushed through the doorway, watching the guard shift from one foot to the other. Once inside, he glanced back just as the patrol car drove up. The guard waved at the cop. The cop nodded, then glanced into the store and eyed Creasy. He waved at the officer, wondering if they'd already been alerted to a shooting. The officer's gaze seemed to linger, then he continued driving through the parking lot without stopping.

Creasy breathed easier as he saw the black and white disappear into the night. It was time to move on.

Chapter 16

Lapwai, Idaho

As Travis and Frank left the police station, a woman at the front counter waved frantically at the older man. "Chief. Got a message for you."

"Can it wait?" Frank sounded irritated.

Travis looked back to see if Lafata and Baptiste might be coming their way. He imagined the FBI agent would take Baptiste in for further questioning. He did not want to be standing here when they came out.

She shook her head, looking around like she was some kind of spy. "You'll want this," she said, lowering her voice.

Travis heard Frank mutter something, but couldn't make it out. They angled toward the counter, Frank taking the lead.

"What is it, Francis?"

Again, the sideways look like she was talking to 007. "I knew you wanted information on Pete Axtell. His aunt and I are good friends. So I told her that we were really concerned about Pete. How he disappeared and all. And that we wanted to know the minute she heard anything."

Frank nodded, apparently knowing there was no way to get this woman to get to the point. She was the kind of person who took forever. Travis hoped that once they finally arrived at the point, whatever she came up with would be worth the wait. He wanted to get out of here before the FBI and Baptiste came through. And he needed to get to Jessie before word got out that Baptiste was under investigation. He hoped Jessie understood that he tried to keep his word.

"So I told her, 'Ethel, you call me—day or night. We wanna know the minute he calls. You hear?' I was trying to tell her how important it was 'cause I really wanted to help you out, Chief. In case it might have something to do with what happened to poor Tommy."

Frank nodded, the muscles around his eyes twitching. "Thanks, Francis. And what'd she tell you?"

"Well, like I was saying, I had that conversation with Ethel the moment we knew Pete turned up missing. That very moment. I called her from here and stressed how important this information was to us." She paused, eyes searching Frank for praise.

"That's good thinking, Francis. You really showed initiative. And what did Ethel tell you?"

Travis marveled at Frank's patience. This woman might ramble for days.

"She finally called awhile ago." Francis stopped and her eyes widened as she looked across the lobby. Travis turned and saw Lafata and the other agent ushering Baptiste through the building. The two agents looked straight ahead, but Baptiste gave Travis a look of hate.

Lafata must have snitched Travis off to Baptiste. Frank had to have seen the look Baptiste hurled Travis' direction, but the older man remained silent, turning his focus back on Francis.

"And what did Ethel tell you?"

Francis seemed to take a moment to remember where she was in the conversation. "Oh, she said Pete called from a place in San Diego. He's trying to get a job and settle down there. He told her he just suddenly needed a change of scenery. Wanted time to think things out. He didn't want anyone to worry, but he asked that she not tell anyone where he was staying."

"Did she get his phone number?"

Francis beamed. "Better than that, Chief. She got the address where he's staying. A relative of the family." She pushed a folded paper toward him. "I've included the phone number. Hope this helps."

"It will. Thanks."

Her smile widened. "Any time, Chief."

Travis wondered whether Francis might be hinting at more than the job.

Frank led Travis outside. "Come on. You and I need to talk. Right now!"

"About what?"

Frank waited until they'd walked outside, in an enclosed parking lot for police vehicles. He whirled around. "You think I don't know what's going on in my daughter's life? How stupid do you think I am?"

Travis started to feign ignorance, but Frank's angry eyes stopped him. The chief must have found out about Baptiste.

Lafata. The agent squealed.

"Sorry, Frank. Jessie just didn't want you to know about this. I tried to give the information to Lafata and keep you out of the loop. I apologize."

"So the problem Tommy referred to in his computer had to do with Baptiste?"

Did Frank know about this or not? His question to Travis was confusing. "Yeah. He and Jessie dated awhile until he started getting rough."

"And Tommy dealt with Baptiste?"

"Yeah. According to Jessie."

"How long ago?"

"About a year. She doesn't know why he entered it into the computer just before his disappearance."

Frank gazed across the parking lot at the mountains beyond. "Lafata will get nowhere with Baptiste. That boy might have a temper, but he knows better than to harm Tommy."

"Why's that? Tommy too tough for him?"

The older man continued to look up into the mountains as if he saw something Travis missed. "No, although Tommy could take care of himself." He stopped for a moment, apparently realizing that there had been at least one person Tommy could not handle. The person who killed him.

Frank reached in his pocket and withdrew a ring of keys. "No. Baptiste is a coward. I never wanted him on the police force, but politics and family connections got him hired."

"So why couldn't he have harmed Tommy?"

"Because he knew he'd have to deal with me."

Travis saw a look in Frank's eyes that told pages about the man. It was a look that Baptiste must have seen at least once. The look of a father who'd do anything to protect his child.

"You already knew what he did to Jessie?"

Frank nodded with downcast eyes. "Jessie never knew, but I learned what Baptiste was up to and confronted him—apparently before Tommy got to him. I warned him to stay away from Jessie or I'd have his badge and make sure he did some serious jail time. He knew I wasn't bluffing."

"You never let on to Jessie?"

A look of sadness deepened the lines across Frank's face. "I wanted her to come to me with her problems. To trust me. She never did. Instead, she hid it from me and went to her brother for help."

"For what it's worth, I think she never told you because she loves you and wants you to think the best of her."

"I know. But I wanted her to find out she could trust me. With anything. She never took that first step."

"I can't believe you already knew this." Travis shook his head.

The older man's eyes hardened. "I gave you a chance to tell me the truth. Instead, you—"

"—I'm sorry, Frank. But I promised Jessie."

Frank bit his lip, gesturing toward his car. "Let's get moving. We'll leave your truck at your place after you pack a travel bag." He strode through the parking lot.

"But Jessie's at Three Rivers. Why do I need to pack a bag?" Travis said, following.

"We're going to San Diego."

"But I needed to talk to Jessie."

"You can talk to her when we get back. Now, let's move. We've got business to take care of in San Diego."

Creasy felt his cell phone vibrate as he drove toward San Francisco's international airport. He glanced at the number. An incoming call from Idaho. He punched the send button to connect. "Speak to me."

The male caller hesitated. "This a good time?"

"Depends. You got something?"

"Yeah. That guy you wanted to talk to. He's hiding down in San Diego. We got the address."

"Hold on a second. Let me get something to write on." Creasy pulled to the side of the road and grabbed a notepad from his briefcase. He quickly wrote down the address and phone number as the caller fed it over the phone line.

"Anyone else know about this?"

"Frank White Eagle and that white guy he's running around with."

Creasy grimaced. Another complication. He severed the connection. Must beat them to San Diego. Axtell had something he wanted.

Information.

Chapter 17

San Diego, California

A thermometer hanging on the wall of San Diego's International Airport terminal seemed pointless. Travis knew this border city near Mexico beat Idaho out by almost 20 degrees. Travis and Frank each carried a small grip bag for a quick overnighter.

Travis, sweat already dampening his armpits, flagged a taxi out front. They climbed inside, and Frank gave a turbaned driver directions. The man nodded and began circling back toward the city.

Travis stared out the window. Aqua-green waters shimmered to his right. He listened to Frank and the driver exchange pleasantries as they drew closer to the harbor. He saw the masts of the Star of India thrusting upward like tall trees above the decks of the ancient sailing ship lying along the waterfront. A few years ago, he'd traveled down here on a case and spent one evening walking along the harbor. That seemed like a century ago.

Frank leaned back, closed his eyes and lapsed into silence.

Travis saw lines of worry and tension etched on his partner's face. "There's something I wanted to ask you, Frank. Something that's bugging me."

"Just one thing?" Frank opened one eye.

Travis grabbed the door handle as the driver swerved to miss a merging garbage truck to his right. "I thought you didn't trust Baptiste?"

"I don't." Frank glanced at him, both eyes open. "Why are you asking?"

"The day Jessie came to my cabin, he pulled up across the river as if he knew she was there. Said you'd sent for her."

The muscles around Frank's eyes tightened. "Not true. I called dispatch and asked if an available unit might check Three Rivers for her. Figured she'd be somewhere in the area."

"So Baptiste happened to be there? Way off the reservation, I'd say."

"Makes you wonder, doesn't it." Frank looked past Travis to the water beyond. "I've got a question for you."

"Shoot."

"Are you interested in Jessie?"

"Huh?" Travis said, coughing.

"Simple question. Anything going on between you two?"

Travis turned and looked at him. "What'd she tell you?"

"You're avoiding my question." Frank refused to back down.

"We're just friends. She helped me survive the rapids on the Lochsa, and ... well, she wanted me to look for Tommy. That's it in a nutshell."

"I'm not blind, son."

"I don't know what else to tell you, Frank. I like her. She likes me—I think. That's all there is." And he wanted to add *And it's none of your damn business* but after Baptiste, he understood Frank's concern.

The older man gave him a hard look, then leaned back in the seat once again, closing his eyes.

Travis gazed outside, feeling as if he'd landed in the eye of an emotional hurricane.

Jessie.

He wanted to talk to her before leaving Idaho. Before she heard about the FBI picking Baptiste up. Before she believed he'd violated her trust. His head began to pound.

The taxi weaved through traffic, finally reaching northbound Highway 5.

Right now, he wanted to move on. To plan their next move. He turned toward Frank. "How do you want to approach Axtell? Let him know we know about the hidden thumb drive?"

The cab driver punched the horn as a car veered into their path.

Frank opened his eyes and shook his head. "What do people see in big cities? Jammed full with traffic, smog, and ticked-off people. Give me the mountains anytime."

Travis waited for Frank's answer.

"I'm going to tell him everyone was worried when he disappeared. Give him a chance to tell us why he ran."

"You don't think he'll buy the line we're worried about him, do you? And how are you going to explain my presence?"

Frank glanced at the driver, lowering his voice so only Travis heard. "He knows why we're here. I want to give him an opportunity to explain himself. Someone made him run. I want to find out why he's so scared."

"He's afraid of cops putting him in jail for criminal behavior."

"Not that easy, professor. Tommy chose his friends carefully. If my son liked Pete, then that tells me something about this guy. I'm betting Pete had to do something against his will. We don't know why he lifted the casino records. And who was the guy threatening him on the video? We can speculate, but we need Pete to fill in the blanks."

Travis watched as the driver took eastbound Mission Valley Freeway and then turned north on Highway 163. The Friars Road exit loomed ahead and he thought the driver was going to miss it. A second later, the cabbie swerved the wheel to the right and screeched his tires to reach the off ramp in time. They circled around the loop and headed west, passing Fashion Valley Shopping Center.

Travis glanced at the address he'd jotted down before the trip. The apartment where Axtell stayed should be in the next block. A series of condominiums and apartment complexes, embedded into the sheared-off hillside, clung along the roadway. Desert shrubs thrived in the shale slopes behind the building. He wondered how much water must come cascading down the hillsides when—or if—it ever rained. The backsides of the apartments seemed like they might be turned into man-made dams catching whatever moisture ran down the slopes.

Frank grasped his arm. "Look."

Travis peered over the cab driver's shoulder. Fire engines and San Diego's black and whites sealed off the number two lane of the four-lane roadway, emergency lights flashing. Yellow crime scene tape decorated the entire front of an apartment complex on their right. As they slowly rolled past, he glanced at the street numbers above the apartment's main entrance.

Pete Axtell's address.

He saw fire hoses strung from the hydrants through a ground-floor apartment near the main entryway.

Frank banged on the plastic Plexiglas separating driver from passengers. "Pull over here." He slipped the driver more than enough to cover the trip. Both men grabbed their bags and headed toward a squad car.

An SDPD officer in short sleeves sat in the patrol vehicle working on a report. Frank flashed his badge to draw the officer's attention. "We're here to contact a witness. Can you tell us what happened?"

The officer lowered his sunglasses and peered up at them for a second. Without answering, he opened the car door and climbed out, folding his arms across his chest. "There's been a fire. The arson squad's working it. First responders found a body."

"Can you tell me which apartment?"

The officer paused, studying Frank again before leaning through the window to peer at his CAD screen. "Apartment three-oh-one, top floor in the back."

Travis glanced at Frank, nodding. Axtell's apartment. Frank turned toward the officer again. "What caused the fire?"

The officer shrugged. "Let's say it doesn't appear accidental. Like I said, our arson squad's going over the place now. At least what's left. What apartment are you interested in?"

"The one that burned. Can I speak to a supervisor?"

The officer raised the sunglasses to the bridge of his nose, hiding his eyes. "Sure, give me a second." He grabbed a portable and keyed his mike.

As the officer tried to raise a supervisor, Travis walked to the end of the patrol car to wait. A warm breeze carried an acrid scent of charred wood, burned rubber and plastic. Abnormal heat rained down on them from the sky, scorching the roadway like rocks in a sweltering sauna. The city's normal cooling breeze seemed to have faltered at sea, leaving the land drenched in unrelenting heat hurled by an unforgiving sun.

A police sergeant strode up the sidewalk, eyeing Frank and then Travis. He circled around the car and walked up to Frank. Travis moved into earshot.

"My officer tells me you guys want to contact a witness in the apartment where this fire originated?"

Frank nodded. "That's right, Sergeant. A man by the name of Pete Axtell."

"Mind showing me some ID? I wanna know who I'm talking to." Frank pulled out his badge and ID, letting the sergeant examine it. Apparently satisfied, the sergeant pulled back. "Chief, huh. Tribal police? Haven't seen one of those badges in a while. And you?" He turned toward Travis.

Frank peered at the sergeant's name plate. "Huh, Sergeant O'Rourke, this is Travis Mays, a consultant we asked to help in a homicide investigation in Idaho. Murder of one of the men from our tribe."

"A consultant? What do you consult, Mr. Mays?"

"I'm a professor in criminology for one of the universities. "

"Professor, you say. You think this guy Axtell could tell you something about your murder?"

"We don't know," Travis said, shifting his feet. "We're hoping Axtell could clear up some things for us."

"Well, if he is the body we found in the fire, the only person he'll be talking to is St. Peter—if he's headed in that direction. The body's burned to a crisp."

"Died from the fire?" Travis asked, glancing over at Frank and then back at the sergeant.

"I'm no homicide expert, Mr. Mays, but I'd say the guy died from a gunshot wound to the head before someone torched that apartment."

Frank broke into the conversation. "Any witnesses?"

"Nope. A neighbor might have heard a door kicked in. Loud voices. Nothing else until a fire broke out. Whoever did this got in and out without raising any attention."

"Thanks for your help, sergeant," Frank said. "We'll let you get back to work."

"Before you go, give this officer your names and contact numbers. I want your information passed on to our investigators assigned to this case just in case there might be a connection. You mind?"

"Not at all," Frank said. "And I'd appreciate it if we could get reports on this incident forwarded to my office. I'd be particularly interested if you get positive ID on the victim." He handed O'Rourke a business card.

The sergeant glanced at the card and slipped it into his pocket. "I'll make sure this gets into the right hands."

Travis followed Frank across the roadway to a gas station at the next corner. "That might be Pete in that apartment, Frank."

He saw the older man clench his jaw. "Maybe. And that means someone beat us to him. Someone knew we were coming. I guess it's time to contact Lafata and let him know what we've got."

"You trust him? Lafata?" Travis thought about the look Lafata threw his way while standing at Baptiste's desk. "He's already burned me once."

Frank withdrew a handkerchief and wiped his brow. "Professor, you can't always choose who you work with. You take what you get, and move on."

Travis studied the other man's expression. *Was he talking about Lafata or me?* "Speaking of partners, why'd you want to work with me, Frank?"

The chief carefully folded up the damp handkerchief and placed it in his pocket. "I've got my reasons, professor. I've got my reasons. As for trusting Lafata, we don't have a choice."

Travis watched Frank walk up to the front counter at the gas station and request a phone book. After scanning the pages, he flipped open his cell phone and dialed. A moment later, he returned. "Cab will be here in twenty minutes or less. It's time to get back to Idaho and find out who's shadowing this case."

"You think Tommy's death and Pete's death are connected?"

"As certain as I know Judas betrayed Christ."

Travis eyed Frank, remembering the Bible sitting in the chief's office. They were going after Tommy's killer. Someone betrayed Frank and let the killer know they were coming to talk to Axtell. He thought Frank's mention of Judas seemed to fit in this context.

Betrayal and murder.

He also knew the Good Book preached about forgiveness and turning the other cheek. He wondered what would happen when he and Frank stood nose-to-nose with the killer. The one who murdered Frank's son, Tommy. What would Frank do? Would he be able to turn the other cheek?

Travis watched Frank walk outside to wait for the cab. What would he do in Frank's shoes? He did not even have to think twice about it. Kill him. Put him out of his misery.

Travis followed him outside, feeling a stifling breeze sweep over him. Somehow, Frank did not seem the kind of man who'd turn the other cheek.

Only time would tell.

 **Chapter 18**

Spokane, Washington

An overcast sky cast a gray pall over Spokane International Airport as Frank and Travis crossed the skywalk from the main terminal to the parking garage. Travis saw Frank's fist clench as he closed up the cell phone.

"What did Francis tell you?"

"Baptiste was standing right there when she got the call. He acted interested, so she spilled the beans. Told him everything."

"We know he didn't fly down and whack the witness. He was in FBI custody, right?"

Frank shook his head. "They let him go an hour after we saw him with Lafata. He could've beat us to the airport." He approached his parked car, opened the trunk and flung his bag inside.

Travis shrugged. "I just don't see it. Seems a stretch to think he's somehow involved in Axtell's death. Maybe he fed the information to somebody else."

"Who knows until we take a closer look." Frank opened the driver's door. "Oh, there's a message on my cell phone. Jessie wants to speak to you as soon as you get back. She doesn't sound happy."

"You know why?"

The older man smiled. "Not exactly. But if I was to take a stab at it, I'd say she's angry because you snitched her off about Baptiste."

"But you already knew."

"Yeah. But she doesn't know that and you promised to keep it a secret. Right?" He chuckled as he slid into the driver's side.

"I'm glad you're enjoying this."

Frank, his smile turning into a broad grin, started up the engine and drove toward the exit.

They cleared Spokane fifteen minutes later and traveled Highway 195 south toward the Palouse. An hour later, they connected with Highway 95 and began the steep decline to the city of Lewiston, a city wedged between forks of the Snake and Clearwater rivers. As they descended, Travis looked out over the expanse. He'd read about the Lewis and Clark Expedition traveling through this part of the country with the aid of Nez Perce guides over two-hundred years ago.

"Ever wish your people had told Lewis and Clark to take a hike?"

Frank smiled as he looked down on the rivers below. "Many times. But it was like trying to stop the ocean's tide. We just tried to survive."

"And have you?"

Frank shrugged. "We're still kicking."

Travis looked out over the expanse, the Snake River to the south acting as the boundary between the states of Idaho and Washington. The sky seemed to stretch beyond comprehension.

He settled back in the seat and mulled over what he'd just learned. Baptiste. Could he have set up Axtell's murder? The man might have had a score to settle with Tommy White Eagle, but it was not clear how this all fit together. Some pieces were missing. One thing he did know. Baptiste just became a person of interest.

They needed to track him down.

# Chapter 19

Kamiah, Idaho

Jessie White Eagle stood under the shade of a Douglas fir, one of two that graced the stone path to her grandmother's two-bedroom home. A sloping flat roof ahead—shaded by a grove of firs and cedars—crowned the modest dwelling. The house sat on a hill with a view of the valley below. She looked down the slope and saw a ribbon of highway leading past Kamiah toward higher mountains to the east. She listened to the hum of traffic on the road miles away. The sound seemed to sweep up the valley to the mountain tops.

She breathed in the fragrance of early roses, bright petals ringing the front yard like a colorful parade of costumes.

Be calm.

She breathed out slowly, still feeling tension clutching her chest, anger still seething inside after learning the FBI pulled Baptiste in for questioning.

Travis.

She couldn't wait to get in the man's face.

A screen door creaked. Jessie glanced toward the house and saw her grandmother emerge. The woman carried a smile brighter than the flowers along the path. In her seventies, Clara White Eagle moved with graceful strength.

"Jessie. So good to see you." Grandma Clara came closer. "Come here, child, I'm so glad you came."

Jessie looked away as she hugged the older woman, her eyes stinging as she tried to keep grief and anger balled up inside.

Clara put her arm around Jessie's shoulder, guiding the younger woman up the path. "Come, let's go inside and talk."

By the time Clara returned from the kitchen with iced tea, Jessie felt the comfort and safety of this place begin to calm her. Photos of the family hung prominently on the wall above her. She rested on a couch, her grandmother settling down beside her.

"Remember what your grandfather named you as a child, Jessie? When you were only as high as his knee?"

Jessie nodded. She could not trust herself to speak, even in this place of protection.

Clara smiled. "Little Deer ... Little Deer Running with the Wind."

Jessie tried to smile. "That's a mouthful."

"He gave you that name because of how fast you ran. Faster than even the boys your age." Clara leaned over and patted her arm. "Are you running away now, honey?"

Jessie felt her eyes burn as she tried to hold back tears. "I'm embarrassed, Grandma. And angry."

"I can't imagine—"

"—I was seeing a man I knew Dad would not like. I did it ... I don't know why I did it." She covered her face as she started to cry. "I knew this ... relationship would disappoint my father."

"Are you still—?"

"—No. This guy hit me and I left. I tried to hide it from my father, but now he's going to find out."

"Oh, child." Clara embraced Jessie. "He'll understand."

"No," Jessie said, pulling back. "He won't. He never understands. And now, I confided in someone and they told the FBI because they thought it might have something to do with Tommy's death. Because of my big mouth, Dad will find out."

"Why'd they tell the FBI?"

"Because Tommy tried to protect me. And now he's dead. They think maybe this guy—Joseph Baptiste—might be a suspect."

Her grandmother's face looked puzzled. "Who was this person you trusted?"

Jessie clutched the glass of tea. "Travis Mays." She almost spit the words out. "A man I met on the river who teaches at WSU. He used to be a cop, and I got him to help us find out what happened to Tommy."

"Well, maybe he thinks this will help?"

Jessie leaned back and took a deep breath. "Maybe. But he promised to keep my father out of it."

Clara smiled gently, lightly rubbing Jessie's arm. "You've never disappointed my Frank, honey. Never!"

Jessie slowly pulled back. "You just don't know, Grandma. I've never measured up to what he wanted."

"Did you ever stop and think maybe it's the other way around?"

Jessie looked at her, confused.

"Your father has loved you since the day you entered this world. He'd do anything for you. Maybe he already knows about this thing and he's angry with himself that he couldn't protect you?"

"I don't understand, Grandma. He always seems to—"

"Don't guess about these things, Jessie. Talk to him. Find out what he's thinking. The two of you are so much alike, always keeping things to yourselves." Clara smiled, patting Jessie's hand.

"He won't understand—"

"Hush, child. Give him a chance."

Clara took Jessie's hand in hers. The soft touch of those calloused hands, fingers gnarled with arthritis, brought back memories of Jessie's childhood. A time when these hands comforted a frightened little girl. Only seven years old, Jessie watched her mother slowly wasting away from cancer. She remembered the shock of her mother's death and how her father withdrew into his own world. He became withdrawn, quiet, and angry, leaving Jessie and Tommy to fend for themselves. Like a comforting breeze, Grandma Clara became their place of refuge, a shelter from a motherless world.

After Tommy's body turned up, she fled to the comfort of Clara's arms. Her grandmother—with tears of grief streaming down her cheeks—held Jessie in those arms, comforting once again.

Clara's voice brought her back to the present, hands still gently grasping Jessie. "Now, tell me about this fellow. Travis Mays. I want to know all about him."

Jessie looked into the other woman's eyes. "I'll tell you all about him, Grandma. But I don't know how long he'll be alive. This man is going to be in a world of hurt when I get my hands on him."

Clara laughed. "I can tell he got to you, child. So I must know everything."

Jessie folded both hands around her grandmother's. As she opened up, the feelings that poured out surprised her. She watched the gentle face of her grandmother, a woman who never judged, who always forgave, always looked at her with those eyes of love.

 **Chapter 20**

Lewiston, Idaho

As Frank drove into the parking lot, Travis spotted Lafata leaning against one of the patrol cars. The agent's crossed arms and square jaw gave him a chiseled stubborn look, and his frown warned Travis of trouble ahead.

Frank approached Lafata first. "What did Baptiste tell you?"

Lafata straightened, eying Frank with unease. "He's not your man."

"How would you know, Lafata? You didn't keep him long enough to warm a chair."

"We kept him long enough to verify his alibi. He was at the Whitewater Casino at the time of Tommy's death. We have him on security tapes."

"Did you ask him about a conversation he had with Tommy just before the murder?"

"Yeah. We did our due diligence, Frank. Tommy accused him a year ago of stalking Jessie, showing up unexpectedly. He warned Baptiste to stay clear of his sister."

"And what did Baptiste say?"

"He said he didn't need that kind of trouble. That he'd stay clear."

"What about the meeting just before Tommy disappeared?"

"Denied it. Said they never met."

Frank glowered at the agent. "And you believed him?"

"Can't disprove it right now. You got something?"

Travis leaned forward. "Did he ask why you singled him out?"

Lafata shot a glance at Travis and sneered. "Yeah, professor. He asked. And I told him. You know the drill, being an *ex-cop*."

Travis edged forward. "I'm not concerned about myself, Lafata, I'm concerned about Jessie. He knows she talked. If he is the killer, you just put her in the crosshairs. I also know that *smart* interrogators gather information. They don't dish it out to people of interest. That's police work 101 where I come from."

Frank stepped between them. "This won't get us anywhere, guys. So where does this leave us?"

Lafata glowered at Travis, before focusing on Frank. "Baptiste returned to work. And, by the way, he wanted to talk to you as soon as you get back from your little trip."

Frank looked surprised. "He told you about our trip?"

"Yeah. As soon as we left your station. Something about San Diego, finding one of your missing persons. Anything you want to tell me about, Frank?"

Travis saw the agent look from one man to the other, waiting for a reply.

Frank glanced at Travis before speaking. "We received information on a missing person case my office is investigating. We thought it might have a connection to my son, since my son was his friend."

"So, who is this missing person and what did you find out?"

"The guy's name is Pete Axtell. But someone beat us down there. Looks like they killed and torched him before we could question him. Waiting for positive ID."

"Murdered?" Lafata seemed very interested. "You think this is connected to Tommy's death?"

Shifting his feet, Frank took a moment to reply. He glanced again at Travis. "We're not sure. We found a thumb drive the guy hid in his trailer before fleeing. Someone must have scared him off before Pete could retrieve it."

Lafata's face darkened. "What was on the drive?"

"Files on customers from Whitewater Casino, personal and financial information. And a video recording of a man threatening Pete. We can't identify the guy, but he sounds like he might be connected to organized crime. Talked about his people taking Axtell out if he didn't cooperate. They must have got to him."

"And when were you going to share this with me, Frank? This is clearly out of your jurisdiction. Murder of a tribal member falls under FBI purview. You know that." The agent's face was livid.

"Like I said, we still don't know how all this ties in. But if Axtell is dead, then we've got two murders with both victims connected to each other and the casino. That is what I call a strong connection."

"You *think*, Frank." Blood vessels pulsated on Lafata's temple. Travis thought the agent might stroke out on the spot.

Lafata lowered his voice. "I want that thumb drive. Now."

Frank shook his head. "Can't do that, Clay. The drive is evidence seized in our missing person case that has now turned into a murder investigation. I'll have my people make a copy for you."

"I don't want your people to even touch that thing. We'll accept custody of the drive and have our forensics people duplicate it."

"Okay," Frank said. "And while you're at it, make a copy of the unknown man in the video and see if your face recognition programs can put a name to it. He may be Axtell's killer."

Travis heard a cell phone chirp. Frank reached into his pocket and withdrew his phone. "Yeah, honey. What is it?"

Frank nodded and glanced toward Travis. "I'll pass it along." He smiled as he hung up.

"Follow us back to my office, Lafata, and I'll turn that drive over to you. And Travis ..." He paused, a smile deepening. "Jessie wants to see you at my office. She'd like a word with you ... in private."

Travis felt a hurricane heading his way.

 **Chapter 21**

Clarkston, Washington

The Roosters Waterfront Restaurant bustled as Creasy approached the waiter and slipped him a hundred dollar bill. "Something nice and quiet out by the water."

The man nodded, sliding the bill into his pocket while leading Creasy through the bar. "Would you like a menu now, sir?"

Creasy slipped into the chair where he had a good look of the Snake River and those coming and going inside the restaurant. "Two menus. One more guy will be coming."

He watched a fishing boat chugging upstream, then scanned the restaurant one more time. He saw a familiar figure cutting around a table and walking toward him.

"Shane Foster. Right on time." Creasy handed the second menu to his visitor. "Lunch is on me."

"It better be with all the money I've sent your way." Foster appeared nervous. "You think it is wise to meet here in public?"

"Don't worry, my friend. Nobody'll notice us in this crowd." He waited for Foster to sit. "And after today, we'll never see each other again."

The other man's eyes widened. "What are you talking about? You still got a job to do."

Creasy chuckled, but the sound came out strained. "Job's done. Sign. Sealed. Delivered."

"You mean the guy's coming back here to finish the job?"

"Nope. He's gone for good. Sniffing dirt."

Alarm deepened Foster's features. "You ... You killed him?"

Creasy leaned over and grasped the other man's wrist in a tight squeeze. "Shut up and listen." He glanced around before continuing. "What was I supposed to do? Two cops on their way to interview your guy in San Diego. Face it, I did you a favor."

Foster leaned back, grimacing.

Creasy released his hold. "That's the least of your worries."

"What?"

"The cops found a thumb drive with everything you wanted stored on it, including one thing you didn't want. A video of you threatening the dead guy."

"You're kidding." Foster looked sick.

"You fool. That schmuck taped your threats. And the cops have that recording." Creasy waited, watching the other man's face whiten. "Only a matter of time before they identify you. If you've got a place to hide, now is the time to start running."

Foster started to rise. Creasy grabbed his arm once more. "Wire me the rest of the money and I'll never bother you again. Fail to do that, the cops will never be able to find what's left of you when I'm through. Understood?"

The other man sank back in his chair.

Creasy leaned back. "Now, shall we order?"

Foster slowly rose. "I've lost my appetite." He stood, unsteady, shaken.

Creasy chuckled as he watched Foster slowly stagger through the restaurant. He knew where Foster would go. As with all clients he mistrusted, Creasy wired everything they touched—home, office, and girlfriend's apartment. There was nowhere to run if he decided to go hunting.

Creasy turned his attention to the menu as the waiter approached. He leaned over the table. "Ready to order, sir?"

"Yes. I am suddenly ravenous." Thoughts of hunting made him hungry like a lion on the prowl. First he'd eat. Then he'd start stalking his next kill.

 **Chapter 22**

Lapwai, Idaho

Travis saw Jessie—arms rigid—waiting in the parking lot of the tribal police station as they drove up. Her body language made it clear trouble lie ahead.

"Frank. How much money would it take for you to keep on driving?"

"You haven't got enough, my friend." Frank chuckled as he slid the car into a reserved parking spot near Jessie. "See you inside."

Lafata pulled up alongside Frank's car.

Travis opened the car door. "I'll catch up with you two later."

"You mean if you survive?" Frank locked the car, laughing.

Travis walked toward her. As he neared, he watched Jessie cross her arms, one finger tapping a cadence on her bare arm. Not a good sign.

She started in right away. "I trusted you, Travis. I thought you'd keep what I told you confidential. Not blab it all over the county." She stood straight and jabbed a finger at his chest. "I heard the FBI yanked him from his desk and hauled him back to their offices for interrogation. Is that how you keep things quiet?"

"I didn't tell anyone but the FBI. Kept you father out of it until the feds walked in and marched Baptiste out to their car. Besides, Jessie, your dad already knew."

Her eyes widened. "No way! Only Tommy knew."

He shook his head. "Nope. Frank knew even before you told Tommy. He pulled Baptiste aside and read him the riot act. Your dad was prepared to yank his badge and haul him off to jail if Baptiste ever laid another hand on you."

Two officers drove into the parking lot and climbed out of their cars. They nodded at Jessie as they walked toward the station. She nodded back, lips clamped tight with anger. "I can't believe Dad never said anything. Messing around in my life and never mentioning it?"

"He just wanted to protect you. What any father would do."

"Yeah. Any other father would have spoken to their children about it. But not my dad."

"He wanted you to come to him. To trust him with your problem. It hurt when he found out you went to Tommy instead."

"It wasn't his concern. I didn't—"

"You didn't want him to know you dated Baptiste? That you lied to him?"

"That's not what I meant, Travis. I just wanted my private life to be … private."

"Then you should have picked someone else. What did you expect? He wouldn't find out?" Travis saw a young woman emerge from the station. He watched as she walked across the street toward the Indian health center.

"The FBI still has Baptiste?"

"Nope. They released him an hour after they picked him up."

"Just like that?"

"Baptiste has an alibi. He was throwing money away at the White-water Casino when someone killed Tommy. They have him on security tape."

"And now he is out? He probably thinks I'm the reason the FBI picked him up."

Travis leaned against her car. "He knows I'm the one that dropped a dime on him. He gave me a look you wouldn't believe when they snatched him up. Lafata gave me up right away."

"Why'd he do that?"

"I dunno. For some reason I seem to tick him off."

Jessica rolled her eyes. "Well, you do have that effect on people. Is it something you learned or did you just come by it naturally? Oh, wait, that's how you described me."

Travis ignored the barb. "By the way, remember when Baptiste *just happened* to drop by my place when you were visiting. He told us your dad sent him to take you back. Remember?"

"Yeah?"

"Frank says that's a lie. Your dad asked dispatch to have them check for any patrol units that might be close to Three Rivers. Baptiste came on the air and said he was in the area."

Her eyes widened. "Following me?"

"That's my guess. Your dad must not have scared him enough. I'm still not clear why Tommy referenced your problem on his computer just before he disappeared. Any ideas?"

Jessie shook her head. "I thought Tommy frightened Baptiste away. That it was all handled a long time ago. By the way, did Pete Axtell give you any information?"

"You didn't hear?"

She shook her head.

"I'm sorry. I should have told you. Someone beat us to him. Killed him and then torched the apartment. At least we think the body they found is Pete. We'll have to wait to be certain."

Jessie hugged herself as if cold, although it was warm enough for an afternoon sun to toast the asphalt they stood on. "You think the two murders are related? Pete and Tommy?"

"I think we need to consider that possibility."

The car window between them exploded in a hail of glass.

A sniper. He heard a rippling shot from the hill above them.

Travis grabbed Jessie by the arm and dragged her to the other side of a parked car, keeping the vehicle between them and the shooter. "Stay down."

He knew by the sound of the rifle the shooter fired some distance away. The bullet must have passed between them. He low-crawled to the bumper, peering around the car as he tried to place where the shot came from.

Nothing seemed to be moving. Cars slowly passed by the police station. People milled around the street seemingly oblivious to danger.

The shooter might be ready to take another shot.

"Stay right here, Jessie. I'm going for help. Keep your head down and stay on this side of the car. Understand?"

Jessie nodded, her jaw tight.

"I'll be right back."

He sprang from the protection of the car and zigzagged to the front door of the police station. No more shots. He burst through the door. Francis stood guard at the counter, surprise on her face.

"Tell Frank there's a sniper outside. Jessie is pinned down behind one of the cars." He gave out the direction of the shooter, then whirled around and retraced his steps, reaching the car without hearing another shot.

The sniper must be gone.

He waited several minutes, then saw Frank running from the station, a rifle in one hand and several vests in the other. The chief ran toward them, flinging himself on the ground next to Jessie.

"Are you all right?" His eyes searched for injuries.

"Yeah, I'm okay. Who would want to shoot at us?"

Frank glanced at Travis. "Not a clue, honey."

Travis watched father and daughter huddle against the car. First, Tommy gets killed. Then someone takes a shot at Jessie. He thought of where they had been standing. The shot struck between them. From that distance, the shooter might have been aiming at either one of them. Or he deliberately missed.

Two burly officers, each grasping ballistic shields, emerged from the station and crouched their way toward Jessie's car. Frank pointed toward his daughter. "Take her first. Travis and I will bring up the rear."

Both officers nodded. Officers shuttled everyone back to the station in two trips behind their bulky shields, each officer peering through a bullet-proof glass—encased in each shield—to find their way to safety.

Lafata stood in the lobby. Travis scowled at him as they passed. "Maybe you'd better find out where Baptiste is hiding, agent. This could be his handiwork."

The agent shrugged and followed them back to Frank's office.

Chapter 23

Dispatch must have broadcast about a sniper on the loose. NPTP officers and other law enforcement agencies came screaming back in their units, wailing sirens coming from all directions. Travis hastily told Frank what happened, giving him the direction and the approximate distance of the shooter. The chief got on the radio and directed a search.

They listened to spurts of conversation between units on the radio as officers searched the hillside. No evidence. No shooter.

Lafata remained silent during most of the conversations. Finally, he chipped in. "That shot must have carried quite a ways. Either the shooter tried to kill one of you—meaning he's a lousy shot—or he intentionally missed." Lafata glancing at Jessie and Travis.

Travis glanced toward Frank, ignoring Lafata. "Where's Baptiste? Is he good enough to make that shot?"

Frank glanced at Lafata and then back at Travis. "He might be able to make it. He's done a lot of hunting around these parts. I don't have a clue where he might be right now." He called dispatch asking for Baptiste's location. Frank waited several minutes without talking, apparently waiting until someone must have come back on the line. Finally, he lowered the phone.

"He called in and said he'd be taking the rest of the day off. No one knows where he went. They tried to reach his house—no answer. They paged him and tried his cell phone. No response."

Lafata shifted his attention toward Frank. "Why are you checking on Baptiste? We cleared him. Besides, what's his motive to take a shot at these two?"

Travis squared off with Lafata. "You gave him a motive, you idiot. You let him know I was the one who told you about the problem between him and Jessie. He knew Jessie must have confided in me. If he is the shooter, Baptiste might have been shooting at either one of us thanks to your big mouth."

Lafata flinched. "We cleared Baptiste because he had an iron-clad alibi on Tommy's murder. Why would he be stupid enough to turn around and take a shot at one of you? Doesn't make sense."

"Maybe he's a nut job and you gave him enough reason to want us dead." Travis braced himself, hoping Lafata might make the first move. "You set us up and then let him go."

"Get out of my face, Travis. This is still a federal investigation. And as the case agent, I have the authority to kick you off it."

"What case, Lafata? So far, you haven't turned up one shred of information that might help solve Tommy's murder."

"Shut up, you two!" Frank's raised voice silenced the two men. "Right now, all I want to do is to focus on who just tried to kill my daughter and Travis. We need to focus on what happened outside."

The FBI agent stepped back. "With your permission, I'll have my people process the car. Maybe we'll get lucky and find the projectile that was fired. In the meantime, we need to comb the area where the shot was fired. See what turns up."

"Thanks." Turning to his daughter, Frank said, "Why don't you go out and let Francis set you up with a cup of coffee while we get things set up here. In the meantime, Lafata," he said, glancing at the agent, "I'd like to finish telling you what we found from Axtell's trailer."

A look of disappointment crossed Jessie's face as she turned to leave. "Travis, I'll see you in a little bit?" She gave him a fleeting glance before walking out.

He gave her a nod and turned toward Frank.

Frank leaned forward. "Everything get ironed out?"

Travis shrugged. "We got interrupted." He walked around the desk to look over Frank's shoulder, seeing the chief had pulled up data from Pete Axtell's thumb drive. "

"Here's the recording Travis and I found interesting." Frank clicked on the video file. Once it opened, he activated the play button. They watched Axtell and the other man talking.

Lafata seemed fascinated by the recorded conversation. "Can you zoom in on his face?" He leaned closer. "Yeah. Right there." He wrote down the time lapse of the frame. "Give me the thumb drive. I'll have our people run that face through our data base. We can start with known organized crime subjects and branch out from there."

Frank copied the file to his computer and handed the original file to Lafata.

The agent straightened. "I'll contact our office in San Diego and have them monitor the arson investigation. Once there's a positive ID, I'll get back to you. Now, I better get things rolling on the car."

He wheeled around and left the room, leaving Travis and Frank alone. Travis saw Frank squinting back.

"What?"

"I don't think that sniper was aiming at Jessie. I'm betting he was trying to get your attention. Are you bringing any baggage to this case from your past? Anyone dying to get even?"

"Absolutely not."

Even as he answered, Travis played back his career in his mind. Old cases, disgruntled suspects. Anything that might have followed him here. A lot of possibilities. But nothing specific came to mind. Just ancient history he'd rather not dredge up. A few faces loomed, but they were either dead or in prison with no hope of ever getting out. "Just ancient history, Frank. No one I know with a motive to kill me today."

There was a hard edge on Frank's face. "If there is someone out there targeting you, you've just put my girl in danger. No one wants to kill Jessie. That just leaves you."

Chapter 24

Clearwater River, Idaho

Slot machines jingled with falling coins and glittered with flashing lights. Steve Robinette made his way across the carpeted casino floor. Once upon a time these one-armed bandits—with their clanging bells, tinkling coins, followed by the excited yelps from paying suckers—and all the other games of chance in this place gave him an adrenaline rush. The thrill was gone.

Robinette straightened his tie as his image flashed in the mirror next to a bank of elevators. His dark, slicked-back hair and brown eyes contrasted smartly with his Italian-made suit.

A Rolex watch warned he was running out of time.

He repeatedly pressed the button to the top floor after inserting a pass key. The elevator door finally opened. He started to enter before seeing an elderly couple tottering out. He waited until they emerged and then stepped inside. Sedate music replaced casino excitement as the doors quietly closed, leaving him alone inside the lift. A moment later, the same doors rolled open and he hurried down a hallway softened by plush carpeting, finally reaching the door to his penthouse. Only a limited number of pass keys allowed people to this floor.

Robinette's cavernous office was larger than his master bedroom at home. From the corner windows, he could see the glistening Clearwater River although he rarely took the time to enjoy this view. Business seemed to demand every moment of his day.

On his desk was a copy of the *Lewiston Tribune* with a page one story of Tommy White Eagle's murder. Newspaper reports kept harping on the word 'unsolved' throughout the article. Of course it is unsolved, he thought.

Cops would have someone in custody if the case was solved. He read where authorities wanted anyone with knowledge about the case to give them a call.

Right. Like he was going to tell them what he knew.

He glanced at the headlines again, Tommy's memory still fresh in Robinette's mind. He'd watched with pride as Tommy rose in the legal profession. He felt a commonality with the younger man although their birthdays were separated by a decade. He felt almost like an older brother. They both excelled in the academic world; he at the University of California's School of Business, leaving with a MBA; and Tommy, a Berkeley Law School graduate. Tommy graduated with top honors. Robinette imagined many law firms vied for Tommy's attention, but he'd returned to his roots just like Robinette. Tommy jumped at the chance to work at the casino.

And now, Tommy wound up in the morgue, and his good friend turned up missing. Pete Axtell.

That was another problem. He'd hired Axtell upon Tommy's recommendation—a decision coming back to plague him. Rumors started floating through the gambling community about Axtell's association with one particular man. Shane Foster. One of Robinette's security officers described Foster as "a leech who enjoyed sucking financial blood out of gullible customers." He knew Axtell—with access to the casino's financial records—downloaded information on Whitewater customers and handed it over to those "leeches." He must try to keep this information quiet.

Sweat beaded on his forehead and ran down his chin. Robinette worried how it might affect the casino if this information got out. He knew he might lose his job. And there were other things investigators might learn if they started turning over financial rocks at Whitewater.

Information that would cost Robinette more than his job.

Lately, he'd begun fending off telephone inquiries from investigators from the National Indian Gaming Commission. The calls were about casino customers complaining of identification theft and fraudulent use of credit information. He desperately wanted to talk to Axtell face-to-face, but the man simply vanished. No one on the reservation knew where he might be hiding.

An inner-office phone line jingled on his desk. He picked it up.

"Mr. Robinette, an agent from the FBI is at my desk. Agent Lafata. He'd like a word with you." Julie, his office assistant, sounded nervous.

"Give me a second, then send him in." Sweat now ran down his armpits as he lowered the phone. Drumming his fingers on the desk, he glanced around the room looking at nothing in particular. He'd heard of the bureau's Indian Country Crimes Unit and the agent's name was vaguely familiar. He rose as the office door opened.

Lafata strode in and showed his credentials, briefcase in hand. Robinette motioned toward a chair near the desk. As Lafata settled in, he peered across at Robinette. The agent flashed a smile like a shark moving in for its next kill.

"I have a few questions about one of your employees. Just take a few minutes." Lafata withdrew a notebook. "You have a Pete Axtell working here at the casino?"

Robinette leaned back in his chair, his shirt damp with perspiration. "Yeah. But he's turned up missing. Do you know where he is?"

The agent squinted at the notebook and slowly raised his eyes, staring at Robinette with the look of a predator. "We believe he might be dead. Murdered, actually."

Robinette felt his throat constrict, pain shoot through his chest. He gripped the desk top. "Murdered? How? Where?"

Lafata shook his head. "Sorry. That's under investigation. We're still trying to verify the identification of the murdered victim. To determine if it is Axtell."

Clasping his hands together, Robinette perched on the edge of his seat, leaning heavily on the desk top. "That's horrible. How can I help?"

"What was his job here at the casino?"

"He worked in our finance department as a bookkeeper, records keeper. He also maintained financial information on our customers and industry suppliers."

"How'd you characterize his work?"

"You mean what kind of employee? Excellent worker. Hard working, paid attention to details. No complaints from my end."

Lafata reached down and pulled his briefcase onto his lap. The agent withdrew a sheet of paper from a file and slowly pushed it across the desk toward Robinette. "Have you ever seen this guy here?"

Robinette leaned forward and glanced down. It was a grainy photo of a man who seemed unaware of the camera. Surveillance photo? It was not off the casino's security cameras. He would have been warned if the FBI poked around in casino files. He looked closer. He recognized the face.

He'd seen this face posted on an alert from EagleIntel, an intelligence data base sponsored by the National Indian Gaming Association. His security chief regularly briefed him on all criminal intelligence information that might affect the casino.

And he knew the face from somewhere else. His hands felt clammy as he struggled for composure. "Can't say I've ever seen this guy before."

"Can't say or won't say?"

"I've never seen that guy here. I don't know his name." He lowered his eyes for a split second and then met Lafata's gaze. "Sorry. I wish I could be more helpful. Is this guy connected to gaming operations somehow?"

"That's what I'm trying to find out."

"Sorry. I can't help you." He started to rise.

Lafata remained seated. "I need whatever information you have on Axtell from his personnel file. And I need the names of those he works with here. I want to interview each of them."

Robinette slowly sat down. "You think Axtell's murder is somehow connected to this casino?"

"Dunno. But I'd say this kind of place—with the amount of dinero changing hands—warrants a close look. After all, love of money is the root of all evil, right?"

Robinette shrugged. "I wouldn't know about that. We run a clean game here at Whitewater."

Lafata finally stood. "Well, I intend to find out. Now, about that information?"

The casino manager pressed a button connecting him to his assistant. "See Agent Lafata gets all the information he needs from our files. He'll be out in a moment."

Robinette watched the FBI agent stride from the room. He took out a handkerchief and tried to dry his hands. He saw trouble walking out of his office.

He must keep a lid on everything. His life depended upon it.

Chapter 25

Jessie could not sit still. "Someone wants to kill us? It just doesn't make sense."

Travis watched Jessie pacing his front porch. Frank left a half hour ago, after asking them to sit tight until they heard from him. He called the Idaho County Sheriff's Office to request extra patrol during the night.

Her pacing even made Sam edgy. The dog watched her for a moment and then cocked his head at Travis as if to ask if everything was all right.

"I don't have a clue, Jessie. We'll take another stab at it tomorrow." He stroked Sam's head, trying to calm the animal.

They heard an eastbound car on Highway 12 across the river. A van with a family of kids chugged by with camping equipment piled high.

Travis glanced at the backpack lying next to him. Before Frank left, he took Jessie aside for a private chat. Travis used that distraction to slip into the cabin and quietly opened his safe secreted behind a panel in the wall. He removed a rifle and a shotgun, both Remingtons, and placed both weapons just inside the front door. He grabbed a semi-auto handgun, closed the safe and put the panel back in place. He slipped the handgun into a backpack near the front door. He then rejoined Frank and Jessie on the front porch.

After Frank left, Travis motioned toward the cabin. "Why don't you come inside, Jessie." He worried about the target she offered out on the porch. An adequate marksman could easily pick her off from across the highway. Sam raised his head in expectation. Jessie smiled at the dog. "Just what does he have in mind, Sam? Should I trust him?"

Sam barked as if to answer.

She stroked the dog's head. "Man's best friend. Maybe I should ask someone else." Jessie passed through the doorway and saw the guns. "Boys and their toys. Who am I staying with ... Rambo?"

Travis followed her inside and shut the door. "Just in case we need some protection."

He strode toward the kitchen "Can you cook?"

"About as good as you kayak."

"While I try to figure what to make for dinner, why don't you set the table. You can do that, right?"

Jessie grinned and began collecting the silverware. She edged behind him and he heard her pause. "Tell me how we're going to find Tommy's killer, Travis? All we have so far are a lot of unanswered questions. And the shooter today ... what's that about?"

"I'm not a fortune teller, Jessie. We take one day at a time, one piece of information at a time. We're not even sure whether the shooter today had anything to do with your brother's death. I want to keep an open mind."

"You have more enemies that we know about?" She glanced at him from across the kitchen.

"Your dad asked me the same question. I told him—and I'm telling you—no one comes to mind."

He turned toward the stove, hearing her close a drawer and walk toward the table. As she came into view, he saw her forehead wrinkled with worry.

Travis reached for a frying pan. "Don't take this the wrong way, but do you know if your brother was involved in anything that was ... shady? Illegal?"

Her troubled look turned to anger. "You saying my brother might be a crook?"

"You tell me. I need to know if there is anything about his life that might have caused—"

"—He's not a criminal, Travis. I won't have you talk that way about him."

He turned and leaned against the counter. "Look, I need to find answers to all the questions that are spilling out of my head. I need to know the truth. All of it."

"He was a good man. An honest man. He was someone I'm proud to call my brother. Does that answer your question?"

He nodded and turned toward the stove. "Just tell me about Tommy—his work, his life, and anyone he hung around with. Everything. I believe something in his life led to his death. And the fact his friend may have been murdered raises all kinds of questions. Help me find the truth, Jessie."

He glanced toward the table and saw her standing there, crying. Quietly, painfully, her grief poured out in tears. He walked over and circled his arms around her. She laid her head against his chest.

"I've told you everything I know about my brother. He was a good man. A good brother. That's what you'll find out after asking all your stupid questions. He was a good man."

Creasy removed the headset and peered out the van's rear window. A quarter mile ahead, he saw Travis Mays' truck parked alongside the road. The van sat hidden in a grove of trees in a pullout along the river.

He smiled to himself. They didn't have a clue what this was about—least of all Travis. The dog surprised Creasy when he first broke into the cabin.

Sam. Now he knew the dog's name.

It cost him a pound of good steak and a healthy dose of knock-out drugs lifted from a veterinary's office. The dog ripped into the meat and fell asleep a short time later. He'd carefully inserted spike mikes in strategic places in the cabin while the dog lay drugged. The mikes connected to power sources that'd keep everything running hot until he no longer needed them. The transmissions boosted by portable repeaters, nestled in trees across the highway, carried whispered conversations into the van a good half mile away.

Early on, he sensed this woman was a way to get close to Travis. To make those walls crumble that the professor so carefully built up since leaving California and law enforcement behind.

Soon I will welcome you to my world.

Now he had a few more installations to complete so that he might follow their futile investigation. It was time to prepare for another trip to California while these jerks ran around in circles trying to figure out why people kept dying.

They'd never suspect him, even after they started making the connections. A lot of time and money had been squandered. But now, he could hide behind an unbreakable wall of aliases. He would continue to close the noose around Travis' neck until the man finally choked to death.

He'd teach Travis what it really meant to lose someone you love. He'd make sure Travis writhed in pain before he died.

And Creasy intended to relish every minute of Travis' agony.

Chapter 26

Lapwai, Idaho

"Baptiste has no alibi for yesterday," Frank said, as he led Travis and Jessie into his office. "Said he took a hike in the mountains to clear his mind. More likely, he was cleaning his rifle."

Travis was tired. He'd hardly slept last night after he'd learned everything Jessie knew about Tommy. The man was a workaholic, but still made time for his family—listening to their problems, sharing their joys, making them laugh when they took themselves too seriously. Tommy idolized Frank while still fighting his father every inch of the way. "Like two peas in a pod," she told him, "and they never saw how alike they really are ... were." Now, here they were back in Frank's office. Still no answers.

He sat down in one of the chairs facing the chief's desk. "That keeps him on the list of potential suspects. I don't know him very well, but I can't believe he'd take the risk of shooting at us because of what the FBI said. He's too obvious."

"Then who would you suggest capped those rounds?" Frank watched Jessie claim a chair near Travis.

"Someone beat us to San Diego and took out Axtell—if it was Axtell."

"You think Axtell might still be alive?"

Travis shrugged. "I don't know. Until we're sure, I'm leaving every possibility on the table."

There was a knock at the door. Lafata stood in the doorway. "Can I join this party?" He entered without invitation. "I see you're still alive and kicking, Travis."

Frank dragged another chair into the room. "Have a seat, Clay. We're trying to figure out who might have taken a shot at Jessie and Travis yesterday. Any thoughts?"

Lafata sat down, rubbing his jaw. "Probably someone from the professor's past." He gave Travis a smirk. "You know, one of those cases you botched."

Travis tightened his lip. The agent kept hinting around about the past. He wished Lafata would just come out with it. Get it off his chest. Instead, the agent kept hammering Travis with verbal jabs, innuendos, while telling him nothing.

Frank leaned forward. "My daughter could have been killed, Lafata. Enough with the jokes."

Lafata looked over at Jessie, and then turned his attention back to Frank. "You're right, Frank. Sorry." He raised a briefcase to his lap and flipped the latches. "I took a run by the casino yesterday after all the excitement here. Spoke with a Steve Robinette who runs the place."

Frank nodded. "I know Steve. He sent some legal work Tommy's way."

"Yeah, well, this Robinette is hiding something. I showed him that photo from Axtell's video file. The unidentified man."

"He recognized the guy?"

"Says he doesn't know him. But his eyes told me he was lying."

"How about Travis and I take another run at him? Maybe he doesn't trust the FBI, or maybe he just didn't like the way you asked." Frank gave him a thin smile.

"Hey, whatever," Lafata said, easing back in the chair. He looked like a man who'd just won the lottery. "The good news is I got a hit on our John Doe. Our people ran it through our organized crime files. Our mystery man is a lowlife by the name of Shane Foster. Heavy into white collar crimes like identity theft, credit manipulation, and stuff like that. No violence in his record. My gut tells me Foster might not be good for the killings. He has connections, but I don't make him as the trigger man."

Travis glanced at Lafata. "We get confirmation on the body?"

Lafata shot him an irritated look. "No. I just assumed the crispy critter is Axtell." Jessie's groan must have made the agent realize what he just said. "Guess I'm just getting too calloused. I assume the *deceased* is Pete Axtell."

"You know what they say about assumptions." Travis smiled back. The punch line seemed to fit Lafata.

The FBI agent gave him an irritated look before turning toward Frank. "We'll try to locate this Shane Foster. Jam him up with what we have on the video. That might shake him up enough to talk." He stood, glancing at the others. "Keep in touch," he said, finally singling out Travis.

Travis met his gaze. "I'll put you on my speed dial."

"Thought you didn't have a phone?"

"Oh, yeah. Forgot."

Lafata wheeled around and stalked out.

"You shouldn't antagonize him," Frank said. "He has the authority to cut you off from this case at any time."

"He keeps riding me about the past. I wish he'd just spit it out. Whatever is bugging him." Travis stood, stretching tired muscles. "I feel we've been running around in circles here. Let's start from the beginning and work the people who were around Tommy. Clients, co-workers, girlfriends, anybody that might have information as to how he spent his last hours."

Jessica stood up.

Travis glanced at Frank and then toward her. "I'm talking about your father, Jessie. I'd prefer you stayed out of sight."

"I want to be a part of this. He's my brother, or have you forgotten?"

"I know. But we can't focus if we're always worried about whether you are safe."

Frank grabbed his jacket. "For once I agree with Travis, honey. Stay with one of your friends, okay?"

Angrily, she grabbed the phone and dialed. "Lisa, it's Jessie. You off today?" A pause, then Jessica continued. "I need to stay with you for a while. Just for a few days? Great, I—"

"—Have her pick you up here, Jessie." Frank leaned forward. "Leave your car in our parking lot and wait in the lobby. I'll have one of the patrol units follow you to her house."

"You hear that, Lisa. Yeah, I know." She glanced at Frank and Travis, before speaking again. "I'm outnumbered. Tell you all about it when you get here. Thanks, girlfriend."

She hung up, jotted something down on paper and handed it to Travis. "Here's Lisa's number and address if you need to reach me." She walked out of the office.

Travis stuffed the note into his pocket. Frank clenched his jaw.

Travis heard Jessie talking to several of the officers on her way toward the lobby. "You think she'll stay out of this?"

"I'd give it a fifty-fifty chance. She's a lot like ..." Frank paused, and Travis felt the police chief might be comparing his daughter to someone close to him, someone who probably was no longer around. Jessie's mother?

Frank seemed to shake from his mind whatever thought he'd just stumbled over. "Let's get a move on. Where do you want to start?"

"I'll tell you in the car. I'd rather not talk about this case in this building unless we have to."

The older man gave him a quizzical look.

"Someone here is watching you. Remember San Diego? Someone leaked that information and we got beat."

He followed Frank through the outer office to the front lobby. Francis still stood guard over the front counter, talking on the phone. Frank gave her a sign to cut the conversation short. She hung up and folded her hands together.

"That information you gave us about Pete Axtell. Did you talk to anyone else about it?"

She started to shake her head and then stopped. Her face turned red for a moment. "You mean other than Officer Baptiste, Chief?"

He nodded.

Francis glanced toward the ceiling, trying to remember. "Come to think of it, I did speak to someone. He called for you and I told him you were leaving on a trip. He said it was important to know where you were going, so I told him about your trip and the new lead."

"You told someone we were going to San Diego to interview Axtell?" Frank sounded like he wanted to explode. "Who did you tell?"

She cringed. "I thought it was all right, Chief. I mean, you guys work together, right?"

"Who did you tell, Francis?" Frank seemed about to lose it.

"Why, he just left. That FBI guy you're working with."

"Lafata?"

She nodded. "Did I do something wrong?"

Frank whirled around without answering and stomped into the police parking lot. Travis hurried to catch up and found the chief slamming his open palm on the roof of his vehicle.

"Lafata knew all about our trip." Frank looked like he was about to have a coronary. "And he acted like he didn't know anything."

"Makes you wonder what kind of game he's playing." Travis folded his arms. "Let's just keep this to ourselves right now. See where it takes us."

Frank opened the car door. "It doesn't mean Lafata's lying. I know him. That jerk likes to hold things back. It ticks me off, but what are you gonna do? Let's go."

Travis climbed inside. Lafata keeping things about the case to himself? Why? And why did Lafata seem to have a grudge against him? They'd never met before that he could remember.

Baptiste and Lafata knew he and Frank flew to San Diego. And someone killed the person they tried to meet. Travis struggled to find a common thread linking all this together. Anything that might make sense.

Nothing seemed to fit. And he could not shake the feeling that he was running out of time.

 **Chapter 27**

Orofino, Idaho

"I thought your dad wanted you to stay at my place." Lisa Penny signaled to make the left turn over the bridge into the heart of Orofino, glancing over a Jessie with a troubled look. "I don't want your dad mad at me."

Jessie saw the river still running high as she watched a log float beneath the bridge. "Don't worry. The only one he'll yell at is me. But I can't just sit around while they search for Tommy's killer." She pointed ahead. "Make the first right. Tommy's office is down a couple blocks."

"Duh. It's not like I don't know where Tommy ..." Lisa stopped in mid sentence as she followed Jessie's instructions. She pulled into a small parking lot adjacent to a two-story brick office building.

Jessie smiled at her friend. They had rarely been apart since kindergarten when one of the kids tried to pick a fight with Jessie. Lisa—even then, bigger than most of the kids her age—pushed Jessie's attacker to the ground and sat on the troublemaker. She wouldn't let the girl up until the troublemaker apologized to Jessie. They had been close friends ever since.

She watched Lisa ease herself from the car, her friend's weight starting to worry Jessie. Around the first of the year, Jessie suggested they join a gym and work out together. Lisa gave it a try for a few weeks, but family commitments and her job as a busy mom resulted in fewer and fewer trips to the gym. Lisa married a guy from high school who held down a steady job at the Potlatch plant in Lewiston. Two children—a boy and girl—became a part of their family. The children became Lisa's whole world. "Auntie Jessie" made sure she spoiled them rotten. "You have your fun with them and then I've got to straighten them out when you're gone," Lisa always complained. But the love in Lisa's eye told her how much it meant that Jessie loved her children, too. And Lisa would do anything for Jessie.

Cascading sunlight began to chase an early morning chill away as the women climbed the stairs to the second floor. Lisa wheezed as they reached Tommy's office. Jessie kneeled, reaching beneath a flower pot near the door. "Ah. Here it is," she said, brandishing a key.

"What do you hope to find?" Lisa pulled her burgundy sweater tighter. "I thought the cops have been all through this."

"Yeah—FBI, my dad, and Travis—they all took a shot at it. Now, it's my turn. I know ... knew my brother better than anyone. If he hid something, I'll find it."

As she started to unlock the door, Jessie saw a women unlocking the adjacent office further down the landing. The woman glanced at Jessie and smiled before disappearing inside.

Jessie hesitated. "Lisa, here's the key. Let yourself in and I'll be back in a minute." She walked down the landing and knocked on the door.

"Hi. Come on in." The woman stood behind a desk, going through a pile of mail. "Aren't you Tommy's sister? I thought I recognized you."

"Yeah, I am. I'm sorry, I don't think we've met."

The woman extended a hand. "We met a long time ago. My name's Abigail. Just call me Abby. And you're Jessie, right?"

Jessie nodded, shaking Abby's hand. "You heard what happened to my brother?"

Abby frowned. "I'm so sorry. He was such a good man."

"Thanks." She pushed an errant strand of hair from her face. "You must see who comes and goes from my brother's office," she said, glancing at the window that offered a view of the landing in front of Tommy's office. "Anyone in particular come to mind? Anything out of the ordinary around the time he disappeared?" She knew she sounded desperate. It was exactly how she felt.

"I don't know. I try to mind my own business."

"Please," Jessie said. "Anything you can give me would be a great help."

Abby laid the mail back on the desktop. She offered Jessie a chair and sat down herself. "Well, there really wasn't a lot of traffic. A few clients and such, I imagine. Except ..."

"Yes." Jessie held her breath.

"There was one person. A woman. Came to his office several times. In fact, one night when I was working late, I saw her sneaking in. She looked nervous."

"Really? Can you describe her?"

Abby beamed. "Better than that. She's married to that guy who runs the casino. You, know, Whitewater. I think her last name is Robinette. I go there from time to time. Once I met her husband, Steve Robinette. Nice guy. What a hunk. He comped me and my husband dinner and drinks."

Jessie leaned forward. "You sure it was Mrs. Robinette?"

"Oh, yeah. I don't know her first name, but I saw her and Mr. Robinette at the casino several times." She clutched her hands tightly. "I don't know how to say this."

"What?"

Abby flushed, a reddish hue warming her pale cheeks. "The way she carried on I thought maybe Mrs. Robinette and your brother were ... you know."

"Seeing each other? Romantically?"

Abby's cheeks darkened a deeper red. "It might be nothing, Jessie. Like I said, I only saw her a few times." The woman leaned on the desk, clasping her hands. Her blush seemed to pale. "You don't think what happened to Tommy had anything to do with Mrs. Robinette, do you?"

Jessie stood. "I don't know, Abby. Mind keeping this to yourself? At least until we check it out."

"Promise. My lips are sealed." The woman crossed her heart.

"Thanks." Jessie left, joining Lisa in Tommy's office. She saw her friend sitting on a couch near the window. She quickly shared Abby's information.

"Tommy and Robinette's wife?" Lisa said. "Wow. That sounds like trouble."

Jessie sat down at her brother's desk, running her hand softly over the top. "It doesn't sound like Tommy. He wouldn't, you know—"

"Mess around with another man's wife?" Lisa giggled. "You've been hanging out in the woods too long, honey. Have you seen Mrs. Robinette? She looks like she just stepped from the pages of some high-class magazine. All looks and glamour. After all, Tommy *is* a man. A good-looking one at that." Lisa must have seen the hurt in Jessie's eye. "Hey, what am I thinking. I forget he's not ..." She seemed to be searching for the right words.

None came.

Jessie turned her attention to the desk and began searching. She must try to find something that would tell her about Tommy's last day on earth. Some clue he left behind.

Jessie and Lisa failed to see a van following them all the way from Lapwai to the Orofino office. Jessie White Eagle and Lisa Penney. He ran the license plate through the system. He assumed the woman with Jessie was the registered owner. The driver swerved the van to the side of the road and parked as he watched the women approach Tommy White Eagle's office. He saw Jessie walk over and enter the office next door, then return a short time later to join Lisa.

The driver never got out. Instead, he slid from the driver's seat and opened an interior door to the back of the van. He crouched and closed the door behind him. In a moment, he flicked on several toggle switches, adjusted the volume on a receiver, and began monitoring a video feed from a camera hidden inside the law office.

"So Tommy White Eagle was playing around with another man's wife. Bossman is gonna love this."

He reached for a cell phone and dialed. A man's voice answered. "Hey, I followed the girl to her brother's law office. Learned something we didn't know. The dead guy was playing around with the casino manager's wife. Yeah, Steve Robinette's wife."

The man listened to his boss. "You want me to stick with the girl or what?" He heard the man's response. "Okay. I'll let you know what turns up."

He hung up and glanced at the monitor. "Well, baby sister. It's just you and me for a while." He watched Jessie and Lisa rummaging through the office.

He chuckled. "You ain't going to find nothing there, sweetheart. We got to it before the cops. Knock yourself out. I get paid by the hour."

Chapter 28

Brian Wyatt stared at the wire transfer on his computer as he tracked his transaction. A five, followed by four zeros. He'd just returned from his bank in Clarkston after wiring the money to an offshore account. They'd given him a receipt.

He was looking at a transaction that might put him on death row.

After the White Eagle killing, Wyatt searched the internet for information on the death penalty in Idaho. Some twenty inmates were awaiting execution. Death could come by lethal injection or firing squad, apparently at the discretion of the director of the state's Department of Corrections. One man decides whether you get poked with a needle or shot by a firing squad if death from legal injection "was not practical," claimed the article. What makes it not practical?

The thought chilled him.

All over a stinking creek the Indians controlled. A creek that ran through his land. A creek that became heavily regulated, a bureaucratic ruling that might destroy everything his family owned. Years and years of ranching down the tubes because of an agreement between the government and the Nez Perce.

And Tommy White Eagle was the reason Wyatt might end up on death row.

He took a match and lit the receipt, watching the paper curl and blacken in the flames. *In for a penny, in for a pound.* They had to prove the money he shipped out of the country was payment for a killing here in Idaho. And they had to connect him to the murder.

The killer is paid. The deed is done. Tommy White Eagle is no longer a threat.

Now another man took his place. The killer. The only person who could link Wyatt to Tommy's murder.

Creasy watched his online account. Electronic transfer data emerged on the screen, a five followed by four zeros. He was $50,000 richer for killing a man he'd already decided to kill. Getting paid to exact his own revenge. And making them think Tommy boy was playing around with Robinette's wife—just icing on the cake. One more person the cops might suspect killed the Indian.

He closed the website for his offshore account and switched to his favorite airlines. He scanned the flights to California, chose one, and paid by credit card listed in the name of a man who never existed. He had a few more calls to make before his next hunting trip.

One more prey to take care of before tightening the screws to Travis. And then—satisfaction. That moment when he would slip a wire garrote around the coward's neck and watch him do the chicken. Watch him jerk his way into eternity.

Brian Wyatt drove onto the gravel road leading to his ranch. He came to a stop, climbed out of the truck and strolled over to the mailbox. Only one envelope inside. He glanced at the sender's name and froze.

Tommy White Eagle.

Mail from a dead man? He tore it open and scanned the cover letter and a copy of a legal filing. The letter explained a complaint had been lodged against him for violation of the water rights act. A hearing had been set in a couple months.

Wyatt felt his stomach churning. The killing. The money. All in vain. This two-bit shyster filed with the courts before he got whacked.

It was now a matter of public record.

Wyatt opened the truck door with shaky hands. He crawled in, listening to the engine rumbling. He had to figure out how to protect himself. It would only be a matter of time before cops starting putting the pieces together and wound up with his name. It would become obvious he benefited from the killing.

But could they prove it?

They'd find evidence of money transferred from his account and wired overseas. They'd try to track the money, but maybe they can't break down the wall to gain access to that offshore account. After all, that's why people paid all that money to set those things up for privacy. To keep their money away from prying eyes like the IRS, right? So, how would he explain this? An investment? Money for an investment in another country.

Sounds lame. Stupid. He'd have to think up a better story. Who could prove he was lying?

The killer.

The man he'd hired to fix everything. The murderer could link Wyatt to this killing if the cops forced the hired gun to talk. Murder for hire. That had a nasty ring. He knew they'd rather let the killer off easy to get to the person who hired the killer. Happened all the time in the movies.

Let's make a deal.

He must figure a way to silence the killer.

Kill the killer.

Again, he shuddered. The man scared him. This guy enjoyed hurting others. That was the look Wyatt saw when he looked into the killer's eyes. But he is human, made of flesh and blood. He bleeds just like everyone else. Right?

Wyatt would just have to figure how to make this guy bleed. Make him bleed to death.

In for a penny, in for a pound.

 **Chapter 29**

Grangeville, Idaho

Travis handed the cell phone back to Frank. "Jessie's not answering. You sure she went to her friend's house?"

Frank scowled. "How should I know? A father can never be sure what his children will do. She's got a mind of her own."

A patrol car from the Idaho County Sheriff's Department rolled past them and entered the parking area designated for department vehicles. Travis saw a uniformed deputy in green khakis get out and walk toward the station house. "Steele said he'd meet us here in a few minutes."

The ride over with Frank did not go well.

Frank wanted to know where Travis thought the investigation ought to head.

Travis couldn't say. It seemed they'd been churning away like two hamsters in a cage, running on a wheel that went nowhere. Always coming up empty or getting beat to a lead by someone out there in the shadows. He wanted to start from the beginning and take a fresh look at everything. And the beginning was where they found Tommy's body.

Frank's impatience put an edge to their conversation: his son murdered, his daughter targeted by a sniper. Travis knew the cop in Frank wanted answers. The father in him wanted payback.

And Travis was running dry. He just couldn't seem to make sense of anything.

They found Steele waiting in the lobby. "Thought I saw you guys pull up. Let's head to my office where I keep the files." They took the stairs to the second floor and traversed the hallway to Steele's office. The door was locked. "Like to keep things buttoned up when I'm not around." He unlocked it and ushered them in.

Travis scanned the files after Steele explained the filing system. He pulled out one of the files marked *Crime Scene Photos*. "You want to pass on this," Travis said, eying Frank before opening it.

The older man glanced at the box and shook his head. Turning to Steele, he said, "Where can a guy get a decent cup of coffee?"

"Come on. I'll show you. Coffee's on me if you can drink the stuff."

Travis opened the file as he listened to their receding footsteps. He fanned out a stack of photographs on Steele's desk in the order of how they documented the crime scene. He placed the shots of Tommy's body in the center to understand its positioning, the close-ups of clothing and anything else the photographers or detectives felt important. Tommy's eyes were open and staring into the camera lens with a look of surprise. Eyes vacant, lifeless. He shuffled the other photos around the body as he remembered the crime scene sketch.

The body lay on its back, arms spread and legs together. Steele said the coroner confirmed what everyone already knew. Gunshots to the head and chest, each shot potentially fatal. He reached into the box, pulled out the coroner's report and scanned through the autopsy report. The medical examiner determined the body had been moved after the killing. Once at the final resting place, the killer forcibly positioned the body just as the camera captured it.

He peered at several full-body shots. Each shot verified the image in Travis' mind. The killer pushed and pulled Tommy's remains into the form of a cross, arms outstretched, legs and feet tight together: the body laid out on a slope, head higher and feet lower, the sightless eyes taking in the canyon below.

The coroner noted there were two small puncture marks of equal size on the chest in what the doctor described as the pectoralis major muscle. He shuffled through the photos until he saw one showing a close-up of the upper chest. There they were. Two twin-like dots, tiny red marks above the left lung. Glancing at the coroner's report again, he saw that whatever puncture wounds pierced the epidermis, they'd traveled through the dermis and subcuti layer of skin and lodged within the pectoralis major muscle.

Travis had seen these kinds of puncture wounds before.

Someone hit Tommy with a Taser while he was still alive to incapacitate him. One possible reason was later documented in the coroner's report. They found bruising on the right inner arm above an artery, noting a possible injection site. Tommy's attacker shot him up with a drug to stabilize and move him to another location while still breathing.

Where did the killer actually end Tommy's life?

The evidence was clear—Tommy had not been shot where he was discovered. As Travis studied the coroner's findings, matching them to the crime scene, he determined Tommy must have been moved at least three times, maybe four times. At the first location, the attacker must have hit Tommy with a Taser, paralyzing the lawyer. However, for whatever reason, the killer did not kill Tommy and leave his body at that location. Maybe the killer feared discovery. Next, the killer carted Tommy to a second location where he was ultimately shot to death. Then, the killer transported Tommy's lifeless body to a third location where others eventually found the body. The time frame between when Tommy disappeared and when he body was discovered puzzled Travis. Marks on the body indicated Tommy was held captive for several weeks at one or more locations. Why the wait?

He took a second look at a file of lab results from evidence removed from the body and clothing around the body. He saw what the killer must have used to stabilize Tommy after Tasing him. Traces of Propofol, used to induce general anesthesia, indicating the victim was induced into a coma-like state before death. Investigators found samples of animal hairs and wood fibers lodged in or clinging to the body and clothing. As he read the report, he saw the findings were ripe with trace evidence—human and animal hairs, carpeting and wood fibers, food particles, and soil samples.

They had everything but where the killing took place.

This evidence would collaborate where Tommy was murdered if the actual site was discovered. The lab and the coroner's findings concurred on one point—the killer was very close when he pulled the trigger. Trace evidence does not lie.

Travis continue to read each report, and then began going through all the interviews collected in the case. An hour later, he heard footsteps coming. Quickly, he gathered up the photos and shoved them into the file just as Steele and Frank returned. He stood to greet them.

Steele entered first, nodding toward his files. "So, what'd you think, professor?"

Travis glanced at Frank. "You sure you want to hear this?"

The older man nodded. "I need to know, Travis. Need to know everything."

Nodding, Travis sat on the edge of the desk. "The killer got close enough to Tommy to use a Taser. They had to be face-to-face because the probes hit him straight on in the chest. The killer must have intravenously injected a sedative into Tommy's right inner arm to further incapacitate him. Once unconscious, Tommy was moved to a second location where he was held until the time of his death. Either at that second location or moved to another. All three shots fired at close range. The killer then moved the body to the final location where it was found. Once at the final site, the killer positioned the body."

He paused, looking at Frank and then back at Steele, before continuing. "The killer staged the body to appear as if it was crucified. Arms extended, palms out, legs together. I believe the killer might be sending us a message."

Steele nodded. "That was my take on it, too. Now, professor, what was the message? I'll take my hat off to you if you can answer that one."

"Haven't the foggiest. The way the killer relocated and staged the body, I know the whacko was trying to tell us something. It may have nothing to do at all with Tommy. He may have been ..." Travis hesitated, looking quickly at Frank.

"Go ahead, Travis. I need to hear this."

"Tommy may have just been a means to an end. A person the killer murdered in order to accomplish another goal. Another objective."

Frank's eyes widened. "You mean Tommy may have been randomly picked. It could have been anyone?"

"Truthfully, I don't know. There may be dual purposes for selecting Tommy. He might have been killed because of something he did or knew.

He might have been killed because he represented something the killer wanted to attack. Or, it may have been random and the killer's sending someone else a message."

"Who?" Steele put his cup down. "Who might he be sending a message to? One of us?"

Travis shrugged. "I don't know. The killer must know that we would not release details of the body or the crime scene. And the fact this body was found in a remote area would suggest the killer meant to send a message to someone in law enforcement, someone this dirt bag knows would have access to the crime scene. The killer must have wanted the body found just the way it was. In a more urban setting, people might have moved or changed the body before the cops came."

Steele wrinkled his brow. "But wouldn't the killer know animals might go after the body? They could have devoured it before we ever found the body."

"But they didn't," Travis said. "I found that strange until I saw this." He pulled a sheet of paper from one of the files. "This gave me a clue."

Steele read the report and his eyes widened. "I saw this, but I thought it was just some garbage a hiker left behind."

Travis leaned on the desk. "Not garbage. It is an ultrasonic motion activator. A little machine that emits high-frequency waves. Scares off dogs, coyotes and other animals in close proximity. One of the techs picked it up, thinking like you did—just something left behind by backpackers. They did process it later, but the machine had been wiped clean. Also, they found high levels of commercial pesticides and other chemical compounds around the body that would have given off a scent strong enough to ward off animals."

Steele handed the report back to Travis. "Well, the killer definitely wanted us to see the body just the way he left it."

Frank finally spoke. "Maybe I'm the one he's trying to send a message to. Think about it. He murdered my son, took a shot at my daughter, and he knew I'd have access to the crime scene."

Travis put a hand on Frank's shoulder. "It may have nothing at all to do with you. We need to keep working this thing until we get answers. They will come in time." He shoved the remaining reports into the box and pushed it toward Steele. "Would you mind having your staff make copies of the lab reports and coroner's report for me at some point? I'd like to go over this more carefully after I've had time to think about it."

"No problem," Steele said.

Frank glanced at him. "I appreciate you going through this, Travis. I needed to know, but I don't think I could look at it very objectively."

"We'll catch this guy, Frank. He's leaving us tons of clues. Sooner or later, we'll nab him."

Steele picked up the box. "I just hope we find him before he does this to somebody else. It doesn't take a shrink to know this guy is a bubble off plumb."

"There's one more thing we need to keep in mind," Travis said, looking at the other two. "The evidence suggests this guy has killed before. Something is driving this nut, and he is likely to strike again until we understand what he's trying to tell us."

 **Chapter 30**

Kamiah, Idaho

Lisa Penny started in on Jessie the minute they left Tommy's law office. "I know your father did not have this in mind. He was clear—stay at my place out of sight. Now I'm driving you to a guy's house that might have killed Tommy. Are you crazy?"

"Lisa, just shut up. If you don't want to help me, then take me back to my car and I'll go alone."

"Yeah, right. Let you face the killer alone? Your dad would be all over me if I deserted you. Just for the record, though, I think this is a terrible idea."

Jessie smiled. "You're a good friend, even if you're a coward."

"A coward?" Lisa tossed her hair back with indignation. "A coward wouldn't go to a potential killer's house."

"Look. All we know is Mrs. Robinette met privately with Tommy. I don't buy your idea he was romantically involved. Steve Robinette was his friend. My brother just wasn't that kind of guy."

"So, if Tommy is as straight as a monk why'd they go sneaking around at night?"

"I don't know. Maybe she wanted legal advice and didn't want anyone knowing about it."

"Right." Lisa snorted. "Tommy meets a knock-down gorgeous lady late at night in his office-slash-bedroom to give legal help? What turnip truck did you fall off? I know what he was giving her and it wasn't lawyerly advice."

"Watch it, Lisa. That's my brother you're talking about."

"I'm sorry, but this just doesn't make sense."

"And that's why I need to talk to Mrs. Robinette. I know Steve's at work right now so this is a good time to corner her about the truth."

They turned off Highway 12 near Kamiah and drove onto a private road which wound up the mountainside in a gradual climb. They cleared the summit twenty minutes later.

"Look at that view," Lisa said. Beyond the mountain's crest, valleys and other mountain ranges rippled across the horizon like ocean waves swelling up from a sea of green. "I could live with that view every morning."

The loose-gravel road hardened into black-tarred asphalt as they neared the Robinette residence. They drove past twin-brick columns, each red column acting as a support for a massive wrought-iron gate. The gate had been left open.

"This is the place," Jessie said. "Tommy brought me here a few years ago for a party. Steve's wife was out of town at the time."

Lisa gasped. "Wow. This guy must have a few bucks. They live in a whole different stratosphere. Look at this place. This is movie star kind of stuff."

"Wait till you see inside. First time I saw their view from the living room, it took my breath away. You can see all the way down the Clearwater River for miles."

They followed the circular driveway, stopping next to a flagstone path leading to the entrance. Jessie knocked as Lisa peered through a window next to the door. "Someone's coming."

"Lisa! Stop that." Jessie scowled at her before hearing the latch click. A woman swung the door open. She looked exactly as Abigail described her.

Jean Robinette.

Jessie quickly took inventory. Long blond hair pulled back in a ponytail, green eyes that looked back at her with interest, and a tan body that clearly expected to be pampered. The woman carried herself with elegance.

"May I help you?"

"Mrs. Robinette?" Jessie said, not sure where to begin.

"Yes. And you are ..."

"I'm Jessie White Eagle and this is my friend, Lisa." She hesitated for a moment. "My brother is ... was Tommy White Eagle. May we come in for a moment?"

Robinette's eyes widened. "You're Tommy's ...? Oh, I am so sorry to hear about your brother. Please, come in." She swung the door wider. "Let's go in the living room where we'll be more comfortable."

As they entered, Jessie heard Lisa give a little gasp. She watched as her friend gaped at the view, her eyes as wide as Betty Boop's. She turned her attention to Robinette. "You have a beautiful home, Mrs. Robinette. I was here a few years ago with my brother."

"Thank you, Jessie. Please call me Jean."

Jessie sat on a couch alongside Lisa while the woman took a chair opposite them. Beyond Jean, she saw the valley below. The noontime sun illuminated the mountains with rich colors—lushness of green foliage, aqua-blue skies and brown and gray rock formations.

Leaning forward with crossed hands, Jessie took a deep breath. "To get right to the point, I'm looking into my brother's death."

Jean glanced downward, straightening a magazine on the coffee table. "That sounds like a job for the police."

"My father is chief of the tribal police, as you may know. He and others are looking into the murder. I'm ... I'm helping out when I can."

Lisa coughed.

Jessie gave a quick glance toward her friend, her widened eyes and rigid expression signaling Lisa to shut up.

She turned back to Jean and saw the woman studying her.

"That sounds dangerous, Jessie. You never know what you're going to come across. Did they send you here?"

Jessie smiled. "I don't think talking to you is all that dangerous. And, yeah, they know I'm interested in helping solve this case." She shot a quick look at Lisa. Her friend tried to hide a smile.

Jean clasped her hands, resting them in her lap. "How can I help?"

"We've learned you met with my brother just before his death. Can you tell me what that was about?"

Again, Jean began straightening the magazines. "I'm afraid there's been a mistake, Jessie. I wasn't meeting your brother. Maybe someone mistakenly meant my husband. They're friends, you know."

Jessie waited until Jean glanced up. "I'm not mistaken. Someone saw the two of you meeting several times, once late at night at Tommy's office."

The woman dropped her gaze. "I don't know what you're talking about. They're wrong."

"They're not mistaken. And they'd be willing to testify in court that—"

"—Court?" Alarm flared in Jean's eyes. "I didn't have anything to do with what happened to Tommy."

Shifting on the couch, Jessie leaned back. "Look. I haven't told the police about this yet. Just hoping you'd tell us what this was about without getting them involved. So we could—how does my father put it—determine whether it's pertinent to the case. I mean, if you're straight with us, maybe your involvement with my brother might never wind up in court."

Jean looked angry. "Jessie, you don't know what you're getting into. Leave it alone. Trust me. It had nothing to do with Tommy's murder. Nothing!"

Jessie felt herself getting angry. She stood, glaring down at the woman. "First you tell me there was nothing. Now you tell me whatever happened between you and Tommy had nothing to do with his murder. Are you lying now or were you lying a minute ago?"

Jean stared back, speechless.

Jessie hammered away. "I wanted to give you a chance to explain things. For Tommy's sake. Some people might think there's something going on—"

"—There was nothing going on between us. Nothing." Now Jean sprang up, facing Jessie. "And if anyone tells you otherwise ... they're lying."

"I know my brother. He was an honorable man. But I do know you two were meeting about something. Are you going to tell us what it was about?"

Jean slumped down in the chair. "I can't tell you. Please don't ask."

Jessie looked at Lisa, gesturing with her head towards the front door. "Think about it, Jean. Sooner or later, I'm going to have to pass this information to my father. His people will be talking to you next time."

The woman just shook her head.

"We'll see ourselves out. You know how to reach me if you decide to come clean."

Jean's eyes glistened. "You don't know what you're getting into. For your own sake, just leave it alone."

"I can't. I have to know what happened." She turned and stalked out of the house. Lisa followed her outside.

This interview did not go as Jessie planned. She wound up with more questions and no answers. Jean Robinette knew something. Jean's eyes told her so, the woman seemed too frightened to tell the truth. If she was not having an affair with Tommy, why was she scared?

As Jessie walked toward Lisa's car another question troubled her. What was she going to tell her father and Travis?

She'd have to think about that for awhile.

Chapter 31

Lapwai, Idaho

Less than an hour later, Travis and Frank drove into the secured Nez Perce police lot. An uneasy quietness marked their trip back from Steele's office. Frank kept his thoughts to himself. Travis left him alone, imagining what the older man must be thinking. It was good Frank never saw the crime scene photos.

As they entered the police station, Francis waved them over. "Professor Mays, got a message from the university. They need you back pronto for some kind of seminar."

He started to wave it off, but Francis thrust a note toward him. "I promised I'd give it to you."

He glanced at the note and saw McPeters listed as the caller. Once in Frank's office, he called the number Francis jotted down.

"How's real police work feel?" McPeters asked when the call went through.

"What's this about a seminar?" He did not feel like engaging McPeters in conversation. "You do know we're in the middle of a homicide investigation?"

"I know. I know. But this came straight from the top. The university hired a security firm from Seattle to conduct a threat assessment on each of the departments and provide training to selected members. You're one of those they picked."

"I don't have time for this, McPeters. Get someone else to fill in."

"No way, pal. This has something to do with the eco-terrorist threats we've received for some of the research projects WSU oversees. The bosses want you to attend because of your background with criminal intelligence work on groups like these. They want you to work with this guy from Seattle. His name is John Ares, head honcho of a company called Puget Sound Executive Protection."

"I'll try to fit it—"

"No way, Travis. They want you here. Now. It'll only take a day or two."

"A day or two? I haven't got time to waste."

"Let me put it another way, either you show up or you're out of a job."

"You threatening me?"

"Not me. The university. That's how important they take these eco-terrorist threats. They're willing to can your butt if you don't show up. Your call, buddy." The line went dead.

Travis slammed the receiver down, turning toward Frank who was already seated behind his desk.

"Hey, easy on the phone, partner."

Travis started pacing. "The university insists I return to campus for a couple days. There's nothing I can do about it." He passed on the threat from McPeters.

"We'll try to get along without you."

"You heard from Jessie yet?"

"No. No one's answering the phone."

Travis stopped pacing. "Maybe we ought to stop by and check on her."

"Not a good idea. I think she's ticked off we didn't let her tag along. I'd let her blow off a little steam first." He looked up with a gleam in his eye. "Unless you wanna go round three with her."

He held up his hands. "I surrender. Let's take a stab at the casino. See what we can dig up about Pete and Tommy before I head back to the university. You got a photo of that guy, Shane Foster?"

Frank nodded, grabbing a file on his desk. "I had one of the guys work up a six-pack to include Foster's mug and five other look-alikes."

"Great. Let's see what we can come up with before I have to shoot over to Pullman."

"I'll give Lafata a ring. Let him know what we're up to."

"You really trust him, Frank?"

"Yeah. At least until I catch him in a lie. So far, all he did was omit he knew about the San Diego lead."

"Yeah. And before we could speak to Axtell, someone torched the apartment and left a dead man behind. And this was after Lafata released Baptiste."

"I'm not ready to point any fingers yet. Let's give him a chance."

"Whatever you want, Frank. It's your call."

The Whitewater Casino sign towered above them as they pulled off Highway 12. The word 'Casino' in bright red neon lights drew motorists like moths to a flame. Vehicles were strewn around the parking lot in numbers that suggested the casino might be crowded.

"I wonder what this place pulls in every year," Travis said, watching a big rig pull out of the parking lot.

Frank found a parking space some two-hundred yards from the entry. "I don't have the exact figures on this place, but I know a few years ago they estimated that Indian gaming revenues nationwide were at about $12.2 billion, about ten percent of the total gaming industry in the United States. And I know the Whitewater brings in their fair share of profits. People travel all over eastern Washington and Central Idaho to lose money here."

"Don't you get a percentage of that?"

"I refuse to take any money."

"Why? It's for your tribe. Your people. What do they call it, the *new buffalo* for the American Indian?"

Frank's face hardened. "Let's just say I don't like what it's done to some of my people and leave it at that."

Travis wanted to pry, but he suspected further questioning would be met with silence. He remembered Jessie talking about her father's feelings on the subject, that it was one of many things Frank and his son fought over. Not a good subject to raise at the moment.

Frank turned toward him before they entered the casino, "Let me take point in here. I know the people. And let's try to ask our questions before Robinette intervenes. He was Tommy's friend, but he also runs this place and wants to protect it. Agreed?"

Travis nodded, following him through the lobby. Frank waved at several employees working near the front door. The employees waved back, then focused on Travis with curiosity. Frank and Travis cut through the main floor. Sound enveloped them—music pounding, drinking glasses clinking, and one-armed bandits clattering—like a swelling symphonic crescendo never easing up. Just the noise itself added to the excitement of this place.

They took an elevator to the second floor. Frank led him down a hallway to the rear of the building and into an office marked Financial Services. He saw a list of names on the directory. The older man followed his gaze. "I wonder if that was where Pete Axtell's name used to be," Frank said, pointing to a space where one name appeared to have been removed.

The police chief opened the door. Behind the front desk, a young man sat as if his backside was taped to a steel rod. He had dark wavy hair, combed straight back, and dark penetrating eyes that looked back at them with mounting interest.

"Chuck, how's business?" Frank said, extending his hand.

The young man shook Frank's hand, glancing over at Travis. "Just fine. Just fine. How can I help you, Chief?"

"Could you show us where Pete Axtell used to sit? We're still working a missing person's case on him and thought we might poke around where he worked."

Chuck grimaced. "Mr. Robinette know you're here?"

"I'm sure he wants to cooperate with our investigation, Chuck. After all, Pete is an employee. Right?"

The young man pursed his lips. "I don't know, Frank. Mr. Robinette is really ..."

"Come on, Chuck. You want us to drag Mr. Robinette all the way down here just so he can tell you to let us look around?"

"I guess, if Mr. Robinette is helping you—"

"Now you're cooking with gas, Chuck. Just point us in the right direction and you can get back to work."

Chuck seemed to relent. They followed the younger man down a hallway that opened up into a large room. They heard the hum of voices. The room looked like a giant waffle with rows of cubicles, each with its desk and computer work station. Travis felt like he was looking at an accounting sweatshop. Each work station was partially enclosed with three-quarter partitions, allowing each desk some modicum of privacy. Travis saw several heads over the partitions, people working within their little portioned-off worlds, fingers typing away on keyboards.

"Here's his desk, Chief. Just as he left it."

"Thanks, Chuck. We'll show ourselves out."

The young man lingered.

"We'll be fine, Chuck." Frank said. "Want us to let you know when we take off?"

Chuck nodded, apparently understanding he'd been dismissed. Travis bet the young man would call Robinette the moment he got back to his desk. They had ten or fifteen minutes at best.

He pulled up a chair and sat next to Frank. They were just starting to open drawers when a young woman's face appeared over the partition. "I thought I heard someone over here. Oh, hi Frank. Still looking for Pete?"

Frank nodded. "Yeah, Cleo. By the way, how's your mom?"

Travis saw the girl's eyes soften. "She's doing better, Frank. Thanks for asking. Brought her home from the hospital a few days ago. One of my sisters took off work to stay with her until mom is back on her feet."

Frank nodded and started to turn back to search Pete's desk. Travis saw the girl looking around for a moment.

"Frank," she said, whispering. Travis moved closer, seeing Frank do the same. "Have you spoken to Pete's girlfriend? She might be helpful."

Frank looked puzzled. "Girlfriend? I didn't know ..."

Cleo squinted at them with a look of conspiracy. "Nobody's supposed to know. Pamela Redfeather's the name. Night janitor at the elementary school."

"Yeah, I know Pam."

"She and Pete are sneaking around like they don't want anybody to know they're together." Her eyebrows danced as she smiled. "For the life of me, I don't know why they wanted to keep it a big secret. Everybody knows."

"Thanks. We'll check it out."

Cleo looked past them in alarm, disappearing into her cubicle like a rabbit returning her safe warren.

"Can I help you, Frank?" Steve Robinette stood frowning down at them. "I was told you're here looking for information."

Chuck wasted no time calling the boss.

Frank stood. "Just following up on Pete's disappearance, Steve. Didn't think you'd mind us looking around here."

"I want to help you, Frank, but I can't have you going through Pete's desk. He was one of our accountants, working on sensitive financial records that we just can't share. It would be a violation of our customers' privacy."

"Would a warrant get us into his desk?"

Steve smiled. "That would go a long way in helping me justify allowing you to search his desk. Thanks for understanding. You get the warrant and I'll personally help in the search."

Travis saw a hint of smugness in Steve's expression.

Frank shrugged. "Okay, Steve. We'll see if that can be arranged."

"You do that. Now, you guys can find your own way out, I trust. Let me know when you've got the warrant." He turned and strode past Chuck's desk, nodding at the young man. Chuck nodded back and the two of them started talking, occasionally looking toward Frank and Travis.

Frank started to leave, then turned toward Robinette. "Steve, I almost forget. I've got some photos here. Could you take a quick look to see if you recognize anybody?"

The casino manager wheeled around. "Sure. Anything to help."

Robinette walked back to join them. Travis watched Frank hand him the photo line-up containing Shane Foster's photo. For a brief moment, Travis thought he saw Robinette's eyes flash with recognition.

Robinette closed the file and handed it back. "Sorry. Doesn't do anything for me, Frank. Isn't that the same face that FBI agent just showed me?" He gave them a blank look.

"Oh, yeah? Lafata showed you that one?" The chief took the file back. "Thanks, anyway. Sorry to bother you." They watched Robinette walk away.

Frank leaned closer to Travis, whispering. "Lafata's right. Robinette's hiding something. He knows Foster and he knows we're hard-pressed to get paper for this desk. Come on, we've got one more stop to make."

They filed past Chuck's desk. The young man busied himself with something in his desk drawer, never looking up as they passed. Frank leaned over the desk. "See you later, Chuck. Thanks for your help."

Chuck gave them a bewildered look.

As they approached the elevators, Frank veered to the left and took another hallway deeper into the building. They stopped in front of a door marked *Security*. Frank entered without knocking. Travis followed. Inside, they came into a room the size of a bank vault. Everything seemed closed in and stifling. On three walls, close-circuit screens flashed a plethora of casino activity from every conceivable angle. Travis saw shots of sections of the main gambling floor, as well as doorways, hallways and elevators. Two men sat at a u-shaped console, looking from screen to screen. By rotating switches and push-button controls, each man could zoom in or out on any of the gamblers. One of the men glanced back. "Hey, Frank. How's tricks?"

"Not bad. Not bad." Frank walked toward the man. "I thought Dizzy worked this shift?"

"Nah. He traded. Wanted to do something special with the old lady. I traded shifts with him."

Frank backed away. "He's out with his wife? That doesn't sound like Dizzy."

The man grinned. "You're right. Dizzy taking time off work for *that* just doesn't sound like him. But what are you going to do? He had the time coming."

Okay," Frank said, laughing. " I'll let you get back to work. Anything interesting happening out there on the floor?"

"Nothing that'd interest you, Frank. Just a lot of people losing their money."

"Makes for good business, right?"

"Not for me, Frank. I get paid either way. Robinette and his crowd are the ones raking it in. Know what I mean?"

"Yeah, take care. Catch you later."

Steve Robinette chewed on his lower lip as he watched Frank and Travis emerging from the security office. He picked up a phone and punched a series of numbers. He eyed another security screen and saw a guard pick up the phone. It was the same guard Robinette saw Frank talking to a moment ago.

"Did I see Frank White Eagle and his sidekick leaving your office?"

"Yeah," the guard said, looking up at the camera he knew linked Robinette's office. "They're asking about Dizzy. Frank thought he was on duty."

"And what did you tell him?"

"Dizzy and I traded shifts."

"That all?"

"Yeah, Mr. Robinette. That's all he wanted to know."

Robinette hung up and reached for a control panel on his desk. Using these controls, he selected the connection to a camera located nearest to the front entrance of the casino. The color monitor came into focus just as Frank and Travis exited the front door and began walking toward the parking lot. He turned to his computer and scrolled down to personnel files. A moment later he found the phone number for Ted Nimmons. Everyone at work called Ted by his nickname, *Dizzy*. He dialed Dizzy's home phone. No answer. A message machine clicked on and advised the caller to leave a message.

Robinette heard Dizzy's message machine signal that the recording had been activated. Robinette started to leave a message and then quickly hung up without saying a word. Instead, he picked up his cell phone and pressed a number on speed dial and waited until the call connected.

A man answered.

"Robinette here. Got another job for you." He laid his plan out. "Let me know what you find out." He hung up without waiting for a reply.

First, the FBI shows up asking about Pete Axtell. Then Jessie White Eagle shows up at his house to interrogate Jean. Then Frank White Eagle shows up at the casino asking about Pete Axtell. He knew they were all chasing their tails unless they started asking the right questions.

He'd make sure they never got that far.

Money carries with it a big stick, and he intended to use that stick to his advantage.

Chapter 32

Clearwater River, Idaho

The black ribbon of Highway 12 snaked along the river's northern edge as Frank drove past Kooskia a few miles. "See that area across the Clearwater?" he said, glancing over at Travis. The police chief drove with one hand and gestured with the other.

Travis saw a historic landmark sign whiz past. "Yeah. Saw the sign."

"No, not the sign. I'm pointing to that area across the river."

Travis looked to the south and nodded.

"That's where Looking Glass' village sat over a hundred years ago."

Travis surveyed the land beyond the river, a tangle of brush, trees and rising mountains. His thoughts were focused on Dizzy and what the casino security officer might reveal. He wasn't up for a history lesson, but he knew Frank had other plans.

"Our people called him Allalimya Takanin. White men named his father *Looking Glass* for a mirror the chief carried around with him. Allalimya took that name as his own when his father died. Looking Glass' people respected him for his leadership as a warrior and buffalo hunter."

"So what happened to the village?"

"Most of it was destroyed," Frank said, looking ahead. "Another example of the cavalry shooting themselves in the foot. Before the war of 1877 broke out, Looking Glass urged other chiefs not to take up arms against the white man. Some listened. Other didn't. And war broke out."

"So Looking Glass joined them?"

"Not at first. He and his people tried to sit it out. To stay away from the conflict, but white men wouldn't leave them alone. Their village stood in that area we just passed, near Clear Creek. Some cavalry and citizen volunteers showed up one day just after hostilities broke out. One thing led to another and they opened up on the Looking Glass' camp—men, women and children. Chaos broke out. Looking Glass and his people fled to the mountains to hide. Several Nez Perce members were killed, including a woman and her child. They drowned in the Clearwater trying to get away. Most fled into the mountains and the white men—angry the Indians escaped—stole more than seven hundred horses. That one stupid act forced Looking Glass into the war."

He waited a moment for Frank to continue. The man remained quiet, gazing across the river once again. "Interesting," Travis said, not sure what to say.

Frank grimaced at him. "You're missing my point."

"I got it. Men make stupid mistakes?"

"It's more than that," Frank said, frowning. "One must not let emotions motivate them to take action. Fear, anger, hatred, vengeance—all these feelings lead to tragic mistakes."

"So, what are you saying?"

"Learn from this. That we must be diligent in our investigation not to allow our feelings to get in the way. I must deal with the fact my son is dead. Murdered. I must learn to put these feelings behind me and try to move ahead with objectivity. Otherwise, like the cavalry, I'll make unnecessary enemies."

Travis shrugged, glancing at the river below.

"What about you, Travis?"

"What about me?"

"Something in your past seems to be troubling you. Will it jeopardize what we have to do here?"

"Look. I don't have the emotional baggage you're bringing to this case, Frank. My son wasn't killed."

He saw Frank wince. "Look, I'm sorry—"

"—forget it." Frank said. The police chief looked ahead for a moment. "I have to say this. I don't think you're being honest ... with yourself."

"You don't know anything about me, Frank. Just leave it alone, okay?"

Frank shrugged, returning his attention to driving.

They traveled in silence until they came to where the three rivers merged. Frank slowed down as the highway began to parallel the Lochsa River.

Travis saw Frank searching the river's edge as he drove. "Is Dizzy his real name?"

Frank smiled. "Nah. His given name is Ted Nimmons. But he's always played around with the trumpet. We just started calling him Dizzy—you know, for Dizzy Gillespie, the jazz player—and the name just stuck."

"So tell me again why you think Dizzy might be on the river and not spending time with his wife?"

"It's trout season. Dizzy would no more spend time with his wife right now than he'd volunteer to have a root canal."

"So when the security guard said Dizzy took time off to be with his wife, you just naturally knew he was fishing?"

"Exactly. This time of year, he might as well be married to the river. He lives for it all year—this and steelhead in the fall."

"Must be a great marriage."

Frank laughed. "Actually, Dizzy loves his wife. And his wife knows he loves fishing. She even comes out with him from time to time. Ah! There he is."

Travis saw a man thigh-deep in water, flicking his line across the water. Frank pulled off the road and grabbed a file from the dash. "Let's see if this drive was worth the time."

They clambered down the bank toward the river, Travis two steps behind the older man. As they got close, Frank cupped his hands. "Dizzy, come here and take a load off?"

Dizzy looked up at them with a scowl. "Man, it's my day off, Frank. See me at the office." He sounded like James Earl Jones' twin, his voice deep and resounding.

"Come on, this is important."

Travis watched as the man cast a wistful look across the water before wading ashore. The waders fit him like a male swimmer in a gigantic Speedo swim suit. Nothing underneath was left to the imagination. Dizzy looked like he'd never passed on a meal.

Frank waited for Dizzy to step on dry land. "It's about Tommy. If it wasn't important, I'd never have bothered you here."

Dizzy face relaxed a little.

"This here's Travis Mays." Frank said, jabbing a thumb in his direction. "He's helping out on this case." Frank did not offer any further information. Dizzy did not seem to need more.

The fisherman lowered his rod and reel, carefully setting them on the ground. "You dropped by the casino?"

"Yep. Just came from there."

Dizzy laughed. "What are you gonna do? I had to go fishing, so I told a little white lie."

Frank slapped him on the shoulder. "Your secret's safe with us, pal."

Travis watched Dizzy reach for a cooler he'd left on shore. The man reached inside and withdrew a diet soda, popped the tab and took a long drink. He sat down on a flat-topped boulder. "What you got that's so important?"

"It's about Tommy's murder and Pete Axtell's disappearance."

"Oh, yeah. Sorry about Tommy, man. He was a good kid. How can I help?"

Frank withdrew the six-pack of photos. "I want you to take a look at these guys and tell me if you recognize anyone."

He handed the file to Dizzy. The man squinted and thrust a finger at one photograph. "Bingo. I know this guy."

Travis peered over Dizzy's shoulder and saw him pointing at Shane Foster's photo.

The security guard handed the file back to Frank. "I remember this guy. We got a security alert on him several months ago, and I saw him floating around the casino recently. Name's Shane Foster."

"He was at the Whitewater?"

"You got that right. Told Robinette about this guy. He said to keep my eye on him."

Frank took the file back. "Robinette knew about him?"

"You bet. I thought it was strange he didn't want us to run this guy off. I mean, that alert went to all the casinos as someone to keep away from the games."

After withdrawing a pen, Frank handed the photo file back to Dizzy. "I need you to date and sign below the photo."

Dizzy started to comply and then stopped. "This going to get me in trouble, Frank?"

"I'll keep your name out of it, Dizzy. If it goes any further, I'll let you know."

"That look of yours spells trouble." Dizzy studied Frank's face for a moment then returned his attention to the file. "Okay, here's my John Henry." He dated and signed beneath the photo, handing it back to Frank. "Any word on Axtell?"

Frank quickly glanced at Travis, then back at Dizzy. "To be honest, I think he might be dead." He gave a quick sketch of their trip to San Diego and the arson fire. "We're waiting for confirmation. Keep that under your hat, okay?"

Dizzy's eyes narrowed. "Man, this sounds serious. First Tommy, and then Pete." He turned to face the river for a moment. "You know, before Pete left I heard rumors that he was running with a shady crowd and throwing a few bucks around. I knew he and Tommy were close. So you think there's a connection between what happened to Tommy and Axtell?"

A crow's harsh cry above caused all three men to glance up. The bird, perched on a branch, gawking at them with piercing black eyes. It squawked at them once more as if scolding the men for trespassing.

Frank glanced back at Dizzy. "Don't know yet. We got a long way to go. Thanks for your help."

Dizzy reached down and picked up his rod and reel. "Any time, Frank. And I'll keep my eyes and ears open. I'll let you know what I pick up." He rose and started toward the water. "Now, get out of here. I need some quality time with the river." He waded out into the water and began working downstream.

Clutching the file, Frank began to climb the rocks. "Come on, Travis. Let's see what else we can find out, now that we know Robinette is a liar."

 **Chapter 33**

Santa Rosa, California

Timothy Heard laced his running shoes, then stretched his calf muscles while pushing against an unyielding pine tree. For the next hour he'd put away his police uniform—complete with brand new lieutenant's bars—and the stress that went with the job. Time to shed a few pounds.

Two women, gasping for breath and drenched from their run, trudged down the path that led to the edge of the roadway. He smiled as they passed, retracing the same steps taken by the women into the woods. A midday sun showered down warmth from a cloudless blue sky. A coastal breeze gently nudged tall grasses on either side of the pathway.

He began a slow gait, until coming to a larger fire trail into the mountains. Once there, he picked up speed. Even out here, he could not keep his mind off the job. After his stint as a sergeant in special investigations, he'd been promoted and sent back to patrol as one of the watch commanders. These changes in duty challenged him, and he missed the adrenaline from supervising task force operations. His investigative unit had been attached to the U.S. Attorney's Strike Force office in San Francisco, hunting down major drug traffickers and other organized criminals who dared settle in northern California. Now, he sat through budget meetings, staff briefings, and citizen complaints.

All this became boring except one frantic call that came into dispatch several days ago. A frantic call from a woman who just found her husband shot to death on their porch. Heard knew the murdered victim. Patrol officers found the body of Assistant United States Attorney Steve Kirkpatrick, gunned down in his home up on the top of Fountain Grove. The killing stunned Heard because he'd worked with the prosecutor on *the* case. The one that caused so much trouble.

Once again, memories began to rob him of the joy of jogging. No matter how hard he pushed himself, his mind refused to forget that one hideous case he'd worked on with Kirkpatrick. In a matter of hours, they'd lost a valuable witness and a brilliant investigator.

Michelle Scarsbourgh and Travis Mays.

In his twenty-five years on the job, sending Michelle back in that night—over Travis' strenuous objections—became the hardest choice of his career. It almost cost him everything. He'd survived—the subsequent investigation and Monday morning quarterbacking by the brass—and he'd gone on to make quite a reputation for himself thanks to Kirkpatrick's quick thinking.

One black mark on his otherwise spotless career.

Kirkpatrick's death unnerved Heard. He knew the AUSA prosecuted hundreds of bad guys, any one of whom might wish the man dead. Could the killer be one of the bad guys he and Kirkpatrick once locked behind bars?

And Travis? The man just slipped from sight. Angrily, Travis turned his badge over to Heard and strode out of the department. The latest words from the officers was that Travis might be somewhere in Washington or Idaho. Heard never followed up on these rumors. Maybe he just didn't want to know where Travis wound up. Better to forget and move on.

Still, it was a shame. Travis was a natural. Good instincts. Able to crawl into the minds of the targets he hunted. One of the best detectives to ever serve in the unit.

What a waste.

Heard and Travis always seemed to be butting heads. The Scarsbourgh woman became their final blow-up. Travis railed about the dangers of sending her back in. But Heard knew there was no other choice. Without her help, they'd never get the paper for wiretaps and the evidence they needed to put the target away. Unfortunately, Travis allowed himself to get close to the witness. He lost all objectivity. Totally unprofessional. Those were the words he used to make Travis back off. Faced with charges of insubordination and failure to obey a direct order, Travis finally relented and stood mute while Heard talked the witness into going back inside the criminal organization one more time. They knew Travis' silence made the woman think everything was all right.

They found her body two days later. And Travis became history.

Heard began pushing himself, as if the pace he set would purge this memory. It never did. The sight of that woman's body still haunted him, never able to shake it no matter how hard he struggled.

Ahead, the path forked. He kept to the left, knowing that it would take him straight up toward Lake Isanjo, a small body of water nestled in the foothills. He pounded away, feeling sweat dripping through his T-shirt and down his back. His breathing became labored as he churned up the path, leaping over several granite boulders and a dry creek bed that had been carved into a small ravine by winter rains.

He finally reached the last stretch of road and spied the lake ahead. He began to slow down as he crossed a small earth dam.

No one in sight. Like having an entire park for your own personal enjoyment. Heard saw a fresh set of tracks on the ground, hoof prints of several horses. He reached a rocky straightaway and began pushing himself once more, long strides and high altitude forcing air out of his lungs. He felt exhilaration as endorphins kicked in.

It was the last thing he felt.

Creasy lowered the rifle after just one shot. He hit Heard straight on, once in the head. It flipped the man back and to the right, the body cart wheeling down the slope, splashing into brackish water. The cop's head and upper torso lay submerged.

The crack of the rifle shot startled a duck nestled in nearby tulles. The bird quacked and furiously beat its wings as it rose into the air. He watched the bird circle the lake and finally settle on the far side. He glanced around the park. No witnesses in sight.

Good.

He slipped out of the sling and carefully placed the rifle in a cloth bag. He'd be gone in just a few minutes, but he wanted to enjoy this moment.

Feast his eyes on one more kill. One more act of justice. He watched the dead man's body gently sway as waves lapped against it.

His business in Santa Rosa completed with this single rifle shot. Now, back to Idaho where he'd bring everything to an end.

Chapter 34

Kooskia, Idaho

Frank White Eagle's cell phone rang as they left Dizzy on the Lochsa River and climbed into the unmarked. He answered the phone, then covered the mouth piece and mouthed "Francis" at Travis in the passenger's seat. Frank laid the phone down and began searching for something in the car.

Grabbing a piece of paper and a pen, Frank brought the phone back to his ear. "Okay, I got something to write on. Give it to me." He jotted the information down and hung up.

"Asked Francis to find Pamela Redfeather's current address. She found an address in Kooskia. It's on the way back to my office."

"Axtell's girlfriend?"

"Yeah. She lives in a duplex. Let's swing by and see if we can catch her at home."

Frank followed Highway 12 until they approached the first bridge into Kooskia. The small hamlet nestled in the crook of the fork where Clearwater's South Fork and Middle Fork merged. From Highway 12, motorists might never see the town if they blinked while passing. A two-lane bridge gave access to the town from the east, and another bridge on the west side of town brought traffic back onto Highway 12.

Frank took the eastern bridge over the middle fork river and continued into town, parking near a squatty duplex. The structure had a flat, sloping roof, with cedar-shingled sides that had long ago turned a weather-beaten gray. An old GMC pickup straddled a common driveway. According to the numbers, Axtell's girlfriend lived on the right.

Travis stood near the car while Frank knocked on the door. The neighborhood seemed quiet for midday. He saw children down the street playing in someone's yard. There were no fences around the dwelling. Vehicular traffic seemed minimal, typical small town protected from the stress of urban struggle while struggling with its own kind of economic survival.

He heard the doorknob rattle and turned to see a woman appear behind a screen as she opened the door. The woman—hair dyed a platinum blond with dark roots showing—wore a tight-fitting sweater with bare shoulders exposed and denim jeans that must have been a struggle to squeeze into.

"Pamela Redfeather?" Frank pulled out his identification and badge. "Frank White Eagle. I believed we met awhile back." He glanced toward Travis. "My partner."

She only focused on Frank. "What can I do for you, Chief." Her nasally voice sounded wary.

"I wanted to ask you about Pete Axtell. Can we come in for a minute?"

"The place is a mess. Can we just talk here?" She glanced over her bare shoulder at something.

"I'd rather talk in private."

Pamela shrugged, opening the screen door a crack. Frank opened it further. Travis followed them inside. She was right about the mess, he thought, looking at clothes strewn over the furniture like a strong wind just swept through the place.

"Sit anywhere," she said, choosing a spot on a sagging sofa. "You wanna talk about Pete? Did he show up?"

Frank pushed aside a rumpled blouse and sat down. Travis decided to stand.

"No. Not yet. We thought maybe you could tell us where he might be."

"Why me? I barely knew the guy."

"We were told you and Pete were ... dating." Frank removed a notebook from his pocket and clicked a pen to begin writing.

"Who told you that?"

"Somebody at the casino. Aren't you?"

"Well, we went out a couple times. You know, for laughs." She pulled out a cigarette and lit up.

Travis felt something brush against his leg. He glanced down and saw a cat rubbing against him, its tail curled. He wanted to give the cat a swift boot, but thought Pamela might object. He let the cat continue to rub.

"When is the last time you saw or heard from him?"

She took another puff, thinking. "It's been awhile. A couple weeks, maybe."

"You know why he took off?"

Pamela took another, longer drag. The smoke slowly curled from her nose and mouth. "He just called me one night and said he needed to leave for awhile. He'd call me when he could."

"Did he say why he was leaving?"

She shook her head. "Nothing specific. Said there'd been a little trouble at the casino and he had to take off until things cleared up. It sounded like he messed up."

"Messed up?"

"You know, got the wrong people mad at him."

"Like who?"

She grimaced. "How would I know? It wasn't like we're married or anything."

"Any idea how he messed up?"

"I told you, I barely knew him. He didn't give me details." She gave Frank a look as if daring him to challenge her statement.

Travis shifted his feet. "Did anyone else contact you about Pete?"

Frank shot him a frown. Travis ignored the look, watching Pamela's face closely. She studied him for the first time as if deciding whether he might be worthy of an answer. "His boss called. Wanted to know where Pete might be."

"His boss? Mr. Robinette?"

"I don't know the guy's name. He just said Pete worked for him at the casino. Said Peter never showed up for work. They were worried about him."

"Those were his exact words—'they were worried about him?'"

His questions seemed to anger Pamela. She puffed several deep drags and pushed the smoke out into the room. It bellowed around her head and floated toward Frank. "That's what I said."

Travis pressed on. "Did anyone else come by here asking about him?" Her eyes flashed. At least that was the look he first thought she gave him. It took a second for it to register.

He was staring into the eyes of fear.

Pamela lowered her eyes. "No. No one came by here. Now, that's all I know. I've got to leave soon. Do you mind?" She gestured toward the door.

Frank slowly stood and gave her a business card. "Thanks for your time, Pamela. If you think of anything else, please give me a call."

She took the card without looking at it. "I don't have anything more to tell you."

Frank followed Travis to the door. "Thank you for talking to us anyway. We'll see ourselves out."

Frank turned over the engine as Travis crawled into the passenger side. Once buckled, Frank turned to Travis. "That girl seem a little nervous?"

Travis glanced back at the house. "She's scared, Frank. I don't think she'll ever tell us who came looking."

"She did say Pete's boss called. I'm assuming that'd be Robinette. So, whatever happened to Axtell, Robinette may not know."

Travis turned the steering wheel. "Or he called up and feigned ignorance to push suspicion away from him."

Frank leaned back. "So what kind of game is Robinette playing? He sure didn't want us to go rifling through Axtell's desk. And yet, he calls the girlfriend trying to find out where Axtell's hiding."

"Maybe the truth lies somewhere in between," Travis said.

Chapter 35

Pullman, Washington

A three-hour drive from his cabin gave Travis time to think. He dropped Sam and his belongings at the rented house in Palouse, then drove another twenty minutes back to Washington State University.

Sam wanted to tag along, but McPeters lurked the corridors during the week. This meant Travis could only sneak the dog onto campus on weekends when everyone else was off enjoying life.

Monday morning.

He had exactly one hour before meeting John Ares, the guy from the security firm WSU hired. He fired up his computer—grown dusty during his absence—and Googled the man's name and his company, Puget Sound Executive Protection based in Seattle.

Hits on the company seemed to verify its legitimacy. He located the company's website, and found links to an array of news articles attesting to the efficiency of the company with Ares listed as CEO and chairman of the board. The company appeared to cater to the elite of the industry, dot. com companies, high-profile manufacturers, and those in the entertainment industry. Publication dates for these articles began several years ago.

One thing surprised him. This young company seemed to attract a high volume of business in a short time frame. Success must sell itself, he thought, exiting the company website. He saw sixty-four e-mail messages waiting his attention. He clicked off the program and watched the monitor darken.

He might get to those later.

Emerging from his office, Travis saw McPeters with another man further down the hallway. McPeters motioned him to join them. "This is John Ares, Travis. The gentleman I told you about." His cordial tone made Travis cautious. "John, this is Professor Mays."

The man was not a pencil-pushing desk jockey. Ares thrust out a hand in greeting, his grip surprisingly strong. Lean and muscular, the security consultant's engaging smile did not conceal the fact he was studying Travis closely. "Glad to finally meet you, professor. Heard good things about you."

Travis glanced at McPeters, surprised, before turning his attention back to Ares. "Call me Travis. And don't believe everything you hear. Particularly from him," he said, thrusting a chin at his boss.

Ares chuckled. "Never believe anything in my business without checking it out first. Only a fool believes things at face value," he said, glancing at McPeters. "Thanks for hooking us up, Kent. See you at the meeting."

McPeters shot a worried look at Travis. "Uh, right, John. See you at the meeting."

Ares waited until McPeters walked away. "That man gives me the creeps." He turned and grinned. "Know what I mean?"

Travis thought it safer to keep his thoughts to himself.

Gesturing toward the exit, Ares said, "How about we walk and talk. The meeting's in a conference room across campus. Like to get some fresh air and a cup of java."

Travis studied the man as they left the building. Ares carried himself like a cop, walking in an easy gait, balanced on both feet, always looking around and taking in everything. Once outside, he heard Ares take a deep breath. "I love this part of the country. Good air, good people, and good hunting."

They climbed concrete stairs leading to the Terrell Mall. As they approached the twin libraries, some students spotted Travis and waved. He returned their greetings, then turned toward the businessman. "Mr. Ares, I'm not sure why I was pulled back here."

"Call me John," he said. "That's right. You're working on some kind of homicide investigation. McPeters filled me in just before we met. Sorry about the inconvenience."

"Yeah. I need to get back to it as soon as possible."

The man's smile vanished. "I understand. And I'll free you up as soon as I can." He pointed toward a bench near the entrance to College Hall. "Let's take a break while I explain."

Ares was not even breathing hard after climbing the hill. Travis started to sit, but he saw Ares remained standing. He rested a foot on the bench, waiting.

"Another satisfied client recommended my firm to the university. Actually, your nemesis, University of Washington on the west side. Go Huskies." He chuckled. "Anyway, WSU came to us about concerns they had over increased eco-terrorist and animal rights activity and threats against several other major universities. Particularly threats against faculty members involved in animal research projects and forest-harvesting development. They want to know how to protect the university against these nuts."

"That's not exactly my field of expertise, John. I haven't a clue about animal research and agricultural projects this university might be involved in."

"I know that, Travis. But here's where you come in. I know you're an expert on criminal organizations similar to these eco-terrorists. Same principles apply whether these criminal organizations are motivated by profit or politics. For example, you worked the Mexican drug cartels — organizations motivated by profit but also involved in the political arena to protect their organizations. We know they use or support terrorist groups whose interests coincide with the cartels. I'd like to pick your brain about how such groups might attack the university here. You are familiar with the university and might be aware of some of their vulnerabilities."

"No offense, but isn't that what your company is supposed to do?"

Ares smiled. "I get paid the big bucks to reach out and find those who can help us provide executive protection for our clients. That means I find guys like you."

"So, you want to take what I know, come up with a protection plan that you can sell, and then get paid by WSU for all this?"

The man's smile turned to a smirk. "They told me you were no dummy. It's called free enterprise, Travis. Everything you need to know will be discussed at this meeting we are attending. Now, when can you get me that information?"

Travis reached down to tie his shoe. *I need to get this guy off my back.* "I should have the information you want in a day or two. Then, I need to get out of here and back to the investigation."

Ares shook his hand. "Thanks for your help. Here's my card. Call me anytime."

Travis watched him move away, the businessman moving like a cat ready to pounce. Taut and agile. At one point in his life, Travis might have been like Ares, always moving, never staying long in one place. Now, all he wanted was to be left alone, sequestered in his mountain cabin with Sam.

He thought of the river near his place, the water flowing past like life itself. He just wanted to sit and watch life pass without getting caught up in the current. Everything changed since his days as a cop. These recent infringements—Tommy's murder and Ares's pressure for information— made him resent the world trying to crowd back into his life.

Jessie, Frank, and now Ares.

The first mistake came when he allowed himself to become involved with Jessie, to be drawn into her brother's murder investigation against his better judgment. He wondered if anyone but Jessie had begged him to become involved in this case whether he would have remained firm. She seemed to have awakened a spark inside him, a feeling that he thought dead for some time.

He'd take this journey one day at a time and see where it might lead.

Change always comes with a cost. Once before it brought him pain. He did not know what the future held, but he never wanted to feel that pain again.

Chapter 36

A graduate student guarded the front counter when Travis returned to his office. She looked up as Travis passed. "Professor Mays, two gentleman are waiting to see you. I let them wait in your office. I hope that's okay?"

"Who are they?"

She stammered. "I didn't get their names. But they showed me badges. Law enforcement from out of state."

His stomach tightened. Badges showing up in pairs and unannounced always means trouble. As he walked down the hallway, Travis saw his office door ajar. He paused, taking a deep breath, then pushed it open.

Two men sat next to his desk. As the door opened they both rose as if they were tied together. The man nearest him smiled.

Tom Kagan.

"Man, it's good to see you," Travis said. "You still in homicide back in Santa Rosa?"

Kagan nodded. "Can't get it out of my blood. And you—a professor? Never would have figured."

Travis shrugged, glancing over at the other man he did not recognize. "What brings you up to my neck of the woods?"

Tom's smile disappeared. "I'll let you get comfortable before we get into it. This is Special Agent Beck Malloy with the FBI." The man was tall, dark, sporting an over-the-collar haircut J. Edgar Hoover never would have approved. Malloy shook his hand.

Travis circled around and sat behind his desk, watching as the others settled in. "Okay, give it to me straight, Tom."

"To be blunt, Travis, I think someone might try to kill you."

Again, his stomach tightened. "Right to the point. I like that."

Kagan studied him for a moment before continuing. "We've had two murders in Santa Rosa within days of each other. I think they're connected."

"Connected how?"

"You worked with both men. The first victim was Steve Kirkpatrick, that AUSA down in the city."

"Yeah, I knew Steve. We worked together on several cases."

Kagan nodded. "The other victim was one of our own. Tim Heard."

"Tim murdered? How?"

"Sniper. Same caliber, same M.O. Hit both of them from a distance. No witnesses. No evidence to speak of."

"You handling the investigation?"

Kagan shook his head. "Not at first. But now, since we see the connection, they've thrown both cases on my desk."

Travis glanced toward Malloy. "And the FBI?"

Kagan and the agent exchanged looks. "We cross-indexed everyone working with Heard and Kirkpatrick over the years," Kagan said. "Your name kept popping up."

"You already told me that."

Kagan leaned forward. "I understand you've been loaned out to work on a homicide case in Idaho? A Tommy White Eagle?"

He frowned, nodding.

"And one of the people involved in that investigation is Special Agent Lafata, right?"

Travis looked from Kagan to Malloy. "Yeah, Lafata's involved. What's this got to do with your investigations?"

"You may not know this, Travis, but you and the two victims worked together. Lafata supervised bureau agents working on that last case you worked. The one where a witness was murdered."

"Lafata was a supervisor?"

Malloy shifted in his chair. "Yep. He never interacted with the investigators in the field, but he monitored the case and worked directly with Kirkpatrick. His name didn't come up on the radar until we cross referenced all the names and Michelle Scarsbourgh. Then bells and whistles started going off."

Travis slammed his open palm on the desk. "I knew I'd seen him somewhere. We had a meeting once in the federal building in San Francisco. Everyone remotely involved in that case showed up. All the locals, prosecutors, FBI and a number of other federal agencies. Lafata was in that meeting, but he never spoke."

Malloy leaned back. "Not his style. He'd rather sit back and pull everyone's chain. At least until the Scarsbourgh case."

Angry, Travis tried to slow his breathing. "What do you mean?"

"When that woman turned up dead, Lafata took a lot of heat from Washington and the SAC for pushing the case and endangering a witness. For forcing Kirkpatrick to send that women back in to get more evidence."

"Lafata was the one who made that call?"

Malloy nodded. "And that's why he got transferred to Idaho. A disciplinary move. He screwed up several other times before, and losing that witness was the last straw for the bureau."

"So why did the FBI send you up here?" Travis said, staring at Malloy.

The agent glanced at Kagan before answering. "I don't work out of California, Travis. I ... work out of Washington D.C. On special assignments."

Travis saw the two men exchange glances. "Are you the man Kagan worked with on that conspiracy case a few years ago? Those white supremacists traveling around the country robbing armored cars?"

"That's where Kagan and I first crossed paths. Since then, we've kept in touch. When Tom came across the connection to Lafata, he gave me a call. D.C. sent me out here to investigate."

"You think Lafata's dirty?"

"Whoa there, professor," Malloy said. "It's one thing to make a bad call and get transferred. It's quite another to say an agent is dirty. All we know is two men connected to the Scarsbourgh case have been murdered, and you and Lafata are on the short list. You both may be the next targets."

Malloy stood up. "I'm up here to make sure both of you stay alive until I can figure out what's going on."

Kagan leaned toward the desk. "And I'm here to try to solve these murders and to make sure you knew what's happening. Unless something new comes up, I'll be heading back to California after we meet with Lafata."

"Not until I buy dinner for you guys. Let me grab a coat and we're out of here."

 **Chapter 37**

Palouse, Washington

Travis' watch showed 10 p.m. as he drove down Main Street in Palouse. He made a left hand turn onto I Street, his house a few blocks up the hillside. As he drove into the driveway, he heard Sam barking from the backyard—sounds of a half-wild dog, used to running free all day through the national forest. The dog hated to be fenced in. His bark was a canine's way of scolding Travis for abandoning him.

Travis knew how Sam felt.

He carried a large cardboard box inside, filled with information Ares dumped on him at the last meeting, and set it on the kitchen table. He continued on through the house until he got to the back door. He unlocked it and the door slammed open as Sam bounded in, the dog's tail signaling forgiveness.

He opened a can of dog food, dumping its contents on a bed of dried kibble. As the dog chomped down dinner, Travis sat down at the kitchen table and began sorting through the files. He tried to concentrate on the documents, trying to work his way through the information as quickly as possible. He hoped to be headed back to Idaho sometime tomorrow.

Thoughts of the two murders in Santa Rosa kept imposing themselves on him. He tried to make sense of Lafata's connection to this whole mess. Pieces to the puzzle floated in his head but he couldn't force them together to form a cohesive pattern.

Other questions vied for attention.

The sniper shooting at them outside Frank's office—related? Who was the shooter aiming at? Based on the two killings in California, the sniper in those murders appeared to be a good shot. The shooter in Lapwai missed. Intentional?

He thought of the weapons at his cabin. Since leaving SRPD, he still felt undressed when he was not wearing a weapon strapped to his belt. Now, he wished he'd followed up on getting a concealed weapons permit here in the Pacific Northwest. At the time, he thought those days of having to pack a weapon were behind him. Teaching was not that dangerous. Maybe he'd get Frank to deputize him and authorize a CCW so he might carry a concealed weapon. He glanced at his watch, thinking about Frank and Jessie. He picked up the phone and dialed the number where Jessie was staying.

An unknown woman's voice came over the line.

"This is Travis Mays. I was trying to reach Jessie White Eagle."

"Just a moment."

Jessie's voice filled his ear. "Travis?"

"Hey, finally caught up to you. Where you been hiding?"

"I'm not going to sit around waiting for you guys to call. I do have a life."

"You didn't go back to Three Rivers, did you?" That would be the first place the killer might check.

"Noooo. They let me take a few days off." She sounded exasperated. "I took care of a few things. Why the third degree?"

"I'm just concerned. Tried to reach you several times but no one answered." He waited for a response. Only silence. "Have you heard from your dad?"

"No." Again, silence. Finally, she spoke. "Where are you calling from?"

"My place in Palouse. Just finishing up with school business. If everything goes well, I'll be back at the cabin tomorrow night." He thought of telling her about the murders in Santa Rosa and Lafata's connection, but decided he'd keep his mouth shut. No point giving her more to worry about.

"Let me know when you're back in the area. I ... I have a little information for you."

"Can you tell me now?"

"It'll wait. See you when you get here." He listened to the disconnect tone humming in his ear. He dialed Frank's number and heard the man's voice after the first ring.

"Hey, how's it going, professor?"

"Not well, Frank." He laid out the information Tom Kagan and Beck Malloy divulged that afternoon. "This thing with Lafata has me stumped."

"That's a puzzler, for sure."

Travis saw Sam had finished his meal and curled up under the table, lying across Travis' feet. "Lafata was the one who gave you the background on me in California?"

"Yeah. But he never mentioned he'd worked with you."

"To be accurate, we never directly worked together. But he should have at least acknowledged we were connected to the same case. Instead, he just kept hinting at my past. Never telling me anything."

"Lafata's a different kind of bird."

"Yeah. I keep wondering if he's some kind of crook. I can't bring myself to trust him."

"Trust is something to be earned."

Sam stirred at his feet.

He wondered if Frank might be aiming that statement at him. "Just wanted to pass on what I learned today. See if it made any sense to you. I should be back at the cabin tomorrow night."

"Good. We'll dive into this when you get here. Until then, watch your back."

Watch his back. He knew from SWAT training that if a sniper zeroed in on your back it was all over. He'd never see it coming.

He hung up the phone and returned to the files.

Six hours later, a glow to the east announced a new day approaching. The dawn light made him feel tired as he finished reading the last document. He made a few final notes before packing up the material.

He'd finish this in his office, make a few calls, and wrap this thing up by noon.

The dog rose and looked up expectantly. "Come on, Sam. Time to go to school." To heck with McPeters. He'd sneak Sam in the back way and hide him in the office. They'd start for the cabin right from school and save an hour's traveling time.

A man sauntered from the Palouse Market on Main Street and watched the truck roll by. A man and his dog. How country. He recognized Travis Mays as the driver. He sipped a cup of fresh-brewed coffee, watching the truck continue west until it stopped at Division Street. The driver signaled a left-hand turn, turned and disappeared from sight.

No hurry. He knew where to find his target. He'd finish this coffee and then continue the surveillance.

The coffee drinker slid into the driver's side of the van and began following the same route taken by Travis. South on Highway 27 to Pullman and left on Stadium Way to the campus. He was beginning to know this area pretty well. The stop at the restaurant last night—watching the cop from Santa Rosa and the fed dining with Travis—made for an interesting evening.

He'd let his boss know the details about those dinner guests and Travis' telephone conversations later. He found the connection to California very interesting, a fact he suspected the boss already knew. But he must pass on everything and let the man use what he wanted.

Creasy always did.

Chapter 38

Selway River, Idaho

Sweat made Brian Wyatt's undershirt cling to his chest. He fingered a handgun lying on his lap. He never thought of killing a man before tonight. All that was about to change. One pull of the trigger and his problem would die.

The cops couldn't prove anything. Another hunting accident in the woods. An unidentified shooter leaving the body behind in a national forest. He'd mulled the plan over ever since the letter came warning him of the pending hearing. He must make this problem go away before investigators made the man talk.

Once this man—this problem Wyatt needed to take care of—slipped and called himself *Creasy*. Odd name. Creasy talked about himself in the third person. Wyatt guessed all killers were a little loose in the head.

Dampness from the sweat made him think about changing his shirt. Creasy might sense fear in Wyatt, somehow smell an odor of fear drenching his clothing. No. Only animals really seem to alert to fear. They either smelled or sensed it, like horses knowing when they carry fearful riders. Maybe people somehow telegraph it by the way they sit, or the way they jerk on the reins, or sit in the saddle. Or that they intended to kill another person.

Creasy was not an animal. Just a killer.

This letter, lying on his desk, came to Wyatt from the hands of a dead man. As if the murdered man lie taunting him from the grave. A blasted hearing to determine whether his family violated waterways to the Selway.

As if the government—and the Nez Perce, for that matter—had any business telling his family how to use their own land.

He remembered a state park ranger mistakenly wandering onto their property when he was a boy. His father damned the creek into a small lake, then stocked the pond with fish considered endangered. The man told his dad they'd have to tear the dam down. His dad pointed a rifle at the ranger and told him to stay off his land and never return.

He laughed as he recalled the ranger scrambling out of sight. The man never filed a complaint and never came back to make sure dad complied. The pond still remained. Now, this letter arrived and threatened everything. The development, the draw to the area, the whole project.

Years after his father passed away, he'd arranged for someone else to forcibly protect the same lake with armed force. Now he'd use a gun to take care of the threat against himself. The problem still remained.

Water rights. Or lack thereof.

He slowly gripped the phone and called the number he'd been given. The call switched over to a message machine. "We need to meet immediately. A problem developed. I'll explain it face to face. Call me at this number. I'll be waiting."

He killed the connection.

Wyatt slipped the gun into a shoulder holster and pulled on his coat to hide the weapon. He'd take care of some chores until Creasy called.

Travis was getting a late start on his way to the mountains. Everything at WSU took longer than he anticipated. Before leaving Pullman, Travis tried the phone number where Jessie was staying. Lisa Penney answered, telling him Jessie was heading up to her own cabin.

"Jessie has a cabin?" he asked. "Where is it?"

"She needs to be alone," Lisa said, refusing to tell him its location.

A phone call to Frank got him that information. Frank sounded worried. "She dropped by my place on her way to the cabin. I told her about the murders down in Santa Rosa and the connection to Lafata."

"I wish you hadn't done that, Frank."

He heard the other man breathing hard. "Travis, she was quite upset you failed to mention it to her when you called. I think she's feeling left out, and she's taking Tommy's death hard. It might be good for you to check in with her."

Travis hung up and finished boxing up the files for Ares. "Come on, Sam. Let's get this delivered and get out of town."

The dog wagged his tail in excitement, tired of being cooped up in Travis' office all day. Ares was still on campus, and accepted Travis' intelligence information with enthusiasm. "Man, this'll help tremendously. We'll be in touch."

Travis hit the road fifteen minutes later. As he left the city behind, he wondered what he faced on the other end. Maybe he should have told Jessie everything, but now it was too late. Beside, it was not his style to reveal everything that turned up. He'd never worked that way in the past, and he wasn't about to change.

Not even for Jessie.

The mountains turned a deep purple as the sun settled beyond the horizon. He flicked on his headlights, and leaned back for a long drive. Sam sat attentively on the passenger side, head sticking out the window.

"Well, boy. Is she going to play nice when we get there or do I need to dive for cover. Speak up, dog. She likes you. Put in a good word for me, okay pal?"

Sam looked at him with a canine's desire to please. If only the dog understood.

Travis turned his attention to the road. Trouble or not, he realized he was looking forward to seeing her once again. Even when she was a pain in the butt.

A smoky dusk darkened the mountains by the time Wyatt finished chores. He'd checked for messages several times throughout the afternoon. No one called. Creasy always returned Wyatt's calls in the past. Maybe Creasy felt less inclined to call now that Wyatt transferred the money into the killer's offshore account.

Wyatt returned to the barn and began currying the Appaloosa. Brushing the horse seemed to calm his own nerves. He felt the bulge under his coat, near his armpit. The gun gave him a safe feeling.

He stroked the horse with his left hand while his right hand rhythmically brushed the hide. He saw the horse's ears raise a moment before he heard Creasy's voice.

"Here I am Wyatt."

Creasy stood in the doorway to the paddock, hands crossed, a heavy coat opened in front.

Wyatt felt the gun under his coat, pressing against his skin. A long way to reach with Creasy facing him a few yards away. "You came here? I ... I thought we'd meet somewhere—"

"Where people might see us? Don't be stupid."

"No. I meant somewhere quiet where we could talk alone."

Creasy glanced around the barn. "The only ones listening to our conversation are the animals. We are alone. So ... start talking."

Wyatt fought the urge to reach for his weapon. He wondered if he'd be able to move fast enough to kill. Fast enough to pull the trigger and watch his problem crumple to the ground.

He assumed Creasy carried a gun.

Wyatt considered whether this man sensed what was about to happen. He'd made it very clear in the phone message he wanted Creasy to call, not just show up at the ranch. He lived alone here, but anyone might drive up. One of the neighbors. One of the hired hands he used to work the cattle.

He tossed the brush into a bucket at his feet, his hands finally free. Creasy watched him closely, a smile playing across his lips. Wyatt stood with his hands to his side, struggling to find some courage to finish this thing.

He played for time.

"A letter from that attorney arrived here warning me he'd scheduled a hearing in a few weeks. A complaint about me violating the terms of the water rights agreement."

The other man shrugged. "Sounds like your problem, not mine."

Wyatt clenched his fist. "If the cops start poking around and see this guy was filing a complaint against me ... and they realize he turned up dead. Don't you see? They'll start suspecting me."

"Again," Creasy said, shifting his stance, "that's your problem, not mine."

The moment had come. He started to reach for the gun.

"Surprise," Creasy yelled. Wyatt froze as he saw the man holding what looked like a gun. At least until he looked closer.

He stumbled backwards.

Wyatt saw an odd weapon in Creasy's hand.

A second later a thousand volts of electricity struck his chest. As he lay jerking on the ground, his muscles twitching helplessly, he saw Creasy move forward. A moment later, Wyatt's world turned to darkness.

Creasy slung the unconscious man over the back of the Appaloosa. Wyatt would be out for some time after the injection. He'd saddled up the horse to help him carry the load where he wanted to end this thing.

Let the beast do the work.

He found a trail leading to a mountain ridge above the ranch. It took about thirty minutes in the dark, flashlight in hand, for him to find the spot he sought. He used the time to mull over the connections between Wyatt and himself, intersections in their lives where investigators might put them together. He'd made contact with Wyatt after learning of the problem the rancher had with Tommy White Eagle. Disposable cell phones, purchased with false identification, had always been their communication link. And the money transfer—made to a third party account under an alias to an offshore account—had been moved several times since Wyatt wired the money. Each account—opened in countries where bank secrecy was sacrosanct—immediately closed after each transfer.

The cops were going to run into one blind alley after another.

He finally reached a spot overlooking the Selway River. He positioned the unconscious man with arms outstretched, palms up, and legs pushed together. He slowly withdrew a gun.

"Ashes to ashes, dust to dust." The first shot echoed through the valley, followed by two more blasts.

Brian Wyatt lay dead.

Chapter 39

Lochsa River, Idaho

Travis turned off the road and parked, engine running. He turned on the interior cab light and read the instructions once more. He'd passed Lowell a few miles back looking for a gravel road leading from Highway 12 up the mountainside. Frank said it was exactly five miles east of where the rivers merged.

The Lochsa River was a silver ribbon in the moonlight to his right. He studied his notes and flicked off the light. Nearly three hours after talking to Frank, here he was sitting in the dark trying to find Jessie's cabin. "Well, Sam, I think the road is just ahead. How about I send you in first when we get there. Soften her up for me. Deal?"

Sam gave him a dog smile and a soft bark of understanding.

"Thanks, pal. You are man's best friend."

He found the turnout to the cabin a half mile further. The truck's headlights swept the gravel road, a dense forest on each side. There were deep ruts and he had to drive slowly. Frank warned it would take some time to reach the cabin once Travis left the highway.

As he drove, Travis thought about Jessie—an enigma, a puzzling mystery he barely understood. Why was he drawn to her? She posed a threat to his way of life. And yet he could not shake her from his mind. Is this what a moth felt as it became drawn to a fire?

He'd grown accustomed to his purposefully sheltered world. It was safe, simple uncomplicated. Just himself and Sam. He'd managed to create a shield—a buffer from the rest of the world—by living alone, living in the cabin on the edge of nowhere.

Until she came barging into his life.

Jessie—enticing him into this murder investigation, into her life, into her world. Once again he found himself walking between the living and the dead.

He felt himself floundering. He knew very little about her. And she seemed angry at him most of the time, expecting more than he could offer. Yet Travis caught himself thinking about her when they were apart, replaying in his mind the few times they'd spent together, the way she looked at him.

Sam barked, yanking Travis back to the present. He saw a light cutting through the darkness, a yellowish beam gleaming through curtained windows. As he drew near, the shape of a cabin emerged in the headlights and he saw Jessie's VW parked in front. He slid his truck alongside, killing the engine and flicking off the headlights. Darkness engulfed him.

He saw a crack of light as the door opened. Jessie walked out onto the porch, silhouetted by light from the cabin. He could not read her expression, the light behind her darkened Jessie's face.

Oddly, he felt like an intruder. As he opened the driver's door, Sam leaped over his lap with a bark and dashed toward Jessie. He saw her reach down and pat the dog. Good. Sam breaking the ice for him.

"I happened to be in the neighborhood and thought I'd drop by." He closed the door and leaned on the hood. "You mind?"

"Come on in." Noncommittal, she turned and walked back into the cabin, Sam padding behind her. She left the door open.

A fire crackled and popped in the fireplace as he entered. It was a modest cabin, simpler that his own, but much neater. Two cots, one table, and two chairs comprised all the furnishings. The floors and walls built with planked pine, knotted and aging. Electricity was the only modern convenience. No water or bathroom that he could see.

"Very ... rustic," he said.

"Meets my needs," Jessie said, standing with her back to the fireplace. "Sound familiar?"

He felt out of place. "I just wanted to see how you were doing before heading to my place. And you mentioned some information for me?"

"So this is really about the investigation. Right? Not how I'm doing." Jessie challenged him from across the room. Was she angry?

"No. Seriously. I'm concerned about you. Just wanted to make sure you're okay. That's all."

Her eyes searched his. "I don't mean to come off like a ...." She stopped, wrapping her arms around herself. "It just seems like everything is setting me off right now. Tommy. The shots fired at us. And then I find out about the murders in California."

He nodded. "I understand. Sorry about not telling you. You want to sit down and talk, or do you want me to go?"

She smiled. "No. Stay. We need to talk."

For the first time, he noticed an easel in one corner of the room. He saw several paintings on the wall, and a cloth draped over a number of other canvases.

He sat down in one of the chairs and pointed toward the art work. "Whose paintings?"

She sank down the chair next to him. "How do you like 'em?"

He eyed them for a moment, stood and walked over to one hanging above the fireplace that captured his attention. Two rivers meeting and becoming one. "Hey, I know where this is. Just below Three Rivers where you work. Right?"

She nodded.

It was as if he could walk inside that painting, as if the artist managed to capture nature in all its colors and subtleness. Breathtaking. "This is really good."

Jessie beamed. "Thanks. This is my work, Travis. This is what I live for."

He looked at her, surprised. "I had no idea. I thought—"

"You thought what?" She laughed.

"I had no idea what a great artist you are. I'm impressed."

"Nice save, Travis. You were going to say you had no idea I could do anything but shoot the rapids."

"No, really. I guess I just ..."

"Save yourself and leave it alone." Still laughing, she patted her knee, drawing Sam's attention. "Sam, tell your owner to keep his mouth closed. He'll live longer that way."

Travis settled back in the chair and gazed up at the painting. "I'd like to see your other stuff."

"Later. We should talk. Tell me more about what happened in California." Seriousness spread across her face, vanquishing her laughter.

Travis felt the mood in the room change. "I don't know how much your father filled you in on everything." He began to tell her about Kagan and Malloy and the murders in California. About his contact with John Ares. She let him talk, her face somber and attentive. As he spoke, he realized he had not shared like this with anyone before. It had all been locked inside. He found himself talking about more than facts of the case. He began sharing his thoughts and feelings, everything but what lie behind the case in California he walked away from years ago. He skirted the details around Michelle's death. She sat and listened without interrupting.

Finally, he finished his monologue of painful history, all except the details that really hurt. In silence, he watched her staring into the fire. The crackle and pop of the wood resonated with warmth.

Finally, she stirred. Turning to look at him, Jessie said, "Tell me about Michelle Scarsbourgh."

He felt himself tense, those words bringing back everything he'd fought to suppress. The look on her face told him that this was pivotal to their relationship. If their worlds were ever to co-exist, now was the time for honesty.

He took a deep breath and began.

 **Chapter 40**

Lewiston, Idaho

Clay Lafata closed and locked his office door. The tiny FBI office offered a view of the Snake River and its confluence with the Clearwater. A boat blasted its horn a few hundred yards away. The vessel passed beneath a bridge—a steel connection between the two cites of Lewiston and Clarkston—as it churned a path on the Snake.

He started walking toward the stairway. Frank White Eagle, with Tom Kagan and Beck Malloy tagging along, left Lafata's office an hour ago for dinner. He promised to catch up with them for a beer. He could really use that drink. The murders of Kirkpatrick and Heard rocked his world, and the agent knew their killer might be coming his way.

Michelle Scarsbourgh.

He thought he'd heard the last of that name after the Bureau banished him to this border town office as payback for his mistakes. His biggest mistake—forcing Kirkpatrick and the others to send that woman back inside.

Michelle paid the price for Lafata failing to heed Travis' warnings. Lafata used the chain of command to shelter himself from day-to-day operations. Quietly, he exerted pressure on those supervising the case when the need arose. The case was too important to the Bureau for Lafata to leave it unattended. Kirkpatrick passed on all the heat Travis generated about making that woman return to danger. But in the end, they forced Travis to walk that lamb to slaughter.

Travis never knew Lafata made that final decision. Until now.

In a way, Lafata regretted his harshness to Travis about the Tommy White Eagle case, but just seeing that man after all these years brought memories hurling back. Lafata's failures, his disciplinary sentence, his humiliating transfer to this tiny office. Plummeting from the heights of the San Francisco office to this hick town on the edge of nowhere. If he'd been able to pull off that case without any screw-ups, he knew he was bound for D.C. He'd paid his dues, and knew that case—before Michelle was killed— would be the ticket to elevate him to a SAC into one of the major cities of his choice.

Special Agent in Charge.

Those dreams were over. Instead, he found himself chasing his tail here in these Idaho Mountains looking for another killer, his career as a mover and shaker only a memory. He knew what lie ahead. Someday soon, he would retire from this Podunk office knowing his lifetime of service and dreams would just float away like so much debris on the Snake River. They'd flush him from the Bureau and move on to the next bright star.

Lafata followed the sidewalk to the parking lot, pressing a button on his key chain. Lights from the bureau car he drove activated as well as a short chirp from the vehicle's alarm system.

Lafata took two steps toward the car before his world ended.

Frank White Eagle, sitting across the dining table, started telling them a story about Travis learning to kayak the whitewaters. He saw Malloy flinch, then reach into his pocket to retrieve a cell phone.

Tom Kagan eyed Malloy. "Can't you even take a break for dinner?"

"Look who's talking," he said, flipping the phone open. He covered one ear to block out restaurant noise as he raised the phone to listen.

Frank saw the agent's face blanch, his eyes narrow and jaw clench. Malloy began speaking to the caller. "I'll roll from here. Yeah. Yeah. I'll handle it." He pocketed the phone, his face grim.

Frank leaned forward. "What happened?"

Malloy glanced at both men. "A sniper just took out Lafata as he was leaving the office. Lewiston PD notified our communication center."

Frank grabbed the check. He started to rise, then froze. "We got to get to Travis. He'll be the next target."

Kagan stood. "Where is he?"

"Up in the mountains with my daughter. No way to reach them by phone."

Kagan slipped into his coat. "Malloy and I will head over to La-fata's office, and you jam up to alert Travis. We'll let you know what we find out."

Frank nodded. "I'll alert Idaho County SO, see if they can't get a unit rolling." He threw money on the table next to the bill and dashed for the door. He felt time was slipping from his grasp.

Every minute counted.

Chapter 41

Lochsa River, Idaho

Comforting light flickered from the fireplace as Travis struggled to tell his story. Jessie curled her legs underneath, luminous brown eyes kind and gentle as she listened intently.

The pain and hurt he suppressed all these years struggled to rise to the surface. He fought for control. "I received a telephone call from a woman who later identified herself as Michelle Scarsbourgh. I remember it was springtime, one of those perfect days. She asked if we could meet some place outside the police station. Wanted to pass on some information, but wouldn't talk specifics over the phone. Sounded very mysterious."

He clenched his fists, struggling to put into words how his own world crashed and burned. "I suggested we meet at a restaurant on the wharf in Bodega Bay, a little hamlet west of Santa Rosa. I started to tell her what I looked like. She stopped me, saying she already knew. Saw my picture in the newspaper a year ago for an award ceremony I attended. Some service club wanted to acknowledge me for a case I worked on. She'd read about the investigation and decided to contact me."

He glanced down at Sam, lying on the floor sleeping. "We hit it off from the start," he said, clasping hands together. "She was a CPA who'd been hired to keep books for a local businessman. Later, I came to understand he hired her for more than her accounting abilities. Michelle started recognizing irregularities in this guy's accounts. Payments for products not ordered, payments to non-existing businesses, large transfer of funds to foreign accounts. In short, she'd stumbled upon a major money laundering operation with ties to one of the largest Mexican cartels. Funds derived from drug trafficking, illegal alien trafficking, and other criminal enterprises. A snake pit of criminal activity."

"And Michelle found this out through the books?"

"Not at first. All the accounts were computerized. She came across another set of books that she was not supposed to see, and began to compare those financial records to those she was supposed to be keeping for the company. She suspected something was off. We started checking out the people involved, running backgrounds and surveillance, and slowly the story emerged. She became our inside contact."

"That's what got her killed?"

Travis hung his head. "I'm the reason she died."

"You?"

"I talked her into going back into that hell hole."

"What happened?"

He stood and grabbed a poker, stoking the fire. He laid another log on the blaze, watching it slowly catch fire. He sat down to face Jessie.

"She slipped us some of the business's records on the QT and we ran it through a contact I had in the IRS. Those names and transactions started a federal chain reaction. We started getting hits on SARs from all over the country—"

"SARS?" She had a blank look.

"Suspicious Activity Reports. Banks are required to file SARs on any suspicious activities. After 9/11, the Patriot Act and other bank regulations fired up and put the banking industry under close scrutiny, forcing them to monitor and report all suspicious transactions of their clients."

"Sounds pretty intense."

"Right. But the banks learned quickly they had to pay attention. This was not like old times when the government pretty much looked the other way. Now the feds were deadly serious. Each suspicious transaction banks missed—a cool $10,000 per day for every day the transaction goes unreported. We're talking millions of dollars in penalties. Anyway, the next thing I knew the entire federal government—U.S. Attorney's Office, FBI,

IRS, ICE—crawled all over us for information. Together, we formed a task force and launched an investigation into this company."

"Sounds like an interesting case."

"Addictively interesting," he said, shaking his head. "I got so caught up in the case I found it hard to keep my priorities straight. We're talking major federal task force operation with almost unlimited funds to take this case wherever we had to take it. My frequent flyer miles were off the chart. New York. Miami. Honolulu. Chicago, Seattle. I lived out of my suitcase for months."

"And what about Michelle?"

"Yeah, Michelle." He clenched his hands together as painful memories came back to hurt him like a dentist striking raw nerves. "Michelle and I grew very close. I knew better than to get personally involved. But I fell for her."

"How about her?" she asked, raising an eyebrow.

"We were both head over heels as they say."

"And she was still working with the crook?"

"At first she gradually pulled herself away from that business. We thought with the initial information, we could independently corroborate everything and keep her name out of it. The problem was these guys rushed things, pulled her out before we knew whether our case would stand without her. The case got so big it became an investigation by committee. We couldn't do anything unless they ran it up the flag pole, all the way to DC. And then some muckety-muck—after treading water for months—finally decides we need to send her back in for more information. By then, she'd been pulled out for her own safety."

"So you sent her back?"

He felt tension in his chest as he relived that moment. "Not at first. I really fought against it. The problem was I'd become emotionally involved, and I wasn't sure whether I was letting my feelings cloud my judgment. Somebody found out about Michelle and me, and they hammered me with that in an open task force meeting after I balked at their plan. They insinuated they'd make my department bring me up on charges if I jeopardized the case."

"Jeopardized?"

"They knew the fastest way to end this case was to send her back in. They needed me to talk her into it. I became their Judas, their Benedict Arnold after they assured me she would be well protected."

Jessie's eyes held no judgment. She waited for Travis to continue.

He leaned toward the fire. "What infuriated me was we could have gotten the same information by other means. Extended surveillance. Rolling over informants. Following the paper trail we did have. The problem—in their minds—all this just took too much time. Using Michelle was the fast way. The easy way. Everyone was under pressure to make this case happen."

He paused and took a deep breath. "Deep down, I knew I was right. I knew it was impossible to protect her. These were some pretty cutthroat individuals." He shook his head. "And now I find out Lafata was the one pressuring Kirkpatrick to push Michelle back out there."

Jessie's hand still clasped his arm, her touch warm and soft. It made what he had to say even harder. "So I met with Michelle and persuaded her to go back in one more time."

Sam suddenly sat up, his ears perked. He began to growl. He rose and slowly edged toward the door.

Travis heard a vehicle coming up the gravel road. "Anyone else live up here?"

She shook her head. "We're the only ones."

"Stay in the shadows, away from the fire," he said, edging toward the door. He pulled the curtain to one side and peered out. He saw headlights cutting through the trees where the road curved toward the cabin.

He relaxed when he saw emergency flashers. A patrol vehicle, an SUV with Idaho County SO markings, rolled up the road and stopped in front of the cabin. He opened the door and met a deputy getting out of the vehicle.

"Are you Travis Mays?" the deputy asked, flashlight in hand. He bathed Travis in the light.

"Yeah."

"And is Jessie White Eagle with you?"

"That's right, deputy. What's up?"

The man seemed to relax. "Got a call from dispatch. Detective John Steele from our agency wanted a unit to come up here and sit tight until he and a police officer from the reservation arrived."

Jessie brushed against Travis, clutching his hand.

"They called me on my cell phone. Didn't want to put details out over the air. They said an FBI agent has been shot in Lewiston. Some Italian sounding name. A sniper got him."

He felt Jessie squeeze his hand hard. "The victim—Lafata?" he asked.

"Lafata? Yeah. That sounds right."

He turned and slipped his arm around Jessie's shoulders. She pressed a cheek against his chest. "Travis, he's coming for you," she whispered.

He held her tightly. "I'll be ready. This time I'm the one in the cross-hairs. Not somebody I love."

Chapter 42

Another set of headlights weaved over the roadway toward Jessie's cabin. Travis recognized Frank's unmarked vehicle, followed by a second set of lights. Frank was just stepping from his car when John Steele pulled alongside.

Frank approached first. "You heard?"

Travis nodded. "Now we're certain who the killer is targeting. There's only one of us left."

Jessie slipped from under Travis' arm and walked back into the cabin. She returned a moment later to stand next to him as she slipped into a sweater. Frank seemed edgy. Travis could not tell whether the older man appeared agitated because of Lafata's murder or seeing Travis' arm around his daughter.

A broadcast from the deputy's vehicle seemed to catch Steele's attention. He must have left his portable inside the car because he walked back to the unmarked and leaned inside. Travis watched him activate the mike. Dispatch came back with a broadcast that made Steele swear. The detective threw the mike inside the car and shook his head.

"We got another one, Frank. A ranch hand found his boss just south of here, off Selway River. Shot three times and spread out like Tommy."

Frank ran his hand over his jaw. "Who's the victim?"

"They won't give the name over the air. But they got positive ID at the scene. I've got more people rolling. I'm heading over now. Wanna tag along?"

Travis glanced at Jessie and then looked in Steele's direction. "You mind if the three of us come? Frank and I ought to take a look. All things considered, I'd rather not leave Jessie alone."

Frank was not smiling. "I'm not sure—"

"We need to take a look, Frank," Travis said, feeling Jessie's closeness. "I don't think she ought to stay here by herself." It was more than a gut feeling. The shooter had taken a shot at both of them. In his mind, Jessie might still be a target.

She squeezed his hand gently. "I'll be okay, Travis. You and dad go and find out what you can."

Frank's face tightened.

Steele beckoned to the deputy standing nearby. "How about this, Frank? I'll leave a unit here while we head over to the scene. He'll stay with her until you guys can clear. Fair enough?"

Frank shrugged. "Travis, jump in with me. Better we just take one vehicle." Steele was already climbing into his car.

Travis turned toward Jessie. "I'll be back as soon as I can."

She reached up and touched his cheek. "I want to hear the rest of the story. And ... I've got something to tell you."

Travis squeezed her hand gently. "See you later," he said, turning to follow Frank. He wondered what Jessie wanted to tell him. He glanced back one more time and saw her standing on the porch, arms crossed. She held his gaze with her own.

Travis turned toward the car and saw Frank watching. Both climbed in, Frank on the driver's side. Silence hung between them like an invisible barrier. Travis peered into the darkness, trying to figure out where he fit in this triangle. Jessie, Frank and himself. The police chief—sitting stoic and rigid—drove away in silence.

They followed Steele's red taillights through the night.

Steele sprang out of his vehicle as soon as they arrived at the ranch house. Travis realized the crime scene must be somewhere else. The detective waved them over. "Okay, the victim's name is Brian Wyatt, a rancher whose family's been around for years. This is all their land," he said, making a wide sweeping motion.

"Where's the body?" Travis said.

Steele pointed up the mountain side. "Quite a hike. About a half mile across rough terrain. Here's some flashlights. Watch your step." He led the way at a fast pace.

They reached the ridge twenty minutes later. Deputies stood near the body chatting. Steele yelled out, "Harry, thought I told you to rope this area off. Get back from the body, fellas."

The deputies backed away, except for one holding evidence tape. "Didn't think we needed to use this stuff up here, John."

"Well, you guessed wrong, Harry. Now I got footprints all through my crime scene."

Travis followed Steele toward the body, stopping a ways back to take in everything. He flashed his light on the victim. The killer staged this just like Tommy's murder. Same position of the body, same positioning of the arms, hands and feet. Same number of gunshot wounds, at least what he could see from this distance.

"Saw the tracks of a horse as well as a set of boot prints, John," he heard Frank tell Steele. "Must have carted the body up here and dumped it."

Steele took a closer look. Travis stayed in place. Frank was a few steps behind him. He turned toward the older man. "Same killer, Frank."

"You think?" Frank said, staring at the body. "All these bodies. Tommy and this guy. Lafata and the three murders down in California. The sniper shooting at you and Jessie. Why can't we catch a break on this?"

It was a question Travis could not answer. The bodies were piling up and he was no closer to the truth. And he was certain the killer planned to make him the next victim.

An hour later, they regrouped to head down the hill. Before they left, Steele met the coroner's unit and field techs assigned to process the scene. The detective walked them through the scene, telling them what he wanted them to focus on before the coroner removed the body.

Travis, Steele and Frank headed back toward the ranch house. As they approached, Steele said, "I'm going to start putting paper together for this place. That's going to take time. Let's do a security sweep of the house for right now." Steele raised his hands and made the sign of quotation marks around the words "security sweep" as he spoke.

Travis knew what he meant. They were well past the legal limit for a security check of the house. The law allows law enforcement a warrantless sweep of a building to make sure that there were no other suspects lurking around or victims in need of help. The sweep must be made in a reasonable amount of time. They were hours beyond reasonable.

Steele opened the door and motioned them inside. "Don't touch anything. But go ahead and take a quick look. On second thought, here are some extra gloves. Put them on, just in case."

The three men gloved up and entered through the front door. Steele found a light switch near the door and flicked on several switches, bathing the entryway in harsh white light. As they walked through the house, more lights were turned on until the place was filled with light.

Once inside, they went their separate ways. Travis walked down a hallway and came across a room that looked like an office. There was a small desk to the left and a larger table to the right. On the table was a model of a proposed construction site titled *Three Rivers Development*. He saw a lodge and a series of cabins placed along the edge of what appeared to be a small lake. He guessed the development was on this ranch, based on the proximity to the Selway River, also identified on the scaled model.

He walked over to the desk and sat down. He glanced at the files on the desk, fanning them out, looking at each title. Nothing seemed to grab his attention. There were two sets of pullout-drawers on each side of the desk. He pulled each drawer out and glanced inside. Again, nothing of interest.

He started to stand up when he saw the edge of a piece of paper sticking out beneath a plastic blotter. He raised the blotter with one hand, and with the other withdrew the paper. It was a court document listing the dead man—Brian Wyatt—as a defendant.

Travis sucked in his breath when he saw attorney of record—Thomas White Eagle.

He read the document carefully. It was a claim against Wyatt et al for violating the terms of a water rights agreement.

"Frank. Come here!" Travis yelled.

A moment later Frank came through the doorway, followed by Steele.

Travis handed the document to Frank. He watched as the older man scanned the paper. Frank's eyes widened. "Tommy sent this letter."

Travis nodded. "I would say we may have found a connection between two of the murders."

Frank handed the letter to Steele. "Yeah, but who's left to talk about it?"

Travis pointed toward a filing cabinet near the desk. "Whoever pulled the trigger. If this was a contract killing, we need to follow the money trail. I would say let's start right there. What we have are parties on both sides of this legal action killed by an unidentified person. Why? Who benefits?"

The three men stared at the document, each wrapped up in their own thoughts. Finally, Steele broke the silence. "Leave that where you found it, Travis. I'll go get paper and we'll tear this place apart. The answer has to be in here somewhere."

Steele walked out of the room. Frank and Travis looked at each other. Travis stood. "Come on, Frank. Sooner or later, we'll get some answers."

Frank turned and left without saying a word.

 **Chapter 43**

Palouse, Washington

Travis carried two bags of groceries into the house. Jessie followed with a third. He sat them on the kitchen counter and began turning on lights, switching the gas heater to full blast.

Jessie sat the bag down and took a look around. "This is where you come to do your professor stuff?"

"This is where I come to get away from nosey people. Hungry?"

She nodded. "What can I do?"

He pulled out two frozen dinners and brandished them. "Relax. I'll do the cooking."

She laughed and sat at the kitchen counter, watching as he slid one of the dinners in the microwave. "A regular Martha Stewart."

A half-hour later, they'd eaten and cleared the kitchen. "Now, it's time for me to get to work."

"Can I help?" She followed into a second bedroom he used as an office.

Pulling several boxes from the closet, he heaved them onto a desk. "Maybe. Let me get things set up."

The boxes were not marked on the outside. He flipped the top of the first box and pulled out a handful of files. "These are all the documents I kept from that case in California. We never found out who actually killed Michelle, although I know who ordered it. I kept these files just in case some day I might be able to hunt down whoever pulled the trigger."

"What do you hope to find?" she asked, peering over his shoulder. "And where did all this come from?"

"Something I'm not remembering from Michelle's past," he said. "I copied all the case files before I left."

He opened one file labeled *Michelle Scarsbourgh*. "Here's the background information I collected on her before we started working together. Needed to know who my source was in the case."

"Your source? You make it sound like she's some kind of tool."

He grimaced. "Yeah, that was part of the problem. I'd got so used to seeing people as a means to an end, as a way of developing a case, that'd I rarely thought of them as people."

"Even Michelle?"

He nodded. "At first, until she and I ..." He opened the file without finishing the sentence. Flicking through the pages, he came to one section listing family and acquaintances. "We never really talked much about her family, but I remember she spoke about her brother. Here it is. His name is Phillip Scarsbourgh. In the military, serving overseas at the time she was killed. Never made it to the funeral."

"Why do you want to search her family?"

"Just trying to cover all the bases. If the killer is after all those who put Chuck Coville—that's the name of the CCE guy we nailed—in prison, he'd have to kill off a couple dozen investigators."

"CCE?"

"Continuing Criminal Enterprise. That's what we nailed Coville on. He's doing a minimum of one hundred and twenty years in prison. Virtually a life sentence with little hope of getting out."

"Sounds like he'd be motivated to come after you guys."

"With what? We took everything he had, and others in his organization took over where he left off. Even his own people don't want him out."

"So that leaves who?"

"Someone who had a personal stake in what happened. He killed off those who had a direct hand in setting up the situation that got Michelle killed. The only one left is me."

"That's why Dad was upset about me coming up here with you?"

"Can't blame him. It only makes sense the killer might be stalking me. In fact, I wasn't wild about you coming here either."

"We talked this out, Travis. I don't feel safe right now on my own. I'd rather be up here, away from things, and let Dad and the others track him down."

"But what if he follows us here?"

"That's why Dad deputized you and let you carry a gun. So you could protect me—you big, strong guy." She batted her eyes and weakly flicked her wrist, mimicking a Southern belle from the movies.

Sam barked.

Travis laughed. "See. Even the dog doesn't buy it. I saw what you can do on the river. Don't give me the 'I'm just a weak little girl' routine."

She nudged him hard with her hip, almost throwing him off balance. "Okay, maybe I'm not that weak. But I do feel better hanging around up here with you than waiting for someone to take a shot at me down along the river. So where do we begin?"

"I'm going to review the files. You—relax and keep Sam off my back. How about the two of you get comfortable in the living room while I start poring over this stuff?"

"Fine. Do it all by yourself."

She snapped her fingers, catching Sam's attention, and the two disappeared from the room. He read through Michelle's family history. Mom and dad deceased. Brother, Phillip, a sergeant in the Marine Corps stationed overseas at the time of her death. He jotted down the brother's file information. He pulled out his wallet and found Beck Malloy's business card, dialing the agent's cell phone.

"Agent Malloy? Travis Mays here. Look, I'd like to run a name through your data base." He read Phillip Scarsbourgh's description from the file and filled the agent in on the brother's background. "Let me know what you find out about this guy." He thanked the agent and hung up.

Several hours later, he finished reading everything and put the files back in the storage boxes without coming up with any new leads. Exhausted and frustrated, he carried each box back to the closet and closed the door. Turning off the light, he walked into the living room and found Jessie curled up on the couch reading a book. Sam lay next to her. The dog perked up his ears as Travis entered.

"Tomorrow, I'm going to head for the campus to make some phone calls and use the computer. Want to come along?"

Jessie closed the book. "Sure, I'd like to watch a professor in action." She reached up and grasped his hand. "You never finished the story, Travis. About Michelle. Unless you'd rather ..."

Sam laid his head down, sighing. Travis sat down, turning toward her. "There's not much left to tell. We pulled her out of Colville's business long enough that sending her back in raised suspicions. Or maybe he was already suspicious, and had been watching her movements. Maybe he saw us together. I just don't know what happened."

"Did she want to go back in?"

"No. Scared to death. She did it because I asked her. She thought I'd keep her safe."

"You mentioned last time that this guy wanted to hire her for more that accounting. What did you mean?"

Travis reached down to stroke Sam's head. "Michele was a knockout. I mean, men turned to look when she walked by."

"So this crook wanted her romantically?"

"Yeah. She made it clear she wasn't interested, but the guy just didn't give up. The first time she left, she told him one of the reasons she was quitting was because he wouldn't keep his paws off her."

"And still she went back?"

Gloomily, he nodded. "Thanks to me, she agreed to go back one more time. Told the crook that if he'd keep his hands off her, she'd come back. Said she was having a cash flow problem."

"What happened?"

"We couldn't wire her up for fear they'd find it. She was supposed to go in and just act normal."

"They didn't buy her story?"

"We thought so at first. Everything seemed to be going along just fine. We couldn't monitor her very well, and we couldn't wire the place because we couldn't get court authorization with what we'd gathered up to that point. Once we got her inside, she was to feed us information and we'd be able to get paper. Search warrant. Wiretaps. The works."

"What went wrong?"

He glanced down, staring at the dog. He clenched his jaw as that night came into focus. "We were waiting outside at the end of the work day. Most everyone in the office left. We waited. She never came out."

"What did you do?"

"Just stayed outside and watched. Later that night, we got a call from the sheriff's office. One of their patrol deputies found her body dumped along the river near the ocean. Left like so much garbage."

"Oh, Travis. How could you have known?"

"Decent people don't send those they love into harm's way." He took a deep breath before continuing. "The main guy, Colville, came up with an unbreakable alibi. A lot of witnesses in another place said he was with them the entire time. One of his hired killers must have done the job. Never found out who actually pulled the trigger. That night after finding Michelle, I turned in my badge and walked away."

A utility van, parked about fifty yards from Travis's house, shook slightly as the man inside shifted. He lowered earphones, letting the tape run. "You didn't run far enough, pal," the man muttered to himself. He'd listened to every word of the story. Dialing a cell phone, he waited until the call went through and a man's voice came on the line.

"Got something for me?"

"Yeah. Confirmation on what you already knew. He just confessed to sending her in and getting her killed. Got it on tape."

"Good work. Keep that recording safe. Stay on them until I clear you. Got it?"

"Yeah. Yeah." He disconnected and pulled a blanket over him. It was going to be another cold night. And it did not look like his targets were going anywhere until tomorrow.

He placed the headset back on and began to listen once more. Maybe he'd hear a little bedroom music tonight. These two lovebirds were getting pretty cozy. He heard Travis talking to Jessie, and shook his head. He heard Jessie heading for what appeared to be the bedroom, Travis told her he'd take the sofa for the night. He heard the bedroom door close.

Soon the house was quiet.

Chapter 44

Clarkston, Washington

Shane Foster heard the blast of a horn from another vessel chugging past his sailboat, his boat tethered to a slip in the marina. He stooped in the galley, preparing dinner. Fresh bass he just caught straight from the river. The blast made him jump.

He'd wired the money to Creasy as demanded, but decided not to run—just hide. He knew Pete Axtell's murder wouldn't fall on him, in spite of that ominous recording the cops found.

Creasy was the killer.

And that wacko operated beyond the scope of his contracted duties with Foster. The orders were clear—locate Axtell and report back. Nothing about killing the guy.

It was not his fault Creasy took it to the next level. However, Foster's attorney warned he could be implicated in the murder since Creasy went after Axtell on Foster's orders. A weak case, said the attorney. They ought to be able to beat it in court. More money for legal fees down the drain.

So Foster was staying put. He would stay out of sight until he knew how things were going, hiding comfortably on this sailboat he purchased under an alias.

No one could track him here.

As he reached up to close the hatch cover, he saw stars twinkling against a black-velvet sky above. He decided to leave the hatch open and let in fresh air. He could see the dark sky from his bunk. He settled into it and soon fell asleep.

A creak above Foster's head startled him awake. He glanced at his watch. 3 A.M.

He heard another creak. Someone slipping on board.

Foster reached under his pillow, withdrawing a Smith and Wesson .38 he always carried. He slid from the bunk and worked his way from the cabin, down the galley to the steps leading to the top deck. Now he wished he'd locked the hatch cover.

The creaking stopped.

He waited a moment, hoping the intruder would keep moving so he might track the person's movement.

Nothing.

He slowly climbed the stairs. One of the steps creaked under his weight. He froze, listening. Nothing. Cautiously he crept upward. He carefully raised his head to peer around the deck.

Something hit him in the back of the neck. A jolt of electricity. Then blackness.

Foster never woke up.

Chapter 45

Pullman, Washington

Sam growled as Kent McPeters marched into Travis' office. The department chairman whirled to face the dog. "I thought I made it clear—no dogs here." The man warily backed away.

Travis struggled to hide his smile. "Oh, sorry, McPeters. Just heading back to Idaho, and I didn't want to drive all the way back to Palouse to pick up the dog."

"Absolutely no dogs." McPeters repeated. Only then did he see Jessie sitting in the corner. "Oh, good morning, Miss ..."

"White Eagle, Jessie White Eagle." She stood, extending her hand. The man beamed until he glanced back at the dog. "Welcome to WSU," he said. "How's the case going?"

Travis stood. "Not good, McPeters. At least two people dead. Not counting three other people murdered who I used to work for."

McPeters face tightened. "You're looking for some kind of serial killer?"

"I don't know what we have right now. Did you want something?"

McPeters glanced over at Jessie before giving his full attention to Travis. "Oh yeah, John Ares wanted to know the next time you're on campus. Saw your truck parked in the lot, so I gave him a call. He'll be dropping by any minute."

"Hey, I really don't have—"

"Make the time, Travis. Must I remind you how important this is to the school? And when are you going to get a cell phone, a pager, something from this century so we can reach you when we need to?"

"I'll get right on that, McPeters." Travis saw Jessie smiling. Ares walked up behind McPeters.

"Harassing the staff again, McPeters?"

The department chairman whirled. "Uh, Mr. Ares. Just telling Travis you wanted to drop by."

"Well, I guess he knows I'm here. You're dismissed."

Travis saw McPeters flush, then try to chuckle. "Well, you gentlemen take care. See you around, John."

Ares grimaced as McPeters left the office. "Pencil pushers. Detest them." He noticed Jessie in the corner. "Sorry, lady. Just call them as I see them."

Travis came around the desk and stood near Ares. "John, this is Jessie White Eagle. We're ... working together on an investigation."

"That's what I'm here about."

"Really?"

Ares leaned on the desk. "I hear things in that case took a turn for the worse. Several people dead and that agent killed. I wanted to offer any help my company might be able to give. We have analysts and profilers on staff. I'd be more than willing to have them come in and take a look at what you've collected. Try to figure out where this killer might strike next."

"I appreciate your offer, but—"

"Not to mention our surveillance capabilities."

"We're not budgeted for those kinds of services."

Area waved his hand. "This will be on the house. If we're successful, the publicity will be worth its weight in gold."

"I'll have to pass right now, John. Thanks."

"Don't mention it. I would have offered earlier, but I don't know how to get a hold of you. No cell phone, pager, anything?"

Travis laughed. "McPeters was just on my case for the same thing."

Jessie laughed. "He's a dinosaur, Mr. Ares. Wants to hide in the woods and be left alone."

Ares eyed her. "I bet he'd come running if you called."

Something about the way the man looked at her made Travis wince. Jessie seemed oblivious.

For the first time, Travis felt Sam leaning against him. The dog was standing, silent, the hair on the back of his neck bristling.

Ares glanced down at the dog. "Wow. Think I'd better go. That dog doesn't look all that friendly." Ares turned and disappeared down the hallway.

Jessie knelt by the dog. "I've never seen him like that."

Travis watched her stroke Sam's head. The dog seemed to relax. "He just needs to get back to the mountains. First, McPeters and then that guy. Time for him to run free."

Jessie stood, grinning. "Two peas in a pod. Come on, time for all of us to go home."

As Travis gathered his things, he thought of what she had just said and realized he liked the sound of those words. Particularly the way she said them.

Time to go home.

 **Chapter 46**

Clearwater River east of Kooskia, Idaho

Travis saw flashing emergency lights flicking ahead from a parade of deputies' vehicles parked along the roadway. Travis tightened his grip on the steering wheel when he realized the cars were across the highway from his cabin.

Jessie, seated on the passenger side of his truck, sucked in her breath. "Oh, no. What happened now?"

He slowed down to a crawl until a deputy motioned him to stop. He rolled down the window as the lawman approached. "What happened, officer? I live right over there." He pointed at the cabin just visible through the trees.

The deputy gave him a hard look, and glanced over at Jessie. Suddenly, the deputy's attention shot to something behind Travis. He glanced in the rear view to see what caught the deputy's eye and saw Frank White Eagle pulling up in his car, lights flashing.

Frank's voice called out in the darkness. "Deputy, that's my daughter in the truck ... and a friend of mine."

The deputy relaxed and returned to directing traffic.

Frank leaned into the car. "Just got a call from Steele. They found another one." He nodded his head at the mountain slope above them. "This time the killer dumped the body just above your house, Travis. It's time to get Jessie out of here."

Travis nodded, glancing over at her. She did not look pleased.

"Where am I supposed to go, Dad? This guy could be anywhere."

Frank leaned against the door, his jaw taut. "Right now, this killer has his sights on Travis. I don't want you caught in the crossfire."

"I know you mean well, dad, but I need to make my own decisions. Right now, I feel safer with Travis."

Travis knew Frank was probably right and he did not want to make another mistake. He would not be able to bear it if any harm came to Jessie. "How' bout we find out what happened here. Then we can decide?"

Frank stepped away from the door as Travis climbed out. He heard Jessie's door close. She came around to join them. He saw Steele working his way across the road toward them. Sam poked his head through the open window.

"Stay, boy," Travis said, stroking Sam's head. The evening air was beginning to cool. He heard the sounds of the river below, almost muffled by the sounds of police activity.

Steele approached, nodding first at Frank and then to the others. "We got an ID on the body. Shane Foster. The guy in the video with Pete Axtell."

"And the body?" Travis asked, already knowing the answer.

"Same as the others. Arms spread, palm up, legs together. It's like the killer staged the body just for you. Some sick twisted message telling you the killer's got you in his sights."

Steele scratched his shoulder, shaking his head. "And we came up with something on Brian Wyatt's finances. We traced $50,000 wired to an offshore account just before his murder. It looks like the contract killer took care of loose ends. Wanted to make sure Wyatt didn't spill the beans."

A thought suddenly struck Travis. He leaned against the truck for a moment, dizzy. "John, were you able to make copies of the lab reports and coroner's reports on Tommy's death?"

"Sure. They're in my trunk. I was just bringing them over to Frank's office." He walked over to his unmarked, opened the trunk and withdrew several files. He slammed the trunk closed and walked back to where Travis and the others waited. "Here you go."

"Thanks," Travis said, taking the file and grabbing a flashlight laying on the dash of his truck. He flicked on the light and laid the files on the hood. He opened one file containing lab results on Tommy's body and clothing. He leafed through the document until he came to the page he needed. He scanned down until he saw the list of what had been analyzed. His stomach tightened.

Jessie touched his arm. "What's the matter?"

He shook his head. "Just a hunch. We need to get over to my cabin to check on this. I hope I'm wrong." He opened the door to his truck, letting Sam leap to the ground.

Travis led them to the cable that ran across the river. He pulled the seat to him, whistled to Sam, and the two of them traversed to the far bank. He sent the chair back and waited until the other three made it to his side of the river.

Once they were all gathered, he led them into his cabin, still carrying the flashlight. He flicked on the overhead lights and glanced around the room, finally focusing on a large throw rug in the middle. He pulled the chairs off the rug, knelt down, and rolled the rug into a tight cylinder. Placing the rug to one side, he flicked on the flashlight and used its illumination to cast a direct beam of light across the timbered floor.

He clenched his teeth as the light lit up three bullet holes, in almost a perfect triangle. The wood around the holes was freshly splintered, the floor recently scrubbed clean.

Travis slowly rose to his feet.

Frank edged forward. "What is it? Why are we here?"

Travis pointed to the holes in the floor. "This is where he killed Tommy."

Chapter 47

Steele ordered a secondary search team dispatched to start processing the cabin. Travis waited on the porch with Frank and Jessie for the team to arrive. He felt Jessie brush against him, her arms embracing herself like a person trying to hold things together. He gently put his arm around her.

He no longer cared what Frank thought.

Steele looked frustrated. "I've got to tell you, Travis. I haven't a clue where this case is going. All I know—everything points to you."

Travis felt Jessie shudder. He said, "My guess is he wants to save me for last. Somehow it is tied with Michelle's murder, the only common link. But why all the guys in law enforcement? One of the crooks actually killed her."

He heard a phone ring. Frank reached into his pocket and withdrew his cell phone. The older man answered, his eyes shifting toward Travis. He held the phone out. "It's Beck Malloy."

Travis pressed the speaker button to allow the others to hear. "Beck, I've put you on speaker. John Steele and Jessie are here with Frank and I."

The lift across the river activated. Field techs started arriving, filing into the cabin one by one to set up. Travis moved to the far end of the porch. "Go ahead, Beck."

"Okay. Here's what I dug up on Phillip Scarsbourgh. Until his sister's death, he was serving in the Marine Corps, mostly overseas. Assigned to their Force Recon units and served in all the hot spots—Afghanistan, Iraq, Africa, you name it. Travis, guess what his specialty is?"

"Sniper?"

"Bingo. And from all reports, he's good."

"What happened? Where's he now?"

Static crackled on the line. "What was that, Travis?" Beck's voice sounded broken, and then the line cleared.

Travis repeated his question.

"Phillip separated from the Marines right after his sister's murder. They cut him loose on a medical discharge. Actually, due to psychological problems."

"And they lost track of him?"

"Simply dropped out of sight. Never put in for benefits, pay, nothing. Just vanished. I've checked all our databases—driver's licenses, criminal records, voting records, you name it. He just ceased to exist on paper."

"He trained for any other duties in the Corps?"

"How to survive behind enemy lines. He knew all the tools of the trade—all he needed to seek and destroy targets. Until the end, he had an excellent record. Earned a number of medals for valor and courage in the field. Quite a good Marine. They tell me something snapped."

Travis nodded. "My guess, Michelle is what happened. She was all the family he had."

Malloy's voice broke in. "Now, his enemy—target—changed. You're it, Travis. For whatever reason, I'm guessing he holds you responsible for her death."

Travis glanced at Jessie. "Well, I am responsible for—"

"No you aren't, Travis" Jessie cut in. "Chuck Coville—that CCE guy and whoever he sent to kill her—they're responsible for her death."

"I was the one who sent her back in, Jessie. I can see her brother's point."

Malloy cut in. "I'll keep checking to see if we can pick up a trail on this guy. Check back with you." The line went dead.

A field tech emerged in the doorway. "Detective Steele, you'd better take a look at this." The young man held a flat cylindrical object half the size of a small button with a wire dangling from it. "We severed the connection when we spotted it," he said, holding it up for Travis to see. "We've used these ourselves on occasion."

Travis recognized the object, a pin-hole camera with audio capabilities. "He bugged my cabin. He heard everything we've said." He saw concern in Frank's eyes.

The technician slipped the bug into an evidence bag. "We'll do a complete sweep before we leave."

Steele nodded as the young man reentered the cabin. He turned toward Travis. "This twisted wacko's been listening to you the whole time."

Travis shook his head, thinking back over the last few weeks. The only time he spoke inside was with Jessie. And just now, when he'd found where Tommy had been killed.

Phillip Scarsbourgh targeted him from the start. Even before Tommy died. Somehow, Tommy's murder became part of a twisted scheme to get at Travis.

He glanced at Jessie. The killer must know Travis' feeling toward her. He was not going to let another person be killed on his watch.

Never again.

The driver fired up the van—parked a quarter-mile from Travis' cabin—and made a u-turn on the highway, heading west on Highway 12. The driver hit the speed dial on his phone, listening for the connection. A man's voice came on the line.

The driver glanced in his rearview mirror as he spoke. "They found the bug and the body," he said, passing on the information Travis learned of Michelle's brother and that the cops found Foster's body.

"Bring me the tapes and pull back. I'll take it from here."

The driver acknowledged the order. It was just as well. He didn't want any part of whatever his boss planned next. Surveillance, wiretaps, and that kind of activity he loved to do.

Killing was not his bag.

Chapter 48

Lochsa River, Idaho

Frank stood on Jessie's porch, listening to the Lochsa rushing below in the darkness. Learning where Tommy was killed hit Frank hard—the hurt and pain striking deep into his heart once more. His eyes followed the sharp upward slope of the mountain in the moonlight as it rose to greet a darkened sky. Behind him, he knew the historic Lolo Trail cut a mountainous swath, a forested highway his people used for centuries. He closed his eyes, remembering his own travels over that trail in his youth, sensing the history of his people traversing those ancient lands.

He heard Jessie and Travis quietly conversing inside. A younger generation with modern ways of living on this land. So much has been forgotten, lost, as civilization cast aside the history of his people to allow progress to move forward.

Once he'd studied maps of the lands that belonged to his people. The immensity of this area—covering three states—staggered his imagination. Boundaries shrank over the years after the treaties of 1855 and 1863 when they ripped the land from his people's grasp. Before the white man marched into their world, the Nez Perce nation stretched from Oregon's Wallowa Valley north to the Palouse River traversing Washington and Idaho, and all the lands east to what is now Montana. His people moved like wind-driven clouds in those times, crisscrossing the mountains in search of food, trade and shelter.

As he listened to Jessie talking to Travis, he thought of his peoples' own language, a language teetering on the brink of extinction. Less than a hundred people fluently speak the language today in a culture once believed to number in the thousands.

Tommy's fear of extinction for the Nez Perce—tribal language, culture and lands—drove him to fight to protect what was left. Frank understood this passion. But his son never understood that Frank's belief in God—his refusal to accept traditionalist beliefs of the tribe—did not mean the father cast aside his culture, his heritage. It was this misunderstanding that seemed to drive them farther and farther apart.

And now, the killer snatched away Frank's opportunity to heal wounds between father and son. He would not let this killer take Jessie away. He coveted every moment with his daughter and he wanted to make sure she understood how much he loved her. And the people he'd sworn to protect.

Lord willing, he and Travis would stop this killer from striking again.

Travis watched Frank sitting on the porch through the open doorway. Jessie sat next to him on the sofa. They'd driven to her cabin until field technicians finished processing both crime scenes. Steele promised Travis access back into his cabin once they'd collected evidence. "Best stay away until tomorrow."

Gently, Travis took her hand in his. "A deputy will be coming by to stand guard while Frank and I continue with the case."

She gripped his hand. "I don't want to stay here just because my dad thinks it's safer."

"He just wants to make sure you're okay. And hanging around with me right now might be fatal to your health."

"I don't feel safe anywhere. I'd rather stick with you guys."

Sam wandered from the woods, bounding through the front door until he saw Travis inside. The dog took one look to make sure his master was in sight, then wheeled around and disappeared into the woods. At least the dog seemed to be enjoying himself.

Jessie straightened. "Oh, there's something I forgot to tell you. Kind of forgot about it in all this excitement."

"Oh? You solved the case?"

"No. But Lisa and I tried to help," she said. "We went to Tommy's office to see if you guys missed anything."

"That wasn't smart, Jessie."

She ignored his statement. "I saw one of his neighbors entering an office when we got there, so I chatted with her. Nobody had talked to her yet, Mr. Investigator."

"Okay, So what'd she say?"

"That Jean Robinette, Steve's wife, visited Tommy in his office several times, and at least once she came there late at night. The next-door neighbor thought they might be having an affair."

"And you?"

Jessie shook her head. "Not Tommy's style, sneaking around with his friend's wife. Even if she is a real looker."

Travis raised an eyebrow. "Maybe I ought to go talk to her."

She dug her elbow into his ribs. "Forget it. Beside, Lisa and I already did that."

Her laughter caught Frank's attention. He walked into the cabin. "What's so funny?"

Jessie glanced at Travis. "I was just telling Travis I learned Steve Robinette's wife visited Tommy on several occasions. The woman in the office next to Tommy's thought they were ... you know."

Frank smiled. "I know Tommy better than that."

Travis though he'd keep his opinion to himself. "Jessie says she went and interviewed Jean Robinette."

Frank's smile vanished. "I told you not to go anywhere near this case."

Jessie shrugged. "I knew—woman to woman—she'd be more likely to talk to me than a couple of guys. Particularly since I'm Tommy's sister."

"So she opened up?" Frank took over the questioning.

"No. She denied anything between 'em. Wouldn't even admit to meeting with him. When I mentioned court and testimony, she freaked out. Said I should leave it alone. That she was not responsible for Tommy's death and that I did not know what I was getting into."

Travis faced her. "Did she tell you what she meant?"

"No. Just clammed up. Even after I threatened to tell the police what I knew. Nada. Something frightened her."

Travis glanced at Frank. "Think Steve Robinette is at the casino?"

Frank nodded. "Now might be a good time to have a chat with the wife."

"I'm coming with you," Jessie said, standing.

Travis smiled at Frank. "Kind of bullheaded, isn't she?"

"Boy, you don't know the half of it."

Travis whistled as the Robinette residence came into sight. "This must be how the other half lives." Frank trailed behind Travis in his unmarked. Jessie sat on the passenger side in the truck.

She glanced at the house. "I can only imagine what a place like this must cost to buy and keep up. Steve must make a lot more than I thought."

Travis slid from his seat and closed the door. He came around and opened her door. They waited for Frank before approaching.

Jean Robinette opened the door just as they reached the front steps. "Oh no. Something happen?"

Frank stepped forward. "We have a few questions, Mrs. Robinette. If you have a moment."

Jean looked at Jessie as if betrayed. "I've nothing to say, Chief. Nothing."

"My son—Jessie's brother—was murdered, Jean. If there is anything you can tell us—"

"—I told you I can't help. There was nothing between Tommy and me."

Frank took a step closer. "Okay. Then just let us come inside for a few and tell us what you do know."

Travis saw Jean waver, her shoulders finally sagging. She opened the door wider, silently signaling them to enter. Jessie and Travis followed Frank inside. Jean led them to the living room overlooking the valley below, moonlight casting a silvery pale across the mountains. The woman lowered herself into one of the chairs. Frank and Jessie took a seat across from her.

Travis chose to stand off to one side while the others talked. He leaned on a bookshelf built into the wall around the fireplace. The shelves were filled with photographs, a few books and several rows of medals.

As Frank spoke to Jean, Travis curiously eyed the shelves. Almost all of the photos were of Steve Robinette standing with celebrities. He recognized a few statesmen, sports figures, and a couple of Hollywood types. Only a few photos included Jean. On a higher shelf, he saw rows of trophies. His eye caught the word *Biathlon*. He peered closely and saw Jean's name on several of the trophies, including a silver Olympic medal.

He waited for a lull in the conversation. "Mrs. Robinette. You were in the Olympics?"

Jean seemed distracted for a moment. She looked at Travis blankly, then seemed to gather herself. "Yes. A long time ago ... before I met Steve. In fact, we met at the Olympics where I won that medal. He still calls me his trophy wife." She did not seem pleased with Steve's tag.

Travis pointed to it. "Quite impressive. Skiing and rifle shooting. Takes a lot of discipline."

"Thank you. Shooting's something Steve and I once shared together. We liked to go over to Montana for a little getaway now and then. We haven't done that in years." For a moment her mind seemed to have taken her to another time, then Jean turned toward Frank and Jessie, giving them her attention.

Frank leaned forward. "Jessie tells us there's a witness that saw you and Tommy meeting several times at his office."

Jean shook her head, saying nothing.

"You say you and Tommy weren't ... seeing each other. And I believe that. But you were meeting him for some purpose. Now's the time to get it out."

Travis saw the woman's eyes glisten, her shoulders began to shake. "I can't ... Steve will ..."

"You're afraid of Steve?" Frank asked, gently.

She nodded, her eyes filling with tears. They began to course down her cheeks. "You don't know him."

"Tell us what you talked about with Tommy."

She wrung her hands, as if the gesture might draw courage she needed. "I wanted Tommy to help me get a divorce. Tommy tried to talk me into getting help, of saving my marriage."

"You think this has anything to do with what happened to Tommy?"

"I don't know," she said. "I just don't know. Steve has a temper, but ... to kill him?" She shook her head. "Tommy was his friend."

Frank leaned back, glancing up at Travis. "Did Steve know you were seeking a divorce?"

She shook her head. "No. I was scared to death he'd find out. Tommy said he'd talk to Steve. Try to get us into counseling."

"So, he did talk to Steve?"

"Yeah. I think so. I never spoke to Tommy after he spoke with Steve. We talked just before he ..." Jean buried her head in her hands, sobbing. "Oh, God. I hope it didn't get him killed."

Frank and Jessie stood to leave. He watched as Jean rose, trembling, leading them toward the door.

Travis followed. Might her relationship with Tommy have been just that—trying to end or save a marriage? As he looked around the house, he thought there must be a lot of community property. A lot of stuff Steve Robinette might hate losing. Including his *trophy* wife.

Travis knew one other thing—Steve Robinette may have been the last person to see Tommy alive. Was there a link between the casino manager and the killer? The more they dug for answers, the more questions sprang up.

 **Chapter 49**

Lapwai, Idaho

They reached the Nez Perce Police Station shortly before nine in the morning. Francis came rushing up just as Frank ushered Travis and Jessie into his office. "I was in the ladies room when you came in, Chief. They just told me you got back."

"Can I help you, Francis?"

She waved a pink message slip. "You got a call from a police officer in San Diego. I think it's about Pete Axtell." She handed him the note, hovering as Frank read it.

"Thank you, Francis. Anything else?"

"Uh, no Chief. Guess I'll get back to the counter." She shuffled off, and Jessie followed her out the door.

Frank dialed the number and asked for Sgt. O'Rourke.

Travis remembered meeting O'Rourke outside the fire-gutted apartment in San Diego. He watched as the police chief identified himself to the San Diego PD sergeant. Suddenly, he saw Frank's eyes widen.

"You sure?" The police chief hung up a moment later and made a sound like air escaping from a tire. "Pete Axtell is still alive."

Travis straightened. "You're kidding. Then whose body got torched?"

"Pete's cousin. And the coroner said someone did shoot the victim before setting the place on fire."

"So where is Axtell hiding?"

Jessie walked back into the office. "What'd I miss?"

Travis shook his head. "Someone just returned from the dead." He gave her the news.

Frank stood. "Now, we need to find him. And fast."

"Let me borrow a copy of Axtell's thumb drive?" Travis asked. "If you don't mind, I'd like to borrow a desk and a computer and take a closer look at what Axtell kept on that drive. Maybe I can come up with some reason why he ran off. And, more importantly, who might be looking for him since Foster is out of the picture. I'll give you a call if I find anything."

Frank exchanged looks with Jessie. "Let's grab breakfast. We'll give the professor a little space, let him use my office."

Jessie glanced at Travis. "Okay. But we won't be far."

Travis smiled. "I'll give you a call if I come up with anything."

As soon as the others left, Travis downloaded Axtell's files on the computer and made a back-up disk. Once he knew everything was saved, he started to examine each file, reviewing all the customer information stored on the disk. He estimated there were several thousand names listed, each entry listing that person's name, address, contact numbers, and amounts won or lost at the casino, including all expenditures.

After an hour, his back began stiffening from working at the computer so long. He got up and stretched, wandering over to the coffeemaker. Armed with a large steaming cup of java, he strolled back and sat down once again.

He started running all victim and witness names he and Frank had uncovered in the investigation and comparing them to names listed in the computer files. The first name he recognized was Brian Wyatt. He searched Wyatt's records, but found nothing that caught his attention. Small amounts, average losses, nothing significant. The man was clearly playing for fun.

Another name immediately caught his attention. Kent McPeters. The man's transactions through the casino seemed staggering. Some days, McPeters dropped thousands of dollars at a time, his losses far outweighing his earnings. Professor McPeters appeared to have a gambling problem. He closed the professor's file and moved on.

Some other names he recognized popped up on the monitor. Shane Foster, John Ares and Clay Lafata. All their files indicated normal, recreational-only gambling. Losses and winnings generally balanced out.

He was about to close out the last file in the data base. He flicked on the Windows Explorer function and typed in *Three Rivers Development.* A moment later he was directed to a sub file listed as 'Diversion.' Under this file, he found a listing for Three Rivers Development. Clicking on this, he found himself staring at a list of names listed as shareholders in the development. As he scanned the names he felt his pulse quicken.

Listed as major shareholders along with Wyatt—Steve Robinette and Shane Foster.

His eye ran to the far right of the ledger. Each man had contributed $400,000. Brian Wyatt's contribution listed as land and property rights for the development. Travis recalled Tommy White Eagle's legal filing against the development. If the suit had successfully halted the development, all investments might have been lost. Worthless. The projected earnings were in the millions of dollars.

This was a motive for murder.

On a hunch, he searched for one other name. John Ares. A few seconds later, a file popped up on the screen. Travis leaned forward to read the file. What he saw made him smile.

He dialed Beck Malloy. Time to get the feds involved.

Chapter 50

Clearwater River, Idaho

Beck Malloy dispatched an agent out of the Lewiston office to hook up with Travis. Between the agent, Frank, Travis and an assistant U.S. attorney, they drafted an affidavit and search warrant which a federal judge signed off with hardly a comment.

Court order in hand, they descended on the Whitewater Casino. The search warrant covered just about any transaction they might want to take a look at. The FBI provided a computer forensic team to help retrieve and store whatever they seized pursuant to the search warrant.

The FBI—along with Travis, Frank, and Steele—found the casino manager sitting in his office. The security monitors had been switched off by the time they walked into Robinette's office. Travis glanced up and saw the darkened screens. He knew Steve Robinette must have been watching them approach.

Good. Make the man sweat.

Two agents stood guard over Robinette in the hallway, while Travis and the others fanned out to begin their search. Casino operations came to standstill as all financial functions became frozen. Agents seized, marked and stored for removal all hard copy files of any transactions for Three River Development, and any of the principal shareholders. Every financial record—wire transfers, credit cards action, checks and bank accounts—surfacing from these entities was seized, identified, and tagged.

Agents from the National Indian Gaming Commission joined the small army of searchers. Travis watched as they spread throughout the casino, focusing primarily in the finance department and the administrative wing. A team of agents began sorting through all of Robinette's office files, searching his computer, and making his day worse by the minute.

Robinette stood outside, fuming. He saw Frank and Travis standing at the end of the hall. He pushed toward them, his two guards tagging along. "Frank, you know how important this casino is to our people. How could you let something like this happen?"

"Talk to the Feds, Steve. This is their case."

Robinette eyed the search team in his office. He turned to face Travis. "I heard you think I'm somehow mixed up in whatever you're investigating."

"Who did you hear that from?"

Robinette smirked. "People talk."

"We're investigating several murders. Beyond that, I won't comment."

"What does murder have to do with the casino?"

"Money's a pretty big reason to kill. And there seems to be a lot of that around here."

"This is ridiculous We run a clean operation. Just ask anybody."

"The judge who read and authorized the warrant thought otherwise. Maybe he was just one of your sore losers." Travis smiled as Robinette's face darkened. The casino manager marched away.

Frank leaned over. "You enjoy yanking his chain?"

Travis nodded. "I hate men who slap women around."

"As a father, I'm glad to hear that."

Travis wondered what Frank thought about the relationship between Jessie and him. When he called to tell Frank what he'd found in Axtell's files, he sensed Frank was on edge. They'd gone out for a late breakfast while he worked in Frank's office. When they returned, Travis saw Jessie seemed upset. Almost angry.

Frank's face gave nothing away.

They'd left her at the police station while they searched the casino.

Steele poked his head out of one of the cubicles and gestured to Travis and Frank. After the warrant was signed, Travis passed several names to Steele just prior to them hitting the casino. He asked to be alerted if they found anything.

They found Steele seated at the computer once used by Pete Axtell. "Got a hit on one of the companies you asked me to keep an eye out for, Travis. Led me to a company identified as Puget Sound Executive Protection."

"Isn't that the company that the university hired?" Frank asked, peering down at the screen.

Travis nodded. "Yeah. The company owned by John Ares. I saw his name on the customer list Axtell had on the thumb drive."

Steele pointed to the monitor. "This is not from a customer list, Travis. PSEP is listed in a vendor's file. They've done some work for Whitewater."

"Whose signature authorized hiring the company," Travis asked.

"Our guy, Steve Robinette."

"And what services did PSEP provide?"

"Threat assessment and executive protection," Steele said. He squinted at the screen and let out a whistle. "They were paid $120,000 over the last eight months."

Travis glanced around the office before speaking. "Frank, let's get a warrant for Robinette's personal finances. Checking, credit cards and other banking records. I'd like to compare those records to transactions through Ares's company and the Three Rivers Development. Robinette came up with a chunk of change for Three Rivers investments. Maybe Ares helped him out. Maybe Robinette has other sources of income we don't know about."

He leaned over and tapped Frank on the shoulder. "Can I borrow your cell phone for a moment?"

Frank handed it over, still watching Steele work the computer.

Travis dialed Beck Malloy's number again. The agent came on the line, and Travis walked away from Steele and Frank, looking for a quiet place to talk. He told the agent about Ares's company and the amounts of money Whitewater Casino paid him through Robinette.

The agent sounded interested. "And you met this guy through the university?"

"Yeah. I'd like to know more about his background and who his business represents."

Travis saw Robinette walking towards him. "And Beck, let's keep this between us right now. You can reach me through Frank." He disconnected the phone as Robinette neared. The man's face was drawn tight, like hide stretched over a taut drum. His eyes, angry. Agents monitoring the casino manager's actions stood nearby.

"I just found out you were up at my house talking to Jean. How dare you come into my house when I'm not there."

"Not something we had to clear with you. We were *invited*." Inwardly, he winced. "We didn't give her much choice. She just wanted to help us find Tommy's killer because the two of you were friends."

"How can my wife help find Tommy's killer?"

Frank saw them talking and walked over. "Everything all right here?"

Travis pointed toward Robinette. "He just found out we went to his house to talk to Mrs. Robinette. I told him she didn't have much choice. That we were investigating Tommy's murder and maybe she could help us." He met Frank's eyes, hoping the man understood what he was trying to convey.

"And I'll ask you again. How can my wife help you find Tommy's killer?" Robinette appeared agitated.

Frank turned his attention to Robinette. "We knew that the two of you were friends with Tommy. That he'd been over to your house a few times. We thought maybe she could tell us a little about who Tommy was running with. People I might not have seen with him."

"Why didn't you come to me?"

Travis leaned toward the casino owner. "Because you lied to us about knowing Shane Foster. We thought you'd just feed us more lies."

"I didn't—"

"Don't even try to tell us you don't know him. You're business partners in a development project even though his name popped up on a security alert through the casino."

Robinette's eyes widened, then narrowed. "I see where this is going. And after all I did for Tommy, you're going to try and stick his murder on me. Unbelievable."

Frank thrust a finger at the man's chest. "What you gave to Tommy he paid back in spades. You know that, so don't get all high and mighty on me, Steve."

Robinette's eyes seemed to harden. He started to say something, checked himself, and slowly walked away.

Chapter 51

Pullman, Washington

Travis squealed tires as he drove into a parking garage buried beneath WSU's main library. He slammed the driver's door shut and trudged toward his office. He wanted to come alone on this interview. Steele assigned a deputy to stay with Jessie while he and Frank followed up on the search warrants on the other end.

Travis felt he must return to the campus. Putting some distance between him and Jessie seemed the safest thing for her right now.

Whitewater files listed Ares and McPeters as regulars at the casino, while other files showed Ares' company providing services for the gambling enterprise. He wanted to question both men about their involvement with the casino.

He'd hoped Beck Malloy would get back to him with information on Ares and the Puget Sound Executive Protection Company before he made contact with either man. But time was slipping away. He felt compelled to move forward as fast as possible, motivated by two haunting visions—Tommy's lifeless body lying on his cabin floor and the threat to Jessie's life.

Inside, he felt anger welling up spurred by feelings of inadequacy, his failure to protect.

In a dream last night, he watched horrified as Tommy's image blurred. The image slowly cleared, and instead of Tommy's body, two others lay on the wooden floor at his feet. Slowly, the first figure's face emerged and he recognized Michelle Scarsbourgh staring at him with dead eyes. Then the second figure's face came into focus – Jessie staring up at him, her eyes filled with fear.

He'd awakened from the nightmare, parched and wet with perspiration.

Once in his office, Travis dialed Ares' cell phone and connected on the second ring. They agreed to meet in a temporary office in the Administrative Annex.

As Travis walked down the hall from his office, Kent McPeters emerged. "What are you doing back here?"

"This is where I work, McPeters."

"Yeah, but you're supposed to be working that case in Idaho—"

"—speaking of which, *Kent*. I need to talk to you about that."

"About what?"

"We served search warrants for financial records of the Whitewater Casino. Your name popped up big time."

"My name?" McPeters' face turned ashen. "You checking on me?"

"You owe substantial gambling debts to the casino. I'm just wondering ... how do you intend to pay them back?"

McPeters' face flushed. "It's none of your business what I do privately."

"Actually—now that your name and gambling habits popped up in our investigation—it is my business. I won't be asking the questions next time. It'll be investigators from the Idaho County Sheriff's Office and the feds."

"I thought they're investigating those murders? What does my gambling have to do with that?"

"Your name is linked to a couple other guys in our case. John Ares, for example."

McPeters looked like he was going to be sick. "John Ares? Nah. What's Ares got to do with this case?"

"Can't answer that. But you'd better start working on your own story."

He left the man sputtering in the hall.

Travis found the temporary office Ares used the last time they met. Empty. Not even dust on the desktop. He turned to leave when he saw Ares emerge from another room down the hall. Ares waved. "Sorry about that. Had to take care of some business." He strode down the hallway. "We'll be pulling out of here tomorrow."

"Back to Seattle?"

"On to the next job. Wherever that is." He pointed to a chair near another empty desk. "Take a load off. Looks like you've been losing sleep."

Travis sat, stretching his legs out in front. "We're busy." He waited until Ares settled in. "I need to ask you a few questions, John. About the Whitewater Casino."

"Yeah? Nice place. Been there once or twice for pleasure."

"Pleasure?" Travis said. "The files we recovered show the casino paid your company $120,000 over the last eight months for threat assessments and executive security."

Ares squinted. "Sounds about right. What's your point?"

"That's a lot of assessments and security for such a small enterprise."

Wrinkles creased Ares' face as he grimaced. "So we did business with Whitewater. I don't see what that's got to do with your investigation? We didn't *kill* anyone. We protected them."

"Ever heard of Three Rivers Development?"

Ares shook his head. "Doesn't mean anything to me."

"Two of the names in that development have been murdered. And they're tied to Steve Robinette, the man who cut checks to your company for services rendered."

"So?" He looked at Travis warily. "I don't see the dots connected here, pal." His voice sounded cool, rigid.

"What services, exactly, did you provide? If they hired you to keep Robinette's friends alive and kicking, I'd say you failed miserably."

Ares' chair creaked as he slowly leaned forward. "Listen. You'd better not start throwing around false accusations." The man jabbed a finger in Travis' face. "I've got a reputation to uphold, and I won't tolerate any false charges leveled at my company."

"I'm not accusing anyone, Ares. Just trying to get to the bottom of this mess before anyone else winds up dead."

"Watch your back, Travis. You make accusations like that and you never know what might happen."

"Sounds like a threat, John."

Ares leaned back and smiled. "Not a threat, Travis. Just a concern for your safety. Now, if you're finished, I've got a lot of matters to close up before we pull the plug here. I trust you know the way out."

Travis reached his office just as his desk phone rang. Frank was on the line with a message from Beck Malloy. "He wants you to call him like right now."

Travis disconnected and called the FBI agent. Malloy answered. "Where are you?"

"In my office at the university."

"You talked to Ares?"

"Just left his office. Why?"

Malloy breathed in deeply. "John Ares is not his real name."

"Who is he?"

"I'm still checking. But up to five years ago, Ares never existed. His name, his social security number, his driver's license, taken from a guy who's been dead for thirty years. The guy used a forged birth certificate to set up this identity."

"You think he's Phillip Scarsbourgh?"

"You are reading my mind, Travis. Can't prove it yet. But I just e-mailed you a photo of Michelle's brother from evidence seized at her house. You've seen Ares. Take a look at the photo and you tell me."

Travis booted up his computer and waited until the system was up and running. He heard Malloy breathing heavy on the line. A moment later, he clicked on the icon to reach his messages. He saw one from Malloy.

He clicked on the message, hit the attachment and a photo slowly crystallized on his screen.

A match for John Ares taken many years earlier.

"John Ares is Phillip Scarsbourgh."

He heard Malloy let loose with an expletive. "I'll call the locals. They and the campus police can be at your office in a few minutes. Let them take this guy into custody, Travis. He's dangerous."

"I think I screwed up, Malloy. He and I exchanged words. He basically threatened me about making false accusations about his company."

"Well, I don't think you have to worry about him filing a lawsuit against you." His voice lowered. "One more thing, Travis. When I pulled Scarsbourgh's military records, I ran into a brick wall. No photos, no listing of assignments. Nothing."

"What do you make of it?"

"I think he was picked up by another agency. It looks like there's been an effort to erase his existence after the Marine Corps and make it look like he was still with them, or they were his last employer. I don't have a good feeling about this guy. He might be a lot more dangerous than I thought. Be careful when you approach."

"He may suspect we're already onto him."

"Just stay there until the cops get there."

"You know we don't have any criminal charges on him right now. Except *maybe* creating a false identity."

Malloy grunted. "Don't worry. I'll roll that into some kind of federal offense if I have too. At least long enough for us to put a case against him. I think he's good for killing Lafata." He heard a click on the line, and Malloy asked him to hold. A few moments later, Travis heard another click and Malloy came back on the line.

"I've got two agents on their way from Lewiston, but it's going to take them awhile to get to you. Work with the locals. If you get your hooks into him, hold him at the local police station until my agents get there."

"I'll let you know what happens." Travis hung up.

It seemed like the cops might never arrive. Finally, two young officers burst into his office like this was their first arrest. That made him nervous. "Pullman PD's on their way to back us up," the youngest officer said. "They'll be here in a few minutes."

"You have radio contact with them?" Travis asked.

They nodded.

"Tell them to meet us at the Administrative Annex on Library Road. We're on the way." He listened as the officer conveyed his message. They hustled after him.

If Ares was still in his office—on the north end of the building—he would not see them approach. It took almost fifteen minutes before a couple of Pullman officers arrived. Travis and the others entered the building and took an elevator to the suspect's office.

As the elevator door rolled open, officers edged down the hallway with guns drawn. Travis hung back, watching. He saw Ares' door, where they'd met earlier. The door was open. Light spilled from inside the office. The first officer crept to the doorway, aiming over his gun barrel as he quickly scanned the room. He saw the officer's shoulders relax as the man lowered his weapon. "Clear. Office empty."

They fanned out, checking restrooms, stairwells, and adjacent offices. Ares had vanished.

Travis entered the office and leaned on the empty desk.

The suspect had just been sitting in that chair a short time ago.

He asked one of the officers for a cell phone. He dialed Ares' number and waited. A moment later he heard an answering ring. It came from the desk. Travis circled the room and pulled out the upper drawer of the desk. There sat Ares' phone, ringing.

Travis hung up, redialed, and heard Malloy's voice. "Get your hooks on him?

"He's gone. The killer's on the loose."

 **Chapter 52**

Clearwater River, Idaho

Phillip Scarsbourgh wheeled the van onto a dirt road, a serpentine artery to the upper ridges of the mountain from the highway below. He turned the engine off and stepped outside. He walked down to the highway, watching and listening.

Nothing. Only blackness tempered by faint light from a quarter moon.

He strung a chain across the roadway and fastened it to a post. From the highway, it looked like a private drive. He got back in the van and continued up the mountainside to a cabin nestled in the crook of a small ravine. Beyond the cabin was a stable. Several horses could be seen in a large corral next to the stables.

Towering groves of fir trees hid the cabin from aircraft. He'd bought this property under another name several years ago. One of several safe houses he'd set up just in case.

They'll all be coming this time. FBI, locals, Indians. So be it.

He'd lived behind enemy lines for so long it almost felt comfortable. He knew how to exist as a human chameleon, blending into the colors and surroundings of the world around him. It was time to fade into that background once more until he was ready to strike.

Laughing, he thought how close he was to his target. The river below, on the other side of the highway, ran right past Travis' cabin. A mortar round could almost be launched here and land on Travis' front porch.

Phillip knew just how to draw the man back to Travis' cabin like a spider luring his prey to an untimely death.

He knew the right bait.

Scarsbourgh packed two saddle bags with supplies. He must move to higher ground until ready to strike. They could search all they wanted, but they'd never find him.

Unless he wanted to be found.

The government taught him how to hide. And now, that same government would be hunting him.

He opened a drawer in the nightstand next to the bed. A photo of a woman lay inside. He picked it up, rubbing a finger gently over the face, the photo taken just before his first deployment to Iraq. The day Michelle earned her CPA license after graduating from Stanford's business school.

He'd been so proud of her.

They'd celebrated at Tadish's in San Francisco. Not that formal, but she loved the seafood and atmosphere of one of the city's first restaurants. She sashayed up to the bar like one of the regulars, drinking a martini straight up. He remembered how flushed her cheeks were from the drink, from the excitement of her venture into the business world. Already she'd been courted by several large companies, a bevy of choice jobs. "I'm going with a small business up in Sonoma County— Santa Rosa," she proudly announced. "Great opportunity. Great benefits." They toasted her success and his survival.

Later, after several combat tours overseas, another government agency came shopping for his special talents. He remained with the cover of a Marine on duty, but he hadn't worn the uniform in years. He worked way beyond what they called Black Ops. He'd been taught how to slip in and out of countries, to operate in the gray, never-neverland of covert operations. He'd been recruited by spies to become a spy. A spy whose specialty was killing. If the Marine Corps ever knew what he'd become, they'd have disowned him. It had all began for God and country. At least that was what he kept telling himself.

Years passed, operations completed. Then word came of her death. He was so far undercover he never made it back to the funeral in time.

After Michelle's death, his world turned blacker. She'd been his beacon of hope, his one glimpse of what life was supposed to be. She was his joy, his love. The only person that made him feel connected. Her death left a void for years until he finally met someone who offered him that connection again. Call it love or whatever. By this time, though, he was driven to rectify the wrong to his family. Until he'd avenged her death, he could not move on. They snatched Michelle away from him. Greed and ambition sought by Kirkpatrick, Heard, Lafata and Travis robbed him of seeing her. All over a lousy investigation.

He pulled a rifle from under the bed. He was going to rain down terror on the last remaining target. The man responsible for leading Michelle to her death.

Travis Mays.

Scarsbourgh picked up the photo again, and saw an envelope lying underneath. The last letter she'd mailed before her death. He had memorized that letter, word for word. Michelle wrote she'd found her true love, a man she trusted. The letter seemed to have been written by a schoolgirl, so excited, so in love ... so naïve.

In love with the man who ultimately betrayed her. Travis must now pay the price.

Scarsbourgh clenched his fist and drove it into the wall. The blow caused his knuckles to bleed. He relaxed his hand and watched the blood drip between his fingers. He might never learn who actually pulled the trigger. Which person actually ended her life. The guy who ordered her death—Chuck Colville—was already locked away in prison doing life. Money had been paid. The man would not be a burden to the state for much longer.

Phillip put the letter and photo back into the drawer and slowly closed it. He had one more job, one more operation to complete. Then he could put it behind him.

Forever.

 **Chapter 53**

Kooskia, Idaho

Frank knocked on the door. Pamela Redfeather's car sat parked in front of the duplex when he and Travis drove up. Chances were good she'd be home.

No one answered.

Travis left the porch and circled around back. A sliding glass door stood open a crack, the edge of a brown-stained curtain wedged between the glass door and the metal frame. He slowly and quietly rolled the door open.

Pushing the curtain aside, he saw Pamela perched on the edge of a chair near the kitchen table as if she was about to sprout wings and fly. She was still facing the front door, immobile.

He took one step inside before she whirled around. "You can't come in here," she yelled, starting to rise. Travis heard Frank knocking on the front door once again. Pamela glanced at the front door, sank back down, glancing toward a closed bedroom door.

"We just need to talk to you for a few minutes."

She leaned over and lit another cigarette, fingers shaking.

He took that as unspoken acquiescence. "Frank, come on in. Door's open." The older man entered, quickly scanned the room, first spotting Travis still standing by the sliding-glass door and then Pamela glowering in the kitchen. He shut the door behind him.

Travis moved to one side so that he could keep an eye on the door leading to the bedroom.

Frank walked toward the table. "Things have changed since the last time we were here, Pamela."

She took a deep drag, glaring up at Travis before turning toward Frank.

"Travis and I traveled all the way to San Diego to talk to Pete. Know what we found when we got there?" Frank moved closer.

She shrugged, glancing away, reaching for another cigarette, not realizing the first one was only half smoked.

"We found the police sifting through his apartment. Someone torched the place and left a body behind with bullet holes. We thought the body might be Pete."

Pamela lit the cigarette without blinking, her face masking anything she may have felt inside. He saw a slight tremor in her hands. She looked at Frank. "And what's that got to do with me?"

Frank continued. "We assumed that the killer got to Pete. Killed him and torched the apartment to hide any evidence. Sounds reasonable, right?"

A wisp of smoked sneaked from her nostrils and floated upwards, creating a hazy halo above her head. Travis wondered how she did that.

The police chief pressed on. "You can imagine how surprised we were when San Diego called and said the dead body was Pete's cousin. That Pete was still alive."

For just an instant her eyes glanced toward the bedroom door again.

Travis faced the door. "Pete. You wanna come out here or do we have to go there and pull you out?"

Pamela shot to her feet. "Hey, you can't come in here and start searching my place. You got no right—"

"—Lighten up, babe. They already know." Pete Axtell stood in the doorway, hair tousled like he'd just climbed out of bed.

"Speaking of the dead," Frank said, shaking his head.

The younger man winced. "Came close to it, Chief. Out looking for work when it happened. Came back to see all the cops and fire trucks. I just started running."

"Pete, it's time you stopped running and tell us everything," Frank said.

"Maybe. I've got nowhere to run." He turned to Pamela. "Mind going to the store for some beer? I'm going to need a few brews before we're through here. And I'd rather you didn't hear all this. I don't want you involved."

She picked up her purse and grabbed a set of keys on the table. "See you in a few, sweetie." She gave him a peck on the cheek and left.

Pete sat and placed his hands, palm down, on the kitchen table. "First, Frank, I wanna tell you how sorry I am about Tommy. I should never have got him in this mess."

Frank sat next to him. "You think this is why Tommy is dead?"

Travis sat down across from them. He'd let Frank take the lead on this.

Pete shook his head. "I didn't know at first. But after what happened in San Diego, I realized they're killers."

"How did you get mixed up in all this?"

Pete studied his hands, slowly clenching each hand into a tight fist. "Because I'm stupid and greedy. Saw a chance to make a lot of money and went for it."

"Who approached you?"

"A guy by the name of Shane Foster. Steve Robinette introduced him as a friend, a friend with a business proposition. He left us at a restaurant to talk alone."

"So Robinette knew you two worked together."

"Oh, yeah. He got a cut through Foster while I took all the chances."

"What did they have you do?"

"Pick out casino customers that might make potential targets. Those carrying a lot of credit potential. Tried to pick people traveling through. You know, out of state suckers stopping in for a little fun."

"What did you do with this information?"

Pete took a deep breath. "I'd compile a database of names with all their personal information—date of birth, social security numbers, credit cards—gleaned through various financial data bases. Once all this information was collected, I'd hand it over to Foster."

"And what did he do?"

Pete scratched his belly. "He'd milk them for everything they owned."

"You mean, credit card scams, that sort of thing?"

"I mean everything. First, they'd run up their credit charges on big-ticket items that could be easily moved on the black market. Then they'd use what was left of the credit to open up other credit accounts, maxing out those accounts. They used the customer's personal information to create fake identifications. Once they were through with a customer, that person's credit history became toast."

"And what did you get out of this?"

"I got a one-time payment of fifteen thousand. Supposed to be the end of it." Pete laughed bitterly. Sweat beaded on his brow and oozed a ring of darkness along the neckline of his stained T-shirt.

"What happened?"

Pete looked over at Travis, then back at Frank. "They wanted more. I knew it was only a matter of time before the cops put these victims' names together and traced them back to the casino—and to me."

"What did Robinette get out of this?"

"I believe he and Foster split everything fifty-fifty. I took all the risks and those two guys were making six-digit scores." He shook his head. "I got chump change, and they wanted me to keep tapping the till. I tried to pull out."

Frank leaned forward. "Pete, we found the thumb drive you hid in the trailer, and we saw the video of you and Foster talking."

Pete nodded. "My life insurance. The customer list and the tape of Foster threatening me. I told Foster I wanted out and if he came after me—well, I told him the cops would learn about everything."

"How come you didn't take the thumb drive with you?"

"I wanted to, but then that other guy showed up. I was walking along the river, trying to clear my head, when I saw him drive up to the trailer. I hid in the trees to watch. That sucker didn't knock or anything. He must have been in there for an hour. Finally, he came out and looked around. I waited until he drove away and then started running. Didn't think it would be safe to go back to the trailer."

Frank reached into his pocket and withdrew a folded paper. "You think you'd recognize this guy?"

"Probably. He was a distance away, but ... yeah, I think I could."

Slowly, Frank opened the paper and pushed it toward Pete. "This the guy?"

Pete leaned over and peered at the photo. "Yep, that's him. Who is it?"

Frank glanced toward Travis. "Phillip Scarsbourgh."

 **Chapter 54**

Pete stood and paced. "So how'd you find this guy?" he asked, pointing to Scarsbourgh's photo. "Is he the one who killed my cousin?"

"We think so," Frank said. "And he killed others."

"Tommy?"

Frank shrugged.

Travis gestured toward Pete. "Mind if I ask a few questions, Frank?" The older man shrugged. Travis looked at Pete. "Hey, you make me nervous walking around like that. Mind sitting down?"

"Sure, man," he said, plopping down in a chair across the table from Travis. "This whole thing's got me wired."

Travis nodded, folding his hands. "How was Tommy involved?"

"Man, I feel rotten about that. I knew he and Robinette were tight. I mean, that's how I got the gig at the casino. Tommy put in a good word for me."

"You told him what was going on with Foster and Robinette?"

"Later, when I thought things were going south. He told me I should report it to the authorities. Turn myself in."

"I take it you didn't like that suggestion?" Travis watched as Pete shifted and scratched his forehead.

"No, man. Now, I wish I'd done what he said. Maybe Tommy and my cousin would still be breathing," he said, rubbing his jaw. "I told Tommy 'no way.' I wanted him to *negotiate* with Robinette and get me out from under them. Get 'em to back off."

"And?" Frank said, eyes narrowing.

Pete glanced at the police chief, then dropped his gaze. "He took a dollar from me. I think he wanted the money to show he represented me in case things got messy later."

Frank continued the questioning. "So what did he do?"

"He arranged to meet Robinette at his office. I waited in the back of Tommy's office behind a closed door. I heard Robinette come in and Tommy called him by name."

"What happened?"

Pete's eyes twitched as he rubbed a finger over his lips. "Heard a lot of yelling. Finally, Robinette just up and jammed, screaming over his shoulder and cussing a blue streak. Tommy never raised his voice. I high-tailed it through a back door and made it to the casino. Thought I could beat Robinette back to Whitewater and grab a few things before I took off. Planned to lay low for a few days and see what happened."

"He see you?"

"Almost. He came barreling into finance. Everyone had left for the day, and I was crouching in my cubicle trying to stay out of sight when he and Foster came in."

"He met with Foster after the blowout with Tommy?"

"Yeah. They talked low, but I could hear everything they said. Robinette told him Tommy knew everything and warned them to stop. Foster got upset and the two of them started jabbering about what they ought to do."

"What did they decide?"

Pete stood up and started pacing again. "Foster talked about a guy they both knew who took care of problems like this. Someone who could force Tommy and me to keep our mouths shut."

"You mean kill you?"

"No, I think it was more like putting pressure on us."

"And when did this all take place?"

"The day before Tommy disappeared. I stayed at Pamela's for a few days trying to decide what my options might be. Then, when I didn't hear anything from Tommy, I started getting worried. My girlfriend went to the market and heard Tommy was reported missing. I really freaked. I took a walk near my trailer, trying to figure out things. Finally decided to go get the thumb drive and some clothes and take off. That's when I saw that guy, Scarsbourgh, breaking into my place. I freaked and took off for San Diego."

Travis leaned back and glanced at Frank. He saw sadness in the older man's eyes as the pieces started to fit. They'd sent Phillip Scarsbourgh to make sure Tommy kept quiet.

And the killer silenced Tommy forever.

 **Chapter 55**

Grangeville, Idaho

A two-way mirror hid Travis' face as he watched Steve Robinette squirming in his seat. John Steele and another detective arrested Robinette at the casino and drove him back to their office for interrogation.

Frank and Travis watched the interview.

Travis hoped he'd get a shot at questioning Robinette. Steele picked away at the casino manager's story after Robinette—in his arrogance—waived his rights. Robinette's confidence seemed to soar once they released his handcuffs.

"Mr. Robinette, this is an investigation into the murder of Tommy White Eagle, Shane Foster, Brian Wyatt, plus the killing of agent Clay Lafata and a man in San Diego."

"You're crazy to think I had anything to do with all those deaths." Robinette's smugness angered Travis. He wondered what Frank must be thinking.

"We have evidence you and Shane Foster were involved in a criminal conspiracy in which you financially benefited. That activity led to the deaths of one or more of those victims I mentioned. That means you're culpable for the murders. We're talking death penalty or life without the possibility of parole."

He saw Robinette flinch. "I had nothing to do with that."

Steele wrote something on a pad, pulled a file from a briefcase and opened it slowly. "I have here the sworn statement of Pete Axtell in which he confesses to a criminal enterprise involving you and Foster."

Robinette's face reddened. "He is a liar and a thief." The man's hoarseness made Travis smile grimly to himself.

John, pull that rope of facts so tight Robinette chokes on it.

Another file emerged from Steele's briefcase. "And we've got evidence seized from your accounts and the casino that not only supports Mr. Axtell's statement, but shows you transferred unaccounted funds to invest in the Three Rivers Development. Two men—Shane Foster and Brian Wyatt—were your partners in that development. They're both dead. And the project's threatened by legal action filed by Tommy White Eagle."

Robinette scratched his nose. Travis saw sweat emerge on the man's forehead. "Shane's dead?" Fear crept into the man's voice, his cockiness gone.

Steele slid a photograph across the table. "And we can prove you and Foster sent this man to take care of Tommy White Eagle. To shut him up."

Robinette's eyes widened in recognition. Phillip Scarsbourgh's photo on the desk was visible through the two-way glass. "You can't prove this."

Steele leaned across the table. "Want to bet your life on it?"

Travis turned from the window. "So Robinette knew Phillip Scarsbourgh and hired him—under the name of John Ares—allegedly for executive protection work."

Frank nodded. "And he and Foster must have had Scarsbourgh kill Tommy."

Leaning on the window, Travis looked at Frank. "I'm not sure, Frank. I mean, no question they sent this wacko to pressure Tommy. But I'm not sure they knew he'd kill Tommy and the others. He may have gone further than they wanted. You heard what Axtell said."

"It seems pretty obvious to me they wanted Tommy dead. Even if they didn't, their actions led to Tommy's death."

"Silenced, maybe. But dead? Look how Scarsbourgh left the bodies. All of them—Tommy, Wyatt, Foster—all arranged the same way. As if he was sending a message."

"A message?"

"Yeah. Look at how he placed them. Arms spread, palms out, legs together. What does that remind you of?"

Frank rubbed his forehead, still watching Robinette in the other room. "Like they'd been crucified?"

"Exactly. And who does that bring to mind?"

"Christ. On the cross."

He saw Frank struggling to understand. "What are you getting at, Travis? Tommy and the others died for someone else's sins?"

Travis held his breath. He wanted Frank to grasp—on his own—what'd been nagging Travis for some time.

"Whose sin?" Frank asked. The older man seemed to be struggling to understand. And then he saw Frank's eye widen as the truth finally came home.

Travis turned away, looking through the one-way window as Steele continued to hammer on Robinette. He couldn't bring himself to look into Frank's eyes. He put his head against the cold glass and closed his eyes. "Yeah, Frank," he said, gritting his teeth. "They died for my sins."

Chapter 56

Lolo Trail, Idaho

Phillip Scarsbourgh loved the irony. He was horseback riding on the historical Lolo Trail, used for hundreds of years by the Nez Perce people as they traversed the mountains between Montana and Idaho. A mountainous highway used by Lewis and Clark, compliments of Indian guides, as they surveyed their way to the Columbia River and the Pacific Northwest.

And now he used this same trail to elude capture from mostly white men.

Moonlight showered the ancient trail with silver flecks. He planned on using a night-vision scope, tucked away in one of the saddle bags, when he neared the target. But for now, splashes of cold light made the trail gleam with white clarity.

Scarsbourgh could track his prey with help from modern technology even at night. Electronic markers, planted along the trail weeks ago, guided him within inches of the target.

He could almost do this blindfolded.

A pack horse—plodding behind him—gave a deep, rumbling sneeze. Horses never traveled quietly. He'd chosen nighttime to traverse this famous trail to avoid backpackers, hikers and other travelers, those forced to move around by the light of day.

The last twenty-four hours whirled by in its own little hurricane. Travis almost caught him yesterday at the university. An electronic bug placed on Travis' phone alerted Scarsbourgh to slip into obscurity and elude capture. The cops finally figured out his identity. He smiled as he imagined Travis traipsing into his empty office. Leaving his cell phone behind was a nice touch, a psychological slap in the face.

Before he pulled his surveillance crew, he'd learned the FBI had discovered his identity. Only a matter of time. He'd already planned several other aliases for the future and stashed them in a safe place until needed.

He pulled out his GPS tracker, scanning the screen. Several more miles before he swooped down for a surprise visit.

Stealth became a matter of survival. He knew they'd already posted an arrest warrant in the system with his name on it. He'd checked just before leaving civilization. Time seemed to spin backwards up here in the mountains, back to a time before all the complexities of modern conveniences made this world so complicated and impersonal. He rather enjoyed this simple life. Well, almost simple. He stashed the electronic monitor in a pocket.

He quickly covered ground. The first marker beeped to audibly remind him to turn off the trail and begin his descent. From now on, he must approach on foot. He slipped from the saddle and led the horses deeper into the forest, off the main trail. He tied them to a tree, tugging the lines to make sure they were tight. The last thing he needed was for his four-footed friends to get spooked and run off. It would be a long arduous hike back to his place without them.

Scarsbourgh slung the rifle over his shoulder, and adjusted his backpack. He felt balanced with a holstered sidearm on his right hip, and a Taser on his left. The moonlight surrendered to shadows as he melted into a denser part of the forest. He slid his night vision goggles on and watched as the night—illuminated by minuscule dots of starlight and faint traces of moonbeams through the tree boughs overhead—became almost like day illuminated by alien-green light.

Slowly he worked his way down a game trail, carefully choosing each step.

Silently.

Quietly.

As he neared his destination, Scarsbourgh slipped off the goggles, allowing his eyes to regain night vision, before pulling a thermal infrared imagery camera from the pack. He flicked it on and scanned the trail ahead.

Two heat sources flared up about three hundred feet away. One figure, a woman, appeared to be moving inside the cabin. The other, a man armed with a shotgun and handgun, stood outside, maybe on the front porch of the shack. The fool probably thought his enemy stupid enough to just drive up and present a target for him to shoot.

Satisfied that he saw all the warm bodies ahead, he slid the camera back into his pack and activated his night vision scope again. Quietly removing his sidearm from the holster, he edged forward while bringing the weapon to eye level, a round, already chambered.

Locked and loaded. No one saw him coming.

Frustration drove Jessie to pace across the rough, wooden floor. Travis and her father should have been here several hours ago with news on the case. Steele and the others scooped Robinette up and drove him to Grangeville for questioning. Travis mentioned he thought the casino manager might break and testify as to who murdered Tommy and the motivation behind the killings.

They all believed Scarsbourgh to be the shooter.

Jessie flinched every time she heard a strange noise. A twig snap here. A branch pop there. All the sounds of night one might normally sleep through.

The deputy stationed outside did little to ease her stress. She knew this killer used shadows to approach his victims like a cougar stalking its prey. She knew he was good at killing. She heard the deputy—his name tag showed Paul Clemmons—stir on the front porch. His boots thudded on wooden timbers as he marched back and forth, pausing to frequently listen. He rarely sat down and seemed as nervous as she felt.

Glancing around the cabin, she wished she'd brought her own weapon. Guns had always been in their family. She became a better shot than Tommy, a fact that made for sibling rivalry—good natured, but still there. Her father taught the children marksmanship early in their lives. They used to hunt together as a family before everyone became caught up in their own separate worlds.

Grasping another log, she carried it to the fireplace. She heard a pop just as she threw the log on the burning embers.

"Paul," she yelled. No one responded. "Deputy Clemmons?"

She crept toward the door and peered out. The deputy was gone.

Jessie opened the door wider and stepped out onto the front porch. She reached behind her and felt the rough-hewed logs of the cabin wall as she slowly edged to the right. Moonlight gave her some visibility, although just leaving the lighted cabin made her momentarily blind.

It took a few moments to adjust.

Slowly, she was able to make out images in the darkness. Jessie crept to the edge of porch. Nothing. The deputy simply vanished. She started to turn until something made her glanced down. She gasped. Deputy Clemmons lay sprawled on the ground face up just beyond the porch.

Motionless.

She leaped down and crouched next to him. "Paul?" She reached out to touch him. No response. She cradled his head in her hands and felt something warm run between her fingers. Light from the open cabin door cast a weak beam across the deputy's face. His eyes stared back, sightless. One bullet hole visible in his right temple.

A twig snapped. She whirled.

A man in dark clothing sprang from the shadows. Something hit her in the chest and she felt a jolt of electricity. Muscles convulsed. She seemed frozen in place. Helpless, she dropped to the ground and jerked convulsively.

The man leaned over and grabbed her arm. Jessie felt a sharp prick.

A moment later, woozy darkness swept her into another world. Like traveling down an unseen water slide into uneasy twilight. She felt numbness before unconsciousness engulfed her.

 **Chapter 57**

Grangeville, Idaho

A deputy rushed past Travis and banged on the interview room door. John Steele turned with an annoyed look. The deputy pushed the door open. "John, you need to come out here. Something's happened."

Travis felt his chest tighten. His first thought—Jessie.

Frank walked toward the door. Travis followed. Steele stepped outside and closed the door behind him. "This better be good, Steve. I'm right in the middle—"

"—dispatch can't raise Clemmons on his radio. Units are responding Code-Three, but it'll be a while until the first one gets to the scene."

Steele glanced at Frank. "That's the deputy I left with Jessie." He grabbed the deputy's arm. "Look, put this guy in lock-up. Tell dispatch I'll be responding."

Frank started toward the exit. "We'll follow you, John." They rushed from the building and climbed into Frank's unmarked. Emergency lights flashed in the darkness as sirens wailed with a sound that made Travis's breath quicken. The sound always signaled disaster, trouble, someone in need. He'd never gotten used to it.

They saw Steele's car shoot out from the parking lot. Frank pulled behind him and began to follow, a silent emergency run with flashing lights only. Steele paved the way through the night. At normal driving speeds, Travis knew the distance took over an hour to get to Jessie's cabin. He glanced at the speedometer. At these speeds they'd be there in half the time.

If they survived.

He tightened his seatbelt and braced against the door. Frank drove with one hand, flicking over to the Idaho SO band with the other. They listened to radio traffic squelching over the car speakers. Deputies responded from all over, their sirens wailing in the background as they answered up over the air. Most were smart enough to kill their lights and siren before getting too close. Approach quietly until they knew what dangers lie ahead.

So far no one was on scene.

Twenty minutes into the drive, Travis heard the first unit go 10-97. Everything shut down over the airways. Everyone listened for an update.

A few minutes later the deputy came over the air. "Dispatch, officer down. No one else on scene. Suspect GOA." The deputy broke the transmission. A moment later, the deputy came back on the air, his voice shaken. "Dispatch. Be advised. 10-55."

Frank hit the dashboard with his fist and increased his speed, keeping pace with Steele. They both knew what the codes meant—a deputy had been killed. "Oh God, no."

Travis glanced at Frank, not sure if those words were a prayer or a curse.

Frank glanced his way. "You know what that means?"

Travis nodded. "Scarsbourgh has Jessie."

"You think he'll ..."

"No, I don't, Frank. He snatched Jessie because she means something to me. He wants me—not her."

"How do you think he'll communicate?"

Travis leaned back in the seat. "Dunno. But you can bet he has a plan."

He saw Steele's emergency lights far ahead in the night. The lights shone for a minute and then disappeared. A second later, he saw the lights flashing through the trees as the vehicle climbed the hill toward Jessie's cabin.

 **Chapter 58**

Lochsa River, Idaho

Emergency lights from a train of police cars lighted the dirt road leading to the cabin. Frank pulled off the rutted road into a patch of ferns and grass. The two men rolled out of the car and scrambled toward a small army of deputies. As they drew close, Travis saw Steele emerge from the cabin. He knew by the detective's expression things were bad.

"Frank, Travis, hold up." Steele stepped down off the porch, making a wide berth where the slain deputy lay. In his gloved right hand, Steele held a torn piece of paper. "This was tacked to the wall. It's to you, Travis."

Travis caught Frank's look. Steele handed him a pair of gloves. "Put these on before you read it."

He nodded, slipping on the gloves before taking the note. Steele pulled out a flashlight, flicking it on for Travis.

Travis,

Go to you cabin and stay until you hear further. Jessie's life depends on you following orders.

Time to pay for your sins.

God's avenging angel,

Creasy

"Creasy? Mean anything to anybody?" he asked, looking at the other two men. Steele shook his head. Frank didn't respond at first. "Creasy? Sounds familiar. I just can't seem to—"

"I'll have dispatch run it through the computer," Steele said, pulling out his portable radio. He passed it on and lowered the radio. "Why don't you guys head back to Travis' cabin, and I'll let you know if anything turns up."

They nodded and started to head down the mountain.

"Travis," Steele said. "As soon as this nut job contacts you, let us know immediately. I'll be by your place as soon as I coordinate things here."

Travis nodded and followed Frank down the road. They'd just reached the car when someone came running up behind them. Steele again.

"Hey, dispatch just called. They Googled 'Creasy.' Guess what they found? Remember that movie *Man on Fire* with Denzel Washington? In the flick, his character's name is John Creasy. Not sure what Scarsbourgh is trying to tell us, but I wanted you to know. Maybe it'll help figure out what this whack job is thinking."

Travis nodded and climbed in the car. Frank fired up the engine and drove out onto Highway 12, heading west. They did not speak.

He knew what was on both their minds. Somewhere out there in the darkness a killer held Jessie hostage. Would he kill her before she could be saved?

Travis felt the coldness of night seep into his soul. The moon no longer offered up its light, hidden behind dark clouds rolling up the valley. A nauseating chill shook him. All this—Tommy, Lafata, Wyatt, and the others—dead because he'd failed to do the right thing years ago. He should have told them to take a flying leap back then. Back when he had an opportunity to do the right thing.

Guilt paralyzed him. He'd lost the woman he loved because he'd been a coward, because deep down he wanted the case to happen. He wanted to make things work out the way he wanted. Ego and pressure clouded his judgment, stood in the way of what he knew was right.

Now this killer held Jessie and expected him ... to what? Admit his guilt? Cut his wrists in remorse? He wanted to pay the price if it meant Jessie might go free. What was the price? A life for a life?

Bringing Jessie back safely might save whatever he had left inside. He'd do the right thing this time even if it cost everything.

"Don't beat up on yourself, Travis." Frank glanced over for a moment before turning his attention to the road. "I know what you're thinking."

"You can't know, Frank. You're not the person who could have stopped all this."

"We all make mistakes. Some carry more consequences than others."

"If anything happens to Jessie—"

"—stop that kind of thinking. It won't do Jessie any good." Frank sternly looked his way. "Guilt and anger has a way of eating away at your soul. You need to let it go, Travis. Trust me, I know."

Travis looked at Frank, wondering what kind of guilt Jessie's father hid behind that stern look.

Frank continued. "It took me years to understand that evil and bad things happened. You have to have a belief in something more than yourself. That God has a plan in all this. All I can do is trust in Him ... whatever happens."

Travis looked away. "With all due respect, Frank. God has nothing to do with any of this. A man has to make his own way in the world. I learned that early. We pay for our own sins—one way or the other. There is no forgiveness."

"I'm sorry you feel that way."

Travis looked back. "That's just the way life is, Frank. Nothing more. Nothing less."

Travis looked way. Forgiveness is not something he really understood. One cannot undo what has already been done. There are always consequences. And now, Jessie and Frank are suffering the consequences of his sins. How fair and just is that?

Frank reached the pull-off near Travis' cabin. As Frank locked the car, Travis listened to Sam barking across the river. The dog must have heard them drive up. He knew Sam would be waiting at the edge of the river, impatiently waiting for his master's return. A dog's love seemed unconditional. Simple. If only life could be lived that way.

Travis crossed first, sending the chair back to Frank. He felt Sam's tail slapping his leg as they waited. Frank finally crossed over and Travis led them up the hill.

Frank broke the silence. "I've got that movie, you know ... *Man On Fire*."

Travis glanced back. "Saw it once. Didn't think all that blood and gore would be your style."

"I liked the movie because of the main character, John Creasy. Remember he's an ex-CIA, ex-assassin, who hit bottom."

"You mean he lost his way in life?" Travis said, hearing the soothing ripple of water down the Clearwater as they neared the cabin. "Yeah, I remember."

"Good way to put it. Lost his way."

"So you're saying that's Scarsbourgh?" He glanced at Frank.

"Yeah. In some twisted ways, he's looking for redemption like the rest of us. He talks about your sins, Travis, but in the movie Creasy struggles with his own. His own evil. By saving that little girl Creasy tries to atone for past sins by saving this innocent one."

"That doesn't quite add up here, does it? I mean, his sister's dead. No salvation there. He can't save her by killing me and the others. So what's he after?"

"Maybe to rid himself of guilt. Sort of like you, Travis. He wasn't able to protect Michelle. And whatever he did for the government, whatever evil they forced him to commit, he feels by exacting justice for his sister he is able make amends for his own sins."

"Sound like psycho-babble to me, Frank. This guy's a nut job and he likes to kill. And he wants to kill me."

"Bear with me for a moment. In one part of the movie, Creasy delivers the child to a private Catholic school where he meets a nun. She asks Creasy if he sees the hand of God in what he does."

"So Scarsbourgh thinks God wants him to kill?"

"No. Listen. The sister starts to quote a part of Romans ... *Do not be overcome by evil, but overcome evil with good.*"

Travis straightened. "That doesn't make sense."

"Creasy interrupts the nun and finishes quoting the verse, quoting her verse and chapter. And then he tells her, 'I'm the sheep that got lost.' You see? Scarsbourgh might be trying to find his way back by earning his redemption, by killing those who do evil."

"Hey, I'm not a religious guy, Frank, but even I know Christ didn't teach killing was a good thing. Or did I miss that Sunday school lesson?"

Frank shook his head. "No, Christ taught the only way to salvation, to redemption, is to recognize we can't redeem ourselves of the evil inside us for the sins we've committed. That we must ask God's forgiveness."

"If that's true, Scarsbourgh missed the boat. He's trying to save his own soul. Earn his ticket to the Promised Land by sending everyone responsible to hell."

Frank started up the steps. "Yeah, a lot of people think that way." He glanced at Travis as he passed. "And then there are those living with their guilt and think there is no salvation."

Travis trailed behind. He knew Frank was talking about him. Frank was wrong. The only salvation he wanted right now was to get Jessie back safe and sound. He knew there was no salvation for people like him and Scarsbourgh. Only guilt and retribution. In a way, he and Scarsbourgh might be rowing the same boat. That thought made Travis squirm.

 **Chapter 59**

Clearwater River, Idaho

Travis saw a tape recorder on the table when he flicked on the cabin light. Next to it laid a map. "Frank. He's already been here."

He pressed the play button and heard Scarsbourgh's voice:

"Hello, professor. By now, you know I have Jessie. By the way, your side-kick there? Hi, Frank. Now, back to business. On the map I've made a notation. There is a mileage marker at that exact location I want you to be at tomorrow morning. Early. I've taken the liberty of noting the mileage printed on the marker so there's no confusions about where you need to be. As you see, the marker is along the Lochsa River upstream from Jessie's cabin. At first light, you're to go to that spot, then to the edge of the river below that marker. You will find I've left a few presents and instructions on the next leg of this journey. Do exactly as I tell you and Jessie just might stay alive. Failure to comply ... well, you know the rest."

It sounded like the message ended except for a low rasping noise on the tape. The killer's voice returned:

"Travis. I want you to say goodbye to Frank. Once you get to the marker, I expect you to be alone. Any sign of cops—helicopters, planes, unmarked cars, strangers in the area—and I'll end Jessie's life. Don't insult my intelligence by carrying a tracking device, a transmitter, or any of the surveillance goodies. Been there, done that. I'll know if you're clean. Ciao!"

The recording stopped.

Frank leaned on the table. "He'll be able to kill you at any time. We need to figure out a way to cover your back."

Travis laid the recorder on the table. "You know that will be impossible, Frank. He's an expert. Knows all the tricks. We can't take that risk."

"And I can't send you out to be slaughtered."

"You don't have to send me," he said, "It's my call."

Frank started for the door. "We've got to tell Steele—"

"Stop and think, Frank. You tell Steele, and he'll have to put people on this. He can't accept liability of sending me out unprotected. The county would be all over his butt if something happened."

Frank sank down in a chair. "I can't just sit here and watch you—"

"I have to do this alone. You have to let me do this ... for Jessie's sake." He glanced at his watch. "We've got almost five hours until daybreak. I'm going to try to get a little shut-eye. I suggest you do the same."

Frank looked incredulous. "You're going to sleep?"

He shrugged. "In combat, you eat when you can and sleep when you can. Because when the fighting starts, it goes until you or the other guys are dead. Besides, there's not much else we can do right now."

He grabbed a blanket, slipped out of his boots, and stretched out on the couch. He set the alarm on his watch and closed his eyes. Sam came over and rested his head on Sam's leg. Travis patted the dog. "How did he get in here, Sam? I thought you were guarding the place?" Sam gave him a look as if the dog was trying to understand. Travis rolled over and he heard Sam's nails clicking across the floor as the dog made his way outside. Tiredness struck him hard. Listening to the dog was the last thing Travis remembered.

An owl's hoot woke Travis from a shallow sleep. Darkness filled the cabin. He saw Frank's dark form stretched out on the bed. He switched off his wrist alarm so that it would not wake the other man. He rose quietly, grabbing his boots, tiptoeing to the door.

"Good luck." Frank raised his head from the bed.

"See you later," he said, slipping into his boots and grabbing his jacket, hanging on a peg near the door. "Take care of Sam."

Five minutes later, he piled into his truck and started his trek east-bound on Highway 12 as the first hint of dawn lightened the sky. He timed it about right. Dawn was in full bloom just as he reached the marker noted on Scarsbourgh's map. Steam mystically blanketed the river below while morning crept across the sky, adding some clarity to an otherwise confusing day. He could see for miles in this light.

So could the killer.

He climbed out of the truck, quickly scanning a full circle. A million places to hide if you knew how. He worked his way down the steep bank toward the river. A grove of birch and firs graced the riverbank near him.

As he drew closer to the river, he saw the dark-green bow of a kayak resting on the bank. Inside the craft, he saw another tape recorder and a bag of clothing. He picked up the recorder, pressing the play button.

"Good morning, Travis. I trust you're alone. Remember, you never know when I'll be watching. Take off everything you have on—including the watch—and toss it into the river. I want to see you with only what you came into this world with—skin. Turn 360 degrees and then put on the clothes I've provided. Once dressed ... Bon Voyage. If you've followed my instructions to the letter, at some point today—somewhere along the river—I'll appear and motion you over. Follow my orders and I might let Jessie live. Disobey and you both die." Abruptly, the tape ended.

Gritting his teeth, Travis slowly began to disrobe in the chilly morning air.

Chapter 60

Lochsa River, Idaho

Scarsbourgh must be watching. Travis tried to figure how the killer might be monitoring. Not a sign of civilization out here. Not even another fisherman or rafter. Only a few cars passed on Highway 12 since he shoved off into the river. Anyone spotting him in the kayak wouldn't think twice about his actions. Just another whitewater rafter heading downstream.

If Jessie wasn't sitting somewhere waiting to die, she'd get a good laugh right now watching him navigate this river. He'd already rolled once and gotten a good shock of cold water.

Several times he glanced at his wrist to check the time and realized his watch was at the bottom of the river. He kept scanning the banks hoping to see a glimpse of Scarsbourgh. He'd seen two fisherman. As he swept by them, they'd glanced his way. One guy waved. The other scowled.

He neared the Grim Reaper and hoped he'd stay afloat this time, Jessie's warnings still clear in his mind. Start to the right, move to the middle, then back to the right "unless you want to get slapped silly by that boulder on the left bank." He smiled as he recalled her laughter after they hit this part of the river. She seemed to know he'd capsize.

This time he'd make it through.

He picked up steam, slanting to the right and then shooting toward the middle, narrowly missing the boulder he struck last time. He lunged toward the middle and then paddled to the right once more, shooting past the last boulder before entering calmer water.

The rookie triumphed. As he paddled away from the rapids, he discovered his breathing was jagged and short. He realized he had been more tense than he thought. His triumph made him feel a little better. He might have enjoyed this little victory if Jessie's safety was not at stake. He kept paddling, never slowing down.

Further downstream, he recognized the bank where he and Jessie saw the dead elk. No more birds. The carcass probably picked clean by now. He glanced around him and realized that Tommy's body had been left almost directly to the south, on the mountain crest towering above him. What if he'd acquiesced that day? What if he'd agreed to search for Tommy instead of weeks later? Would that have changed the outcome? What if ... ?

He thrust the paddle into the water. He might never know for sure. He knew one thing—Scarsbourgh wanted him dead. At some point. After what? After he saw everyone he cared for destroyed?

The sun worked its way higher in the sky. He guessed it to be early afternoon, maybe later.

Where was this guy? He hoped Jessie was still breathing.

This operation cost Scarsbourgh some serious dinero. He flicked from one camera site to another. Mini-cams, each linked to a satellite-connected computer, had been strategically placed along the river. Each mini-cam and computer powered with enough battery life to last this operation. He'd watched Travis tossing his clothes and contents of his pockets into the river before climbing into the kayak.

Good boy.

He'd enjoyed watching Travis struggle on the river. Any discomfort suffered by this scumbag pleased Scarsbourgh. By nightfall, Travis would reach the point on the river where they'd meet face-to-face. Unless, of course, he failed to follow orders. If so, slight change of plans. Kill Jessie as retribution, and then take Travis out from a distance.

He wanted to watch Travis die up close. The first option allowed him to watch Travis suffer slowly, painfully. The alternative would end his life quickly. Mission accomplished either way.

Scarsbourgh preferred to take it slow. To savor every moment.

A scuffling sound caught his attention. He rose from the table, leaving the laptop open. He walked into the bedroom of the cabin. Jessie lay across the bed, handcuffed.

"How we doing this morning, Princess?" He beamed at her, enjoying the sight.

Jessie's eyes glinted with anger.

"Oh, the silent treatment." He laughed, walking towards her. "I've been watching your boyfriend trying to navigate the Lochsa. You're a pretty good teacher, Princess. Only rolled a couple times this morning. But the day isn't over yet."

He started toward the next room. "Relax. If everything goes well, you and he will be reunited by nightfall. You'll be able to tell him goodbye before he meets his untimely death. And if you're a really good girl, I'll let you watch."

He laughed at the fear in her eyes. "Get some rest. It's going to be a long day."

Steele tiredly walked toward his car. It'd taken all night to finish the crime scene at Jessie's cabin. Not that there was a lot of evidence to gather. One of his deputies, a guy who doubled as a tracker during hunting season, spotted boot prints approaching the cabin from higher up. The same boots lead away from the cabin, only more weight pressed down on the boots.

The killer must have carried Jessie on his shoulders.

The tracker ascended until he reached the Lolo Trail, where he saw evidence the killer had two horses tied up. After that, only the horses left a trail, working their way west. They'd brought dogs to track the scent, but Scarsbourgh must have sprinkled a chemical agent across his path. Whatever it was, one whiff and the dogs howled in pain. Search over. The horse tracks were soon lost in brush, stream beds, and forest.

He couldn't seem to get in touch with Frank White Eagle.

Tried the cell phone several times, but no one answered. He ordered deputies to spread out east and west on Highway 12 looking for any suspicious vehicles. One deputy traveling east called in a truck registered to Travis Mays.

Travis disappeared.

Frank disappeared.

Steele got on the phone. People were disappearing on him—Scars-bourgh, Jessie, Frank, and Travis—and he was getting tired of being the last to know anything. It was time he put some eyes and ears up in the sky.

Time for a full-court press.

Chapter 61

Lochsa River, Idaho

Travis winced as he heard the whoosh of helicopter rotors sweeping up a ravine. He furiously dug into the water with his paddle, rushing toward a grove of trees, branches hung over the river like a protective umbrella.

As soon as the bow hit the bank, Travis sprang out and dragged the kayak deeper into the tree line. Just as he pulled the craft out of sight, through the branches he saw the metallic bird working its way upriver. The aircraft zigzagged a path back and forth like a giant pendulum, swinging first to one side of the valley and then the other.

Travis tightened his jaw. If Scarsbourgh knew the chopper was here he'd end Jessie's life right now. Had Frank warned Steele?

Maybe Steele spotted his truck parked along the highway. If he'd talked to Frank at all, Steele might have guessed.

The detective knew Scarsbourgh was going to contact Travis based upon the note left behind in Jessie's cabin. Placement of Travis' vehicle upriver from his cabin gave Steele a grid to search. He grudgingly gave the detective credit; the lawman instinctively knew Scarsbourgh sent Travis upstream. If he'd been in Steele's position, an aerial search seemed a logical choice.

Travis just hoped it did not mean Jessie's death sentence.

He waited until the chopper moved further up the river. Once the aircraft was out of sight, Travis pushed the kayak back onto the river. He pushed off once more. From now on, he'd have to be on the alert if that chopper came back this way. If Scarsbourgh was watching—and the man had to be watching somewhere on this river—he'd see Travis trying to avoid detection.

That should be worth some brownie points. Just enough to keep Jessie alive.

As he floated downstream, Travis rubbed his chest and arms, trying to stimulate some warmth to his body. He glanced under his outer garments and saw his bare skin looked like a plucked goose, the color of blue ice except for large red splotches where the skin felt burned by the cold. His fingers and toes tingled with numbness.

He hoped Scarsbourgh would show his face soon.

Creasy lunged for his gun when he saw the police helicopter hovering above Travis. As he eyed the monitor, Creasy turned to face Jessie as he slowly took a bead on her forehead as she lay on the bed. Mouth taped. Eyes wide open in fear. A single tap to the head and he'd be on his way.

Travis apparently cared more about saving his skin than freeing Jessie.

He took one more look at the monitor before squeezing the trigger. He saw Travis scrambling out of sight and dragging his kayak into the trees. Creasy waited to see what happened. The helicopter continued on its search further upriver, away from Creasy's operation. He saw Travis slip out from the trees, obviously trying to conceal his position.

Good. He'd keep her alive a little longer. Until his prey arrived. Creasy released his pressure on the trigger and re-holstered the weapon.

Okay. The professor seemed to be trying to play by the rules.

If Frank and Travis disobeyed, Travis wouldn't be trying to hide from the aircraft. Maybe the deputies saw Travis' truck and started their search based upon its location. Made sense.

He flicked to the next mini cam he'd set downstream, waiting for Travis to come into view. Travis emerged, paddling furiously.

Creasy chuckled as he saw Travis beating himself trying to stay warm.

He leaned back and relaxed. Let the cops keep looking. He'd be gone before they ever figured it out. Didn't they know he wrote the book on cover and concealment, hiding and killing all his life. This is why he was created. To hunt. To kill. To disappear again.

Bring it on.

Frank started toward his car. He'd promised Travis he'd avoid Steele. Keep him in the dark. And he'd kept that promise.

But this was the life of his daughter. He could not stand by and do nothing.

He'd studied the map left by the killer. He knew this river better than most and knew where Travis started his trek. If he was in the killer's shoes, he'd want to make sure Travis was not followed. That meant a slow trip down the river where any surveillance would stick out. Aircraft, suspicious vehicles along the highway, anything.

And he had a hunch where Travis might end up. Killers, like people, are creatures of habit.

He glanced at his watch. Must work quickly. He picked up his cell phone and saw the battery died. Angrily, he realized he had forgotten to leave the charger in his car.

He crossed the river, and began driving to Three Rivers. Minutes later he made it to the resort and asked one of the owners if he might use their telephone. Quickly, he started making calls, telling those he called exactly what he wanted. He called Nez Perce County dispatch and made sure that all his calls were forwarded immediately after borrowing a cell phone from a friend. As long as he was in range, he'd get those messages. If not, the others knew what to do.

An hour later, a truck turned off Highway 12 onto the Three Rivers property pulling a horse trailer. Frank walked toward the truck as the driver emerged. He clasped the driver's hand.

"Thanks, Jim. If you'll unload the horse and saddle him up, I'll go grab my gear." The driver's long black hair tied back, his dark eyes, and chiseled features telegraphed his Nez Perce heritage. Jim turned toward the trailer and lowered the rear gate.

Frank strode over to his car, pulled out a rifle and a box of ammunition. He returned in time to see the horse tied to the trailer and saddled. "Are you Superman? How'd you do that so fast?"

Jim softly patted the horse's neck. "Knew you'd want to move out quickly, Frank, so I had the horse ready to go before I took off. Good hunting."

Frank hoisted himself up into the saddle and grasped the reins. "Thanks. And keep us in your prayers."

"Godspeed, brother." Jim waved as Frank wheeled the horse toward the roadway.

Frank crossed the road and began to look for a shallow crossing where he might ford where the two rivers came together. The two merging rivers—broadened at this point—provided a shallower crossing than further downstream where they became the Middle Fork of the Clearwater. He edged the horse into the water and slowly crossed, allowing the animal to search for its own footing in the swift current.

Time was running out. He needed to move fast before the killer appeared.

Chapter 62

Clearwater River, Idaho

Long shadows stretched across the floor of the valley, a purple shroud darkening the river and the lower reaches of lands. Darkness came quicker in these mountains. Phillip Scarsbourgh glanced at his watch. He made one last check on the computer and saw his kayaker struggling.

Just a few more miles, fool. Then you're all mine.

Travis paddled steady, but his thrusts seemed weaker. It was good that the river's flow slowed down at this elevation. The pathetically-weak professor was just passing the Three Rivers Resort as dusk approached. He still had a ways to go.

Keep paddling, fool. Don't stop now. Not if you want to see your woman one more time.

Love is such an incentive.

Scarsbourgh stood and entered the bedroom. Jessie lay sprawled across the bed, her eyes closed. She opened them as he entered. He reached into a cabinet drawer and pulled out a syringe.

"Time to go night-night."

He watched her struggle with the handcuffs, the metal cuffs firmly attached to the metal railing of the bed. "No use fighting it, Princess. Soon you can say hello to Travis. Won't that be special."

He held down one arm with his knee and thrust the needle into her skin. He pushed the plunger and watched her face. Slowly, her eyes closed and she stopped resisting. He reached over and dragged a back-pack toward him. He reached inside and withdrew a roll of duct tape. He tore off a piece and covered her mouth, making sure her nasal passages remained clear.

"Don't want you making a loud fuss until your boyfriend arrives. Once I've got my hands on Travis, you can scream all you want." He knew she never heard a word.

He turned his attention back toward the computer. On the screen, he watched Travis passing the last marker he'd set up. He picked up a hand-held portable.

"My boy's almost here. You set?"

Two squelches over the air gave him the answer he sought.

The trap is set.

Travis hit himself repeatedly, trying to beat warmth and circulation into his veins. An hour ago, his legs started cramping and he began to lose feeling in his feet. He hoped when the time came he'd be able to stand.

Crawling was not an option.

Darkness crept across the waters as dusk settled down the canyon. He recognized this part of the Clearwater. Home was not far ahead. Things started to make sense. He must prepare himself because he knew the killer would appear soon. He paddled to the bank for a quick break. It was too dark to see what he was doing now.

He tried to step out of the craft onto the rocky shoreline, but his knees buckled. He kneeled on the ground and slowly pushed up until he half stood, half crouched, supported by extended arms in an ape-like stance. Slowly, painfully, he raised himself to a standing position.

One step at a time, he tottered in a circle, watching the banks on both sides of the river. He knew this madman somehow managed to watch him most of the trip. Scarsbourgh might be watching even now, untroubled by the cops swarming the area and police aircraft patrolling the skies. He knew this guy could blend into the countryside like a leopard blending into vegetation.

Somehow he must figure how to outsmart this guy. Everything depended upon it. A quick scan of the trees and mountain slopes revealed nothing. Darkness was both a friend and foe. Creasy could not see him, nor could he see the killer. He suddenly realized everything seemed unnaturally quiet. Even the birds and animals remained silent.

Too quiet.

Again he looked around one more time before climbing back into the kayak. He shoved off and began paddling. Glancing up the river bank, he began to recognize places just upstream from his cabin. He was close to home.

He wondered how much longer Scarsbourgh might force him downstream. Surprising Travis by taking him to his own cabin made sense as long as Frank left. Where was Frank?

No one would think to search Travis' place. The cops would do drive-bys while searching the general area. They'd think the cabin would be the last place the kidnapper might bring her. After all, Travis and Frank were known to be staying there. Right?

It made the perfect place to stash his victim. A place cops might never think of checking. So did he hide Jessie there?

Just the thought of Jessie with that killer angered him. It was like fighting a phantom, always elusive, never right in front of you. Scarsbourgh, so far, always one step ahead. That was before they knew who he was—and knew the fury that drove him.

He tried to get inside Scarsbourgh's mind, sick as it was.

Ultimately, he knew Scarsbourgh wanted him. Wanted to watch Travis die for what he'd done to Michelle. First, however, the killer wanted Travis to understand and suffer the same pain Michelle's death caused him. He wanted Travis to be deeply hurt before dying.

Jessie would be that tool, that sacrificial lamb placed upon Scarsbourgh's altar of revenge.

Travis's only hope rested on one assumption—this killer kept Jessie alive long enough to draw Travis into his trap. Once caught in that trap, he must figure a way to beat Scarsbourgh at his own game.

So far, this guy held all the cards.

He heard a vehicle heading his direction along the road further up the canyon and moving fast. He estimated it would pass in a couple minutes. Not enough time to pull off the river out of sight. Nothing to hide behind here. He cradled the paddle in his arm, letting the current carry him as he waited.

A Ford F250 pickup, a dusty green with a white cab over, loomed into view. He saw the driver peering down toward the river, but in this light he thought himself close to invisible. Twilight's dusk shielded him from anyone getting a clear look at his face. The truck continued down the road.

No cops in sight.

Travis resumed his paddling downstream.

"**Frank, can you copy?** This is Charlie."

Frank reined in his horse and pressed the send button. "Yeah, Charlie. I copy."

"Just passed that cabin you mentioned. No lights. No activity that I could see."

"Copy that, my friend. I'll be in touch." He sent Charlie past Travis' cabin to spot any activity. Charlie, in his green pickup, would wait further down the Clearwater until he heard back from Frank.

He started to put the radio back into its holder when he heard a squelch and Charlie's voice on the air.

"Frank, you still with me?"

He punched the send button again. "Hear you loud and clear."

"Spotted that guy you mentioned on the river. Upstream less than a mile from the cabin. Barely see him in this light. Copy?"

"Yeah, thanks again." Frank nudged the horse forward.

No lights at the cabin. Maybe he had been wrong. He shuddered to think he'd misread everything.

If he was wrong—Jessie would be killed.

Chapter 63

Travis's arms and back ached as fiery pricks of nerves fired through his tired muscles. Exhaustion sapped his strength, his thigh muscles twitched in agony as cramps returned. He must push on.

Every moment counted.

He heard the helicopter returning and scrambled for cover on the bank as the chopper's blades beat closer. Through the tangle of branches, he watched as the copter flew overhead, its searchlight piercing darkness with enough candlelight to blind. Who were they searching for—the killer or him?

He hoped Frank kept his word. If any cops stopped him now ... he shuddered at the thought. The killer would simply end Jessie's life with a bullet, slipping away into anonymity to return later to put Travis out of his misery.

For the first time, he wondered if Scarsbourgh might be working with others. The man's actions seemed so bizarre, it seemed reasonable to assume that no one in their right mind would work with him. But the man appeared sane enough to fool Travis. He'd actually done work for this wacko.

The helicopter crew moved on in their search. He slipped from cover and began the journey once more.

Travis found he could still navigate the river in darkness, the current calmer on this stretch of water. He knew he would not face any more whitewater challenges. The darkness was not completely black as his eyes adjusted to the night. A pale moonlight began to send its cold light across the sky, casting a ghostly pall.

Ahead, he saw the span of cable across the river leading to his cabin. Home just ahead. He knew he could not stop, but he liked being on familiar turf. He knew this area well.

A voice broke the silence. "Travis. That's far enough."

Phillip Scarsbourgh.

Scarsbourgh saw Travis paddling through the water. He scanned the river with his night scope, watching everything in the green light of the lens. Darkness evaporated into a green sheen as he saw the kayak loom nearer. Travis looked tired as he slumped forward.

Good. He wanted his enemy dog-tired, unable to fight back. He wanted the man alive just enough to suffer for a while, then die at just the right time.

As Travis drew closer, Scarsbourgh lowered his rifle and brought it to the ready, flicking off the safety. If the little coward tried to run, this piece of equipment would cut him down before he finished the next paddle stroke.

Glasses in hand, Scarsbourgh ordered Travis toward the shore. Travis jerked at the sound of the command, then immediately obeyed. Scarsbourgh stepped back in the darkness of the brush and waited until the craft's bow struck shore.

"Now. Once you get out of there, raise your hands slowly. Any false move and you're dead. Understand?"

Travis nodded.

"I said, do you understand?"

"Yeah, I understand." Travis slowly pushed himself out of the craft and stood on dry ground, tottering as if his legs might be cramped.

"Now, lay on the ground, put your hands behind you. Face in the dirt. Do it now!"

Travis obeyed.

"Don't move." Phillip crept forward with a flex cuff and looped it around Travis' wrists. He savagely yanked on the cuffs, plastic cutting into the wrists.

"Now. Get to your feet. I'm going to pat you down. When I'm sure you're clean, walk toward the cabin. You know the way."

He saw Travis looking around. "Looking for Sam? The mutt's dead."

He saw Travis clench his fists together. "Don't worry, man. Soon it won't matter anyway." Chuckling, he patted Travis down and then shoved him forward with enough force to cause the man to stumble and fall. He waited until Travis struggled to his feet. "Now, let's go see your girlfriend."

Jessie heard footsteps coming.

She gave one tug at the metal handcuffs binding her wrist. With her free hand, she tried to loosen it to no avail. The killer cuffed her to an eye-bolt deeply embedded into the wall near the fireplace. Frustrated, she felt the cuff tighten even further. The more she struggled, the more metal bit into the skin.

The floor creaked beneath as she shifted, eyeing the doorway. More footsteps. It sounded like several people coming up the path. She looked around, wondering where Sam might be hiding if he was still alive.

Phillip fired one shot at the dog when they first arrived. Sam yelped and ran off into the forest. She feared the dog might be dead. That had been hours ago and the animal never returned.

Creaking sounds came from the porch as she listened to at least one set of boots striking the ground. The door swung open. Travis stumbled inside. The moonlight caught his face on the threshold. She knew that he could not see her in the darkness.

"Travis. I'm over here."

"Shut up unless I tell you to speak." Scarsbourgh shoved Travis further into the cabin before entering himself. The killer propped both the wooden door and the screen door open. "Sit on the sofa. One more word and I'll kill you both right now."

Jessie watched Travis slump down on the sofa, glancing around and looking for her. Darkness made his search useless.

A match flared up and Scarsbourgh's face loomed above a lit candle. "Isn't this romantic?" He cackled as he blew out the match. Harsh laughter of a madman.

Feeble light from the candle struggled to push back the darkness. Jessie caught Travis' gaze for a moment, his look giving her hope. She tried to read his mind, to decipher his plan.

Then an overpowering wave of panic struck her like an emotional tsunami, destroying any ray of hope. The truth of the situation crushed down upon her. This crazy killer would soon end their lives like the match he just extinguished. And there was nothing they could do to save themselves. She could not move. Travis' hands were tied behind him, and his face telegraphed his exhaustion from the river. Even if he broke free, he might not be able to put up much of a fight.

Scarsbourgh seemed to have planned everything in his favor.

She studied Travis' face once more in the candle's flickering light, to memorize the face she'd grown fond of in such a short time. Was this love?

Jessie desired to paint that face into her very soul. It might be her last work of art.

Chapter 64

John Steele scanned campsites at Three Rivers and saw Frank White Eagle's car parked near the lodge. Night descended, but light from the resort illuminated the parking lot nearest the camp store. He parked near the chief's car and killed his engine. One of the camp's employees strolled across the parking lot near the parked cars. He recognized the man.

Steele motioned him over. "Harry, you seen Frank White Eagle around? I see he left his car here." He motioned toward the unmarked.

"You bet, John. Saw him on horseback several hours ago. A friend of his came by with a horse trailer and dropped off his ride."

"Where did he go?"

Harry scratched his head, thinking. "I recollect he went that way," and pointed toward the west where the rivers merged. "I think he rode down the Clearwater."

"Which side?"

"Now that I can't tell you. All I know—he headed downriver."

Steele thanked him and got back in his car. He left the campground, pulled along the river off Highway 12 and parked. He flicked on a flashlight and scrambled down the bank to the river's edge, working his way upstream.

Fifteen minutes later, Steele found signs of fresh prints in the mud. He kneeled down to get a closer look. A horse had been ridden to this point and then the hoof prints veered toward the water.

Steele studied the swiftly-flowing blackness of the Clearwater. Frank must have forded the river here to reach the south side of the river. Steele glanced downstream and smiled. He knew where Frank might be headed. Travis' cabin was on the other side a mile or so downstream. Frank had quite a ride ahead of him if that was his destination.

Steele began walking back to his car. Why didn't Frank tell him what he planned to do? He should have known there was no way Frank would stand by while a killer held his daughter. But what was he up to? And where was Travis?

He'd start doing a little reconnaissance of his own.

Frank reached the mountaintop towering above Travis's cabin. Darkness hid details of the canyon floor below, though moonlight combed the mountain peaks with cold streaks of silver. He would take the horse halfway down the slope, and then go on foot the rest of the way. Everything would depend on stealth.

Sliding off the horse, Frank pulled out his binoculars and scanned below. He knew the cabin was hidden by the forest, but he'd hoped to see some activity near the roadway.

Total darkness.

Frank searched with the glasses a few more minutes before tucking them away, his stomach tightening from the stress. He couldn't help but think he'd misjudged this killer. So sure where his daughter might wind up. But the darkness below only made him begin to question his confidence.

He might be wrong.

God, help me. I can't lose another child.

He climbed back on the horse and began working his way down the steep rock-strewn slope. The horse stumbled several times, catching itself before moving on. Frank leaned back in the saddle over the animal's withers, letting the reins loose in his right hand, trusting the horse to find its way safely.

Thoughts of Jessie forced him to think about his son. Losing Tommy had hit him hard. So many unanswered questions. Why must Tommy die so young? Why'd the killer snatch Jessie? These thoughts—fears—rattled in his brain as he tried to hold fast to his faith.

Frank reined in the horse. He tied the horse to a branch, slipping his rifle from its sheath. He'd go the rest of the way on foot. Patting the horse on the rump, he shouldered the rifle and began to silently tread down the mountain slope.

He left his bitterness and anger on the mountaintop. It was time to focus on saving his remaining child.

Time to focus on the living. Later, he'd mourn the dead.

Travis felt the flex cuffs slicing his wrists. Each movement tightened them more. The cuffs started cutting off circulation.

He shot Jessie a look of encouragement before facing Scarsbourgh. The killer stood near the doorway after lighting the candle, the flickering flame threatening to extinguish at any moment as a slight breeze came through the open door.

Travis wondered why Scarsbourgh left the door and the screen propped open. The light might not be strong enough for anyone to see them from the highway. But who knows? Maybe they'd get lucky and a passing deputy might get suspicious. Steele must be wondering why he and Frank slipped off his radar. He might have deputies watch this place.

If only they would come in time.

He turned his attention back to their captor.

Scarsbourgh leered. "Think someone's gonna rescue you at the last minute?" He laughed, bitterness searing his words. "Maybe like Michelle thought you'd come and save her just before they ended her life?" Hate gleamed in the man's eyes.

Travis heard a horse whinny. A second horse answered. He glanced toward their abductor, wondering if the man heard the same sounds.

A sneer crossed the man's face. "Don't get your hopes up. Those are my horses. You think the two of us hiked here?"

Scarsbourgh edged closer. Travis heard a click. A knife blade flashed in the candlelight.

The killer held a switchblade in his hand. "Now, let's get down to business."

Frank froze when he heard the horse call out below. A moment later his own horse answered further up the mountainside. A sick feeling curled his stomach.

Someone is down below. And they know I'm coming.

He carefully made his way down the slope, moving quickly and quietly. Time was running out.

In the moonlight, he saw Travis' cabin less than a hundred feet ahead. Two horses tied up in back.

Where was Travis?

At least he was right about one thing. He'd correctly read the mind of this madman. Now he knew Jessie was close. He prayed he might get there in time.

Chapter 65

"Stand up, lover boy, and face your girlfriend. Keep your back to me." Scarsbourgh barked his command. "One wrong move and I'll end it right here."

Travis wondered if Scarsbourgh intended to bury the knife in his back.

The man seemed to be reading Travis' mind. "I want your hands free so that you can write something for me. Your confession. Now, stand up."

Travis faced Jessie a few feet away. He saw panic in her eyes. He heard Scarsbourgh move closer.

"And just in case you think of using any of the kung fu stuff, I've got a gun to your head." Scarsbourgh gave a low, rasping laugh. "A bullet beats a karate chop any day of the week."

Travis felt the knife blade cut through the plastic cuffs with a powerful tug. He felt his wrists were free and brought his hands around in front. He fought the urge to swing around and slam his fist into the man's skull. He could not make a mistake here.

The horses whinnied again, and then he heard another answer further away. He wondered if Scarsbourgh also heard it.

Slowly, Travis turned and saw the barrel of a 9mm Beretta semi-automatic pistol leveled at him.

The gunman waved it toward the ground. "Now, sit down and do what I tell you."

Scarsbourgh stepped back and pulled a folded piece of paper from his pocket. He gestured toward a pad of paper on the table, tossing the rumpled paper from his pocket and a pen on top of the pad.

"I want you to write your confession, Travis. How you killed my sister and tried to hide from your sins. I've taken the time to write it out for you. Copy it word for word. Then sign and date it."

Travis glanced at the paper and back at Scarsbourgh.

"You know I didn't kill her."

"You were responsible. Now, sit down and start writing." The killer swung the gun barrel toward Jessie. "Do you want me to give you an incentive?" He cocked the hammer, glaring at Travis.

Travis quickly sat down. "Okay, okay."

Scarsbourgh gave him a mirthless smile. "Get started, slick. Before you lose another girlfriend." Glancing at Jessie, the gunman said, "Hey. You could do better than this guy. He only thinks of himself. Look what he did to my sister. Got her dead so he could make a name for himself. Some hero, huh?"

Travis gripped the pen hard. "That's not what happened."

The gun barrel swung back toward Travis. "Oh, so you didn't send her back in to get what you wanted? To make your case?"

"Okay. I sent her in, but I thought she'd be safe. We needed—"

"—you thought she'd be safe? Then how did she wind up dead?"

Travis bowed his head. "Look. I've regretted that decision ever since. I wish I could take it back."

A sharp pain exploded in Travis' head and he fell forward.

Jessie screamed.

Dizzily, Travis tried sitting up. He realized Scarsbourgh had struck him with the butt of the gun.

"You regret getting her killed?" The killer cut loose with a string of epithets that made Travis cringe. "I ought to put a bullet in your head right now. Shut up and write."

The blow made Travis woozy. He struggled to stay upright.

"Do as I say or I end this right now," Scarsbourgh screamed, trembling with rage.

As Travis leaned over to write, he heard a faint clicking noise in the silence that followed Scarsbourgh's outburst. He gave a quick glance toward the door and saw Sam in the doorway, crouched and coiled, moving like a mountain lion ready to spring.

"Did you hear me? Start .... writing ... now!" Scarsbourgh's screams filled the cabin, drowning the sounds of Sam's approach.

Travis glanced toward Jessie. She stared at the door and then back at him. He shook his head and bent over to appear as if he began writing. He waited to see what the dog might do.

"Okay, man. I'll start writing. Just chill—"

Sam sprang toward Scarsbourgh, sinking his teeth deep into the man's right calf. The killer howled and whirled to fire at the dog.

Travis leaped from the sofa and grabbed Phillip's gun hand. The two men struggled for control until he felt a sharp pain in his side. He'd forgotten about the knife. The blade sliced into his side. He felt Scarsbourgh yank upward on the knife as it filleted his skin. His entire side burned like someone tossed searing coals onto his skin. He clung to the gun with one hand, trying to stave off another blow with the knife.

They collapsed on the ground. He tried raising himself, but felt his strength ebbing on one side where the knife must have hit muscle.

In a daze, he felt Scarsbourgh wrench the gun free and saw the gunman strike Sam on the head with the butt of the gun. The animal went limp.

Scarsbourgh turn and struck Travis across his temple, slamming his head against the wooden floor. Dazed, Travis watched the killer heave himself to a standing position. Breathing heavy, Scarsbourgh limped back a few feet, still pointing the gun in Travis' direction.

Spent, Travis lay on his back looking up. He knew what was coming.

Scarsbourgh slowly raised the gun. "Forget the confession. It's time you paid for your sins. I've waited a long time for this."

Travis cringed as a gun fired. He heard Jessie scream.

Scarsbourgh fell on top of him.

Chapter 66

Scarsbourgh's body pinned him to the floor. Travis felt a sharp pain in his side as he pushed the dead body off. Struggling to raise himself, he heard Jessie gasp and glanced toward the doorway.

He heard someone walking across the porch. At first, darkness outside hid the person's face, body silhouetted in moonlight. Then, as the footsteps drew closer, the face became illuminated by faint candlelight.

Frank stepped from the shadows.

"Dad." Jessie tried to stand, one arm still shackled to the wall.

Frank looked from his daughter to Travis. He grasped a rifle in his right hand and started walking toward Jessie. "Jessie. Thank God. Let me find a—"

Frank lurched forward, a surprised look on his face. Travis heard the report of a rifle echo in the distance.

Another shooter.

Jessie screamed.

Travis hurled himself toward the candle, sweeping it to the floor. Darkness drowned the room, bathing them in its protection. Outside, the moon cast its sheen of light across the river. The darkened trees stood like a silent army washed in a silver glow.

He crawled to the doorway, peering out. Jessie sobbed in the darkness, calling out to her father, "Daddy, Daddy ..." Frank lay still. Travis scanned outside, trying to pick up any movement. Everything seemed deathly quiet. Nothing moved.

He slowly moved across the floor toward Frank. The shooter—after the blast that struck Frank—must have lost his night vision for at least a few moments. Just enough time to check on Frank.

Travis groped in the darkness until he felt Frank's face. He lowered his hand until he could feel the chief's carotid artery. Great. A strong pulse. Frank's alive. He tugged at Frank's belt until he pulled the man from the doorway and behind the wall for protection.

"Jessie. Stay where you are. Don't move."

"Is Dad ..."

"He's alive. I just moved him out of the way of the shooter. Stay put until I can get you free. Okay?"

Travis heard her acknowledgement. He crept over the floor toward Scarsbourgh's body. He heard Sam stirring. "Sam, lay down." He heard the dog sink back to the ground, his tail thumping on the wooden floor.

Scarsbourgh's body still felt warm as Travis began searching through the killer's pockets until he found cuff keys. Glancing through the doorway, he slowly began crawling toward Jessie. A bullet might be coming his way any moment if the sniper used a night vision scope. He made an excellent target with the moonlight streaming through the doorway after extinguishing the candle. He could not wait. Frank needed help and Jessie lay in an exposed position.

He heard Sam whimper.

"Sam. Lay down, boy. Stay."

The dog obeyed.

He crawled forward, fighting a wave of nausea from the pain in his side. He continued crawling until he felt Jessie. She reached out and touched his face with her free hand. They clung to each other for a moment.

He reached toward her shackled arm, felt the cuffs and worked the key into the lock. He felt the key slip in and the cuffs loosen. He opened them up to free her. She circled him with her arms.

He grimaced as she accidentally pressed against his wound. "Jessie. Stay real still. Don't move. I don't think the shooter is in a position to see this part of the cabin. I'm going to try to get help."

"How's Dad?"

"He's still alive. I don't know where he's hit or how bad. But we can't risk turning on a light right now. Okay?

"Yeah."

He turned and began crawling toward the front door when he froze. Footsteps on the pathway, crunching on the gravel.

Sam growled.

"Sam. Quiet." Silence inside the cabin.

"Travis" Jessie hissed his name.

"Shhh." He frantically started feeling around the floor where Scarsbourgh lay, looking for the killer's gun.

Heavy boots crunched on rocks only yards away.

He raised himself and began clawing at the dead body, desperately feeling around for the feel of cold metal. Where was that gun?

He heard steps on the porch. Heavy boots.

Travis gave up on the gun and tried to stand. If he could only make it to the door he might be able to attack before the killer got inside.

He tried to stand, but lightheadedness forced him to his knees.

A flashlight flicked on and illuminated the room, drowning him in light. He froze, waiting for the sound of the gun.

Instead, he heard a man's voice.

"Travis. It's me ...John Steele."

As Steele entered the room, Travis heard sirens wailing in the distance. The wails drew closer.

"I've got units coming. But I think the second shooter's gone." Steele knelt and cuffed Scarsbourgh. "How are the two of you doing?"

Travis felt his side. "I'm going to need some help. Scarsbourgh nick-ed me with a knife. Not life-threatening. Need to get help for Frank first."

Steele nodded and rose to his feet. He began spitting out commands over the portable radio. "Requesting an air medevac. Location Code-4. Suspect 10-55. Two victims need medical attention. One in serious condition. Code-3 run."

Staccato commands. Travis welcomed the man's command presence.

Sirens kept coming.

After finishing the broadcast, Steele flashed the light around the room and switched on the lights. He glanced at Travis. "Hey partner, you're going to need some help yourself."

Travis glanced at his side and saw redness drenching his torn shirt. A fold of skin lay loose like a partially-filleted salmon. Blood oozed, turning everything into a river of dark scarlet.

Jessie clamored over to Frank the moment Steele turned on the lights. He saw her gently raise her father's head. A bullet creased his scalp. Travis had seen wounds like this before. The velocity must have slammed Frank to the ground, knocking him out.

Steele peered over Travis' shoulder. "I think he'll be all right if they can keep the swelling down. He'll have one heck of a headache when he wakes up."

Travis glanced up. "How'd you get to the cabin?"

A smile crossed Steele's face. "I followed Frank. He took a horse across the river. I figured out where he was probably headed—your place—and jammed back to Three Rivers to borrow a raft. I crossed over upstream from here and worked my way as close as I could get in the dark. Sorry I didn't get here sooner."

Sam's wet nose searched Travis face. Travis reached over and patted the dog. "I thought Scarsbourgh operated alone. At least until I saw him leave the front door open and the screen door propped. Couldn't figure that out until the second shooter clipped Frank. I should have known."

Steele nodded, glancing through the doorway. "Yeah. I heard the first shot when Frank popped Scarsbourgh. Tried to get here as fast as possible. Then I heard the second shot. Once I realized what happened, I flashed my light up the hill trying to draw the shooter off. I think the light scared him away. I'll get my deputies to start combing that mountainside, but I figure the shooter's long gone."

Travis nodded, looking down at Frank, still lying motionless. "First, let's get Frank to the hospital. Then I want to start looking for the shooter. Until we find that person, this is not over."

He glanced at Jessie, her face tight with concern as she stroked her father's cheek. She looked up. "Find him, Travis. Find him and end this before anyone else gets hurt."

He knelt and put his arm around her. "I'll try, Jessie. I'll try."

He heard sirens cut out as each patrol vehicle arrived. Their emergency lights continued to light up the night. Twenty minutes later, he heard the blades of a chopper cutting through the night.

First things first. He had to make sure Frank was taken care of and his own wounds patched up. Then, he'd start tracking this second shooter after they safely stashed Jessie away.

As he waited for the medical crew, he thought about the case and where he'd gone wrong. He must start over and look at everything with fresh eyes.

Everyone.

Already an idea started to form, a suspicion burrowed deep in his brain like a splinter festering under the skin. Something he'd seen and failed to understand. Maybe if he'd been smart enough to pick up on it at the time, all this could have been averted.

Maybe. Could have. Would have. He was tired of second-guessing himself. For the past. For the present. Right now he would only focus on the here and now.

As he thought about it, another thought began to take shape like sculptor struggling to see how a hunk of marble might be chipped away until a clear image emerged. He remembered a small detail that escaped his attention at the time. And now, like a movie camera bringing everything into focus, he began to see clearly.

He'd been looking at this all wrong. Travis thought he knew where to start hunting. Not all the pieces fit, but a big part of the puzzle just fell in place. There were connections in the records seized from the casino that he'd glossed over, connections that fell in the 'so what' category. Until now.

He needed to go back over the records.

 **Chapter 67**

Grangeville, Idaho

Steele rushed Travis to St. Joseph's Regional Medical Center in Lewiston. At first Travis resisted until he learned the medevac team airlifted Frank to a trauma unit in Spokane with Jessie onboard. Once he knew they had protection, he acquiesced taking a ride to Lewiston.

Steele insisted. "I've got protection for them once they touch down. Now, let's get you to the hospital."

Doctors and nurses repaired Travis' knife wound. Hours later, they wheeled Travis from the emergency room with orders to give his stitches a break and take it easy. Bed rest and light duty.

Travis pushed himself up from the wheelchair and eased into Steele's car. "Get me to your office, detective. We've got a case to finish."

This time, Steele agreed.

Steele set up a temporary work station at the sheriff's office to give Travis a place to operate. Once set up, Travis started to read the interview notes again. He called the hospital in Spokane and left a message for Jessie where he could be reached.

His mind struggled to grasp everything that had happened in the last few days. Part of it made sense. Other parts seemed complete garbage. The whole case depended upon finding the right key, the right piece of information linking Scarsbourgh to those with a common interest, a common goal.

One of those common interests seemed to be Travis.

It didn't take a lot of gray matter to figure out why Scarsbourgh wanted Travis dead. In the killer's twisted mind, he held Travis responsible for Michelle's death.

But why might others come after him?

Maybe they needed what Scarsbourgh offered. So they worked in concert with him so everyone got what they wanted. The problem he wrestled over was a motive for the co-conspirators. Money? Power? Revenge? What?

And who were they?

Travis felt like he was getting nowhere. One name kept surfacing. One person who'd been in the background. But he needed to be sure. And he needed to understand the motive before exposing his hand.

He jumped as a phone rang on the desk. For a moment, Travis let it ring, trying to get back to his thoughts. The phone kept ringing. He snatched it up.

"Travis Mays."

"Travis ... it's Jessie. Steele gave me this phone number." She sounded tired and worried. "They say Dad is stable, but listed him as critical. They're doing everything they can."

"Is he ..."

"Dad's unconscious." Jessie's voice cracked. He listened as she struggled to speak. "They say that's a good thing. He needs to be real still."

"That's good, I guess."

"How are you doing?"

"A little sore, but otherwise, I'm fine. Just sitting here trying to make sense of all this."

"Any luck?"

He hesitated. "I've got a couple things to follow up. If they are successful, I'll give you a call."

There was a moment of silence before she spoke. "I miss you. Just be careful," she said, before cutting him off.

"I miss you too, Jessie," he said to a dead line.

Just as he replaced the receiver, the phone rang a second time. "Jessie?"

"Tom Kagan here, Travis."

"How'd you get this number?"

Kagan laughed. "I'm a detective, remember? Steele called and updated me about Frank and everything that happened at your cabin. He told me you'd be sharing an office. You near a computer?"

Travis glanced at the monitor in front of him. "Yeah."

"I've shipped out a copy of a video taken from the city's surveillance camera in personnel. I downloaded the video for the days you asked and shipped it to your e-mail account. Call me back when you've had a chance to see it."

Travis hung up and went online to access his account. As the program opened up, he saw Kagan's message sitting in his inbox along with a number of unopened messages. He clicked on the attachment link and saw a video clip load. Embedded controls allowed him to zoom in where desired. He let it run in fast forward until one scene caught his attention. The camera lens captured everyone approaching the front counter. A second angle gave a shot of the front door. Hours of tape went by in minutes. The view ran a split-screen, with both cameras' vantage point running in sync.

He tapped his finger on the mouse as he watched the video unfold. In one segment of tape, he saw a man enter. Something about him looked familiar. Travis stopped the clip and reversed it. He hit the button and let the video run in real time.

The film caught a quick glimpse of his face. Travis froze the picture and zoomed in on the face.

Kent McPeters.

He hit the print key. A black-and-white copy of the photo rolled out of the printer next to him.

Travis straightened in his chair. McPeters traveled more than a thousand miles to access Santa Rosa city personnel files. There could only be one reason. He let the tape continue playing until a woman returned with a file in her hand. He saw McPeters sign and open the file. He stopped the frame and zoomed in on a photo pasted in the upper left hand corner. He zeroed in on that image. It was a headshot of Travis. Here was proof McPeters traveled there to go through Travis's personnel file.

He grabbed the phone and punched Kagan's number. Kagan answered immediately. "You saw it?"

"Yeah. Kent McPeters. Department chairman here at WSU. My boss. Can you find out what story he gave them to see my file?"

"Already checked into it. Here's the scoop. Personnel said this guy identified himself as heading up a federal DOJ grant research project requiring top-level security clearance. He was assigned to do a background check on you for the school. He'd contacted the city before arriving and mailed a letter—allegedly, signed by you—authorizing him to take a look at your personnel file."

Kagan coughed. "One more thing. After McPeters saw the file, someone else may have accessed it. All the pages were left unstapled as if someone ran off a copy. No one signed it out, so we may have someone here in the city with access to these files who may be in cahoots with one of your suspects."

Travis struggled to think this through. "Somebody accessed it after McPeters."

"Uh-huh."

"So that's how McPeters found out about Michelle."

"Exactly. He learned about the personnel investigation when DOJ complained about you not playing ball with them. Your statement about what happened, and how you felt responsible for her death. All that became part of the record."

"This was before Scarsbourgh knew of my involvement. Up to that point, only Clay Lafata, Timothy Heard, and Steve Kirkpatrick knew any details. So how did Scarsbourgh wind up with the information?"

"It's clear to me McPeters told him or that other person here who has access to our files."

Travis tried to make these facts fit. "I don't know, Tom. McPeters isn't the sharpest tool in the shed. How'd he learn about Scarsbourgh's identity? It took us a lot of digging, and Malloy used a federal database to put it together."

"Maybe McPeters is smarter than you think."

"I know the man. Trust me, he's not that bright." Travis smiled to himself.

"Okay. Who told him? It certainly wasn't Scarsbourgh."

"Maybe he just wanted to know more about me."

"McPeters? Maybe." Kagan sounded doubtful. "Anyway, you've got at least one more suspect to work on. Happy hunting. And let me know about Frank if anything changes."

"You got it. And thanks, Tom." Travis hung up.

He rifled through several boxes of records seized from Whitewater Casino. Inside, he found a file on all customer transaction breakdowns by date and time just before Tommy's disappearance. He pulled these out and located McPeters' name, a regular loser at the casino for months before Tommy's disappearance. And then, McPeters' transactions dropped off completely. He jotted down the time periods. These transactions showed a pattern to McPeters' financial demise; a bar tab, then dinner with more booze, and then gambling chips.

Thousands of dollars on credit.

From a contact sheet he and Frank created, Travis scanned down until he came to the name he sought. He dialed the number connected to that name.

Dizzy's vibrant bellow resonated. "Whitewater security."

"Travis Mays here, Dizzy. You got a minute?"

"Sure. Got all the time in the world. Just sitting here watching people throw their money away." His Earl Ray Jones voice softened. "How's Frank doing?"

Travis gave an update. "Anyone else listening to this conversation, Dizzy?"

"Nah, man. My partner hit the head a few minutes ago. I'm solo right now."

"I'll make this quick. How far back do your security tapes go?"

"As far back as you want. We keep everything by date and time."

"Fantastic. Can you get me in to review the tapes made just before Tommy disappeared? Need to look at the last four weeks prior to him disappearing."

"Sure man. Anytime."

Travis wasn't certain how to phrase his next request. "I'm working out of the Idaho Sheriff's office here in Grangeville. I don't want to get you into any trouble, but I want to check on a couple of customers who popped up on the casino's financial records. I'll need to look at the tapes. I can be there whenever you can set it up."

"Tell you what. How about I bring the tapes to you? Too many eyes here."

He heard footsteps over the phone line. Someone coming back into the office.

Dizzy's voice changed. "Sure enough, sweetheart. See ya after I get off tonight. I'll bring those movies you wanted. Meet you about midnight? We'll spend some quality time after that." Dizzy hung up.

He glanced at his watch. The dial read 8 p.m.

Four more hours.

 **Chapter 68**

Clearwater River, Idaho

Dizzy stretched and looked over at his partner. "Hey. Mind if I wander outside and stretch my legs? Be back in about twenty."

The man laughed. "You're going to do more than stretch your legs, Dizzy. Your wife know your messing around with some of the girls here?"

Dizzy fumed." I don't mess around, partner. Like the surgeon general's warning on cigarettes, messing around on my old lady would be harmful to my health. Besides, I get all I need at home."

The other man waved him off. "Get out of here. Go tell your lies somewhere else. And remember, I've got you on camera."

As soon as Dizzy left the security office he slipped into a nearby darkened office, picked up an in-house phone and dialed a number. "Hey, angel. Dizzy here. Could you do me a favor?"

"Anything for you, sugar." The woman's hearty laugh drew a smile.

"You don't know what I'm going to ask."

"Hey, your wish is my command, big boy, as long as your sweet wife doesn't mind."

"That's my girl." Dizzy laid out his plan and hung up.

He exited the office and slowly wandered down the hall looking over his shoulder. He knew all the blind spots where cameras could not probe. A locked cabinet, bolted to the wall nearest him, was one of those spots. Only seconds elapsed as he took out a key from his pocket and unlocked the cover. Using a handkerchief he reached inside and removed a security access card, making sure no fingerprints were left inside or on the card he retrieved. The cards—this one identified as granting access to the casino's security files storage room—only to be used by Robinette or his designated representative. Dizzy was not one of these chosen few.

Quickly, he locked up the panel and retreated down the hallway.

Several minutes later, Dizzy reached the storage room. He knew security cameras did not cover this part of the building, although in light of what he was doing right now he wondered why they left this place blind. Definitely an oversight by security experts. He slid the access card through a scanner and heard the door click. Once inside, he pulled the door closed and flicked on a penlight he always carried. A bead of light fell on rows of security disks, floor to ceiling. Dizzy quickly scanned for the date and time sequence Travis requested. Four disks. He took those and slid them under his coat before flicking off the light. He quickly left the room, pulling the door tightly closed behind him.

Muffled voices reached him, coming from a few yards away where the hallway angled at ninety-degrees to the right. Footsteps just around the corner. He hesitated, wondering if he should try to slip back into the locker room. Just as he pulled out the access card, voices faded away and he heard a door close.

Silence. He started breathing again.

As he rounded the corner, Dizzy saw someone had left a laundry cart midway down the hall. He took the tapes and buried them under a pile of soiled towels. He started to relax as he pushed the cart toward a service elevator. As he pressed the down button, he heard the elevator already moving. Someone was using the lift.

There was no time to hide. The cart could not be left unattended. He'd have to take a chance. The elevator stopped on his floor and the doors rolled open. Steve Robinette strode out, glancing at Dizzy and at the cart next to him.

"What you up to Dizzy?"

Dizzy felt his voice thicken. "Just tidying up, Mr. Robinette. This cart was left in the hallway. Thought I'd take it down to laundry for the night crew."

"Let someone else do that, Dizzy. I pay you good money to keep us safe."

"Yes, sir. And that's what I'm doing. But I like to help out wherever I can. You know, always trying to be the employee of the month and get that special parking place." He grinned, trying to lighten the tension.

Robinette scowled. He shook his head, glanced at the cart again as he walked away.

Dizzy's shirt felt like he'd just dived into a swimming pool, perspiration making his shirt cling to his skin. Robinette had been a pain to everybody at the casino every since the cops let him go after the interrogation. They had more things to worry about—Jessie kidnapped, Frank shot—than hassling Robinette at the moment. Rumor had it Robinette could be expecting legal action at any time. This made the casino manager edgy and he had become suspicious of everyone in the casino since the arrest.

Dizzy pushed the cart into the elevator and hit the basement button. Once there, he pulled out the tapes and wrapped them inside one of the towels. Leaving the laundry room, he glanced around once more before walking into the employee's locker room.

He was alone.

Another blind spot from the security cameras. Quickly, Dizzy unlocked his locker and withdrew a gym bag. He spied a discarded paper bag from the casino's gift shop left near an overflowing garbage can. He put the tapes inside, and stuffed the paper bag in with his gym clothes. Looking around once more, he shoved the gym bag back inside his locker and fastened the lock.

As he left the lounge, he made one more phone call from an inner-casino phone. "Okay, angel. Everything's set." He gave her the combination to his locker, hoping no one bothered to monitor this call. He hung up and returned to duty.

Dizzy glanced at his watch. Ten o'clock. He rose, glancing at his partner as he slipped into his jacket. "See you tomorrow. Don't let the boss catch you sleeping." The other man looked up with tired eyes. He grunted and turned back toward the wall of security monitors.

"Enjoy your hot date, Dizzy."

REVENGE   305

Laughing, Dizzy took one last look at the monitors. He'd lost track of Steve Robinette since their encounter at the elevators. "I think the boss went home early."

The other man grunted.

No one in the employee lounge when Dizzy arrived.

He went to his locker, pulled out his gym bag and saw the gift bag missing. He headed for the exit, looking over his shoulder and scanning the room.

Everyone on the main floor seemed uninterested.

He sighed with relief and strode toward the front door. He was several feet from the lobby when he heard someone yelling at him.

"Dizzy, wait right there."

Glancing back, he saw Steve Robinette and two men walking toward him.

He felt his heart rate jump. He halted, glancing once toward the open door.

Robinette came closer, his face taut. The two men with Robinette were strangers. But one glance at these men told him all he needed to know. Hired pit bulls. Rippling with muscles and short on brains.

His boss eyed the gym bag in Dizzy's hand. "Leaving a little early?"

"Nah. Boss. Got off a few minutes ago. Just heading home."

"What's in the bag?"

Dizzy felt his heart beating harder. He'd never been challenged like this before. Robinette must know something. "Just my dirty clothes."

"Nothing else?" His boss did not smile.

"No."

"Then you don't mind if my men make a quick check, do you? Just a routine security check."

Gritting his teeth, Dizzy held up the bag for inspection. One of the muscle men snatched it from his grasp and began pawing through it. The man reminded Dizzy of one of the muscle builders he saw at the gym. Spent most of his time looking in the mirror at his own reflection. After finishing the search, muscleman looked at Robinette, shaking his head.

Robinette's face flashed disappointment. "We're tightening up security measures across the board, Dizzy. I'm sure you understand. I want these gentlemen to escort you to your car, where they will conduct a brief search. Strictly voluntary, you understand."

Dizzy stiffened. "That's illegal, boss. You know that."

Robinette gestured. "Like I said, this is strictly voluntary. But if you refuse, it might make me wonder what you've got to hide. And I can't worry about what my security personnel are doing, now can I?"

Glaring at Robinette, Dizzy snatched his gym bag. "Let's get this over with." He marched outside, the two pit bulls trailing behind. Dizzy glanced over his shoulder and saw Robinette standing near the entrance watching every move.

Dizzy reached his vehicle, hit the alarm button and heard the locks automatically spring open. His car's interior lights flicked on. "Make this quick," he said, standing back, watching the two men closely. They searched quickly and efficiently, one taking the interior, while the other goon opened the trunk. Both men tossed anything that got in their way.

After trashing the car, the men emerged and gave Robinette a thumbs-down gesture. They began walking back toward their handler.

He took a deep breath and climbed into the car, throwing his gym bag into the back seat. After backing out, Dizzy carefully looked into his rearview as he drove from the parking lot. No other cars followed. Slowly, he pulled onto Highway 12 and turned east while still glancing into his rear mirror for any surveillance. No suspicious cars tailed him.

A mile further he pulled off the highway and into a gas station. He stopped near one of the pumps and climbed out. No other cars followed, although several vehicles whizzed past on the highway. He entered the mini-market and saw a woman loitering near where the refrigeration units stored cold beverages. The woman gave him a big smile.

"I thought you'd never make it." The woman seemed nervous.

He grinned. "Angel, you're a sweetheart. I'll tell you what's going on as soon as a friend of mine figures it out. Until then, this is our little secret, right?"

She seemed to relax. "I'm really good at keeping secrets, Dizzy." She handed him the gift bag he'd left in his locker. "By the way, you need a deodorizer in that locker of yours. Tell your wife to freshen up your clothes once in a while."

"And what if she asks why you're nosing around in my locker?"

"That's your problem, Dizzy." She gave him a hug and walked away.

 **Chapter 69**

Grangeville, Idaho

Travis rubbed his jaw, feeling bristles sprouting on his unshaven face. It had been nearly twenty-four hours since he enjoyed a shave or a shower. His eyes felt like someone was grinding sand into them every time he blinked.

He felt the cell phone vibrate, the phone another gift from Steele for this investigation. The caller ID on the display made his heart skip a beat. Sacred Heart Hospital in Spokane.

Frank?

He punched the send button and raised the phone. Jessie answered.

"Everything okay?" His heart beat faster when she paused before answering.

"Everything's more than okay. Dad regained consciousness a little while ago. The doctor says the next twenty-four hours will be critical, but it looks very promising." A catch in her voice hinted at the concern she tried to conceal.

"And you? How're you holding up?" He waited. The sound of her voice jolted his tired body like getting an intravenous shot of caffeine.

"I'm doing fine, Travis. You?"

"Good. Just needed a little good news. Thanks."

He suddenly felt awkward, like a school boy on his first date. The thought made him feel stupid. *Man, I'm almost forty. Grow up.* Still, he plunged ahead.

"I ... miss you." There, it was out.

Jessie laughed.

He felt his face heat up. "You're laughing."

"Sorry," she said, although he heard a stifled giggle. "I never thought a hermit like you missed anyone. I'm touched."

"You're touched, all right," he said, already wishing he'd kept his mouth shut.

"How's the case going?" Finally she gave him a break.

"Good. Dizzy dropped off the tapes I requested last night around midnight. I've been going over them ever since."

"You've been working on that for eighteen hours? Without sleep?"

His watch read 6 p.m. Now he understood why his eyes burned. "I'm almost through."

"Anything interesting?"

"Not yet. I've focused on McPeters and the people he met."

"And?"

"Nothing yet. I'll give it a couple more hours. Maybe something'll leap out at me."

"No idea who he's working with?"

"I've got a couple ideas. I'll finish with the tapes and cross-reference it with phone records."

"Get some sleep, Travis. Don't run yourself down."

Concern in her voice made him feel strange. A long time since someone cared about him. "Thanks. I'll take it easy. And tell Frank I'll be up as soon as I can break free."

"He'd like that," she said. "And so would I."

As Travis lowered the phone, he felt rejuvenated. Energized.

He turned toward the computer, fast-forwarding the tape until he spotted McPeters perched on a bar stool. The man seemed to spend hours inhaling booze. He saw his boss push himself away and wander toward one of the card tables. A cocktail waitress trailed him, plying the man with free drinks. Travis wondered how McPeters stayed upright.

Several hours later, according to the tape's time recorder, McPeters wandered out into the parking lot and lit a cigarette. A moment later, he pulled out a cell phone and dialed a number.

Travis froze that frame, noted the date and time on the screen, and pulled out all cell phone records for the case. He thumbed through until he found McPeters' cell phone calls and scanned down the page until he reached the date and time on the sheet which matched the time stamp on the video.

He highlighted the phone number McPeters called. Writing the number down, he began a search of all phones connected to every subject listed in the case. The numbers had been entered in numerical order by area code and telephone number.

It only took him a minute to locate the number. His finger followed the dotted line from the number to subscriber information. As soon as he saw the subscriber, he felt his pulse quicken.

He finally found the connection. He grabbed the phone and dialed.

John Steele answered.

"John, how quick can you get back into the office?"

"Half an hour."

"Make it fifteen. We've got a break." He lowered the phone and smiled.

 **Chapter 70**

Clearwater River, Idaho

Travis watched Steele fidgeting. He knew what was troubling the lawman. Suspect baited and hooked. Now—will the fish take a bite?

As soon as Steele arrived, Travis began laying out his plan. They'd driven to the Three Rivers Rafting Company parking lot to make the phone call to McPeters. Travis was not certain where McPeters might be at the time of the call and he wanted to be in place before contact. McPeters said he was in Pullman, a three-hour drive away.

"I gotta be honest with you," Steele said, shaking his head. "I'm not wild about this idea of yours. Let's just move in and make the arrest."

"No. We've got to stick to the plan. This way, you'll have all the proof you need."

"How'd you know he'd take the bait?"

"Because he has everything to lose. I just told him if he didn't meet with me, I'd go straight to the administration with what I knew."

"He bit on that?"

"Yeah. I let him know I expected a little monetary compensation for keeping my mouth shut. McPeters is all about greed. That's what he understands."

"And what if he tries to kill you?"

Travis smiled. "McPeters doesn't have the guts. Besides, I'm counting on you to cover my back. You've got a couple hours to get your men in place."

Steele nodded. "I'll do my best." He climbed into his unmarked and rolled down the window. "I'm going to meet SWAT a couple miles down the road. I'll give you a jingle when we're set up. You sure he'll come?"

"Worried about the overtime?" Travis smiled. "He'll come. As sure as I know the sun will rise tomorrow. He can't resist."

"So, you'll be set up in this parking lot when the suspect arrives. Right? And remember, don't move from here. We can't cover you if you go mobile."

"Got it. I won't budge. I'm going across the river to grab a bite to eat. I'll be back here in plenty of time."

"And don't forget to switch the power on. That jacket I gave you has a mini-camera transmitter that gives us audio and visual. But only if you flick it on."

"Okay. Don't sweat it. I'll power up when it's time."

John looked dubious, but whatever doubts he harbored he didn't share. "I'll give you a call when we're set up."

Travis waved as Steele pulled away. A pain shot through his side and the bandages pulled as he raised his arm. He tossed the bullet proof vest into his truck. There was plenty of time to put that thing on. He pulled on his jacket and felt for the switch inside his pocket.

Standing on the porch of the Three Rivers rafting company, he listened to music from one of the campsites. Voices carried through the darkness as campers settled in for the night. He gazed at the stars, unfettered by any clouds. Coolness from the night made him zip up his jacket.

Travis was reeling from the last twenty-four hour whirlwind of events. Following up on a hunch, he called Tom Kagan back in California asking for help. Kagan sent back his findings which cinched what Travis suspected. For the last couple of days, he'd slept a total of three hours. With Steele's help, Travis poured over all the case files—security tape from the casino, financial records and computer data linking Scarsbourgh with those he'd been in contact with, and all phone records—trying to match his suspicions to the names in the files. Finally, he'd hit pay dirt. With this information in hand, he'd talked Steele into supporting a plan to flush out the shooter. At least, he hoped the plan would work.

His own survival might depend upon it.

Travis glanced at his watch. Eight p.m. Plenty of time for dinner across the river in Lowell. McPeters would not show for another couple of hours.

A new waitress was serving when he entered. Becky must have taken a night off. Travis picked the same table he and Jessie used that first time they met here. He sat where he could see Three Rivers in the distance. Lights flickered from campsites on the other side of the highway and the river.

The young girl, maybe nineteen, took his order — steak, baked potatoes, corn, and a salad. He felt like he was having his last supper. It had been a while since he ate a full meal.

Another customer left a newspaper on a nearby table. After the waitress returned with his meal, Travis grabbed the paper and began reading.

He had plenty of time to kill.

Travis' cell phone vibrated as he sat in his truck trying to take a nap. He pulled it out and glanced at the caller's number. John Steele. He glanced at his watch and saw it was almost 11 p.m.

"Travis, we're all set. You got the vest on?"

"Nah. I was about to get suited up."

"Well, hurry up, partner. This may be going down real soon."

Travis hung up. He was about to slip the phone into his pocket when he felt another vibration. Another call coming in. He looked at the phone screen and saw the caller display.

McPeters.

Ahead of schedule. Travis reached inside the jacket and flicked on the monitor before he answered the phone.

"Travis, here."

McPeters' voice sounded wary, guarded. "I see you in the truck. I'm watching. Here's what I want. Drive down the road and park where the Lochsa and Selway meet. I'll be waiting ... and watching."

There was a long pause. Travis started to kill the line.

McPeters spoke again. "Don't call anyone. If I see you use that phone, I'm history. And your friends — dead. No one will be able to protect them. Understand?"

"I understand," Travis said, although he thought McPeters' warning strange. He knew the man did not have the guts to kill anyone himself. So, he must be warning Travis that if McPeters disappeared, the killer would be close behind to finish the job. Someone else—whoever McPeters worked for—was the real threat.

Who is McPeters fronting for?

Travis thought of Steele's last admonishment about staying in place. He wondered if surveillance could cover his back once he went mobile. He hoped someone picked up the transmission from his jacket during the phone call. The phone line died. McPeters severed his connection.

He felt his phone vibrate again. Steele? He dared not even look at the display. He let the phone ring until the caller gave up. He couldn't take a chance. He slowly backed up.

He hoped the transmitter hidden in his jacket could reach Steele's receiver. "If you hear me, Steele, here's what McPeters wants." He quickly relayed the suspect's orders. "Sorry to go mobile. But I don't have a choice. He could be watching everything I do."

Travis drove over the lip of the roadway near where the three rivers joined. He got out and started down the embankment, slipping on loose gravel in the dark. Rushing waters filled the night air with the sounds of churning power. The noise threatened to drown any conversations he hoped to record with McPeters. Maybe if he moved closer to the target, he'd get the mike to work. McPeters might want to keep his distance.

He reached the bank and started working downstream. He trudged about twenty yards, using the moonlight's casting halo to guide him in the darkness, when a figure stepped from behind a tree. "McPeters?"

"Who'd you think would be out here?"

Travis edged closer. "Thought you'd bring the person you've been working with."

"Don't get any closer, Travis. And let me see your hands." McPeters started to step back in the shadows, closer to the trees. "Any tricks and I'm history."

Travis held up his hands. "No tricks. Just questions."

"You mentioned we could work out a financial arrangement here. That you'd keep your mouth shut." McPeters appeared to be looking for surveillance. Travis hoped Steele's men—if they were out there—knew how to stay hidden.

"That was before I knew you had a partner."

"A partner?"

"Yeah. I started looking at the security tape of you at the casino. Twice I saw you meeting with Steve Robinette. Just friends or were you guys working together?"

"What are you talking about?" McPeters looked puzzled. Travis could not be sure whether the man purposefully feigned ignorance or if he might be truly confused.

"Look, I know you went down to Santa Rosa and looked up my personnel files under some pretext. Then you must have handed that information off to Phillip Scarsbourgh. How much did you make on that deal?"

McPeters grimly shook his head. "You don't know what you're talking about."

"We don't have to be coy here. After all, you're going to pay me money to keep my mouth shut. That makes us partners, right?"

Travis saw a red dot on McPeters' chest. A laser beam. The dot slowly climbed his chest. One of Steele's snipers? Or someone else?

Dread clenched his stomach.

"McPeters. Anyone else know about this meeting?"

The man shot a glance up the mountainside before quickly turning his attention back toward Travis. "Are you crazy? Who'd I tell?"

"The person who's planted a big red dot on your chest."

"They—" was the last word McPeters blurted out. His head jolted back and he fell to the ground. The shooter hit McPeters with one head shot.

Travis heard the rifle shot echoing a second later. He dove for cover, crawling like a crab for the nearest tree. Once there, he slowly stood up, placing the tree trunk between himself and the shooter. He remembered Steele might be listening.

"Someone took McPeters out. Move in fast."

Before he got the words out, Travis heard men rushing through the brush and sirens howling further down the highway.

Steele closing the trap.

Several men darted across the highway and scrambled down the embankment, Steele leading the charge.

"Travis, you alright?"

"Yeah, I'm fine," he yelled out, coming out from behind the tree. The shooter must be long gone by now with all this activity. "McPeters coded out. A sniper blew the back of his head off. That wasn't friendly fire, right?"

"My men know better than to take him out unless I give the green light."

"That just leaves one person."

"Yeah, but we're stuck here for awhile. I'll call the boss for a shooting team to respond. Did he give you anything that would give us exigent circumstances?"

"On whose place?"

"Robinette's."

Travis shook his head. "No. He never had a chance to give me any names."

Steele drew closer. "Then we're stuck. We'll serve paper on the casino manager as soon as we can get free. That was who McPeters called from the casino? Robinette's home phone?"

"That's what the subscriber records show. We never had a chance to follow up on Robinette after Jessie was taken. We cut him loose in all the confusion so we could find Scarsbourgh. We need to see if there is a paper trail connecting Robinette and McPeters."

"I wonder what McPeters and Robinette were cooking up."

Travis looked at the crumpled man at his feet. "McPeters can't tell us anymore. Someone made sure of it."

Chapter 71

The shooting team kept Travis sequestered for nearly twelve hours before his interrogation. He had curled up on a cot at the sheriff's office and caught up on his sleep while waiting. Earlier, they let him call Jessie so she did not hear it on the news first. He brought her up to date.

Frank was slowly recuperating. "He's as feisty as ever," Jessie said, laughing.

Frank insisted on getting on the line. Travis repeated the news. "So you think Steve Robinette is good for the McPeters shooting?"

"Maybe," Travis said. "What about you?"

"I don't know. I've known Steve since he was a kid. He might be a lot of things, but I don't see him as a killer."

"Maybe not. But all the evidence seems to match up. Maybe I'll know more later when we hit the house."

"Don't be so sure. Just keep your eyes and ears wide open."

"I will, Frank. You take care."

"What else can I do? With Jessie here, I can't even go to the head by myself."

Once the interview was over, they cleared him to return to the case.

The investigation pushed back the intended search warrant on Robinette's residence until Steele and everyone involved in the shooting case could return to full duty.

A search team, armed with warrants, converged on the briefing room for patrol officers. It was mid-afternoon before they regrouped to execute the arrest and search. John Steele briefed everyone and led the caravan to

Steve Robinette's residence. Travis followed them, leaving his truck parked at the bottom of the road below the suspect's house. Travis climbed into Steele's car. He hoped to head up to Spokane after they hit the Robinette house if everything went as planned.

Steele and a couple of his men marched up to the front door, while others fanned out to cover the exterior. Travis trailed behind Steele.

Robinette yanked the door open before Steele finished his knock and notice. "What now?"

Officers crouched, leveling their weapons at the suspect. Steele stepped forward. "Mr. Robinette. I've got a warrant for your arrest and a search warrant for these premises. Stand back, turn around and place your hands on your head."

"Do you know—"

"I said, stand back and place your hands on your head."

Reluctantly, Robinette raised his hands and turned.

"Interlock your fingers," Steele ordered, bowing the man out after grasping his hands and bringing him slightly off balance. The detective pat-searched Robinette before cuffing him.

Jean Robinette emerged from the living room. "Steve?"

"Get my attorney on the phone," Robinette said, glaring at Steele until he saw Travis. "You behind this? Can't make a real case, so you go on a fishing expedition?"

Jean disappeared, one of the deputies trailing her. Other officers began a security sweep to make sure no one else was in the building. They returned a few minutes later empty-handed.

Steele marched Robinette into the living room, and sat his prisoner down on the sofa, after searching it thoroughly.

Jean came down the hallway, the same deputy shadowing. "I got hold of the attorney. He said to say nothing until he has a chance to talk with you."

Steele motioned for the woman to sit down in one of the stuffed chairs opposite the sofa. Steve Robinette looked at them with contempt. "So what did I supposedly do?"

Jean leaned forward. "Steve, the attorneys said—"

"Shut up. I know what I'm doing." He glared at her before turning his attention toward Travis. "So what do you think you have on me?"

Steele interjected. "Mr. Robinette, I need to advise you of your rights. You have—"

"I know my rights. I don't need you to read them to me."

"Are you waiving those rights?"

"Are you a moron? I'm talking , aren't I? I've got nothing to hide."

Steele nodded to Travis.

Travis walked around to face Robinette. "Mr. Robinette, Detective Steele is recording our conversation. I want to advise you once again of—"

"Don't bore me. Let's get down to business."

"I take it that you've waived your right."

"Take it however you want. Just answer my questions. What do you think I did?"

"I think you hired Phillip Scarsbourgh—"

"Who?"

"You knew him as John Ares. You hired him to fix some financial problems you thought Tommy White Eagle created to halt the Three Rivers development."

Robinette looked at Travis for a moment, understanding creeping in his eyes. "You think I ordered Tommy killed? You're crazy."

"And you had the killer try to take me out. When he failed, you shot Frank White Eagle and later killed Kent McPeters to shut him up."

"Who? McPeters? You mean that drunk from the casino?" Robinette laughed. "That guy doesn't have the brains to even play a good hand of cards. Why'd I want him out of the picture?"

"Just before Tommy disappeared, McPeters called you here at your home."

"That's a lie, I never ..." Robinette stopped, glancing from Travis to his wife. His eyes widened for a moment, then narrowed in anger. "I've got nothing else to say. I want to talk to my attorney."

Travis looked at Steve Robinette and then at Jean, sensing these two finally reached an understanding that did not exist a moment ago. Travis strived to understand what sparked this understanding but their eyes gave nothing away. Steve's eyes seemed to tighten with anger. Jean's eyes remained expressionless. They told him nothing.

Twilight cast a gloominess across the valley below as Steele and his men finished their search. A setting sun silhouetted the mountains in dark purple while painting the sky a pink glaze. Travis waited outside, watching the last rays of sun slipping behind the western mountain range. Footsteps on the porch drew his attention back to the house. Steele strode toward him.

"Anything interesting?"

Steele shook his head. "Hard to tell. We took every scrap of paper we could find, all the computer files and hard drives, and seized every phone. I've got them tagging and bagging every weapon in the house. A small arsenal in there. Maybe we'll get lucky and match one to the shootings."

A deputy marched Steve Robinette out of the house with hands cuffed behind. The deputy protected Robinette's head with a black-gloved hand as the casino manager backed into the rear seat of the patrol car. Steve settled in, glowering at Travis as the deputy slammed the door shut.

Travis heard a garage door open and turned to see a black Mercedes sedan backing out.

Steele followed his gaze. "We let Mrs. Robinette go. Said she had to get out of the house. This hit her pretty hard."

Travis watched Jean angle the Mercedes, turning the wheel to give her a straight shot on the circular driveway. Her backup lights seemed brighter as twilight gave way to the blackness of night. Watching the car pull away, Travis fished in his pocket for his truck keys. "Unless you need me for something, I'm going to head up to Spokane and check in on Frank and Jessie."

Steele nodded. "No. I think this is a wrap. We'll have plenty of time to go through this evidence. And Steve Robinette's arrest report will practically write itself. I'll let you know if we come across any surprises. Want a ride down the hill?"

Travis nodded and climbed into Steele's car. "Let's get out of here."

As they neared his truck. Travis turned toward Steele. "Jessie talked about a cabin Phillip Scarsbourgh held her in before he moved her to my place. You guys ever find it?"

"Man, we've been up to our eyeballs in paperwork and follow-up. It's on my list of things to do. Ever since Frank shot him, we've put it on the back burner. Why?"

Travis shrugged. "Just loose ends. One of those things that's nagging me." He stepped from the car and leaned in through the window. "Jessie said she thought it was close to my place. Just the other side of the river and up the mountainside a ways. There was a path leading past it down the mountainside to the highway."

"Yeah. Well, we'll get to it one of these days."

"Mind if I poke around?"

"Not at all. Just one more thing my office won't have to follow up on."

"Great. Mind if I borrow a flashlight? I think I'll check that out before heading up to the hospital."

Steele reached across the seat, flashlight in hand. "Here, take mine."

Travis grabbed the light. "Thanks. I'll let you know if I find anything."

Steele waved as he drove away. Travis climbed in and started up his truck. In a few minutes, he was on Highway 12 heading east. He wondered where Jean Robinette was headed. Probably anywhere she could get away from her husband.

He punched the accelerator. Sooner he checked this out, the quicker he'd be in Spokane with Jessie. The thought made him drive faster.

Chapter 72

As Travis reached his cabin, his cell phone vibrated. Steele's number flashed on the phone's LCD screen. He quickly accepted the call.

Steele sounded angry. "Robinette clammed up and demanded a lawyer. We got nothing out of him."

"Thanks for the update," Travis said. "You won't be able to reach me for awhile. I'll be looking for that place where Scarsbourgh held Jessie. Check with you later."

Travis hung up and grabbed several flashlight batteries from his cabin, sticking them in his backpack. He stuck a .40 cal auto in his waistband, and slung his hunting rifle over one shoulder. He knew it made more sense to wait until light, but the mystery surrounding Phillip Scarsbourgh continued to haunt him. And the sooner he could find out about this man, the more he might understand why all this happened.

And zero in on the second sniper.

Scarsbourgh drugged Jessie before moving her from his cabin which accounted for her distorted memory. The hideaway needed to be accessible from the Lolo Trail after the kidnapping. Crossing any main highways or roads with Jessie in tow would have been a risk. He wouldn't want to bring her across the highway to Travis' place unless absolutely necessary. Search teams crisscrossed the main roads looking for Jessie and her abductor during that time.

Travis crossed to the highway-side of the river and began searching along the roadway. A full moon crested to the east, and cold light began to rain down upon the canyon floor. The tall trees basked in the glow of moonlight, their dark branches coated with silver, the outline of trees dark against a blue-black sky.

He knew Scarsbourgh used horses to move Jessie, so he began flashing a light along the brush on the north side of the road working his way east. He trudged for a half mile before seeing impressions in loose soil. Horseshoes pressed into fresh dirt, ending at the edge of the highway. This is where Scarsbourgh must have crossed over.

He began to follow the telltale signs of horses up the mountainside, knowing the Lolo Trail ran among the ridges above. A few hundred yards into the woods, he saw the print merge with a shoulder-width fire trail snaking its way up the hillside. He began following the trail and the still-fresh markings left by horses. Fresh tire tracks told him this trail had been used as a driveway by someone.

He heard an occasional vehicle whoosh past down below on the highway. He listened to the sounds of night as he walked; crickets calling to each other, an occasional squawk from birds nesting above, and the ever-rushing Clearwater River below.

Winded, he came to the first ridge top. The path began to descend beyond its crest, a trail still marked by fresh U-shaped horse tracks.

An inner rush, fueled by a mixture of curiosity and adrenaline, drove him forward. This familiar feeling always came to him when he felt a case might be coming together. At one point in his life this *chase*—this is what he liked to call it—took over and seemed to consume him. Blinding him to everything else. All that changed after Michelle's death when he realized the brutal consequences of charging ahead without considering the cost to those around him. Tonight, his compulsion to find the truth was tempered with what this case already cost others.

Tommy, Frank and Jessie.

He hoped to find more answers. But he knew what was really important. He was doing this to end the threat against the lives of those he cared about, and not to quench an inner need to find out the truth regardless of the cost.

Travis' only hope of getting into Scarsbourgh's mind and identifying the second killer—after the murders of McPeters, Wyatt, and

Foster—seemed to be looking for what the killers left behind. A diary of Scarsbourgh's insanity would be nice. Anything that might help Travis understand this man's twisted mind and identify his partner. Everyone seemed to think Robinette was good for second chair in these serial killings, but something he saw in Robinette's eyes made him think the killer might be someone else.

Travis' flashlight started to dim. He slipped off his backpack and felt for fresh batteries inside. His fingers located them. He flicked off the light, and quickly replaced the worn with the new. Another flick and light illuminated the ground at his feet.

He just started down the trail when he heard a horse whinny ahead.

Flicking off the flashlight, he stood in the darkness, listening.

Silence.

The sounds of night he heard earlier seemed to have died. Only stillness descended.

How long could he play this waiting game? Standing here all night would not get him to Spokane. And he knew he needed his flashlight to follow the trail. He felt foolish standing here in the dark. Most of the suspects in the case were either dead or in jail. There was no reason to go tip-toeing through the forest.

Unless Robinette was not the second shooter. Unless someone else shot Frank and killed McPeters.

That killer might still be on the loose.

A good reason to proceed with caution. But still, he couldn't stand here all night. And he needed light to continue.

He flicked on the flashlight and started down the trail. The horse he heard probably belonged to someone living up here. An innocent party not involved in this case. Besides, sounds carry in the dark. That horse might be a long way off.

At the bottom of the next ravine, the path rose once more. A few hundred yards further up the slope, it leveled off into a small meadow. Moonlight filtered down between the trees and illuminated grassland.

What he saw ahead made him flick off his light.

Two dwellings loomed before him, a cabin on the right near the edge of the meadow and off to the left, a small stable. He heard a horse calling from a paddock. Windows revealed the inside of the cabin to be blacker than the night sky. He slipped out of the rifle sling, lowed the weapon to chamber a round, and brought it up to the ready as he entered the meadow. Jessie's mind had been foggy, but she described her place of captivity as similar to this layout. And this was the direction Scarsbourgh came when he brought Jessie down from the mountain.

He skirted the edge of the forest until he neared the stable. A dirt road entered the meadow from below. Somehow, he'd missed where this road connected to the highway below. Something else he'd missed.

Travis glanced over at the darkened cabin, then inside the stable. He worked his way around the meadow until he came to the stable. He quickly peered inside. No one. A horse sharply raised its head as Travis entered. He slowly walked toward the animal, calling to it as he looked for any tack left behind. If this was Scarsbourgh's place, maybe he left one of his horses behind.

The animal had access to a corral through an opening on the far side of stall. He saw fresh hay pitched on the ground. Someone visited this place since Frank shot Scarsbourgh. Fear wrapped its fingers around his throat. He felt like a target with a huge bulls-eye pinned to his back. He forced himself to calm down.

He stood in the shadows of the barn, eyeing the meadow outside and the cabin beyond.

Nothing moved.

Once outside, he gripped the rifle and edged toward the darkened cabin, again feeling like a moving target as bright moonlight poured upon him. It seemed like an eternity before he crossed the open grassland and neared the cabin. Wood creaked beneath his feet as Travis climbed the stairs to the front porch. He put his ear against the door for a moment.

Nothing.

He saw only darkness through the windows. Gingerly, he shouldered the rifle, withdrew his handgun and turned the doorknob. It rotated in his grasp.

Unlocked.

He thrust the door open, flashing his light—up and at an angle with his left hand—while griping the pistol in his right.

Empty.

He scanned the room as his breathing returned to normal. An unmade bed, a sea chest, and a couple chairs near the fireplace. He saw an oil lantern sitting above the fireplace. He holstered his sidearm and searched until he found some matches. Grasping the lantern, he lit the wick and returned the flickering oil burner to the mantle, its mandarin-orange flame struggled to push away darkness. He lowered the rifle from his shoulder and left it leaning on the wall near the fireplace.

He continued to use the flashlight in his search for brighter illumination. The sea chest sat at the foot of the bed. He knelt down and undid the clasp, raising the lid to peer inside. Men's clothing—shirts, underwear, and denim jeans—carefully folded inside. He felt beneath the clothing, grasping a leather binder. He placed the binder on the bed and opened it.

There was a yellow envelope nestled inside. He opened the envelope and pulled out a half dozen photographs. He began to go through each photo, one after another. Somewhere in the middle of the stack, one photo immediately captured his attention and made the hair on his neck rise.

It was a photo of himself and Michelle Scarsbourgh taken at Doran Beach in California.

It felt like someone just punched him in the gut.

This was Scarsbourgh's cabin.

A branch cracked outside. He stopped breathing, trapping air in his lungs as he strained to hear. Slowly, he reached down and quietly upholstered his weapon.

No more sounds.

He flicked off the flashlight, doused the lantern, before creeping toward the doorway. He'd left the door standing open. He quickly stepped out on the porch and shifted to one side where he could stand in the protection of darkness.

No sounds. Nothing moved.

He slowly relaxed. Must be hearing things. Stepping off the porch, he edged his way around the cabin with his back to the wall, searching for any movement.

Again, nothing.

After returning to the front porch, Travis went back inside and closed the door. He re-lighted the lantern before kneeling by the bed to go through the photos one by one. The others were Michelle with friends, and one photo of brother and sister. It looked like the photo had been taken at Fisherman's Wharf in San Francisco. He could make out the Pier 39 sign in the background.

Once he examined each of the photos, he left them on the bed and returned to the chest. He removed the clothes and saw a stack of letters bound together at the bottom.

The letters were written in a woman's handwriting, and addressed to John Ares using his business address in Seattle. The sender was not identified. He opened the first letter and began reading. A love letter. He turned the letter over to see who signed it.

The name written on the letter made him clench his teeth.

He heard a sound outside. The horse gave out another whinny.

Travis snatched the bundle of letters, his flashlight and crept toward the fireplace. He quickly extinguished the lantern and stood in the dark, listening. Now he had the advantage. It was darker in the cabin than outside. He edged toward the window and peered out.

The meadow seemed void of life. The forest crept within a few yards of the cabin to his left. Otherwise, an expansive pasture spread outward, giving him a clear view of anything or anyone approaching.

He scanned outside. Still nothing.

The only area that made him wary was the edge of the forest to his left. He could not stay here. Once outside, he'd make a dash for the trail and return to the highway. He had the letters. Tomorrow, he'd bring John Steele and the others back here for a better search.

Right now, he just wanted to make it out alive.

He took one last look outside. Maybe his mind was playing tricks. He slipped on his backpack, shoved his handgun into his waistband, and grabbed the rifle. Slowly, he turned the knob and opened the door. He pushed it open with his foot and waited to see what might happen.

Silence.

He crept through the doorway and made it halfway across the porch when he saw a red laser beam aimed at his heart. He froze, unable to bring his rifle up in time. The shooter had the advantage.

"Travis, move slow and easy. I'll take my letters, thank you."

Jean Robinette stepped from the clearing, a rifle leveled at his chest.

Chapter 73

Jean Robinette stood only yards away. Moonlight seemed to fill the night with illumination as if breaking from a cloud. Everything became almost as clear as day. She sighted down the bore. "You know I'm an excellent shot, Travis. You've seen the trophies. No sudden moves or you'll join the others."

He stood in place, watching her.

"Now, very slowly, lower that rifle to the ground."

He obeyed.

"Again, slowly pull out that handgun by two fingers and throw it on the ground. Now."

Travis bit his lip in frustration. He felt like a rookie cop. Frustrated, he followed her commands, clutching the flashlight in his left hand.

"Good boy. Now, I'll take my letters, thank you."

Travis clutched them with his right hand, his flashlight still in his left. "You made two mistakes, Jean. The first mistake was Frank. You missed him—he survived."

"That's a mistake I'll rectify later. Right now, I've got you in my sights. And I can't miss from here." She squinted at him. "What do you mean two mistakes?"

"You missed shooting my dog before he attacked your boyfriend."

The woman's face tightened. "I was looking for humans to shoot. The dog surprised me. He attacked before I saw what was happening. But now I can correct everything ... starting with you."

Travis began to slowly slide to his left, closer to the edge of the cabin. He started talking, trying to distract. "I don't get it, Jean. You were in love with Scarsbourgh?"

"I don't expect you to understand. Yeah, I loved him in my own way. And he was my ticket to freedom."

"Freedom? You had everything. A beautiful home, plenty of money. What more did you want?"

He saw the front sight of the rifle lower slightly as she spoke. "I was trapped. Steve only wanted to show me off like some kind of big game he'd bagged. He never loved me. But Scarsbourgh—Phillip— in his own way loved me. Without any strings attached."

"Okay. But why'd you involve McPeters?"

Jean raised the rifle, pointing it once more at his chest. "McPeters is a drunken fool who thought I *might* love him. He saw a chance at money and love. He'd have done anything I told him. But in the end, he was just another weak man."

Travis nodded. "You have answered another question I had about Phillip taking Jessie."

"I never said anything about that."

Travis edged a little closer. "I wondered how Phillip could be in two places at once. He kidnapped Jessie from her cabin. At the same time, he left a tape recorder and note in my cabin telling me what I needed to do to get her back. There was no way he could have pulled that off by himself. By the time I got to my cabin with Frank, Phillip was still high up in the mountains with Jessie working his way back to his cabin. Right?"

Jean shrugged, slowly moved closer. They were now only a few yards apart. "Took you long enough to figure that out. Too long. Now, I'll take those letters."

"Here they are," Travis said, slowly raising his right hand toward her.

"Just put them on the ground and move away. Slowly."

He placed them on the ground and began to step back. As Jean reached down Travis flicked the flashlight directly into her eyes and then flicked it off. Just enough to blind. He leaped to the left as he heard the first rifle shot. The bullet slammed into the wall as he dove around the edge of the cabin.

He scrambled into the woods a few yards away before Jean could round the corner. He heard her running after him. He dove deeper into the tree line, running and stumbling in the dark.

He had one advantage. At least momentarily, he'd destroyed her night vision with the flashlight. Her sight would quickly return. By then, he hoped to be deep into the forest. Travis circled around until he knew he was the near the trail. He paused, listening. No footsteps followed. Just silence.

Then he heard the horse from the stable. A short time later he heard hoof beats through the meadow. Jean was riding away. A sense of relief swept over him for a moment. Then panic struck.

He remembered Jean's last warning about Frank. A mistake to be rectified. She was on her way to kill Frank and Jessie.

He used the flashlight to find the path down the mountain, running and crashing through brush. He knew he'd never beat her to the highway.

The horse gave Jean a significant head start.

Travis finally burst out of the forest and began dashing along the highway toward his truck. He flicked off the flashlight, moonlight giving him enough light to find his way. He'd left the cell phone locked inside. He kept looking over his shoulder looking for the woman.

Jean Robinette seemed to have vanished.

He anticipated horse and rider might bear down at any time, but he saw nothing at the moment. Maybe she stashed a vehicle nearby, already on her way to Spokane.

Travis raced toward his truck twenty yards ahead. He took a deep breath and slid behind the steering wheel, groping along the seat until he found where he'd tossed the cell phone. He activated the phone, starting the engine while waiting for the phone's signal to reach a cell tower. Once the display announced service, he punched in Steele's cell phone number.

Placing the truck in gear, he started down the highway just as a horse and rider cleared the forest directly in his path.

Jean Robinette.

He floored the accelerator and leaned over to use the dash as a shield. He peered over the dash, keeping his right foot on the gas pedal and tossing the cell phone onto the seat, still activated. He heard Steele's voice calling out.

No time for phone calls.

Jean aimed her rifle at his windshield,

She fired once. Glass began to spider across the front window from a single rifle shot, the bullet whizzing past and smashing the rear window behind his head. Another shot cracked the glass further as he swept past. A third shot shattered the forward window, passing through the rear broken window and narrowly missing his raised head. The last shot passed through the broken rear window and zipped past his raised head.

He sat up once out of range, glancing for the phone's glow. He snatched the phone up and heard Steele yelling.

"What the heck is going on there, Travis? That gunfire?"

Travis glanced in his rearview, Jean Robinette no longer in sight. "We got the wrong Robinette, pal. Jean is the shooter. Just took out the windows of my pickup."

"You alright?"

"A little glass in my hair. Otherwise, fine."

"I'll start sending units now."

"She'll be long gone before they arrive. I think she'll be going for Jessie and Frank. I'm heading up to Spokane right now. Can you get Spokane PD to sit on them until we set up?"

"Sure. I've got three deputies with them right now. Just to be safe, I'll ask for reinforcements until we can shut down that part of the hospital."

"Great. I'll fill you in on the details later. At some point, we need to get some people up to that cabin I told you about. I'll give you the 10-20 later. I suspect you'll find more evidence."

"We're stretched thin right now, but I'll see what I can do. My priority right now is to make sure our friends at the hospital survive."

Travis started breathing easier. "Thanks, John. I don't think she's crazy enough to take on the cops. But I'd feel better knowing there's security around them until we can get our hands on her."

He heard Steele chuckle. "Two of a kind, huh? Jean and Scarsbourgh. Bonnie and Clyde."

"Yeah. Let's get her in custody."

"I'll start working on that right now." Steele hung up.

 **Chapter 74**

Spokane, Washington

Travis reached the hospital several hours later. Steele kept his word. His men stood locked and loaded, one inside Frank's room and two others outside. A field supervisor from Spokane PD dropped by and added more security.

Jessie was sitting by Frank's side when he entered. "Willie boy has been busy." She smiled, her eyes retaining the sparkle he remembered the first time they met.

He laughed.

Frank gave him a weak grin. "Man, I pull your bacon out of one fire, and you turn around and jump right back in. What's it with you and women?" Frank winced. "Sorry. Must be the drugs."

"Or a case of stupid," Jessie said, putting her arms around Travis' waist, hugging him. "It's good to see you."

"Thanks. And Frank, don't sweat it. I'll never be able to repay you for saving our butts. You can spout off whatever you want."

"Okay. How about this? What's your intentions toward my daughter?"

Jessie gasped. "Dad. Please."

Frank gave Travis a stern look, and then broke into a grin. "I guess that crack on my head did more damage than I thought. Just couldn't resist." He pointed to a chair near him. "Now, let's get down to business. What's this stuff about Jean Robinette? I have to confess, I didn't see that one coming."

Travis circled the bed. "Me either, Frank. One thing bugged me after you shot Scarsbourgh. Everyone thought McPeters was the killer's go-to guy. I just didn't see him as backing Scarsbourgh's play. Too stupid, if you ask me. I would have put money on Steve Robinette."

Frank nodded. "So where do you think Jean's hiding?"

"She could be anywhere. I just want to make sure she's not lurking around here."

Frank waved his hand. "She'd be stupid to try anything here. If she had any brains, she'd be in Canada by now."

Travis nodded, drawing up a chair and sitting down next to Jessie. "Well, we'll just have to wait and see."

The hospital door opened and John Steele emerged. He smiled at Travis and Jessie, turning to Frank. "Good to see you sitting up and talking, Chief. You had us worried."

"Thanks. Any word on the woman?"

Steele shook his head. "We found her car abandoned along the river. She just vamoosed. We put a BOLO to everyone, and gave her photo out in a press release. It should be plastered all over the news in the next few hours. She won't be able to go anywhere without people spotting her."

Travis thought of his encounter with Jean at Scarsbourgh's cabin. "I don't think she'll run, Steele. She's got another agenda."

"Like what?" The detective glanced at Travis with curiosity. "She'd be crazy to stick around if everyone is hunting for her."

"Something drew her to that cabin. I think it was letters or memories."

"She thought they might reveal her involvement?"

"Nah. I think it was more than that. Her feelings for Scarsbourgh ran deep. She risked everything to return to that cabin. To get those letters. They represented the only thing left of Scarsbourgh. That and her memories."

Jessie leaned over and hugged her father. "I just want this woman caught and have this whole mess behind us so we can get back to normal."

A frown furrowed Jessie's brow. Travis guessed she was thinking of Tommy. He knew it would be a long time before anything seemed normal again. He would watch over these two as if his life depended upon it.

Until they nailed Jean Robinette.

Two weeks passed as law enforcement searched for Jean Robinette. She simply vanished without a trace. Travis hovered around the hospital until Frank received permission to return home to recuperate. "I'd like the two of you to stay at my place until this thing blows over. Easier to protect you there until she's found," Travis said, already seeing Frank starting to protest. "Come on, Frank. It's the least I can do after what you did for me."

He glanced over at Jessie and her father as the doctor approached. "And I've got a little surprise. A friend of mine—from one of the surveillance companies I've worked with in the past—loaned me some state-of-the-art stuff. We'll have 360-degree coverage around my place. You can relax and get well without any worry."

Frank finally gave him a scowling consent just as Travis wheeled him from the hospital. Officers trailed behind them while others took point as they passed through the corridors and out into the parking lot. Temperatures hovered in the low 80s, as warm breezes gusted through the parking structure. Jessie entered the truck cab first, followed by Frank. Travis swung himself behind the steering wheel after placing Frank's luggage in the bed of the truck. He'd replaced the damaged windows since his run-in with Jean Robinette and swept up the broken glass.

Steele arranged for an escort back to the Clearwater. Travis followed one of the patrol vehicles from the parking lot, while another deputy followed behind. "Sort of like a presidential convoy, Frank. They must like you down there."

Frank shrugged. "Nah, they just want to prevent one more shooting case. They've got enough to handle right now."

"Steele said they're stretched thin, but he still coughed up enough guys to baby-sit you. Nice touch, this escort."

"Just get me out of here, Travis. It's time to go home."

 **Chapter 75**

Clearwater River, Idaho

A beeping red light on the console made Travis rush to the monitor. He clicked the mouse to link the numbered light to the triggered web cam. He caught a glimpse of a dark shadow retreating into the forest.

Someone tripped the alarm beam nearest his cabin.

"Frank, Jessie. Kill the lights."

Darkness swept the cabin except for a white sheen from the monitor. The shadow never returned. He knew for sure the figure he saw was human, not animal. He wondered what scared off the intruder. He heard Sam's tail beating the floor.

Only one person still alive cared whether he and the others were in this cabin.

His fingers gripped a holstered firearm at his side. Travis flicked off the monitor, letting darkness bathe the room in its protective shield. His hands found the rifle, leaning against the wall next to him.

"I'll be back in a while," Travis said, opening the back door a crack. He scanned the forest with a night scope. No movement. "Sam. Come!" He felt the dog nudge, starting to whine. "Hush!"

Jessie moved close. "Be careful, Travis. Don't take chances."

He smiled into the darkness. "I started taking chances the day I met you. Why stop now?"

Her hand brushed his cheek. "You know what I mean."

He clasped her hand gently. "Give Steele a call and tell him the alarm's tripped. Tell him I'm checking it now." He slipped through the door, closing it quietly behind him.

Moving further into the trees, he sat on his haunches, listening, and waiting. He used the night scope to scan in the direction of the alarm.

Still nothing.

He sat motionless for another ten minutes. He'd hired a specialist from the old days to install a security blanket around his cabin — trip laser beams hidden along selected paths, surveillance cameras and web cams, replete with night vision scopes.

A mini-CIA encampment.

No longer could Jean sit on the other side of the river and take sniper shots at them. He'd shuttered the windows and the front door remained closed and locked. They never crossed over to the highway unless Steele had set up a perimeter of deputies for protection.

Still, it felt like prison. He had to figure another game plan. This search for the killer might go on for some time.

He learned something about Jean Robinette that night she cornered him at the cabin. She would never disappear. Not until she finished her task. Revenge would bring her back like an unrelenting wave. Somewhere along the way, Scarsbourgh enticed her into his world of twisted logic, of right and wrong that only made sense to two twisted individuals. A world in which she felt justified in killing Travis and others.

And now she had nothing left to lose but her life.

He stayed there for another half-hour, Sam lying at his feet, alert but quiet. A gray dawn crept through the trees, giving a hint of the day to come. Forest sounds returned, telling him whoever approached the cabin must have left. A plan began to form in his mind. He quietly rose and walked back to the cabin, knocking twice on the rear door. "It's me, Travis."

The door creaked. Jessie stood in the threshold. "She's gone?"

He nodded, closing the door behind him. "I have an idea. Were you able to raise Steele?"

Jessie shook her head. "Couldn't get through. Dispatch said he was out on a call, and the closest deputy is an hour away. They won't run lights and siren unless the danger is imminent."

He nodded, turning to Frank. "My guess is she's headed back to Scarsbourgh's cabin. I'm going to take Sam and try to track her down. You two hold down the fort until Steele and his deputies arrive. Okay?"

Frank nodded.

Jessie cut in. "Hey. You're not leaving me stuck here. I'm coming with you."

"Jessie, I can't concentrate on what I've got to do if I'm worried about your safety."

Her chin jutted out. "I'm not just going to sit around here and twiddle my thumbs while you're traipsing through the woods. Dad's in no shape to go and you need back-up. Besides, I'm a better shot than dad."

Travis glanced at Frank. "She's kidding, right?"

Frank grinned. "She's the best shot in the family. I think you're stuck."

He felt his stomach tighten. "I can't let you—"

"—you can't stop me, Travis. You need me."

Frank looked at him soberly. "I think she's right. I'm no use to you right now, and Jessie can—"

"—Okay, okay," Travis said. "I give up but you've got to do exactly what I tell you. For your own safety. Agreed?"

She fluttered her eyes. "Oh, Travis. I always listen to what you say, don't I?'

"You've never listened to me." He tried to look stern, until he saw Frank smile. Travis shook his head. "Okay, let's get our gear and move out." He turned toward Frank. "Keep trying to get in touch with Steele. Tell him where we're headed."

He watched Jessie gather her things as he tried to make himself believe this was the right move, but he couldn't shake the belief he ought to go it alone. Just he and the dog. The last time he let someone change his mind, someone wound up dead.

Chapter 76

A few minutes later they finished packing, slung rifles, and quietly slipped out of the cabin by the rear entrance. Travis learned from his last encounter with Jean Robinette. A night scope, attached to his rifle, and a pair of night-scope glasses were part of his tools this time.

Travis led them to where he last saw the intruder.

"Sam, here!" he said, pointing to a boot impression in the earth. The dog sniffed the ground excitedly, growling in a low snarl. "Sam. Find."

Sam wagged his tail and bounded forward through the woods. They moved quickly, keeping the dog in sight. From time to time, Travis let out a low whistle which brought the animal hustling back. The dog led them in a large circle, first in an easterly direction and then a slow arching curve to the river below. Travis saw where horse hooves churned up the riverbank, wet hooves digging up dry soil.

"She brought a horse and crossed here," He pointed to the far bank. "Ready to get a little wet?"

Jessie nodded. Travis led them across the riverbed, water reaching his chest at midstream. He looked back and saw Jessie holding her rifle above her head with both hands, water almost reaching her shoulders. Sam paddled ahead and leaped ashore before Travis, shaking water from his fur while eyeing them.

Once across the river, they clambered up a boulder-strewn embankment, crossed the highway, and found the trail continuing on the far side. The prints led into the woods and up the mountain slope.

"It looks like she's headed back to the cabin," he said, pointing north. A few moments later he saw Sam go rigid, the dog staring into the brush. Travis motioned to Jessie to take cover.

Sam stood still, barely moving even his tail, finally turning back toward Travis as if seeking instructions. He motioned the dog toward him. As Travis rubbed Sam's head, he scanned the trees and brush where the dog alerted.

Only silence. Nothing moved.

The only movement was an early morning breeze rustling the leaves of a bay tree. He edged up to where Sam had stopped and glanced down. There, two sets of hoof prints—one leading east and another continuing up toward Scarsbourgh's cabin.

He crept back to where Jessie lay behind a tree. "Jean had help," he whispered, still looking for movement. "Now we have two horses, each now going in separate directions."

"Someone else? Which one should we follow?"

"Let's head toward the cabin."

Jessie shrugged and shouldered her backpack. Travis grabbed Sam by the collar to get him following the trail leading to the cabin. The dog resisted, giving a low whine and tugging in the direction of the prints leading away from the cabin.

Quietly, Travis leaned down and spoke softly to Sam. He pointed to the tracks he wanted to follow, trying to make the animal understand. The dog finally relented and they pushed on into the woods.

He signaled them to take a break a half hour later near the top of the first ridge. Jessie came and sat near him, whispering. "Why do you think Jean might head to the cabin?"

Travis put his index finger against his lips, signaling they needed to speak quieter. "My guess is the cabin is a place she feels safe," he whispered. "And it was the last place they shared together before he kidnapped you. She knows the cops already searched this place, so she figures it is safe to return."

Jessie matched his whisper. "But she knows cops must be watching the place. Why would she risk going back?"

"Maybe there's no other place to run and she is playing the odds."

"That's crazy," she said.

"Not that crazy. Gives her a place to hide close by while trying to nail us."

Jessie rose, shaking her head. "I sort of feel sorry for her."

Travis scoffed. "Remember, she tried to kill your dad. And she's trying to finish the job on all three of us."

"I know." She gave him a half smile. "But to lose someone you love. It must hurt. That's all I'm saying."

Travis shouldered his backpack. *Women.* He started up the trail, mulling over Jessie's comment. Losing someone you love does hurt. He knew that feeling and never wanted to experience it again. He regretted bringing Jessie here. Once again putting someone he cared about in danger.

Jean and he might have something in common after all. Painful loss.

And Jean? A person driven by loss and revenge. He thought of that for a moment, thinking Jessie might be right. Maybe, in a small way, he should feel sorry for this woman. And then he thought of Frank lying on the ground, bleeding and unconscious. No. He did not feel sorry for her. She'd made her choice. Now it was time to face the consequences.

Travis shouldered his rifle and trudged up the trail. He'd make sure Jessie and Frank never fell in Jean's crosshairs again. He'd be ready this time.

And he'd make sure they survived.

Travis was wrong. Tracks at first led toward the cabin and then began to veer away up the mountainside. All the way up to the Lolo Trail. Morning gave way to afternoon, and afternoon slowly gave way to another sunset. They trudged ahead, mile after mile, until the sun was starting to set. As dusk settled, the trail seemed to finally circle back and lead them in the direction of Scarsbourgh's cabin once again.

Quietly, Sam lead the way and Jessie followed behind Travis. Even the dog seemed to sense stealth meant survival. Jean Robinette appeared to be very cautious about approaching the cabin, leading a wide circle to the backside of the property.

Darkness enveloped them. He knew the cabin was just below. He called Sam back, signaling the dog to lay down.

Several times during their hike, Travis heard the rotor blades of a helicopter overhead, sweeping back and forth across the mountain slopes. Must be Steele's crew searching. The copter always pulled away, leaving the forest in its own kind of silence.

Travis thought he heard a horse near the meadow. Not in the stable area, but further to his right, beyond the cabin, somewhere in the forest beyond. Whatever moonlight they had earlier seemed to gain in intensity. There was almost no need for the night scope except to peer into the shadows. There was enough illumination—between moonlight and the night scope—to get a clear look at everything. He lay sprawled out on the ground and eyed every square foot of land between the cabin and the stables.

No movement.

Jean might never see them approach if she was inside.

He motioned to Jessie to slip back into the brush. "I'm going to try to get close to the buildings to see what I can. Maybe we can end this now."

"Be careful." Jessie wrapped the rifle sling around her arm and sighted down the barrel. "I'll cover you from here."

Travis handed his rifle to her. "Take mine. It's got the night scope, and I've got night-vision glasses. That way we both will be set."

Sam sprang up, growling. "Sam, stay! The dog crouched down, quivering. "Keep him here," he said without looking at Jessie. He studied the terrain for a moment.

The dog continued to growl. Travis turned and saw the dog glaring into the brush behind him. He reached out to try to quiet the dog, but no amount of petting would silence Sam.

"Sam, shut up!" Travis said, trying to keep his voice above a whisper and still carry force. He shook the dog's collar with force. It did not help.

A branch snapped behind him. Travis whirled around to see a rifle aimed at his head.

"Don't move."

John Baptiste stepped from behind a tree, rifle raised.

 **Chapter 77**

Scarsbourgh's cabin

"Keep your hands where I can see them. Both of you." Baptiste looked from one to the other. "And make that mutt shut up before he gives us away."

Travis reached out and patted Sam. The dog crouched down, warily watching Baptiste.

Jessie slowly shifted her position. "What are you doing here, John?"

Baptiste ignored her, looking at Travis. "I just didn't want the two of you shooting me before I could explain." He lowered his weapon. "I've been on horseback for two days near your cabin, thinking this woman might try again. Saw her cross the highway about the same time I heard SO dispatch a unit. Tried to catch up with her, but she gave me the slip. You've been stupidly following my trail—nor hers."

Travis rubbed his forehead. "So she was heading east. That's why Sam was trying to drag me in that direction."

"Smart dog. I got here some time ago," Baptiste said. "I knew about this cabin after your last run-in with her. I set up here awhile ago. Saw her arrive about a half-hour ago. Waited until she put her horse in the stall. I was going to catch her between the stable and the cabin—out in open. But then I heard you coming and pulled back. Haven't seen her since. You might have spooked her."

Jessie broke in. "Why are you here?"

Baptiste shifted his gaze toward her for the first time. "Because she tried to take out your father."

"But I thought—"

"That's your problem, Jessie. You never understood anything about me."

Travis slowly raised himself. "Now that you're here, let's have Jessie provide cover while we try to get close to the cabin. Maybe get the jump on her."

Baptiste still focused on Jessie. "Well, professor. You still got it in you? Police work, that is?" He finally turned toward Travis.

Travis met his gaze. "You sure she never left the cabin?"

"That's what I said."

"You can't see to the left there, where the forest reaches the edge of the cabin."

"I'd have heard her leave, professor. I got the drop on you, didn't I?"

Travis stood and motioned Sam to follow. "Stay here or follow me. I don't care, Baptiste. Just don't get in my way."

Baptiste raised his rifle and laid it on his shoulder. "Let's do this."

Travis glanced down at the dog. "Sam. Come." He turned and began working his way through the trees, listening to the other man following. He looked back and saw Jessie blending with the forest. If he did not know exactly where she lay hidden, he could not have spotted her. He turned and began to quietly descend, trying to move noiselessly through the dry underbrush.

Sam padded silently ahead.

Minutes passed before they neared the cabin. The last twenty yards, he crouched down and began to low crawl through the brush. As they got closer, Sam began to turn away trying to lead him back into the forest. Travis grabbed the dog's collar and silently motioned the animal to lay still.

Something seemed to be spooking the dog.

Once Travis quieted Sam, he began to crawl toward the cabin where the forest grew closest to the cabin, branches scraping against log walls.

This was the same approach Jean took the night she surprised him. Now it was his turn.

Baptiste swung to the left so they'd have the cabin in a crossfire.

He signaled that he was about to approach the front of the building. After Baptiste nodded in recognition, Travis started creeping forward using the cabin wall as cover while tightly gripping his rifle. He rounded the corner and scanned the front porch.

Empty.

He slowly raised himself up to peer through a window pane.

Only darkness inside.

Travis slung his rifle and pulled out a handgun before taking the stairs and edging toward the front door. A board creaked under his weight. He froze, listening to any sounds that might warn him of the killer's presence.

Silence.

He grasped the handle with his left hand, slowly turned until he knew the door would open with a push. In one swift motion he flung it inward and dove into the darkness.

Silence.

Gradually, his eyes grew accustomed to the darkness. Moonlight filtered in. Jean was gone.

A thought gripped him. Could Baptiste be lying?

He carefully peered through the doorway. Baptiste was still planted in the same spot. Travis rose to his feet, keeping the handgun at his side. He slowly strode across the porch and walked toward the other man.

"I thought you said she was in the cabin?"

Baptiste looked at him, squinting. "Empty?"

Travis nodded.

"Then that means ..."

Travis hurled off his backpack and fumbled for his night vision scope. He flicked it on and dashed to the corner of the cabin. As he raised the glasses, he focused where Jessie lay hidden. It took a moment for him to scan the ground above them and find where they'd left her.

He felt his stomach knot as he adjusted the sight.

Jessie lay on the ground, a rifle pointed at her head.

Jean Robinette glared back at them, a sneer on her face. He saw a night scope in her other hand. She'd been watching them from above, her face contorted with hate.

Chapter 78

Jean Robinette called out. "We're coming down, Travis. You've got one minute to drop your weapons—both of you—and move out into the clearing where I can see you."

Travis moved to comply, laying his weapons on the ground.

"And the dog—I'll kill him if it gets anywhere near me."

Baptiste stood. He paused, glancing at Travis for a moment. Finally, he shrugged and laid his weapon on the ground. Together, they moved clear of the cabin, standing in the grassland between the dwelling and the stables. Jean had cover and concealment going for her. From her high elevation—and with a gun on Jessie—she had them in a kill zone they could not escape.

The women slowly descended, Jessie walking a few yards behind. As they drew near, he saw Jean looking from one man to the other. "Both of you. Kneel down and let me see your hands."

The men obeyed, Sam came alongside Travis. He looked down at the dog. "Sam. Lay down!" The dog obeyed. Baptiste knelt a few yards to his left.

Jean motioned to Jessie as they drew near. "You, too. On the ground." Jessie complied.

Travis watched Jessie kneel on the ground next to Sam. "Now what? You've got our weapons. You can just ride out of here and disappear."

Jean looked at him, scowling. "Do you remember that famous line when Sitting Bull's braves descended on Custer and his troops?"

Her words chilled him. Travis shook his head, fearful he knew where she was taking this.

She scowled at him, clenching her jaw. "Sure you do, Professor. He took a look at the cavalry and said, 'This is a good day to die.'"

Travis tensed. "It doesn't have to be this way. You have all the advantages. No one has to get hurt."

"You think I'm going to let you just walk away? After what you took from me?" She seemed to hurl the words at him like bullets, as if the impact would be enough to make him want to curl up and die.

Rotor blades of a helicopter beat the air in a deep throbbing rhythm, the aircraft heading in their direction. Travis tried to draw Jean's attention to him. "Took from you? What are you talking about?"

"I'm talking about Phillip. Money. My ticket out of this hell-hole."

"He was going to kill us, Jean. What were we supposed to do?"

Jean swung the rifle in his direction. "It was all your fault. You set everything in motion. You're responsible for his sister getting killed."

"I can't change the past. If you want revenge, you've got me. Let the others go."

The helicopter drew closer.

"I want you to suffer for taking Phillip away. I want you to feel pain before I kill—"

A helicopter crested treetops and a searchlight bathed them in dazzling-white blindness. He saw Jean glance up and knew she'd be momentarily blinded.

He lunged to his feet and tried to dash toward the killer. His feet stumbled over a rock and he almost lost footing. He quickly regained balance, only to see Jean swing the rifle toward him.

A shot exploded. Jean jerked back as if struck in the chest.

Another shot echoed to his left.

Baptiste rushed forward, gun in hand. He fired two more times at Jean. Her body twitched as each bullet struck home.

Travis approached and saw Jean staring up at the hovering helicopter, the aircraft still bathing them in light. Jean glanced back at him for a moment with a look of hate before she ceased to move. Her lifeless eyes stayed locked on him.

Travis signaled a Code-4 at the helicopter crew. The craft veered off to settle in the grassy meadow fifty yards further down the hill. A figure jumped out and dashed toward him.

John Steele.

"Had a devil of a time tracking you. Frank told us you headed up in this direction, but our heat-tracking camera came up empty the first few times we did a fly-over. It wasn't till we topped those trees this last time our cameras picked you up. By then it was too late."

Travis watched Baptiste standing a few yards away. "If it wasn't for him, I'd be face-down in the dirt right now."

Steele shook his head. "Started out I thought he might be one of the shooters. "

Travis shrugged. "Me, too." He patted Steele on the back. "Thanks for the back-up." He began walking toward Baptiste. As he approached, he extended a hand.

"Thanks for saving my bacon, officer. Much obliged."

Baptiste's eyes narrowed, his hands remaining at his sides. "Still think I'm involved?"

Travis glanced over as a deputy stood over the dead woman's body. "I'd say all this tells me you're one of the good guys."

"I didn't do it for you, professor. I did it for the chief and—" He let the sentence drop without continuing.

Travis saw Jessie talking to one of the deputies. "Officer Baptiste. Something is still bugging me. So ... I'll just ask you straight out."

"What?" Baptiste gave him a wary look.

"Frank and I—"

"Chief White Eagle." The man's face hardened. "His name is Chief White Eagle."

"Okay, Chief White Eagle." Travis tried again. "The chief and I found a notation on Tommy's computer where he'd typed 'Re: Jessie's Problem' a few days before he disappeared. At the time, we thought he meant you." Travis waited for the officer to speak.

A puzzled look crossed the man's face, then he smiled. "Oh, yeah. Tommy probably meant me."

"So you acknowledge you're Jessie's problem?"

"*Was* Jessie's problem. In Tommy's eyes the matter had been handled. He knew his dad spoke to me about it a year ago. We settled things between ourselves after he knew Jessie and I were a thing of the past. Maybe Tommy did not want to put my name down on the computer, so he used those words to identify me."

"So you did meet him just before he—"

"Yeah. His buddy, Axtell, was having problems with a guy. Tommy got the crook's name from Pete and asked me to check him out without the chief finding out."

"And did you?"

Baptiste hung his head. "No. I never got around to it. Tommy disappeared right after that. Then you guys started thinking I was the shooter. That just ticked me off and I forget all about it until everyone turned up dead. By then I figured it was too late."

Jessie walked toward them and reached out and touched Baptiste's arm. "Thanks, John."

Baptiste tensed for a moment before nodding. He turned away without saying a word. Travis watched him start up the hill, finally disappearing into the brush.

"I can't figure him out, Jessie."

She took his hand in hers. "Neither can I."

Sam brushed against his leg. "I guess Sam's telling us it's time to go home. Steele knows where to find us." They collected their weapons and equipment and began the trek down the mountain.

"Let's see how Frank's doing."

# Chapter 79

Lochsa River, Idaho

Travis felt an adrenaline rush as his kayak stayed afloat. Jessie held her position downstream, waiting, as he finally cleared the *Grim Reaper* a second time without capsizing. Just three months ago, these same rapids turned him upside down and buried him in ice-cold water.

Today, he conquered it once again.

"Hey, Willie-boy. Not bad." Jessie grinned as she paddled toward him.

"Thanks. I've got a great teacher."

"Face it, professor. You've got the best."

"And yet, so humble." He laughed as she made a face. "Let's take a break. I brought lunch."

They pulled to the bank and dragged their kayaks onto the rocky shore out of reach of the current. The blue sky, heavy with late-summer heat, made the day near perfect.

He selected a large flat rock where he laid a lunch box, pulling out a bag of Kentucky Fried chicken and a couple cans of cold soda. Next to them he placed, several paper plates, bunches of Concord grapes and two candy bars.

"You must have spent ages in the kitchen," Jessie said, looking skeptically at the food.

"All finger food. My favorite. And no dishes." He started on a drumstick.

Jessie grabbed the grapes, popping one in her mouth. "You really need a woman. It's scary thinking of you surviving all these years on your own."

"Hey, I managed."

Travis saw her expression change, a smile turn to a frown. She looked out over the river, holding the grapes in her hand. "Where do we go from here, Willie boy?" She turned and looked at him.

He weighed each word carefully as if he was treading on a precarious bridge suspended over a chasm. Each word he chose might send him crashing. "Wherever *here* might be," he said, "I want you in the picture. And you?" Just as quickly, he'd shifted the question back to her. Her answer meant everything.

Jessie looked away without answering.

All summer Travis and Jessie seemed to avoid this inevitable conversation. Frank healed and returned to work. Life returned as close to normal as all these events allowed. He and Jessie became friends, and when he was away he found himself thinking about her. But each time he returned, it seemed they needed to readjust to each other because whatever might be between them had not been settled. Never clearly stated. As if each of them were trying to figure out what the future held without actually talking about it.

Today, Jessie seemed determined to settle this thing.

To celebrate the summer's end, she had suggested they take one last trip down the Lochsa. The river ran mildly slow this time of season, nowhere near the threat of a few months ago. And here they were, traveling the same river that first brought them together. The end of summer flows were tame compared to what they faced a few months ago.

Jessie glanced at the sky before speaking, her voice drawing Travis back to the present. "I want us to be together, Travis. Does that scare you?"

"Scare me?" He saw a quizzical look on her face. "Yeah. But in a good way. After all that happened, I feel that if we stick together — you and I — we just might survive."

"You talking about us or surviving this river?" Her smile returned.

"Both ... Pocahontas. Let's see what's around the next bend."

Laughter seemed to dance from her eyes. "Okay, Willie boy, you sure you're ready?"

He watched the river for a moment, locking this point in time in his mind. "Yeah, I'm ready." Travis stood and took her hand. "Come on. Let's get started."

Together they walked toward the river. An eagle flew over as they climbed back into the kayaks. He saw the majestic bird circle once and then dive, snatching up a trout that swam too close to the surface. Watching the bird, he thought of Jessie's last name and realized he never asked her how her family came to be called White Eagle. He'd have to find out one of these days. There was a lot to learn about Jessie, her people, and this land.

He paddled out to the middle of the current and waited for her to catch up. A hot August sun beat down upon the river and the water looked cool, clear and inviting. As she drew near, they turned and began the trek downstream side by side. Like the river that flowed past his cabin, his life seemed to have escape those eddies of stagnation, finally moving forward with a promise of hope. Darkness of the past slowly slipping away as the future began to take shape. Maybe for once his life would become like the river he loved.

Clearwater.

Author's Note

A novel is never a solitary trip, although the author may believe so at times. Many people came along side during this journey to offer helps, advice, and needful warnings. Travis and I may be a little waterlogged by the Clearwater River, but we are mindful of everyone's help given on and off the page of this novel. We want to recognize all those who made this journey less painful.

First and foremost, I want to recognized my wonderful wife, Katie — a published poet, a Renaissance woman, a great editor, and my best friend. Her careful editing has pulled me back from the abyss of some terrible and embarrassing mistakes.

My friend, James Scott Bell, whose encouragement and mentoring allowed me to believe people can learn to create novels. Carole Neal, for her insightful comments. Francine Rivers, whose help, advice, and writing showed me what the future might hold for other writers. Further thanks to Angela Hunt, for her patience and willingness to train others. To Laura Jensen Walker and Jeff Gerke –along with many others that space precludes from mentioning— for their advice, encouragement and editorial assistance.

I would be remiss if I did not express thanks to Dr. Donna Paul, economic professor at Washington State University, for sharing with me a little insight in the world of academia through the eyes of faculty. Any deviance from the real world rest solely on my shoulders. In the interest of story, I may have taken allowances that might never happen at WSU — or might they?

Gratitude to river guide Tonya Lyons, whose knowledge of the river help this story and this author through several rapids, and for pulling me out of the whitewater more than once.

Thanks to writers Joe Konrath and Aaron Patterson, whose motivating blogs for authors has encouraged this writer to launch out as an Indie publisher in this new digital age. The future looks bright for authors.

Lastly, I want to express heartfelt appreciation to all those who helped me gain a deeper understanding and appreciation of the Nez Perce Nation. Chief Leslie Hendrick of the Nez Perce Tribal Police, helping me to understand the difficulties of navigating her law enforcement agency between two worlds, two cultures, and the challenges faced by her officers every day. Dr.

Robin Johnston, archeologist with the U.S. Department of Forestry Services, whose research over thirty years of the Native American cultures gave me a glimpse into this brave Nez Perce nation. Attorney J.Heidi Gudgell of the Nez Perce Office of Legal Counsel, who help me understand the complexities of water and fishing rights held sacred by these peoples. I may not have got it right, Heidi, but I tried. Reverend Art Finney of the Second Native American Presbyterian Church in Kamiah, Idaho, who shared spiritual struggles between his church members and the culture at large. To Olivia Jackson, and her mother, Colleen Lupe, whose Nez Perce heritage came alive as they shared the present and past of their fascinating culture. To Livi: May the voices of the past cease to haunt those living in the present. Finally, to the Nez Perce people who have struggled and survived against insurmountable odds and injustices. May your journey finally bring peace.

Coming Soon by Mark Young

Off the Grid: A Gerrit O'Rourke Novel
(Scheduled for Release, Winter 2011)

Can a hunted man lose himself in this age of technology. His life may depend upon it …

Detective Gerrit O'Rouke has little to lose. Parents killed in an accident ten years ago drove Gerrit to leave the sterile environment of the academic world and become a Seattle homicide detective. Specializing in cold cases, he tries to hunt down his parents' killer and learns that nothing is as it seems. A beautiful federal prosecutor has her eyes on Gerrit, as they team up on a puzzling federal RICO case that begins to unravel. An attempt on Gerrit's life reveals that powerful men have decided he must die for secrets he just uncovered. To survive, Gerrit must shed his identity to survive in a technological world where hiding is almost impossible. He must learn to live *Off The Grid* in order to survive and fight another day. As this new world opens up, Gerrit finds out there are many kinds of warriors living in this gray netherworld of technological warfare. He must learn who can be trusted and who might stab him in the back.

www.ingramcontent.com/pod-product-compliance
Lightning Source LLC
Chambersburg PA
CBHW030013180626
46810CB00001B/12